The Star Dancers

By Jeffrey Caminsky:

The Referee's Survival Guide

All Fathers Are Giants (ed.)

The Sonnets of William Shakespeare (ed.)

The Guardians of Peace series:

>*The Sirens of Space*
>
>*The Star Dancers*
>
>*Clouds of Darkness*

Coming soon:

>*The Guardians of Peace*

The Star Dancers

A Novel

Jeffrey Caminsky

NEW ALEXANDRIA PRESS
LIVONIA

Published by New Alexandria Press
PO Box 530516
Livonia, Michigan 48153
www.newalexandriapress.com

The quote attributed to Edmund Burke first appeared in 1775, in his *Speech on Conciliation with America.*

Hardcover Edition:
ISBN-10: 0-9790106-7-5
ISBN:13: 978-0-9790106-7-5

Softcover Edition:
ISBN-10: 0-9790106-4-0
ISBN-13: 978-0-9790106-4-4

Quantity discounts are available on bulk purchases of this book Special books or book excerpts can also be made available to fit specific needs. For information, please contact *sales@newalexandriapress.com* or send written inquiries to New Alexandria Press, PO Box 530516, Livonia, Michigan 48153.

Printed in the United States of America

10 9 8 7 6 5 4 3 2

2008934584

To Nonie,
with hope for the future....

Author's Note

IN VOLUME I OF THIS WORK, THE Author tried to provide some insight into the historical context of the ensuing volumes through excerpts from a timeless historical work written by an award-winning historian of an era yet to come. That particular work, however, focused on the development of civilizations tracing their origins to Planet Earth, and offered few insights into alien cultures and customs. In addition, as press deadlines neared for this volume, the source proved to be unavailable, for reasons which have not been explained to the Author's satisfaction.

Alien cultures have been a source of endless fascination since the days of Marco Polo, and speculation about extraterrestrial life is a passion for many in our own day. The menace of alien invaders has been a common theme for generations, and as the scientific advances of the Twentieth Century brought space travel from the realm of fantasy into the dreams of visionaries, speculation about what may await us in the vastness of space became a source of endless fascination. Curious readers can obtain information in a wide variety of places, but the most authoritative sources are not yet in print in this section of the Galaxy. To help those interested in learning about the our nearest galactic neighbors, the Publisher has once again been gracious enough to share some information about what the Future may hold in store—this time taken from the historical records of our sister races.

Unfortunately, current translations appear to make some of the accounts even drier than the originals. It is the Author's hope that future editions of this work will be able to take advantage of any improvements in linguistics as they become available.

Annuls of Cru'Shenagla CCLIX , *circa 15,247 BC:*
And it thus and verily proved to be that the blood rage of the Translucent Ones was the result not of evil nature, but of fear; not of murderous intent, but of the panic of desperation. For even as they pursued the Followers of His Worthiness, they fell upon several who, previously injured, had lagged behind and were taken. And unto the darkness of night, the shivering Followers grieved for their lost companions, amid dark visions of evil rituals and unimaginable feasts.

Yet upon the dawning of the Seventh Day, as the anxious Followers awaited the arrival of rescuers from beyond, a Strange One approached, carrying a small child who had been taken. And the injured child cried for his mother, who came to the child and held him in her arms. And the Strange One gave them to understand that other Followers needed assistance that their Strange Sciences could not provide. And so unto the Seventh Night, a man of medicine followed the Strange One to their encampment, as the others spent the sleepless night in fear. And with the Eighth Day, two more Stricken Ones returned to their families; and still the rescue awaited.

And on the Tenth Day, word came that a Follower had died among the monsters. And yet the medicine man, returning with the rest, assured them that the Strange Ones had done nothing to cause harm, and that only fear and panic, reflected in the Followers's own hearts, had resulted in the breaking of bones and the flowing of blood. And the Returned Ones attested also that they had received kindness from their hosts, and that no harm had come to them deliberately.

And as rescue came with the Twelfth Dawn, the rescuers wished to slay the Strange Ones to claim Atonement. But the Followers told them that the Strange Ones had done them no harm after the first hour, and had saved many Followers who had been given up as lost, and had shared what little food and water they had with them. And so the rescuers and the rest left in peace, leaving food and drink in payment. And soon thereafter, the Strange Ones found rescuers of their own to fetch them away.

* * *

From Galnas, trans, *Falashi's The Clash of Alien Cultures and the Rise of the Grand Alliance: An Annotated Translation of the Original 8,759 BC Edition*, (New Alexandria, cc:292-8316; 2954 OE; 918 Is):

Following the near-disaster, emissaries sent a message to our Crutchtan neighbors, hoping to avoid any similar misunderstandings in the future. Within a year, formal discussions between the two races had begun, and a line of division was drawn through the skies between them. Each promised to observe the boundary, and not to pass into the other's space uninvited, and soon traders of both races were plying their wares along the trading outposts built along the mutual border. Although each side tried to impose strict limits on their scientists, books and goods were freely exchanged, and before long the curious on both sides had turned the border into a sieve. A peace treaty soon followed, and the Agreement between the Veshnans and Crutchtans would form the basis for the Establishment of the Consortium, two millenia later.

* * *

TRANSLATION COURTESY OF THE PUBLIC RECORDS DEPARTMENT, TRANSLATOR'S BUREAU, VESHNAN GOVERNMENT, PUBLIC AFFAIRS DIVISION:

OFFICIAL GLINCIAN HISTORICAL RECORD, *circa 4 BC:*
Having grown from the mistrust arising from our First Encounter, the animosity between ourselves and our Landoran neighbors seemed at the time to be visceral, and almost instinctive. The dispute concerning the contested sectors set both races on a course that seemed to admit no winner, for concessions by one were viewed as victories for the other, and neither side wished to appear weak. Though the perspectives of history show them to be petty and trivial, the disagreements began to extend beyond the mere rights of passage, and began to assume the flavor of a mating struggle among lower animals. Proffered solutions by one were taken as no less than rights due by the other, and for two generations the leaders on both sides were chosen largely for their unwillingness to bargain or compromise with their perceived adversaries....
Finally tiring of the unending squabbles, the High Council imposed a solution on the contending sides over the objection of both sides. The disputed regions were taken from both races, and administered in trust by a commission appointed by the Council. The commission controlled exploration in the area, and managed the

development of any resources found by explorers of any race. But while this arrangement suited the needs of the moment, the nature of the solution was ripe for exploitation by the unscrupulous. The Crutchtan representatives having secured a firm majority among the Full Members, the governing commission came to be dominated by Crutchtan industrial interests, who came to favor their own national interests in awarding Licenses of Development and Letters of Patent and Franchise. Within a generation, the Landoran representatives had converted the Crutchtan majority into a Landoran one, supplanting Crutchtan industrial favors with those of their own.

At the same time, pending final resolution of the matter, the Glincian application for full membership in the Consortium was deferred indefinitely.

* * *

IT IS 2551.

Four years after Terra's first encounter with an alien civilization resulted in a bloody massacre at Hawkins Star, warnings about the alien menace still fill the halls of the Terran Senate. Pirates are stepping up their raids in the shipping lanes along the frontier. Intrigue fills corridors throughout the galaxy...and peace talks are set to resume on an alien world.

THE PLAYERS

The Cosmic Guard

Yeoman Lars Anderson, *shift supervisor*
Commander Jeremy Ashton, *ship's systems officer*
Denny Barrett, *crewman*
Ens. Roberta Blount, *a junior gunnery officer*
Lt. Jerry Burdick, *security officer*
Captain Tom Chandler, *a starship captain*
Admiral Porter Clay, *commander of the Eastern Fleet*
Yeoman Chief Gregory Connors, *supervisor of enlistees*
Roscoe Cook, *a native of Planet Isis*
Ens. Kirkland Dexter, *apprentice systems officer*
Captain Brian Fitzgerald, *a starship captain*
Ens. Tom Gerlach, *apprentice weapons officer*
Commodore Jefferson McKinley Jones, *senior wing commander, Demeter Command*
Andrew Larsen, *crewman*
Jim Martindale, *crewman*
Ens. Mary Mathison, *apprentice radio officer*
Commodore Jason McIntyre, *senior wing commander, Looking Glass*
Ens. Connie McKenzie, *apprentice navigator*
Commodore Peter Medwick, *commander of Starbase 117*
Lt. Janet Mendelson, *ship's helmsman*
Commodore Abdul Mohassan, *Ishtar Command chief of operations*
Lt. Karen Palmer, *weapons officer*
Yeoman Rick Sillars, *shift supervisor*
Tom Sullivan, *crewman*
Lt. Ronald Talbert, *ship's navigator*
Ens. Ishao Takira, *junior radar officer, Starbase 117*
Captain Art Tanana, *a starship captain*
Lt. Dennis Underwood, *communications officer*
Lt. Cmdr. Bruce Van Horn, *ship's chief engineer*
Yeoman Kevin Ward, *shift supervisor on Looking Glass*
Admiral Winthrop Weatherlee, *commander of Demeter Command*
Commodore Miriam Wright, *commander of Looking Glass*

Spacers and Assorted Riff-Raff

Cyrus McGee, *spacer and former pirate*
Mason McGee, *brother of Cyrus*
Janey, *housemate of the brothers McGee*
Chad Herzog, *a spacer*
Kenny McKeller, *a spacer*

Clintus Rafferty, *a spacer*
Kate Riley, *owner of Riley's Station*
Lars Swenson, *a spacer*
Chadborne Wilkes, *a space pirate*

Terrans
Andrew Cook, *Roscoe's father*
Cornelius Cook, *Roscoe's uncle*
Thomas Cook, *Roscoe's grandfather*
Jonathan Osborne Grant, *Terran Ambassador*
Duncan Heathcoate, *senior senator from Demeter*
E. Emerson Hollenbach, *senior senator from Earth*
Irene McGinnis, *senior senator from Isis*
Nicholas Schiller, *a Demetrian industrialist*
Mikos Sarkisian, *President of the Terran League*
Suzie Yang, *presidential aide and journalist*

Veshnans
Munshi, *a translator*
Zatar, *a diplomat*

Shuli, *a diplomat*
Zatsami, *ambassador and solon*

Crutchtans
Cra'Jenli, *Imperial Foreign Minister*
Balshadra, *consort to Cra'Jenli*
Bra'Lendt, *scientist at Outpost Shun'Galanga*
Dra'Lani, *ambassador and solon*
fl'Shenda, *servant at the Court of Gr'Shuna*
G'Rishela, *the Imperator's ambassador to Terra*
gal'Fondro, *family retainer for Galgravina clan*
Ga'Glish, *Havenmaster Supreme of the Crutchtan Empire*
Ga'Glishek, *father of Ga'Glish*
Gal'Shenga, *brother of Ga'Glishek and uncle of Ga'Glish*
Glishenda, *mate of Ga'Glishek and mother of Ga'Glish*
Ja'Rend XCVI, *Imperator of the Crutchtan Empire*
Jerenda, *servant at the Court of Gr'Shuna*
La'Stala, *a commander*
Lanshana, *mate of Shl'Lanasha, mother of Shl'Glisen*
Ls'Sala, *the Imperator's emissary*
ls'Shen, *first apprentice to Ra'Henl*
Ra'Henl, *Grand Foodmaster at the Court of Gr'Shuna*
Shl'Glisen, *a young boy*
Shl'Lanasha, *mate of Lanshana and father of Shl'Glisen*
Sra'Chenga, *senior deputy to Ga'Glish*
Ya'Glankha, *groupleader of Outpost Shun'Galanga*
Ya'Lisha, *Lord Deputy of the Imperial Foreign Ministery*

Other Members of the Consortium
Drubid, *a Glincian ambassador and solon*
krHarata, *a Fidrei ambassador and solon*

A SELECT GAZETTEER
OF OBSCURE HEAVENLY BODIES

Athena, *a Terran planet*

Balarium, *seat of the Grand Alliance of the Consortium*

Ceres, *a Terran planet*

The Crutchtan Cloud, *a vast natural formation of rocks, gases, and precious elements*

Demeter, *third most populous Terran planet*

Earth, *former capital of the Terran League, most populous Terran planet*

Gaea, *a Terran planet*

The Great Divide, *the Crutchtan name for the Neutral Zone*

g'Khruushte, *ancestral home and capital of the Crutchtan Empire; also, Crutchan Empire*

Gr'Shuna, *a Crutchtan planet and regional capital*

Gutterman's Gap, *a narrow passage to Isis through the Nakahashi Storms*

Hodges Binary, *an agricultural colony east of Ishtar*

Ishtar, *Terra's easternmost planet*

The Ishtari Belt, *a formation of rocks, gases, and precious elements near Ishtar*

Isis, *Terra's westernmost planet*

Khu'ukhana Rift, *a narrow passage through the Crutchtan Cloud*

Looking Glass, *colloquial name of Starbase 102*

Mullinberry's Star, *the star dominating the Demeter system*

The Nakahashi Storms, *a large and intense formation of gases and rocks east of Isis*

New Babylon, *capital of the Terran League, second most populous Terran planet*

New Calais, *a Terran planet*

Pirate's Alley, *a dangerous stretch of space from the Ishtari Belt to Demeter*

Riley's Station, *a private starbase and interstellar port of call along the Terran frontier*

Shun'Galanga, *a Crutchtan scientific outpost*

Valhalla, *a Terran planet*

Zarathustra, *one of two inhabited Terran planets west of Earth*

I SWEAR UPON MY SACRED OATH to renounce all bigotry, racial and religious; to forswear for my term of service all planetary allegiance; and to serve Humanity as a guardian of peace, dedicated to preserving human life wherever it wanders. I swear to uphold the laws of the Terran League and all its member planets, and to conduct myself at all times in a manner consistent with integrity and justice. I pledge to serve my superiors faithfully and obey their lawful orders, and to treat any discretion that befalls me as a sacred trust not be abused, nor perverted for personal gain or aggrandizement. And I pledge full devotion to all of my appointed tasks, no matter what the cost to myself.

To fulfill my duties to Humanity, and to the Cosmic Guard, I pledge my name, my life, and my honor.

CosGuard Oath of Allegiance

The Star Dancers

Magnanimity in politics is not seldom the greatest wisdom; and a great empire and little minds go ill together.

EDMUND BURKE
Old Earth Statesman
1729-1797

Prologue

THE HOT SUN hung in the summer sky. Even the sweat gnats, in their maddening swarms, gathered in the shade of a bush or tree rather than venturing out into the heat. Heedless of the elements, two young boys inched quietly through the tall grass. At the top of a small hill, they parted the weeds and peered at a solitary tree in the middle of the field, forty yards away.

"Shhh," whispered one, holding a grimy finger to his lips. "It's the pirate camp."

"We've stalked them through a dozen star systems," said his companion. "Roscoe—we can't let them escape this time."

"Let's surround them," Roscoe said, as softly as he could. "You go that way."

"You always lead the attack. I want to do it my way this time."

"Marcus...," Roscoe began sharply, only to cut himself short and roll his eyes in disgust. This mission was too big for bickering. The pirates had slaughtered countless thousands across the length and breadth of Terra, capturing and torturing both of them three times in the last two days. It was time for action, not squabbling. And if that meant that Marcus McWilliams had to lead the assault, then so be it.

The boys narrowed their eyes, studying the enemy's lair. There was no movement—except for Nancy Davidson, who didn't know better than to cut through a pirate camp on her way home from Dora Gottlieb's house. Fortunately, the pirates took no notice of her. Otherwise, the boys would have been duty-bound to rescue her. It was somewhere in the Honor Code of the Cosmic Avengers; both of them were sure of that, though neither could actually remember reading it. And that was more than either of them could stomach.

"They're asleep," Roscoe announced.

"How many are there?"

"How many do you see?"

Marcus shrugged.

"I see a hundred and twenty," said Roscoe.

"Yeah."

The boys sat back in the grass. The still air hung over them like a death shroud.

"We probably won't get out of this alive," Marcus said grimly.

"There are too many of them," agreed Roscoe. "And there's no time to send for help. But Omicron-6 can't go unpunished. And we can't let them get away again." He reached for his laser-blaster, which was cleverly disguised as a stick.

Marcus clasped his comrade's shoulder. "Goodbye, Roscoe."

Roscoe's eyes hardened like tempered steel. Life was a parade of adventure and tragedy, he thought, but the end was no time for faintness of heart. "Goodbye, my friend, and may Fortune smile upon you until we meet again."

They resumed their crouch, coiled and tense. They peered through the grass for a last look at their quarry before they attacked.

"Follow me!" screamed Marcus. "Take no prisoners—Victory or Death!!!"

"Ayyaya!" answered Roscoe. "Chee-arge!!"

"*Odl-odl-odl-odl...!*" bellowed a flock of panic-stricken grousefinches, rudely disturbed from their afternoon refuge in the grass and rising from the battleground in a fusillade of flapping.

"*Mo-o-om!!*" cried the two terrified commandoes, as each boy raced toward home.

Chapter 1

SHL'GLISEN—COME INSIDE. Your death shall come with the very wind if you do not hurry to shelter."

"But Mother...!"

"Come inside."

"But Mother— ! "

"Come inside, Young One. Tomorrow will come soon enough."

Shl'Glisen kicked the dirt with his boot but knew that further protests would be fruitless. He was already bundled like an infant and could hardly move. It pained him to be treated like one as well. Slowly, he walked toward the hut, dragging his feet in defiance. Though the sun was still an hour from setting, the large planet loomed full on the eastern horizon, its wide bands lending color to the sky.

It was unfair, he thought. Though the native birds sang as merrily as those of home, the days on this moon called *Shun'Galanga* were cold as a morning stone. Even the alien summers failed to warm the blood. But with the warm clothing they had brought to ease the chill there was no reason to keep young ones from enjoying the daylight. It was simply unfair.

"Shl'Glisen."

"I come, Mother."

The young one scurried forward, stopping just before the entrance. His mother's face carried a look of severity; deference to elders was a lesson her son had not yet mastered. But her eyes spoke amusement, and Shl'Glisen felt her good humor. She reached to touch his cheek with her hand, and soon met her young one in reconciling embrace.

"We shall eat soon, anyway," she whispered. "And your lessons need tending."

"Yes, Mother."

Her smiling eyes followed the young one inside before drifting to the moon's mother planet, now rising in the east. Ribbons of clouds laced the arching sky, and along the horizon the distant mountains loomed over the nearby treetops like royalty. If it was a cold world to which Fate had brought them, at least it was one filled with beauty. Just the same, the probes of the giant planet were nearly finished, and she would be glad when their work was done.

She breathed deeply in the chilled air. The results of their endeavors were most promising, or so her mate had told her. Organic compounds filled the atmosphere of the giant planet, and the richness of its clouds and nearby planetoids meant that this moon was a prime candidate for settlement—provided, of course, that they could find souls whose heartiness would supply the warmth lacking in the climate.

Her eyes flared in quiet amusement. The planetary engineers could warm the moon— in a generation or two, if all went as planned for the first time in the history of the Imperator's Colonial Expedition. But if she could believe what she read in the journals from home, *Shun'Galanga* was better suited to the Terrans. After the wastelands they inhabited, this world would seem balmier than a still night on *Gr'Shuna*. And as far as she was concerned, they could have it.

Shivering, she opened the door and stepped inside, rubbing her hands together to help restart her circulation. If the longnoses could live on worlds where the setting sun turned breath into clouds of frost, she knew many half-frozen *g'Khruushtani* who would depart with glad hearts.

* * *

As SHL'GLISEN devoured his dinner, and a nameless planet rose in the darkening sky over his lonely settlement, far to the east a transmission monitor's fingers worked to adjust a receiver, vainly trying to focus long-awaited words from a long-overdue mission.

But the broadcast was hopelessly garbled. A storm in the Shunite sector was the cause, raising static on all channels. The pilot's voice was all but lost, like a lone gull's cry amid the crashing waves.

"I hear, but yet hear not," said the monitor. "Perhaps the augmentor—"

"I hear and understand," said the Tall One beside him. "You may proceed. I shall later return."

Ga'Glish of *Gr'Shuna*, Centurion of the Imperator and Havenmaster Supreme for the entire Shunite sector, strode from the Monitorium and walked down the hallway, his footsteps sounding briskly over the brightly colored tiles. The halls themselves rang with excitement, for all knew that the Ship of Grand Horizons was nearing. But on the centurion's order all monitors had been restricted to stations, so word of the storm had not yet become common knowledge among the rest of the Haven. There was yet no need for worry, and as the need might never arise, spreading useless words was unnecessary.

Ga'Glish thought briefly of returning to his abode. His mate would be home by now and the soft pillows of his bed would do much to ease his weariness. But he concluded that the time for such indulgence was so short as to be unthinkable. The Imperial Haven was responsible for the safety of all the Imperator's subjects in the Shunite Sector, from *Gr'Shuna* westward to the Great Divide. As Havenmaster, Ga'Glish was charged with preserving safe passage in the sector not only for ships of the Empire, but also for those of the Imperator's allies. Storms were common in this portion of the Empire, a grim gift from the swirling gases and luminescent spirals of the Great Cloud. It made his task among the most difficult in the Colonial Arm of the Ministry of Expanse Services. As if he had not problems enough, the exalted rank of the diplomats of the Grand Alliance on the ship bound from Terra—and now caught in the storm—made him answerable to the Emmissariat as well.

But the Ship of Grand Horizons had safely traversed the Expanse and was almost to port. The storm it faced was a minor one, and posed little real danger. More pressing was the tempest raging among the diplomats now infesting his domain. Already, they buzzed with word that the Terrans would soon be coming—for in another quarter-cycle or so, Terran emissaries would be meeting with those of the *g'Khruushtani* and intermediaries of the Grand Alliance on his own home planet. Such a turn meant securing the Expanse from the intrusion of privatecraft, and even restricting movements of the Patrollers, all to guard against revealing any secrets of state. The presence of government officials on his Haven had always meant trouble, and last month's communiqué—announcing the Terran visitation—had sent the Imperial Government into a flurry of protocol. Besides, the Imperator's representatives rarely issued compliments; they constantly searched for ways to leave an impression. This meant finding fault, and fault, of course, implied correction.

As he strode down the hallway, an aide overtook him; it was his senior aide—Sra'Chengla, son of Sr'Cheng. He brought word that the high diplomats of the Grand Alliance awaited his presence in the Hall of Formal Discussion.

"Word from m'Lishen?" Ga'Glish began.

"The transmission is undecipherable still," sighed the aide. "The monitor tries, but the disturbance grows and spreads. The augmentor will be scant help until it abates."

Ga'Glish closed his eyes to relax. He had hoped for word from the ship before the meeting. It would have made the ensuing gathering less unpleasant, but Fate had otherwise decreed.

Wearily he stepped up his pace, as his aide escorted him to the Hall.

EIGHT DOZEN astronautical units from the Great Divide, *Gr'shuna* lay nearly half of the way from Terra to the Outer Planets ringing the perimeter of the Crutchtan Basin. Concealed from Terran long-range sensing devices by a prominence emanating from the Great Cloud, it had long been the farthest outpost of the Empire, the lone island of civilization in the wilderness of the Shunite Sector.

As in all things, progress in science altered the circumstances of life, and as scientists from the Imperial Institute arrived to spark exploration of the Cloud, change had swept the sleepy planet like a tropical storm. Industries sprouted like mushrooms in the forest, and colonists from all reaches of the Empire came to join the Millennial Outreach. For the first time since the *g'Khruushtani* helped form the Grand Alliance nearly eight thousand cycles earlier, the excitement of discovery had taken root, and in the dozen duodecades since, the Colonial Ministry had brought fully six-dozen planets into the Dominion. Imperial scientists reduced many of the most promising to habitability, all within sight of the Great Cloud, whose gentle grace across the night sky was as familiar to the outermost reaches of the Imperial Domain as the milky streamers of the Galaxy. The first settlements beyond the Shunite Prominence had occasioned much celebrating, from the humblest worlds to the sacred soil of *g'Khruushte,* and breaching the Wisps of the Cloud had come to symbolize an end to the limits of the past and the dawning of the New Age.

But the same advances which carried the Imperator's subjects to newer worlds brought new concerns as well. Toward the Galactic

Core were the Glinci—a race of wingless birdmen whose appetite for shiny baubles rivaled the legendary monsters of the Sheregal. Toward the Galactic Periphery were the Atkvalo of the Large Eyes and Hideous Countenance, who dwelt below ground in hermaphroditic abandon, with strange ways and odd ideas that threatened the time-honored Ways of the Third Empire of the *g'Khruushtani*. Both races cast covetous eyes at the riches of the Cloud, and both races chafed under terms of the Charter, which long had placed most of the Cloud within the Empire's domain. Each had demanded alterations, but as each full member of the Grand Alliance had right of veto over new admissions, the Imperator's Emissaries to the High Solonic Council could deny voice and vote to the interlopers. They remained junior partners in the council chambers—able to share the benefits of membership, but lacking a means to press for change.

Then the Terrans rose to throw the Alliance into turmoil. Their sudden appearance in the western skies meant a limit to the westward expansion of the *g'Khruushtani*. Worse than this, they gave both Glinci and Atkvalo a wedge to thrust toward the Great Cloud. Imperial policy long had placed highest importance on developing the regions beyond *Gr'Shuna*, to give the Imperator a bulwark against encroachments by the neighboring races. But the primitive Terrans, blocking the way west, provided a vacuum as clear as the blackness of space, there for any ambitious race to claim. And if Terra fell under the sway of Glincian lies or Atkvali blandishments, the efforts of a dozen generations would crumble into dust, for all the diplomats at the Imperator's command could not change reality. If beset by hostile claims on three sides, the Charter's boundaries would fall as surely as a rock thrown from a mountain.

These thoughts filled the mind of Ga'Glish as he made his way to the Hall. He was certain to face an Inquisition by diplomats from all corners of the Grand Alliance. None wished to be left out, and all professed great concern over the progress of talks, but the interests of most lay in watching the competing forces contend for advantage, and the contenders each had their own interests to advance. Only the Veshnans seemed truly interested in promoting the common good, but they had always struck Ga'Glish as rather an odd race.

No sooner had the Centurion entered the Hall than the diplomats began assailing him with questions, each speaking his own tongue—

aided, as need arose, by a translating device, or by one of the many translators, who sat by the wall nearest the door until summoned by a dignitary.

"Zatar is due when, Ga'Glish?" demanded the Fidrei ambassador. The Fidrei were a short race, with webbed feet and long, flat bills, from far to the South of Veshna. Self-important to the point of pomposity, they were constantly at odds with the subjects of the Imperator—and likely allies of the Glinci, if events forced them to choose sides.

"He is due soon." Ga'Glish took his seat, off to the side. Like the diplomats, he sat on a plush pillow of finest purple velvet. An elaborate tapestry hung from the wall behind him; a mosaic of stone greeted his eyes from the opposite side of the room. Everywhere, the finest trappings of the Imperial court abounded, but like the chamber music at a Grand Feast, none of this impressed the assembled dignitaries. All had long since grown used to the comforts of civilization, and while quick to notice deficiencies, the amenities of life met with as little notice as the air they breathed.

"How soon?"

"As soon as he arrives."

Ga'Glish watched the ambassador rapidly nod his head and flare his fire-orange eyes, as Fidrei did when aggravated. The ambassador was unamused by his verbal fencing, but Ga'Glish reflected that it was ever so with the Fidrei. They saw amusements as trifles.

"A storm delays their arrival, and— "

"A great storm?" asked Shuli, the Veshnan.

"No, a modest storm, but enough to blur communications with the travelers. Still, they are only three units away. The delay will be a few days, nothing more."

"You are aware, are you not," said Drubid, the Glincian observer on the High Solonic Council, recently arrived from Balarium to meet with Zatar's delegation personally, "that the Terrans are due in—*achh*, how do you call it? The fourth-part of your year."

"A quarter-cycle, Subsolon?" offered Ga'Glish.

"Yes, yes—a quarter-cycle," continued the Glincian, dismissing the centurion's assistance with a wave of his hand. "We must ensure that arrangements proceed apace. You must, of course, ready the planet and plan a proper festival."

"I understand," Ga'Glish said coldly, annoyed at the Glincian's arrogance, "that the Terrans care little for festivals."

"Their lack of hospitality does not excuse our own, Ga'Glish," corrected Ls'Sala, the Imperator's emissary.

Ga'Glish bowed in acknowledgment.

"But that is not his responsibility," continued Ls'Sala. "The Imperial Ministry of Foreign Relations has determined— "

"The jurisdiction of the Imperial Ministry is not conceded," interjected Drubid.

"Be that as it may," Ls'Sala said blandly, though Ga'Glish felt the fire beneath his words. "Arrangements must be made. I suggest that we talk to Zatar before committing ourselves to a particular program. His insights will be of undoubted value."

"So it is agreed," said Shuli, the Veshnan, seeking to make peace among the diplomats, "that we await his arrival? We must, after all, make the most of his presence while we have the opportunity. The High Council will likely wish his presence for a full consultation on Balarium before the Terrans arrive to resume the talks, so we had best ensure ourselves ample time to converse with him before he is called away."

"I will arrange the transportation needed," nodded Ga'Glish.

"And you must secure the Expanse," reminded Ls'Sala. Ga'Glish bowed silently, though it seemed pointless to confirm the obvious. With that, the meeting concluded abruptly, leaving the astonished Ga'Glish grateful that it had not been the roasting he had feared. Without ceremony, the assembled diplomats rose and left; the two g'Khruushtani trailed behind.

"No craft must interfere," Ls'Sala whispered in a hiss unintelligible to the others. "We must not reveal too much to the longnoses—not now, and perhaps never."

"Aside from their escorts—which will keep a proper distance, if you wish it—my own craft alone will sail, while they are en route," returned Ga'Glish.

"No. None."

"I will go to the planet, Ls'Sala. I must look at the Terran craft first-hand, for we must see their ship in operation. The chance may not recur under such favorable circumstances."

"Those are your instructions, Ga'Glish. We do not wish to offend the Terrans. Nor, more importantly, do we want to give them the chance for insight. We will guide them to port because we have no choice. But heed this: no unessential travel will be permitted along their star path. It is the decree of Minister Cra'Jenli, and no one less. Your duty is to obey."

The havenmaster frowned, but purged his mind of defiance. When he and Ls'Sala parted company, he turned toward the Arborium gate. He wanted the time and peace to contemplate his alternatives, and the gardens of the arboreal walkway soothed his mind like the countryside of home.

His reverie was interrupted by the appearance at his side of Sra'Chengla. The Young One showed much promise and often offered insights as sharp as a woman's tongue. They left the corridor and walked together toward the garden, where plants and vines flourished in the artificial light. As they slowly strolled, Ga'Glish advised him of all that had transpired.

"So Drubid and his allies are still angling to control the negotiations, all the while staying out of view."

"They will try," nodded Ga'Glish. "But they must first contend with Zatar, and the Veshnan is unlikely to lose the encounter."

"And Ls'Sala is determined— "

"Ls'Sala is but an errand boy for his superiors. Foreign Relations is vying with Expanse Services for the Imperator's ear. It is simple as that. They will cut us out to serve their ends in the capital, whatever the cost to security."

"What is our recourse? It seems to me...."

Amusement flared in the eyes of Ga'Glish. "I will find a way, Son of Sr'Cheng. I trust the Terrans very little, but I trust our brother races even less. And I trust Ls'Sala and his kind not at all. So I will go to *Gr'Shuna*—if not as Havenmaster Supreme, then simply to visit my parents. And in the end, do you doubt that the Imperial Emissary would bow to form—or imagine that any would dare deny Ga'Glishek a visit from his own son?"

Chapter 2

A S IMPERIAL POLITICS PRESSED upon the heart and mind of Lord Glishek's son, the days passed like years in purgatory for the bridge crew of the starship *d'Artagnan*, fresh out of Ishtar Command and fully entangled with everything that could possibly go wrong on a ship's shakedown cruise.

"Palmer...."

The blinking control lights of the weapons station marked each passing second, as events led the senior weapons officer to wonder again why she had once found space duty so irresistible. Her jaw set firmly, she waited for their local god to exact his peculiar justice. After all the difficulties they'd had getting their ship ready to sail, the mission was simply not going according to any of the Skipper's plans. While this came as no surprise to anyone, including the increasingly annoyed captain himself, it was making life difficult for everyone on the bridge. As she knew it would, when judgment time finally did come the captain's voice dripped with disappointment.

"Palmer...Palmer...Palmer.... "

"Yes, sir?"

Rocking in the command seat, Roscoe Cook slowly shook his head. All Karen Palmer could do was sit and wait. It was a ritual that had quickly become routine, but familiarity couldn't keep her from getting uncomfortably warm. Finally signaling that the ordeal would continue on schedule, the captain raised his index finger.

"Seams, Lieutenant," he said ponderously, like a judge delivering a weighty verdict.

"Yes, Captain."

"On my ship, we aim for the seams."

"Yes, sir."

"The seams in the enemy's shields."

"Yes, sir. The seams."

"Now you're following me so far?"

"Yes sir," Palmer gritted her teeth. "Aim for the seams."

"And be sure to time your shots to the correct rhythm when I give the command to fire. Unless the order is to fire at will, it's fi-re-*boom*...fi-re-*boom*! Three beats, exactly in tempo, and you fire on the third. That way, the power surges straight from the engines into the guns without being caught in the buffer. It saves us about two-and-a-half beats if we get the rest of the sequencing right."

"Yes, sir," Palmer sighed.

"All right," Cook smiled tightly, then turned his chair forward, to face the helm. "Mendelson— "

"The helm is still sticking, sir," said Janet Mendelson, staring stiffly ahead at the helm station. "I'm still trying to iron out the problem."

"Remember—you and I have the job of making sure that the weapons officer has a clear shot at cutting through those seams, rather than bouncing our shots off the fat part of their shields."

"Yes, sir."

"Sticky helm or not."

"Yes, sir."

Overhead, the viewer showed the passing stars as they burned in the blackness of space. Cook just nodded and continued rocking, as if critiquing his senior officers' performance was no more interesting to him than chatting idly about the interstellar weather.

"Mr. Talbert?"

Talbert stared sullenly at his control console. The navigation screen had returned to the plot he'd chosen for the last approach—which hadn't been perfect, it was true, but was the best he could do in the time allowed him. He knew that he was not performing up to Cook's standards. Those standards were impossibly high, and everyone knew it. And he hated this slow torture Cook put them all through. Before long, the navigator could stand the wait no longer.

"Sir?" he said at last.

Though his voice was calm as ever, Cook's eyes narrowed intensely. The sarcastic tone of his voice pierced the navigator's ego more painfully than the sharpest nails. "Let's try to get it right next time, shall we? We were off again that time—nearly two points off, if you care to check the track. And you know, Commander—you do tend to be slower than Moses. Let's try to pick up the tempo, shall we?" the captain said, clapping his hands for emphasis.

Talbert had no audible reply; Cook rose from his chair to stretch his legs.

"Practice, people—that's all we need. That's all any of us need. That's why we do this and that's why we keep running the same drills day after day after day. Practice—that's all it takes. Practice can make a little talent go a long way."

Janet's cough caught his attention—and for the first time since they'd left IshCom, he'd caught her smiling, and the corners of his mouth turned up when she cast a quick glance toward his station. It wasn't until he saw her face flush a bright red that he remembered.

Quickly, he resumed his seat. "Let's have another go," he barked. "Same exercise., different random variables. Dexter, take systems. McKenzie to navigation. Jeremy, you take the chair for this one."

As his executive officer set the computer for another drill and rose from the systems station to come to the command seat, Cook cleared his throat, recalling the line from his past—"Practice can make a little talent go a long way." It was a perfectly innocent remark. And however trite, it was an observation well worth remembering.

Of course, he smiled, last time it was a slightly different context.

* * *

THREE HOURS LATER, Jeremy Ashton found himself in front of the door to the Science Lab. Feeling very foolish, the ship's executive officer stood and waited, summoning the resolve to enter.

Like every Academy graduate, he'd spent his share of time in a lab, but this one made him uneasy. Like the laboratory on any starship, it was as cramped as a storage compartment, less than half the size of a research lab at any respectable starbase. Yet what kept him on edge was not the spartan surroundings. He simply felt uneasy around the ship's science officer, a dark and mysterious Valhallan named Hatfield, whose eyes bulged whenever he smiled. A research biologist, Hatfield seemed better suited as a character in a book of supernatural terror than to duty aboard a ship of the Cosmic Guard. Jeremy kept expecting to wake up one day to find the ship taken over by a resurrected fetal pig, or overrun by an army of freeze-dried rodents.

Not that he was prejudiced against biologists. In earlier days it was his favorite science. But shortly after they'd put out from IshCom, he ventured labside, looking for some spare wiring to fix a minor glitch in his computer console. There he'd seen Hatfield, alone in the lab, cutting into some pickled amphibian from New Babylon or elsewhere, his face a vision of rapturous delight. It made Jeremy's skin crawl, and ever since he had avoided the lab and their science officer whenever possible. Cook said that Hatfield knew his field, and the captain seemed a keen judge of talent, but it didn't make the slightest bit of difference to Jeremy. The young Valhallan made him nervous.

The door to the Science Department swooshed open and Jeremy stepped inside. His eyes, used to the brighter lights of the hallway, saw nothing but darkness. As his eyes adjusted, only the bubbling sounds of heating compounds rose to catch his ear.

Suddenly, a hand gripped Jeremy's arm; he flinched convulsively, emitting a frightened yelp that was swallowed by the soundproofed walls.

"Sorry, Commander. I d-didn't mean to startle you."

It was Hatfield. His high-pitched voice burned with an eerie breathlessness, and he spoke with a stutter.

"That's all right, Lieutenant. I'm looking for— "

"The Skipper's in C-cubicle Number T-t-two," smiled the young Valhallan. "That's straight down the hall, s-second room on the left."

Jeremy strode directly to Cubicle Two, arriving to see Cook sitting on a stool and oblivious to the rest of creation, staring intently at a half-finished, makeshift gravity bell perched in the middle of a large black counter. Unlike the rest of the lab, the room was well lit and littered with bits of scientific junk. Cupboard doors and drawers were opened around the room, showing a scattered collection of beakers and tubes, wires and cutting instruments, in closets, on tables, and everywhere. More than anything, it looked as if Cook had gone into every corner of the room, looking for this and that, and had forgotten to close any of the drawers when he was through.

After waiting for a few moments, and shifting uncomfortably from one foot to the other, Jeremy audibly cleared his throat. When it became clear that this would do no good, he knocked gently on the wall and entered the lab.

Cook looked up, a puzzled look crossing his face.

"You sent for me?"

"Right," Cook nodded tentatively. He couldn't quite remember why he'd sent for his executive officer, and it took a few moments to recapture the thread of his thinking.

"Oh, right!"

Cook motioned for Jeremy to take the empty stool across the counter, then handed his executive officer a pad of graph paper. The captain's eyes brimmed with the pride of a schoolboy bringing home the best report card of his life.

Jeremy grimaced in befuddlement. The paper was filled with vector markers and lined with indecipherable hieroglyphics. Arrows pointed this way and that, and equations with no apparent meaning were scattered throughout. The only thing he recognized was a small disc-shaped object in the upper left quadrant. It was probably a starship, he concluded, though he wouldn't have given odds on his chance of being right.

"What's this?"

"A new maneuver," grinned Cook, starting to lean back in the lab stool and catching himself just before falling to the floor. "Well, it's not exactly new. It's been noodling around in my head for quite some time, actually. I just needed some practical experience on a starship to get the ideas moving again. And I think I've finally solved the problem."

"But what— "

"You see, Jeremy, I never have been satisfied with the turning radius. On a starship, that is. Actually, on any ship, but especially a starship."

"You mean, the parabola of change? But it's— "

"I mean, given the hull's stress tolerance—and the raw power available for maneuvering...well, it's bothered me since my days at the Academy. It's just too narrow. Too damn constricting."

"And what about the laws of physics?"

Cook waved his hand contemptuously. "Achh—details."

"I beg your pardon?"

"*Wellll*...physics is a dynamic science, Jeremy. I mean, after all, nothing really immutable about it. With each new advance in our understanding of the Universe, it's constantly changing. It's not some holy writ carved in stone on some moldy mountain in eons past."

"Yes, but— "

"Five hundred years ago, the laws of physics held it impossible to sail faster than light."

"I know, Skipper, but— "

His eyes filling with mischief, Cook wagged a pedantic finger at his second in command. "And five hundred years before that, scientists declared flight to be physically impossible."

"But what does that have to do with— "

"Besides," Cook took the pad and nodded, his brow furrowing intently. "It works. At least it does on paper."

"Uhhm—?" Jeremy took the pad, squinting in confusion.

"Well, it almost works. Close enough for now, anyway. Just a few minor bugs to iron out and then we should be set. Of course, we still have to think up a name for the damn thing."

"But, Skipper— "

"Besides, considering the bridge drills of the past few days, looks to me like we need something to capture everyone's attention," Cook shook his head gravely. "We've reached a plateau, Jeremy. And we need a reason to keep up the pace or everyone will get discouraged. Actually, I suppose I'd be the one getting discouraged, but then that's rather beside the point."

"Yes, but— "

"So it's settled." Cook rapped the counter with his fist and gave a vigorous nod of his head.

"What is?"

"We start tomorrow. Well, maybe the next day. We'll need to double-check the repair job on the Helm, first. And I want to have Van Horn give the engines the once-over. We don't want to short circuit anything, now do we?"

"Oh no—this isn't going to— "

"Now just calm down, Jeremy. There's nothing to worry about. Nothing can go wrong."

"But— "

"Well, nothing we can't fix, anyway."

"*Skipper!*"

"So it's settled, then," laughed Cook.

* * *

AS THEIR CAPTAIN amused himself by running his executive officer around in circles, the junior officers of the Quarter Watch were waiting their turn at the simulators in the Computer Room Annex.

"I still think we should be spending more time on the bridge. Off hours I mean."

"Why is that, Dexter?" Tom Gerlach winked a mischievous eye at Connie McKenzie, the apprentice navigator. She flashed a captivating grin in return, and they waited as patiently as they could while the chronometer pulsed along interminably. The room was large—forty feet across—divided into sections by three rows of domed simulators. The three of them stood next in line, and the hour was about to strike, freeing the simulators for the next shift. The furnishings were sparse and functional: no chairs or tables, just the simulators and the clock on the wall.

"Well," said Dexter, pushing his thick glasses off the tip of his nose, "simulator practice is fine for basic skills, but it really gives us no feel for the ship itself. It's like limiting small craft practice to class work, rather than taking the scouts into space ourselves."

"Oh, I don't know, Dexter," said Connie. "We've made progress."

"Ha!" snorted Gerlach. "Hardly enough to please the Skipper."

"No," she smiled at Gerlach. He'd had a particularly bad day with the captain, who couldn't understand why the weapons station always seemed to develop so many technical problems whenever the apprentice weapons officer took over the seat. Only the navigator, it seemed, took more abuse than Gerlach. Of course, she thought, the captain could expect Talbert to know his job. After all, he'd been at it for quite a while.

"But our progress is pretty steady," she continued. "In no time at all, I'll bet, we'll be ready to take anything he has to dish out."

The hatch to Simulator Number Three swung open, and Roberta Blount walked out, shading her eyes to give them the chance to adjust to the stronger lights. Short and heavy-set, her dour face spoke a bitter disappointment over her first assignment, the ancillary guns in the ship's weapons section. She felt a bitter coldness toward Gerlach for besting her for the post of weapons officer apprentice, and was still angry at the captain for telling her that she hadn't even made the first cut after she protested her assignment. Without so much as a sideways glance, she ambled toward the hallway, her face wooden and humorless.

"Go ahead," smiled Gerlach, motioning for Dexter to move ahead of his place in line.

"You sure?" said Dexter, his eyes widening as he looked up at his companions. Of all the new blueshirts, he was the only one who actually followed the captain's directive to work with the simulator at least a cosmic hour each day. Even worse, he actually seemed to enjoy practicing. The trait had not endeared him to the rest of the ensigns.

"I mean, you guys were here first and all. It just doesn't seem fair, to go and—well, you know— "

"No, I insist," Gerlach said, his brows furrowing jovially. "Besides, I'm not done talking to Connie. With the watch ending, another dome is sure to open up any time now."

Dexter smiled broadly. "Gee, thanks Gerlach." He turned and walked ahead to the simulator.

"Don't mention it," Gerlach said. He waited until Dexter disappeared behind the closed hatch and then motioned to the others in the room, a fiendish glint in his eye.

"*Quiet*," he whispered, motioning for Bruno and Curtis, who were standing beside the storage closet door, to unfasten the latch and open the door.

" 'All right Mr. Underwood,' " a voice with a pitiable Isitian accent called from inside Simulator Number Three. Gerlach rolled his eyes and snorted derisively; Connie tried not to giggle. " 'Sound battle stations.' 'Aye, sir.' "

As Dexter added his peculiar sound effects to the simulation, Shrewsbury and Savich, two ensigns currently assigned to help supervise the security detail, entered the simulator room, pushing a broken robot cleaner that Gerlach had found in the hangar deck machine shop. They grunted mightily under the weight, groaning angrily for someone to help them. It was box-shaped, about three feet high, with a smashed electronic eye and a broken left wheel. Gerlach and the other men ran to help support one side of the cleaner, while Connie ran to stand by the entrance, to make sure no one was coming.

"'Helm, slow to C-2. We've no need to be showing off just yet, Mendelson. Not till the rest of this group can handle the basic Level Four Simulations.' 'Aye-aye, sir.'"

Grunting under the strain, the five men wheeled the cleaner to Dexter's simulator and, gently as possible, pushed it up against the hatch—which, for safety purposes, opened outward on all the simulators.

"'Range, Mr. Dexter?' Uh—just let me check, sir," Dexter said from inside, in his own voice. " 'We haven't got forever, Ensign. Enemies do tend to laugh at requests for more time, you know.' Yes, sir. Range, fifty klicks and closing."

Quietly, the conspirators tiptoed away. Everyone but Gerlach headed straight for the door.

"'Palmer—full power to shields and prepare to charge the starboard guns.'"

"Hurry," Connie called from just outside the door. Gerlach reached down, unplugged Number Three, and ran toward the door, joining his companions in a sprint down the hallway.

"Hey, guys—my machine just went dead. Could somebody check the plug?"

After a few seconds of silence, the hatch door started rattling on Simulator Number Three, soon followed by knocks from inside the practice station.

"Hey, guys? Whoops—boy, you want to hear something funny, guys? The door's stuck. Again. What is that, the third time this week? Anyway, I may need some help getting out of here." Dexter rapped loudly on the inside of the hatch.

"Okay, Guys?"

The knocking stopped.

"Guys?"

* * *

```
CC:              143-0635.4
FILE:            Log
ACCESS:          Command.
SECURITY:        Standard
OPERATIONAL STATUS: Shakedown
LOCATION:        43-450339/xx/rF-x
```

We are forty parsecs beyond Ishtar, nearing the limits of Cos-Guard's Training Range. Course holding steady at 045/015-n. Reddish glow of Crutchtan Cloud dominates the forward vista. Interstellar debris of Eisenbraun Range is four parsecs dead to port; Jaimie's Spiral is visible 45 degrees south of starboard beam. Area's dominant star is unnamed red dwarf, two parsecs ahead.

Bridge drills are improved, though much remains to be done. Spacedrive difficulties have forced us back to the simulator.

Though glitch source remains undetermined, chief among suspected culprits are my efforts to perfect "spiral turn" maneuver. (See Log and Supplement, cc:143-0634). I have reduced speed to C-6 to minimize engine drain during repairs. Lt Mendelson has isolated and fixed circuitry cross-wirings in the helm controls. This should increase ship maneuverability, but we cannot test improvements until Chief Engineer solves difficulties that have developed with the engine blocks. Other problems are minor.

No word on Command Request of 142-9994, concerning participation in upcoming maneuvers.

Capt R Cook

Chapter 3

IT WAS HARD NOT TO notice, especially on a small outpost like Starbase 117. Blueshirts were flooding Hallway C, moving quickly toward the central monitors. And thanks to automation, officers rarely set foot inside the Inner Ring, except during emergencies.

It was an arrangement much-loved by the one hundred and ninety-nine crewmen and technicians who did the actual work of the base. The central computers collated and processed data from the base sensors, and from the two dozen or so tracking stations along the frontier that fed their readings into the base centrax. As long as everything went smoothly, there was little need for the blueshirts. Only the officer-on-call stayed past roll call, and even he often left the shift foreman, invariably an experienced yeoman, in charge. This kept the base running smoothly, for experience had proven time and again that most blueshirts were more trouble than they were worth.

So when half the officer's roster came scurrying toward the control room, people took note. Even Commodore Medwick came, and it was exactly the second time that he had entered the control room since arriving from DemCom, eight weeks earlier. Soon, rumors were spreading as fast as the Demetrian Flu; but on a starbase, they were the second favorite source of entertainment.

THE YEOMAN gritted her teeth but said nothing, She hadn't won her chief's stripes by insulting commodores. All the same, she felt sorry for Ensign Takira, the new arrival from the Academy. The young blueshirt's problem was even clearer than his explanation. He may just as well have been talking to driftwood on the mantle.

"You are not making sense, Ensign," snapped Commodore Peter Medwick. Perspiration beaded on his brow, and his stubby fingers looked like raw pork sausages. Short and thickset, his jowls flapped like gills, powered by his robust jaw muscles. His breathing was hard and labored, and his nervous brown eyes darted constantly about him.

"Commodore...," Takira began again, trying again to make clear his concern, but running out of patience himself. He placed a hand on the main console. The crewman at the station kept his eyes focused on the circular motion of the sensor sweep, hoping to avoid the flak he knew was coming.

"The computer shows the same alien ship at Stations Three and Ten. Either they're lying about their identity systems or they're lying about their call numbers. But they're sure as hell lying about something. If you ask me, we damn well better make an inspection transit to investigate."

The commodore's eyes bulged angrily.

"If I may say so, sir," the ensign added hastily.

Medwick frowned darkly. He hated insolent tyros, especially Academy hotshots like this slanty-eyed Earther. More importantly, CentCom hated "incidents," and he'd have none in his sector. Not while he was in charge. He had fifty parsecs of border to worry about, and if the lizards ever took it into their heads to be troublesome it would not sit well with the promotions board. Besides, both starships assigned to his base were on patrol. It would take days for them to arrive; with his available cruisers in dry dock for repairs, he'd have to send a lowly frigate across the boundary to investigate. That, he concluded, was something he simply would not do.

"We have no proof that anything is wrong," Medwick said disdainfully, each word a slap at the young ensign's pride. "A junior officer's speculations are no substitute for hard data. Most likely, it's a simple mistake, or our own malfunctioning computer. And I'll bet you never thought to check this thing with the lizards' Alpha Base, did you, Ensign?"

The young officer lowered his eyes.

"I thought not," harumphed the commodore. "Next time, don't sound the alarm until you have proof. Real proof."

Mumbling ponderously to himself, he waddled to the door, leading the other blueshirts from the room. Red-faced, Takira stared at the floor until they had gone. Even the blinking lights on the viewscreens seemed to mock him. He turned to face the control room crew.

"Carry on," he said. He smiled bravely, but there was pain in his voice. He had been badly hurt. "I'll be in my quarters." Hastily, he stepped past the ramp leading to the control tower, and headed toward the main floor hatch.

"Ensign?" the yeoman said out loud.

Takira stopped, but did not turn. The yeoman, embarrassed for the deflated young blueshirt, shifted uncomfortably on her feet.

"Don't let it bother you, Mr. Takira. Old Fogbrain doesn't seem to have a lot of sense," the sweep of her arm took in all the technicians manning the monitor desks, "though I have ten witnesses who'll swear I never said any such thing."

She looked across the control room. Every redshirt was looking up from his screen; she was speaking for everyone there.

"But for whatever it's worth, I think you're right."

Takira nodded his head and breathed deeply, but the yeoman's words didn't help much. He walked out the door and down the hallway. Then he rode the elevator to the residential deck and locked himself in his room.

Chapter 4

THE BATTLE STATIONS BUZZER had no sooner faded than the alarm bell started ringing throughout the ship. At once, the hallway was in an uproar, as crewmen and yeomen alike scrambled for a safe haven. Everyone knew what the alarm bell meant. Like Pavlov's dogs, they all responded by instinct.

Yeoman Chief Gregory Connors raced from his post in the computer room and darted toward the Library's foyer, two doors down. The walls of the corridor passed him like a tan-colored blur. Breathing heavily, he grabbed a handhold in the outer hatch and prepared to hang on for dear life. The computer room was no place to be at a time like this. Papers, shelves, and anything not tied down would soon be banging the head of anyone foolish enough to stay put. The foyer offered a secluded spot of safety, one of the few choice spots on the Conning Deck that wasn't already assigned, but it had only two sets of handholds. He wasn't the only one to know about it, and rank meant nothing at a time like this. It was every man for himself.

Seconds later, running like a frightened schoolboy, Lars Andersen slid into the hatch, a half-dozen redshirts on his tail. But the yeoman's hands had grabbed the handhold first, so by right it belonged to him. Cursing angrily, the rest of the mob rushed down the bend in the corridor, seeking some other haven until the crisis passed.

"How long—?" began Andersen.

"No idea," returned Connors, still slightly out of breath. "But if we're lucky...."

The movement of the ship cut short his reply. She pitched and swayed beneath them gently as a billowing sea, her soothing motions causing the two yeomen to panic, and they clutched their holds as tightly as they could. "Christ!" muttered Connors, under his breath, desperation turning his knuckles white. "Here it comes."

The rocking soon became sharper, more focused, more commanding, and the ship curved violently beneath their feet, disrupting their sense of balance. Without warning, the fierce whine of the engines engulfed the deck. The ship careened as if out of control, snapping into what felt like a steep, endless curve that drained whatever strength remained in their legs and sent their insides swirling into a violent eddy of time and motion.

"I'm—losing it...."

"Stand fast, Andersen."

"I'm losing it, Chief."

"Hold on. It can't go on much longer."

The swirling stopped as suddenly as it began, and the ship shimmied under the stress of a forced reduction in power.

"Engines are cuttin down," shouted Connors. "We made it."

Andersen made no reply.

The ship seemed to straighten out beneath them, no longer pressing them into the walls. The dizzy, mad whirling started fading like a bad dream, and Connors relaxed his grip.

"There we go...what did I tell ye? No matter what he does, the engines always kick down under the strain. As long as the safety override stays intact— "

Connors looked to see Andersen, already on his knees, his arched back heaving violently. He knelt by to his friend's side, grabbing him by the shoulders to steady him.

Slowly, the hallway started filling again. Crewmen staggered down the corridors, some to their duty stations, most toward sick bay. From beyond the bend came the usual sounds of distress—the moans and curses and sounds of retching. Andersen's stomach was hardly the weakest on board. These days, old hands and greentails alike were making their mess in more than the usual way.

"Let's come along there, Andersen. Let's get ye to the doctor again." Slowly, the Chief helped the ship's second-ranking yeoman to his feet. Connors felt the floor sway beneath his own steps. His mind fought to clear itself, and his stomach struggled to keep his lunch.

As they neared the sick bay, Connors saw what was coming to be a common sight. The Skipper had them lined up into the corridor again. Half the crewmen on board were bent over like withered old ladies, puking their guts out. Connors could only shake his head. He was sure that the Skipper had his reasons for doing this to them. Whatever he did, Cook always had reasons.

Whether they were silly reasons, he thought—now that was an open question. And it was a question being debated on every deck of the ship.

"CAW—THIS rock's a-brimmin. I can feel it in me bones."

"Where are ye, Cyrus? Ye've stepped off the screen...ah! There be ye."

Mason McGee glanced up from the monitor to rest his eyes. The ship was quiet; he'd set the engines to run on batteries. This close to the asteroid's parent star, the power would last indefinitely. Lights flashed on the control panel, as the auto-pilot kept the ship a steady distance above the pockmarks and gulleys that streaked the gnarled surface of the small world below. Mason was intent on tracking the green pinpoint of light on the ancillary screen. His brother was making the first drop to the asteroid, and Mason would not relax until Cyrus returned.

"What's the readin?"

"There's somethin down here, Macey. The instruments show that much. But there's too much iron and nickel mixed in. It's foulin the readin. I can't get me a true fix."

"Maybe it's all just common rock. We seen us false readin's enough this time out to fill a bloody book."

"Maybe. But there's somethin different about this one. It don't add up, if its just common space rock. Maybe I should take out the geophyzer after all."

"Suit yourself."

Mason watched the screen as Cyrus hiked back from the crest of the central swell toward the flats of the plain, where he'd left the lander. Mason's eyes drifted toward the forward porthole; the ship was rounding toward leeward, and the view was toward Galactic Center. A dusting of stars stretched before him, and the Cloud stretched far into the distance toward the east. All around him, the local lights gleamed brightly, in colors as vivid as the blackness in which they floated. They were in uncharted skies, well anticenter from any Cozzie base, looking down the throat of the Neutral Zone and so far beyond civilization that not even the lizards cared to post a sentry. Even the faint signals from Riley's Station had faded into subspace static weeks ago, and Riley's was already beyond the limits of civilization as far as the Cozzies were concerned.

There was a timeless beauty to the endless void he sailed, mused Mason, like a dream floating on an empty sea. He never tired of the stark vistas that greeted him. It fired the wonder in his soul to walk where no man ever stood before. Like the caverns he and Cyrus scoured for riches, an emptiness inside would not let him rest. Yet wherever his wanderings led, space always brought him peace.

Suddenly, he heard Cyrus bellow over the radio.

"Sakes! Ah, ye Demmy-rotted, jack-twistin pile o'space bilge!"

"Cyrus! What's wrong?"

"Like to bash me head a-thund'rin—it's just like the rest, Macey. The bloody stars'll go moldy a-fore— "

"Tell me! What ye be a-seein?"

"It's like the bloody rest, I told ye. It's another bloody cone. A buggered-up metallic cone."

Mason sighed wearily. He was hoping they'd struck pay dirt this time, but was starting to wonder. The metallic cones they'd been finding looked like nothing he'd ever seen, and this region of space had no claimers. So far as he knew, there weren't a half-dozen prospectors who'd ventured this far past the charts. Yet the onion-shaped cones were of advanced design and disrupted their instruments to no end. Sent everything hay-wiring to proper fits, it did; made it look like the rock was loaded with all sorts of heavy metals when it was just a metal cone shooting off sparks. At first, they both thought it was some ore miner's way of misleading the competition. Now, Mason wasn't so sure.

Something registered in his mind, something about the location. This was the third cone they'd discovered on this trip, all in the same general location. He got out the logbook and put it next to the monitor.

"Ye be a-comin— ?" he began.

"Ye bloody right, I be a-comin," Cyrus snapped. "What the bloody hell else ye think I be doin, Macey? I sure ain't be gonna stick around here for me bloody damn health."

Mason sighed. "Take your time, Cyrus. There's no need to be takin chances, now. Even if we find n'more gold this outin, we already got us more'n we can squander in a month. No use losin your temper.

It'll just make ye careless." He watched the screen until his brother was safe inside the lander, and rising from the rock on his way to dock with the ship. He glanced at the logbook; as soon as Cyrus was home, he'd make his checks.

He was sure he'd find something.

He wasn't so sure he'd like the answer.

* * *

"I'M SORRY, sir, but I just don't see it."

"Thank you, Miss Palmer," Cook sighed. "Anybody else?"

At the fore of the bridge, just below the main forward viewer, Cook rubbed his eyes with a weariness born of frustration. This exercise was not going well at all, and he'd had such high hopes at the outset. Freeze-framing images of the computer enemy seemed like such a good idea. He could move the bridge crew along at a pace they could handle, and the whole approach would permit the same Socratic exchange of ideas that energized discussions on the Lyceum Commons back home. Unfortunately, nobody else could keep the flow of events in mind while analyzing all the separate images. Some of them could parse through each frame, but they simply couldn't put the pieces back together. All he had succeeded in doing was confusing everybody—and by now, he feared, that kind of success was becoming routine.

"All right. Next frame...and freeze it."

The bridge was half-empty, and the second team had taken over the systems and communications stations. The side chairs, brought by Maintenance to seat the spillover during bridge drills, were almost empty. Those absent were in sick bay; most of the others had a greenish look about them, as if they were trying to digest something disagreeable. This passed unnoticed by Cook, who seemed immune to the space sickness that was consuming more of his crew with each passing day. His attention was riveted on the viewscreen. He walked toward the forward screen, holding an electronic cursor in his hand. Two starships showed on the screen; the images appeared almost on top of each other, although the computer-guided sensors showed them almost a full astrometer apart.

"As you see, the lead ship has crossed in front its wingmate, so in the course of their maneuvering, they've shifted their relative headings. Now, what does this tell us?" asked Cook. A reddish light circled the enemy ships as he moved the cursor to draw the crew's attention.

Nobody answered. Eyes were all fixed on their respective stations, where the shifting light patterns seemed comfortably familiar.

"Anybody? Except Mendelson, of course. I'm sure she already knows the answer."

Cook looked to see Janet blushing, but across the rest of the bridge he saw only blank looks and averted glances. This, he concluded, sadly shaking his head, was not very Isitian: Isitians did not beat dead horses. At least not very often. For the tenth time since he'd started, he was about to give it up. Maybe it was just as well that they didn't make the inspection cutoff for maneuvers, he smiled to himself. It was one less headache to worry about, and at least this way, they'd have plenty of time to pull things together. Before he could call the current fiasco to a halt, help came, though the rest of his crew found it a decidedly mixed blessing.

It was Van Horn, calling from below.

"Put it over the speaker," Cook told Mathison, the apprentice radio officer; with Underwood in sick bay, she was the acting communications officer for the whole ship.

"Just a minor problem, this time," said Van Horn, when Mathison finally pushed the right button. Across the bridge, faces and stomachs fell in tandem. "Nothing but a glitched-up relay switch, burned out by the power overload. It's easy enough to fix, but for the life of me, Skipper, I don't see a way around the problem. The same thing's bound to happen again so long as you keep trying those new-fangled turns of yours. And we'll still be operating on reduced power until we get an overhaul. Right now, the capability gauge is holding at 60 percent, and I don't see it improving any time soon."

"One step at a time, Mr. Van Horn," laughed Cook. "Let's take one step at time."

Van Horn signed off, and Cook turned his attention back to the bridge. He scratched the back of his head and paused, trying his best not to look like a little boy on Christmas morning, eager to try out a new toy. "I'm sure we all appreciate the Chief Engineer's efforts," he said at last. "Let's take ten minutes to refresh ourselves, before we return to business. Be back here at 900 Hours—*sharp*—for another go at everyone's favorite maneuvers."

"Everyone?" Cook looked to see Janet, her chair turned to face him, smiling the knowing smile of one who shared a secret. Fortunately for the future of the "spiral turn," she also shared his near-immunity to motion sickness. It reminded him of pleasanter times, warming his heart in ways he hoped no one else would notice.

Cook chuckled, despite himself. "Except for those who are—well—indisposed." The rest of the bridge crew was too unsteady to register more than a sullen lack of humor.

"All right, all right. But just this once. We'll work on timing, then. But come 350 Hours tomorrow, it's back to evasive action and spiral turns—even if you all have to leave your bellies in your cabins."

* * *

"CYRUS— "

"What the bloody hell do you want? Don't bother me with tripe. I got enough o'that down on the bloody rock, and I'm in no mood for chitchat."

What they called the galley was a small room, about three meters across, with two stools flanking a single table. They'd made the oven out of a second-hand radio transmitter. Cyrus was too cheap to pay the top dollar that new ship stoves commanded along the frontier these days, and their jerry-rigging worked just fine, anyway. It fit into the rounded side wall, directly across from the door, just below the storage bin hatch. Usually, Cyrus liked nothing better than to relax with a pot of hot coffee and some spacer's biscuits, telling his brother about the old days, or just enjoying the silence. But today, Mason had spread the star charts over the table, leaving no room for snacking. In the best of times, it would have set Cyrus to grumbling; now, it only fanned his temper.

"Ye know somethin, Cyrus?"

"Ye damn right I know somethin. I know a bloody lot o'somethin, and if I had me way ye'd not be askin such dim-witted questions a-fore dinner!"

Sighing to the stars, Mason held his tongue. It was useless talking to his brother when he was like this. Cyrus was like a child throwing a tantrum. The best thing to do was leave him alone until he snapped out of it by himself. Soon, the muttering had receded to a trickle of spacer's obscenities, barely audible beneath his breath. A few moments later, after the storm had passed, Mason tried again.

"Cyrus, remember the other two cones we found."

"I'd rather blot'em from me mind, Macey. And I don't think ye be wise— "

"Listen, they line up, they do. This one lines up with the other two."

"What ye be sayin?"

"Look for yourself."

Mason beckoned his brother to the table. As he'd hoped, Cyrus' curiosity got the better of him. The charts showed an unnatural alignment—a line bending perfectly along with the curvature of the galaxy, leading from the first cones they found to this last batch. The galley's dim lights cast a shadow across Cyrus' scraggly face; he scratched his beard pensively, then compared the local chart with another in a different binder.

"Ye know what these be pointin to?"

Mason shrugged. "Rigel?"

"Not quite. Look-ee here." Cyrus pointed to the second chart. "Ye see? The galactic curve's bringin it short of Rigel's headin by a goodly spread."

"Then what—?"

Cyrus grinned, as much in wonder as amusement at his brother's puzzlement. Mason was a good kid, he thought, though sometimes a speck or two slow.

"Trace it out."

As Mason ran his finger over the chart, Cyrus ran his hand through his shock of hair and shook his head. He had no idea what it all meant, but this was the last thing he expected. It made him wonder anew about the strange markings he'd seen on all the cones. Runes, it seemed—like the random strokes of a calligrapher's pen. "It heads right into the Greater Nakahashi Storm," said Cyrus, "the grandest one in all of Western Terra."

"Well...if these be some kind o'signal, why give a headin right into the teeth of a storm cloud?"

"Look again, Macey."

Cyrus traced out the heading on the chart himself, keeping the course on the same gentle arc set by their cones. "The cones point straight to Gutterman's Gap, smack between the Greater Nakahashi

Storm and the Lesser," Cyrus marveled. "Just like a ruddy compass."
It was positively eerie, he thought: a marker heading straight for the
only pass through the most brutal storms of the West.

"What in God's name.... "

"And ye know what's on the other side o'them storms, Macey?"

Mason shook his head. Cyrus tapped his index finger on the chart,
calling his brother's eye to the only yellow star in the region—
guarded on three sides by permanent storms of varying intensity.

"*Isis*," Mason whispered. A bewildered haze creased his brow.

Cyrus nodded his head, but his mind was racing far ahead of his
brother's. He had long passed wondering how the cones came to be,
or why they pointed to Terra's most distant, most mysterious planet.

He wondered instead what might lie in the other direction.

* * *

"YOU WANTED to see me, Captain?"

Seated beside the communications station in the briefing room of
the starship *Magellan*, Brian Fitzgerald looked up from his viewscreen
to see Helen Bradley, his new executive officer, at his door. She was
a tall woman, with brown eyes, and raven black hair that flowed
gracefully onto her shoulders. She was a fine officer, Fitz thought—or
would be, if she ever learned to relax. Still and all, she made him
nervous. Her tense voice and nasal, Gaen accent seemed out of place
along the frontier. Gaens were not a starfaring people, and only Isis
sent fewer people into the Cosmic Guard.

Even so, she deserved her chance, and he'd often found that people
surprised him, if given a little encouragement. He leaned back in his
chair and beckoned for her to enter. "Have a seat, Braddie, and close
the door behind you."

She walked to the visitor's chair, directly in front of the captain's
oversized desk, and sat down. She noticed a worried look on her
commander's face; gone was the twinkling smile that usually greeted
her arrival—or the arrival of any of the ship's prettier bluebirds, for
that matter. And while she knew that Fitz kept a stern profile in front
of the crew, the same look in the privacy of his own quarters could
mean nothing but trouble.

"You know, I wonder why we bother trying, sometimes," Fitz
sighed, his voice almost sad with resignation. "Nothing seems to make
any sense, and nothing good lasts forever."

Bradley smiled sympathetically. "Couldn't agree more, Cap—but I'm sure that's not why— "

"We're being ordered to the Ishtar Sector," Fitz interrupted, his voice changed from distant to firm, "to help secure the shipping lanes."

"Why?" Bradley squinted as she shook her head. "Surely they have enough ships between here and Ishtar to— "

Fitz turned his screen so that it faced his executive officer. "Read this," he said, concern furrowing his brow.

She looked at the screen; worry soon crept across her face.

```
//II/COMMAND ALERT:
    CC:        143-0640.5/
    TO:        CommandingOfficers-EasternFleet/
    FROM:      FtAdmPorterMClay/
    SECURITY;  CodeBlue/
    PREFIX:    Need-to-Know,Eyes-Only/
    FLAGS:     red1;red2;red3/
```

CosGuard Security Office confirms the presence of Chadbourne Wilkes in Ishtar outlands. Preliminary intelligence reports place him at Allen's Dwarf Station on 143-0638, and trace him to an unregistered schooner which departed toward anticenter-north, then disappeared off sensors into Delabranza Shoals. His present whereabouts are unknown, and CSO is sifting through conflicting reports of recent sightings.

Wilkes' arrival in this sector at a time of increasing pirate activity has elevated CSO concern about the prospect of renewed raids on commercial shipping. In addition, the last direct pirate assaults on fixed EF positions conforms to the period prior to Wilkes' absence from region, while unexplained attacks on Central Fleet bases along Ishtar-New Babylon trunk coincides with rumors of his presence in the western portion of Pirates' Alley. While the significance of his appearance remains unclear, it is feared that his return to this region will escalate the scope and cohesiveness of pirate activity. Surveillance by CSO operatives has detected increased level of communications throughout the frontier.

I am ordering increased security on all outlying CosGuard bases, and am reviewing present deployments with a view toward reinforcing patrols along the most vulnerable shipping corridors. All commanders are advised to prepare for changes in alert status in their sectors, and all ships are advised to prepare for reassignment. Medium Wave Channels 40-60 are now cleared

for emergency use only; all commands will post constant monitors on these channels until further notice. Low Wave Channel 3 is now cleared for security bulletins only; all commands will monitor this channel for further information.
ENCRYPT/TRANSMIT//

"WELL, SKIPPER, that's sure bound to complicate our lives. What do you make of it?"

Alone with the captain in *d'Artagnan's* briefing room, Jeremy looked up from the screen to see Cook lost in thought. It took a moment for his question to register, but when the captain stirred back to life he seemed to dismiss the whole topic.

"Beats me," Cook shrugged, his voice distant and subdued. "But we're too far from the shipping lanes to worry about it." He turned the viewscreen back to face himself. Jeremy noticed him enter the code for the duty roster, then rest his chin in his hand.

"I saw him in action once," Jeremy ventured, returning to the visitor's chair. He saw Cook start entering something into the computer. "It was a couple years ago, when I was first officer on a convoy frigate. He kept his distance. Wouldn't come within spitting distance, even though we had the richest prize moving down Pirates' Alley that month. I never did see what all the fuss was about."

Cook leaned back in this chair, rocking pensively.

"I saw him once, myself," he said at last, his mouth drawing into a tight, humorless smile. For the first since they'd met, Jeremy saw hatred flash in the captain's eyes. It vanished as quickly as it came, but in its wake was a somber, brooding Roscoe Cook that Jeremy had never seen before.

"And what..., " began Jeremy, when he realized that Cook would volunteer nothing more unless prompted.

"What's he like?" Cook leaned back, locking his hands behind his head, gently rocking his chair.

"His maneuvers have an economy of movement that would even make me proud. Almost poetry—stark, lethal poetry. Like a swaying cobra about to strike. My one encounter with his band was just after I'd gotten my frigate. The *Grapentine*, if you remember— "

Jeremy nodded.

"—a second-generation rust-bucket that we kept starworthy by thumb tacks, prayers, and baling wire."

Jeremy leaned back in his own chair. This story was a new one, and he'd never seen Cook so deadly serious.

"One day a call came, sending my squadron to rescue a tramp ore freighter bound for Ishtar down the Anticenter Spike. As we neared, we heard the freighter's skipper begging for his life, and crying into the radio that he'd fulfilled his part of the bargain. Our screen showed him surrounded by a half-dozen brigantines, taking duck-barrel shots at him for their own amusement. As soon as we came into sensor range they finished him off, telling all within earshot that they had to make an example of fools who took too long to surrender his prize.

"And you know what this particular prize was?"

Jeremy shook his head.

Cook leaned back in his chair. Cold fury narrowed his eyes.

"The freighter had given up its gold, and its platinum—and its silver, and half its supplies. But her skipper made the mistake of letting the pirates make visual contact, and they caught a fleeting glimpse of his fourteen-year old granddaughter. Wilkes decided that she should have been part of the old man's offer from the start, so he blew up the ship—after taking the girl, of course."

Cook sighed bitterly. "We gave chase...but, you know, for all its firepower, a frigate is really no match for a pirate's brigantine. Frigates just aren't not maneuverable enough, and they're too easy to shake. At least, for someone who knows what he's doing. We had five of our own to chase after six outlaws, and I sent every one of us after Wilkes. With the whole squadron...well, I thought we had a good shot at him. But then Wilkes cut the smartest arc I ever saw, right into the middle of a cloud bank, and vanished without a trace. And right until the end, he serenaded us over the subspace radio with the sounds of that poor girl getting raped by his entire crew."

The captain smiled bitterly. "And that, Jeremy, is my experience with the famous Mr. Wilkes." He leaned forward and turned the computer screen to face his first officer. "In case it ever comes up, I thought you should have a look at this."

The screen displayed the duty roster, including the ship's formal lines of command. It showed himself and Cook on round-the-clock call, as regulations specified. And it designated Van Horn as next in line during Jeremy's daily stint as early watch supervisor, from Zero

Hour to 500 Hours. Jeremy's eyes widened when he saw the designation for the late watch.

"That's not—regulations are quite specific, Captain," Jeremy sputtered. "You can't—you can't— "

"Achh—details," laughed Cook, dismissing his first officer's consternation with a wave of his hand. "I swear, Jeremy, sometimes that's all you think about. You have to learn to look at the broader picture. See the whole forest, not just the trees."

"But.... "

"And tell me—in a crisis, who would you rather see in charge of the ship? An incompetent navigator—or our gifted helmsman? Besides, I did make one concession to regulations. I did designate Van Horn as senior light comm, though it's not what I'd prefer."

"Talbert won't like it." Jeremy shook his head, protesting more to himself than to the captain, but he'd long since learned that Cook found most of his protests more amusing than helpful. "He won't like it one bit. And I can't imagine how we could justify it to a review board."

Jeremy gulped at the thought that he had just made himself a conspirator; out of politeness, he'd said "we" instead of "you." Cook just chuckled amiably. At times, the captain thought, his first officer could be quite amusing, especially when he wasn't trying.

"Don't be a croaker, Jeremy."

"A what?"

"A croaker…a worrywart. One who harumphs concern to all within earshot, usually about things that aren't worth the effort, most often about matters affecting his own pocketbook."

Jeremy frowned; but it only made Cook laugh.

"No, Jeremy—you see, this roster isn't the one listed on the ship's books, on the standard call-up. The computer won't activate it unless the ship is on red alert. No one will know except you and me—and I certainly won't tell anyone, not even Mendelson herself. There's no need to ruffle feathers needlessly. But when the chips are down, I simply will not have Talbert in charge of my ship, no matter what the rule book has to say about it."

Jeremy sank gloomily into his chair, a reluctant conspirator, his obvious discomfiture doing much to lift Cook's spirits. But the captain was right again. Talbert was all bluster to those below him, a holy terror to anyone he outranked. But in a crisis, the man could crumple like paper. If their lives were at stake, Jeremy thought, he'd much rather see Janet on the hot seat.

"Well," said Cook, settling back in his chair with a self-satisfied smirk, pointing his finger at one of the portraits on the wall behind him, the one with the flowing gray hair and the distant, serene eyes. "Now that we've settled that, let's get back to Hamilton Hawke and the Council of Nine.

Smiling despite himself, Jeremy could do little but shake his head and hold his tongue. Cook enjoyed telling stories, and he seemed to have an endless supply of them, though Jeremy often wondered if any of them were true. Of course, the captain also had an annoying tendency of keeping his first officer away from all the "details" that kept piling on his desk in order to free Cook to contemplate "The Broader Picture." Even so, Jeremy was a willing listener. All the more so because, inevitably, the Captain was full of surprises.

"It was back in the days just before the Terran Civil War—though it's not until after the Fleet sails toward Demeter that the story gets interesting."

"If at all."

"Very funny, Jeremy. You realize, of course, that the Council of Nine back then wasn't noted for its sense of humor—so remarks like that could well have gotten you into as much trouble as the good Master Hawke, but I'm getting ahead of myself."

"Yes, you usually do."

"Now in those days...."

Chapter 5

YOU HAVE CHANGED, G'RISHELA. Is your mind still numbed from the cold, or has life among the longnoses truly altered your outlook?" In the room darkened to receive the holograph from the Capital, a look of wry scorn flashed across the image of Ya'Lisha, Lord Deputy of the Imperial Foreign Ministry.

Ls'Sala's found his own amusement tempered by the fire he felt welling in G'Rishela's soul. His friend had been quiet since the return from Terra, Sala thought, and the few words that Shela did speak were deliberately vague and uncharacteristically subdued. So long as he kept his own counsel, the source of G'Rishela's unease remained imponderable. Now, though, Shela's anger was too pronounced to conceal, and though the image of Ya'Lisha was blind to its depth, Ls'Sala felt it like the midday sun. His friend was usually much too disciplined to let another perceive his private thoughts, but rage was getting the better of him. Ls'Sala hoped that G'Rishela could remain outwardly calm until they could talk in private.

"Surely, Lord Deputy Ya'Lisha would wish his subordinates to learn from experience," G'Rishela replied coldly. "Or perhaps the Imperial Minister himself prefers that his emissaries retain as little as his deputies?"

Fury darkened the Lord Deputy's eyes. "You forget yourself, G'Rishela. And you forget He whom you serve."

G'Rishela refused to accept the correction. "It seems that you have confused servant with master already, Ya'Lisha."

Ls'Sala exhaled a warning rush of air, but it was too late. Indignant, the Deputy Minister rose and nodded to someone out of view. Then he turned his harsh glare back to confront G'Rishela. "You have heard not the last of this, *Emissary*," hissed Ya'Lisha, spitting the last word hatefully. "This transmission is ended." The image vanished abruptly, leaving Ls'Sala and G'Rishela alone with the darkness.

"He is not one to offend needlessly." Ls'Sala could feel the rage slowly die in his friend's soul and clapped his hands, summoning the lights to activation. The walls showed murals of comely females, dancing in the ritual of mating. Near them, on the dining table, a feast stood untouched. G'Rishela insisted that he knew no hunger, and Ls'Sala was too good a host to eat alone.

"He is a fool," G'Rishela replied softly, blinking rapidly to accustom his eyes to the renewed brightness. "We are all fools."

"But Ya'Lisha speaks truly of one thing, my friend. You are not as before. Something within you is changed."

G'Rishela's eyes narrowed in contemplation. Ls'Sala felt a wave of melancholy grip them both. "We are dancing on a bed of eggs, Sala."

"But our duty is clear, Shela. And it comes from the highest authority."

"Folly knows no rank, my friend. And with fools for advisors, the Imperator can be little better than a fool himself."

"Your talk sounds of treason, G'Rishela."

"I talk of danger, my friend, and yet none pays me heed, not even you. Does this betoken wisdom?"

"But speak reason, Shela. The Terrans are but primitives." G'Rishela's eyes bulged with amusement, but Ls'Sala felt a deep sadness in his friend's soul.

"Yes, they are primitives—such primitives as walk the heavens. I tell you, Ls'Sala, and I hope that Time proves me little more than a circus clown, but I cannot but feel the most profound misgivings about our course."

"But the dictates of diplomacy, G'Rishela. Surely, you do not suggest that we permit— "

Smiling, G'Rishela raised his hand to silence his friend, and placed it on Ls'Sala's shoulder. "I know all about the dictates of diplomacy, Friend of Mine. Such things now haunt my days even as I see the Universe changing around me. I only wish that someone would explain it to the Terrans."

* * *

THE GATHERING was in festive mood, for a Celebration of Return was always an occasion of joy. Succulents of all kinds filled the tables, and the bowls overflowed with the remaining stocks of Terran

Ambrosia from beyond the Great Divide. Music wafted through the air, and the lights in the oval room danced as brightly as the celebrants at a Festival of Spring. Dignitaries from all corners of the Grand Alliance shared in the gaiety as well as the food, laughing at the brightly clad jesters and applauding the strolling musicians, conversing on topics ranging from politics at court to the curiosities of life among the Terrans.

In a small room behind a door of carved wood, one floor above the ballroom, Ga'Glish played host to a gathering of his own. The mood of this gathering was markedly less than festive.

ON THE TABLE a glowing orb cast soft shadows into the far corner of the room, as two unlikely friends spoke in the shadow of a sound masker in the hushed tones of conspirators. On the walls hung the portraits of past havenmasters, all forgotten in the river of time. Stillness filled the room, and aside from voices the only sound was the gentle pulse of the clock on the table, marking each moment as it passed into forever.

"And if you forestall, they are likely to grow weary and turn their attention elsewhere, most probably at imagined slights inflicted by the Glinci and Atkvalo, who by then will have tried to befriend them."

Ga'Glish listened over the translating machine, his attention riveted. They were alone and would be, for as long as Zatar's aides could distract the attention of Her Grand Eminence, the Veshnan Ambassador. Even across the abyss of alien cultures, he felt a special kinship for Zatar, as for a kindred spirit, one who shared a common love of Truth and a mocking disdain for foolishness. And as he himself served two masters, so did Zatar—only the contention for the Veshnan's loyalty transcended petty bureaucratic bickering. Zatar owed allegiance to both the High Council of the Grand Alliance as well as to the Veshnan Presidium, and neither would take kindly to finding him sharing insights over tea with one of the Imperator's masters of security. Of course, many such insights were likely to be shrouded by the formalisms of the Veshnan language, but few things in life came as unmixed blessings.

"So given their limited span of attention, you discount the nature of the threat. And so I worry needlessly."

Zatar smiled sadly. "On the contrary, though I stand nearly alone in my concern. It is true that they are primitive by our standards. But they are more awkward than primitive. And though you may laugh at the thought, I believe that they are a race on the threshold of greatness, though in acute danger of falling back into the pit."

Ga'Glish exhaled loudly, venting his disbelief. Veshnans, it seemed, had a gift for hyperbole, and Zatar was among the most gifted practitioners of the art. It was one of their most endearing traits, made quainter still by the stilting limitations of their mode of speech.

"Scoff as you will, Ga'Glish, and I freely admit that I am just coming to understand that of which I now speak, and may well be prattling along in the serenity of ignorance. But note my words: their history is littered with the ruin of war— "

"As are the histories of all. It is the common failing of primitives and one that Terra brings even to the present day."

"Yet their wars transcend the notion of a Supreme Conquest, that final quest for glory that brings peace along as its byproduct. Often as not in the last millennium their wars were battles against oppression, made all the more bitter because they fought for ideas rather than riches, and consequently all the more confusing to their growing moral awareness. They sense a grander purpose to life than mere existence, though as a People they lack the wisdom to perceive its outlines. But I tell you, Ga'Glish—they are groping their way toward enlightenment, and some among them already have the necessary vision. All they need is time to mature.

"And note this as well, my *g'Khruushtani* friend: alone among the races known to Civilization, the Terrans have the energy of youth. If properly guided, they could rejuvenate the entire Alliance. But if provoked to rage, we cannot fathom the consequences."

Ponderously, the Veshnan shook his head. His unblinking eyes stared into the very soul of Ga'Glish, and Zatar's words burned themselves into the Crutchtan's memory.

"The Grand Alliance thinks of them as children, with a child's tiny grasp and small horizons. Yet they are children who play among the stars, with toys that can bring planets to ruin. As with all children, there is a dark side to their nature that cries to be civilized, and it is that which draws our scorn. Yet though their Science be primitive, there is a single aspect in which it is a prodigy."

"And what is that, Zatar?"

The Veshnan smiled sadly. "We may laugh at their backwardness, Ga'Glish. Robbers infest their skies, and their *khasg'arhdh* can barely protect their lanes of commerce. But of necessity, they excel in the science of war." The Veshnan leaned forward and lowered his voice to a whisper.

"And they have been waiting for us, as frightened as your Small Ones at tales of the Sheregal, for the last forty of your cycles."

Ga'Glish rocked back and forth in contemplation. All his old fears were rising to life, like a false Ghilgh'a'sin sowing Terror with the dawn of Spring. Still, he found one small point of satisfaction, though he sadly reflected that he could not confide it to Zatar. He resolved, come what may, that his ships would continue their secret fortifications along the Great Divide, no matter that he was violating the orders of his own Ministry. He would guard the Imperator's flanks, even if it would cost his honor and his rank, if his treachery were revealed.

Chapter 6

"LIEUTENANT—LIEUTENANT, COME QUICKLY."

As the on-call officer made her way to Control Station Twelve, tension spread throughout the Ishtar Command dispatch office. The technician watching the Hodges-Ishtar shipping lane was not the only one whose subspace monitor heard the distress call. In the absence of any designated priority, the computers were programmed to receive and flag any Code Blue alert in all contiguous sectors. And this signal wasn't just any Code Blue. The message from the convoy flagship sent shivers down the spines of all who listened: the Hodges Convoy was under attack.

"You've checked the location?"

"Yes, ma'am, as well as the call numbers against the preliminary navigation plan we have on file from Hodges. It all checks. It's no hoax."

The young blueshirt leaned over to activate the speaker. She pushed the emergency override button, tapping into the base public address.

"Repair Crew Forty-six, please come to Security," she said, using the day's operative code to announce a major emergency over the base public address. "Mr. Potter, please call 8704."

Seconds later, a call came from Admiral Clay's office; it was Abdul Mohassan, IshCom's chief of administration.

"We have a major problem, Admiral."

"What is it, Lieutenant?" Mohassan snapped. His face looked stern and menacing over the monitor, as if to emphasize the trouble sure to befall anyone—particularly a junior officer—who dared to misuse the emergency communications code.

"Pirates are attacking the grain convoy from Hodges, sir. The lead frigate reports heavy losses among the escorts, and— "

"How many bandits?"

"Unknown at this time. But a lot, Admiral. Quite a lot."

"Find out, and get a fix on their position. Then call up all CosGuard ships in the vicinity and have it ready for my review. I'll be there in five minutes—and I may have company, if you know what I mean."

"Aye, sir."

"Send the nearest starship to the scene at once. Tell them that reinforcements will be sent as soon as we analyze the available resources."

"Aye, aye."

"And Lieutenant?"

"Sir?"

"Do not—repeat, do not—breathe a word of this outside the Dispatch Office. Am I understood, Lieutenant?"

"Yes, sir."

"Administration out."

As Mohassan's image faded from the viewscreen, the control desk at IshCom Dispatch transformed into a whirl of activity. Though hardly routine, emergencies weren't uncommon, and pirate raids were a part of life on the frontier. But this one just didn't make sense. Supply convoys simply didn't draw fire. Pirates would not risk their lives for a few kilotons of wheat. Things like that didn't happen—yet there it was, right on the screen, plain as could be. The bandit numbers involved made it clear that this was something quite out of the ordinary.

MASON MCGEE sighed deeply, but it wasn't the emptiness that was getting to him. They'd often spent months at a time with none but themselves for company, listening to static on the subspace radio and having nothing but dust cross their sensors. Spacing was a lonely profession, and those who couldn't take it simply chose some other way to make a living. Mason glanced at this brother. Cyrus looked straight ahead, oblivious to anything but piloting their ship, his hands gliding lightly over the controls.

No, thought Mason, it wasn't being alone at the end of creation that jittered him. It was knowing that someone—something—had been here before. Here, where virgin worlds lie unsullied by human hands, just waiting for such as them to pluck the riches that Nature herself was all too willing to yield. Whatever had come before had left a trail as haunting as it was unmistakable. Over the past four days they'd found another half-dozen cones, all in a line, and all bearing the same strange markings. Now Cyrus had the two of them heading God-knows-where, looking to find God-knows-what.

Mason looked at the navigation screen. They were twenty parsecs past the Neutral Zone, well into the lizards' domain, although the nearest base of any kind, Cozzie or Crutchtan, was so far toward the center of the Galaxy as to render boundaries meaningless. And still Cyrus kept pushing them onward.

The control room lights flickered and dimmed. Mason felt the ship shudder beneath him as her engines wavered, then stabilized at reduced power. By reflex, Mason looked at the control dials.

"Power's fadin, Cyrus, down to point four-seven. An' that's the second kickdown today. Best come up an' recharge."

"Forty-seven percent power's plenty."

"Cyrus," Mason said sharply. "We've no reserve left and there's none about to hear a distress call. It's time to come up. There's a double-green a-comin, off to port. I make it to be one parsec away. Come up and recharge. A day there, maybe two, an then we're off again."

Cyrus turned his head; the dark smile on his lips set his brother's spine to quivering.

"No, Macey...we're bound for the red dwarf, a day or so dead ahead. It's the next system on the cone line."

"But Cyrus— "

"And besides," Cyrus smiled, tapping his fingers on the low frequency sensor to his right. "it's a-callin us, it is."

Mason leaned across the console break for a look. Like a sinking stone, he fell back into his seat, his face white as a sheet. The sensor showed its focus directly before them. Dimly, but unmistakably, it read a low frequency pulse, repeating with mathematical precision every 2.373 seconds.

"Like the heartbeat of a bloody demon," Cyrus grinned coldly, his smirk growing into a callous laugh as his brother's failing stomach sent him scurrying to the head. Cyrus turned his attention to guiding the ship through the sky. Though growing closer with every moment, the star hung in the blackness like a burning ruby, beckoning him like a sorceress, tickling his lust with her alluring mysteries. A thirst flamed in his soul, and he felt only the consuming thrill of pursuit. There was no telling what would greet them when they arrived.

* * *

"WHAT THE—Lieutenant, did you— "

"It's already taken care of, Admiral. I mean, at least as much as we can do about it. I sent the message as soon as word came from the Ishtari home fleet command."

Admiral Clay glared angrily, first at the young blueshirt, then at his administrative assistant, then at the blueshirt again. The fact that this latest development wasn't their fault only added to his frustration. He never liked Command Order 136-0015, CentCom's rule implementing some half-assed federal law requiring the Cosmic Guard to provide the home fleets of all member planets with "not less than one vessel comparable to the most advanced vessel commonly in use in the Cosmic Guard." It was no more than a waste of good starships and a classic boondoggle as far as he was concerned, the politicians' way of grandstanding for votes with the folks back home. But it was as dangerous as it was costly, since untrained oafs trying to play Cosmic Avenger with CosGuard's most advanced piece of equipment—one whose repair manuals were still classified as Top Secret—couldn't help but get in the way whenever they put out from port.

"And?" Clay demanded gruffly.

She hesitated briefly, afraid of the reaction her answer would bring. "Ishtar Home acknowledges the message, Admiral. They say as long as we can't guard their food supply, they'll be taking matters into their own hands. But the convoy's still at least two days off, even at flank speed. Our people will get there first."

"Damn fools!" Clay slammed his fist onto the console top. "All that sand clogs their brains."

"Who's going to the convoy's immediate aid?" asked Mohassan. "Which ship?"

The officer looked at the screen, over the shoulder of the redshirt at the monitor station.

"The *Magellan*, sir."

Clay breathed deeply, and exchanged a tense smile and nod with his second in command. For the first time since the alert came in, he started to relax. Good old Fitz, Clay thought to himself. Brian Fitzgerald wasn't much for style, the admiral thought, but you could count on him to get the job done. And Fitzgerald wasn't one to shrink from doing a proper job on the pirates, from any excess of civilian scruples.

"Another distress call from the convoy," announced the redshirt. She paused for a moment; her face clouded and her jaw tensed. "The pirates just flamed another escort. Commander Schelling reports the situation is critical, and the bandits have turned on the lifeboats."

She turned her chair to face her superiors. "But *Magellan* is closing rapidly. And the convoy won't give up without a fight."

Clay leaned over to look at the radar screen. It showed a few dozen blips, nothing more; from the sterile screen it was impossible to tell who was who. But the admiral had earned more than a few of his gray hairs trying to guard a foundering freighter. Even across the gulf, he felt the desperation of brave men and women, fighting for their lives against an enemy that killed for sport.

"Come on, Fitz," he said softly. "Come on...you can do it."

"MR. HARDESTY?"

"Range, five hundred klicks and closing. Bandits are scattering, sir. But they've broken off the attack."

Fitz grunted an acknowledgment. The pirates' maneuver was not unexpected, but that didn't make him feel better about it. A brigantine was no match for a starship; but a single starship could only chase one of the buggers at a time.

"Helm, maintain C-18 until the engines kick down. Let's put the fear of God into them. Miss Bradley— "

"Sir?"

"Radio the *Yorktown* and have Schelling confirm the bandit leader. If we can only nail one of the bastards, I want to make it count.

"And broadcast the headings of the others. Maybe a backup squadron somewhere can try for the rest."

"Engines kicking down, Cap—to C-16—15, 14...."

"Helm, come to heading 005, two points north. Let's go after the son of a bitch."

"Aye, aye, sir."

"Engines stabilizing at C-12."

"Still gaining on him, sir. Two minutes to intercept and the bandit's engines are failing, Captain. Just dropped three C-levels." Hardesty, the systems officer, briefly turned to grin at his skipper.

"Must've strained a gut trying to waste one skiff too many."

Fitz smiled darkly. The regulations were quite specific about it. Pirates were outlaws, and CosGuard ship commanders had absolute discretion in dealing with them. They might be called before a review board and questioned until the seas returned to Ishtar if a squeamish desk jockey happened to be on the panel, but so long as the captain could show a confirmed attack by the suspected pirate ship, nothing he did would be subject to second-guessing.

"A hundred klicks and closing. Bandit's slowed and is fluttering his shields."

Bradley interjected: "I'm getting a message, Cap. Their incoming hail says— "

"Don't answer the hail," Fitz said sharply. His jaw set grimly, his eyes narrowed coldly, he leaned back in the captain's chair and forced himself to relax. "Helm, slow to C-2, prepare for sublight approach. Weapons, ready the forward guns and prepare to lock on target."

The pirates were worse than animals, Fitz thought as his bridge crew methodically prepared the ship to move in for the kill. They murdered for sport, raped or enslaved any women they could get their hands on, and then begged for mercy whenever they couldn't escape. Nothing under heaven turned a starship captain's stomach more than hearing a cutthroat, having gunned down as many helpless civilians as he could, pleading for his own miserable life.

Fitz wasn't the only starship skipper who felt this way. It was a burning feeling, a hatred that filled his soul whenever he took up the chase. Once those animals lit the skies with innocent blood, so long as it was in his power, he would see to it that some of them died.

Chapter 7

ATOP A STARSHIP'S NORTHERN HULL is the Mast Battery, its main guns arrayed in opposing semi-circles about forty meters across. Beneath the reinforced hull lies the gunnery station, manned by three blueshirts and a repair crew during battle stations but otherwise, like the other weapons batteries, among the quietest duties on the ship. Most crewmen longed for the chance to spend time away from the prying eyes of officers at a post where little happened to disturb the daily routine. But as Captain Fitzgerald and the *Magellan* searched for survivors in the skies far toward the galactic center, *d'Artagnan's* Mast Battery echoed with the flying sparks that had caused the day's gunnery drills to abort, and not all of the sparks were coming from the electrical systems.

"It's inhuman, I tell ye. Bloody inhuman."

Tom Sullivan wiped his brow and returned his handkerchief to his pocket. The gunnery station was small, about twenty feet across, with a circular, multi-screened console right in the middle. Seated aforeside, perched on the resting stool he'd brought for himself, he had a good view of the problem. As Martindale and Larsen fought to remove the troublesome circuitry panel from the gunnery console, he and Denny Barrett analyzed the situation. From their perspective, it all seemed horribly unfair.

"I swear, Denny, everyone else drew light duty today. Even the gunnery guards are nowhere to be seen. All hands but us get to clean up for the bash tonight. The Skipper himself announced half-shifts for tomorrow. Why in blazes do we get stuck pulling the one heavy load o'the day?"

"Dunno, Sully, but it sure don't seem fair."

Suddenly, they heard what sounded like disgruntled voices coming from the two junior members of the repair crew. Sully turned to face the main control panel of the ancillary guns. "So how's it comin, in there? You see the glitch? Speak up, lads. Don't be a stone glitch yourselves, now."

Sweat dripping from their brows, Jim Martindale and Andrew Larsen scooted out from under the station and leaned back against the dark gray base of the console. Their heads almost disappeared inside the collar of their coveralls, but tyros who couldn't afford to buy their own gear had to make due with Standard Issue. Or "substandard issue," as the old hands called regulation equipment, from uniforms to tools. It all made a bad situation even worse.

"The target locks are all cross-wired," sighed Larsen.

"No wonder the gunners can't hit anything," added Martindale, taking off his work gloves and pushing his safety goggles onto his forehead. "The short-circuits have fused half the control panel together." Though softer than when they'd first arrived, the sparks still sounded from deep inside the console.

"Might'a known," Sully said ponderously. "Damn contractors are too busy low-ballin' each other to pay attention to their work. And it ain't changed since I was green at the tail myself. Why, I remember this mint-fresh frigate I drew—back in '27 it was. Or was it '29?"

"Anyway," Larsen interrupted, wiping his forehead with his sleeve, "it'll take days to sort it out, and that's if there's nothing else wrong with the bloody thing. Say, you don't think they'll make us work through the party today? That would be a bit of a rotter, don't you think?"

"A what?" grimaced Sullivan. "Larsen, don't talk like a bloody riddler. What the hell— "

The tyro laughed. "Don't ask me what it means. I just overheard the Skipper say it one day."

"One of Cook's Isitian cryptograms, I imagine," ventured Martindale. "That's probably what keeps short-circuiting all the equipment. The ship can't understand him either." Their laughter was cropped by a voice from behind them.

"I suppose we'll all be short-circuitin ourselves once things get under way." Yeoman Chief Gregory Connors grinned as he watched them start in alarm and hastily jump to their feet. He'd emerged from the station hatch and come upon them entirely unnoticed. It had been years since he stopped wondering why CSO was so particular in screening those it accepted for security detail. For all the hardships, life in space insulated them from so many dangers that it was easy to become careless.

"Chief!" Sully said hurriedly. "We was just taking a breather. All this hard work can leave a man breathless, don't ye know, so we—"

"Save it, Mr. Sullivan," Connors roared, his twinkling brown eyes undercutting his gruff facade. "I'm not here for a fanny roast, much as the lot o'ye deserve it. No, I got overruled on that one. But Lt. Palmer did tell me to come fetch the whole sorry bunch o'ye downside."

"Are you saying what I think you're saying, Chief?"

"Well, I told her there's much to be said against spoilin the redshirts. Sets morale right to flaggin, it does. But I was countermanded and she decided the guns could wait, so you're all to stand down. Once you secure the area, that is."

Connors smiled as the men let out a loud cheer. Cook's style was infectious, he chuckled as he helped the redshirts organize the equipment. By now, even the blueshirts had gotten the word: the crew came first, and nothing in the regulations prohibited treating them like human beings. Like anyone else, the redshirts hungered for recognition and respect, and the affection they gave their captain had proved to the rest of the officers on board that discipline was not incompatible with common courtesy. Beyond this, they all seemed willing to bust their butts for anyone who cared enough to temper the rules with a little human kindness from time to time, or to tolerate a good bit of healthy irreverence. Like this blowout today: the Skipper had seen that tempers were starting to flare and the crew's spirits were sagging. So instead of cracking the whip he looked to the calendar, found that it was Christmastime on Earth, and gave them half the day off to celebrate. It gave morale quite a boost, and if it meant that repairs were put on hold for a time, then so be it.

"Those circuits have fused themselves together, Chief," said Larsen as they collected the gear. "Likely to take a whole day ripping out the panels before we can even think about straightening this mess out."

"Like as not," grinned the chief, "there'll be enough of us who'll be getting fused together tonight—at least, if our missies show proper appreciation for some of the fine specimens we've got us on board."

The rest of the repair team laughed roughly. This would be their first chance to mingle freely with the ship's available supply of women since they signed on board.

"All right, ye lounge lizards," Connors barked as they finished securing the station. "Let's hightail it back to your natural habitat. I'm sure you'll not be strangers to it. And try to look presentable. Stink and sweat might be optional in the engine coils but they're out of place at a proper Cozzie blowout. It's standard reds for all the redshirts. Fatigues'll land ye in the brig, that's the order of the day. And let the lot of ye remember, anyone who refuses to sing or dance when the time comes'll be drawn and quartered and set out for pirate bait, orders of the Skipper himself."

* * *

As *D'ARTAGNAN'S* CREW prepared to seize a few carefree hours from the unremitting press of duty, a party of quite a different sort was taking shape near a metallic body far beyond the outermost outpost along the frontier.

"My God in heaven."

His voice had shrunk to a whisper. Cyrus stared out the forward porthole, transfixed, unable to do anything but shake his head in amazement. Cold shivers seized Mason's spine. He wanted to turn and run, but had nowhere to go; he wanted to scream, but his voice died in his throat.

"Mason—Mason? What in God's name is it?"

Cyrus took no note of his brother's answer. His own attention was riveted on the globe hanging before them in space. Ten billion miles from the twin green stars that dominated the local sky, it crept through the heavens like a ghost. It was small as celestial bodies went, less than ten miles across, but massive enough to hold a ship in orbit. It was unlike anything either of them had ever seen: as smooth as glass, and hollow as a politician's promise.

It was a satellite of some sort, thought Cyrus. It had to be, though the very thought froze his soul. Black markings dotted its surface, black dots on a coating of silver. Cyrus was sure he recognized the pattern, but try as he might he couldn't quite place it. It was driving him crazy.

"We're goin down there," he said at last. "Ye hear me, Macey? We're a-goin down there." He turned to see his brother's face, white as death; Mason's head was shaking as if palsied, his eyes fixed on the phantom that hung outside their ship.

Cyrus shook his brother by the shoulders, each shake harder than the last, trying to break the specter's grip on his brother's soul. "We're goin down for a look, Macey," he said, his voice rising in anger. "If it brings us riches or death, so be it. But one way or the other, we're a-goin down to see."

* * *

EXCEPT FOR a skeleton crew of volunteers on the bridge, *d'Artagnan's* complement scattered around the ship. Some gathered in the galley, to listen to the makeshift trio that had formed to give them the nearest approximation to music found anywhere on board. Some gathered in smaller groups, laughing and dancing together in cabins or corridors. Others ran footraces down the far halls, too sober to pass out, yet too drunk not to respond when a crewmate offered a challenge. A few fortunate souls were busily engaged in quarters, boosting each other's morale. The ship's store of beer flowed freely, and the spirits surged like the storms of western Terra.

In the galley itself, officers and redshirts traded insults and stories, sharing songs and laughter and jeering as they made the tyros gather in groups to sing songs from their native land. Stars dotted the observation screens, passing unnoticed as the ship slipped through the sky. And for a short time in the galley's lounge, seated at the keyboard, the captain himself helped play the accompaniment, along with Yeoman Barrows and Larsen, the redshirt tyro.

Few noticed when the Skipper left to answer a page from the bridge; nobody noticed when he didn't come back.

> *The Cozzie who opens a bottle of rum*
> *And offers his shipmates none;*
> *He won't get any from me when all his rum is done.*
> > *He won't get any from me,*
> > *He won't get any from me,*
> > *He won't get any from me*
> > *When all his rum is done.*

"BEGGIN YOUR PARDON, ma'am," winked Connors, leaning close to be heard over the rollicking chorus. "But I still say that there's hardly a peach-faced, little boy blueshirt aboard what can stand in the same boots as a real spacer. I mean, be reasonable. Ye can't very well expect lads to fill in for a man, now can ye?"

Karen Palmer laughed a salty laugh, and slapped Connors good-naturedly on the shoulder. "Shame on you, Chief," she said. Her face was radiant, her eyes sparkled merrily. "You should know better than to say that to a girl who's sober enough to know what you're talking about."

Connors grinned wickedly and refilled the laughing lieutenant's wine glass to the rim. Of all the bluebirds on board, he found Palmer the most to his liking. She wasn't soft and frilly like some of the others. She could swear a blue streak with the best of them when the spirit moved her, but beneath it all he sensed that she was a sentimentalist at heart—much like himself, though he'd never admit it. It touched a soft spot in the chief's soul to discover that she carried a torch for an ex-husband who vanished without a trace into an ion storm several years ago. Connors himself had some emotional baggage hidden away: a small son, now a young man, whom he hadn't seen in ten solar years.

They moved closer together, better to hear each other over the singing. Soon the passing songs faded into the background, and as they left they barely noticed their crewmates' voices, sounding down the corridors.

* * *

> *The sirens of space are a-calling me, lover,*
> *Their soft, distant lanterns are bidding me come.*
> *'Cross cold winds of fate, chasing riches and treasure,*
> *Cruel fortunes await me, a long way from home.*
>
> *Will I ever return to your eager, young arms,*
> *Or bathe in the warmth of your fertile young charms,*
> *Free of wand'rin's and risin's and empty horizons,*
> *Lonely and lost, and a long way from home?*

"SO WHAT DID he say then?" asked Connie McKenzie, mildly annoyed that one of her companions seemed more interested in the singer than in their conversation. Mary Mathison did appear rather smitten with the tall redshirt, though Connie couldn't fathom the reason why.

"Well," continued Sally Grissom, a portly young lieutenant who ran the personnel office. "It seems that Andersen wouldn't hear of being bested by a mere bluebird, and a tyro bluebird at that. So when Bobbi was finished— "

Mary didn't hear a word of what her friends were saying. She could feel the warmth in Larsen's song, an old Isitian ballad from the time of Terra's Civil War. More importantly, she sensed that he was singing the song to her and he smiled whenever their eyes met.

> *Farewell to you, Love; farewell to the sunshine,*
> *The mountains, the hills, and the valleys below.*
> *I'm up with the sun and off with the morning,*
> *The dawn waits for none and, alas, I must go.*
>
> *The river of time flows slowly and long,*
> *But Life burns so quickly, and then we are gone.*
> *The stars will keep shining, the days will keep flying,*
> *My heart will be crying, a long way from home.*

"Mary? Mary!"

Connie shook her arm, breaking her reverie.

"Really, Mathison, sometimes it's like you leave your head in your cabin."

Anger clouded Mary's face; Connie always seemed to know exactly what to say to make her mad, but dependable old Sal could always turn her anger in a smile.

"I think her head's in the clouds," grinned Sally. "And I bet I know why."

Mary blushed, but smiled good-naturedly and slouched back in her chair. Her feelings might be an open secret, but she really didn't care. She just wanted to listen to the music. And when the music stopped and she saw Larsen start to make his way over, the songs kept singing in her head.

> *So here's to the Spring, and here's to the sprinter,*
> *The laughter of Youth, and the wit of the Sage.*
> *The story goes on, never waiting for Winter,*
> *Outracing the dawn and Humanity's rage.*

Eternity sparkles like jewels in the sky,
To flicker and fade with the blink of an eye,
While jokers keep dancing and Death comes romancing,
It's cold but entrancing, a long way from home.

* * *

"Cyrus?"

"Shut up. Just let me have a look."

"But Cyrus— "

"Shut up, I say or I'll punch out yer mask and pull yer tongue out myself."

Cyrus knew that he'd never do any such thing, and he knew that Mason knew it as well. But his brother was proving to be nothing but a bother, and Cyrus was beginning to regret not leaving Mason back on the ship. His annoyance faded when he looked around. In all directions small, dark markings covered the flat, silver surface of the object. They weren't the same markings he'd seen on the cones; these were mostly black dots of varying sizes, with occasional swirls and odd geometrical patterns mixed into the design. Invisible from the ship, the markings stretched everywhere, and seemed to be projected onto the surface from below, for the surface itself was smooth as a mirror and impervious to dents and nicks.

On they walked, marveling at the hardness of the structure, yet wary and alarmed. Neither had any idea what they'd found, but they both knew that it was beyond the capacity of human science—and prayed that it was beyond that of the lizards, as well. Cyrus looked at the changing patterns on the surface, and an obsessing wave of *déjà vu* gripped his brain. Slowly, it dawned on him that he recognized the patterns, but no matter how he wracked his brain he simply could not remember where he'd seen them. He began to feel short of breath, and started to perspire. Suddenly, Cyrus grabbed his brother's arm and Mason saw fear flash across the old spacer's face. Fear and a stunned look of amazement.

"Cyrus—Cyrus, what is it?"

The fear passed quickly, replaced by a dawning awareness. Soon a sly smile lifted the corners of his mouth and Cyrus ran quickly toward the northwest, his brother stumbling after him. Then, the older

McGee brother stopped, looked up at the sky, and gave an earsplitting shout. As Mason neared, Cyrus dashed due east—then due south, then northwest again until he was back where he'd started, his brother lagging behind him at each turn. Finally catching up to his brother, panting and nearly out of breath, Mason heard an ominous chuckling rise over his earphones.

"Cyrus?"

The chuckling grew louder and louder, until it ripened into a full-bodied laugh. It was a laugh without humor and brought no joy in its wake, sending shivers down the spine of its only witness.

"Cyrus?" Mason asked in alarm. He slipped as he ran to join his brother, but quickly scrambled to his feet. When he arrived at his brother's side, he saw wild and unrestrained glee in his brother's eyes.

"I know what it is, Macey, and it'll take us back to get what's rightly ours. Ain't no bloody Cozzie nor lizard can stop us now."

"What are you talkin about."

Cyrus grabbed Mason by the shoulders. "It's a map, Macey—a bloody damn map, showin the stars and clouds and storms and passes."

Mason's eyes widened. "How— "

"Don't ask me how it comes here. Don't even think about it. It'll just drive ye crazy. But look down there." Cyrus grabbed his brother's helmet and forced Mason to look down at the surface, then jerked his brother's head to force a look at the sky. "And now…"

"It's the same," Mason cried. "It's the same! But how…?"

As his brother gawked dumbly at the heavens around them, Cyrus' eyes were drawn toward what appeared to be a pass, clearly shown on the surface. He looked up at the Crutchtan Cloud directly overhead; it glowered in the distance, its storms and nascent stars casting an ominous, reddish glow. At this distance any pass would be invisible to the eye, but Cyrus knew that he'd find it. It was as certain as Death itself. When he did, the pass would take them into alien space, past the sentries and outposts of Cozzies and lizards alike, right into the heart of Lizardland.

And right to the treasure that the lizards had stolen from them.

All they needed was courage and a little help, and Cyrus knew where they could get both.

* * *

AS IT HAD been for most of the day's liberty, the officers' lounge was almost empty. With the rest of the ship filled with drinking and singing, it seemed more like a library than a lounge. But when songs and laughter filled all decks and revelry churned the ship like an ion storm, some found the peace and quiet too tempting to ignore. As they'd done countless times since the ship put out from IshCom, Janet and Jeremy were sharing a small snack table in a corner of the room. They'd talked about Babylonian seashores and the sands of distant worlds, politics and heroes. But oddly, their conversation always seemed to drift back to a single topic. This time, Janet was laughing, and Jeremy had never heard her laugh so playfully.

"Abraham Lincoln." Nodding ponderously, Jeremy leaned back in his chair and gestured toward an imaginary wall behind him. By this time—after countless monologues which had left him completely baffled—Jeremy had become quite good at mimicking the captain's Isitian accent and most of his mannerisms.

"Now there was a man who never gave up. Deaf as an lead-laden ore freighter and still he kept writing some of the greatest music that Old Earth ever heard. There's a lesson in that for all of us, Janet."

"I'm sure there is, but Lincoln wasn't a composer. You're thinking about one of the other ones."

Jeremy waved his hand, in mock contempt. "Achh—details," he deadpanned, his mimicking voice a clone of the Skipper's. "There's a larger picture here, Janet. A larger picture."

"Maybe so, Jeremy, but I think it's out of focus."

"Yes—but—well, focus itself is a relative concept you see. Or not see, I suppose. But then that's rather beside the point."

Janet and Jeremy both laughed. It was often tough putting up with the captain's idiosyncrasies—his moods, his odd working habits, and his maddening habit of lecturing on the most obscure topics imaginable. But his oddities had a way of becoming familiar, and like most of the crew, they both found Cook's presence on the ship exhilarating, though in different ways and for far different reasons.

"Still and all," Jeremy chuckled, "and whatever his other faults, it's hard to imagine a starship without Cook in the command seat. And except for a few notable exceptions, none of whom are within earshot, I hope, I can't imagine a nicer group of people to be cooped up with. It's almost like coming home and meeting your family all over again."

Janet smiled brightly. She liked being with Jeremy; he made her feel so—worthwhile, she thought. No pressures, no pretensions. Nothing but quiet friendship and a nice time. It was a relief to find someone like that anywhere, but on a starship a friend like that was a godsend. Spacers were a crude lot for the most part, and it was rough staying on guard all the time, trying not to show hurt or embarrassment. For much of the recent past, she'd been insulated from the carnal roughhousing that passed for romance on board ship, but she had enough experience in these matters to know how rough it could be. Now that she was ready to start over again, she felt herself grateful for people like Jeremy. He was so unthreatening, and surprisingly enough he was quite a good listener.

Leaning forward, she wanted to tell Jeremy about her own family, the real one waiting for her on New Babylon, with the doting father and fretting mother, two incorrigible brothers, and a line of aunts and uncles that stretched endlessly into the horizon. All of them brought more pleasant memories to her now, hundreds of light-years away, than they had during the whole of her difficult passage from small girl to young lady. But when her line of sight passed the centerside entrance she started, and sat bolt upright in her chair.

There, at the entrance hatch, was the captain.

And he was beckoning her.

She chided herself for the sudden embarrassment she felt, and resentment started building inside her. She was angry that a perfectly innocent talk with a friend could cause her such grief. But then Cook pointed toward Jeremy as well, and made it clear that he wanted to speak to both of them.

"Jeremy," she began weakly. "Skipper wants us."

When she looked again, the expression on Cook's face told her that the reason he summoned them went beyond personalities. That small bit of knowledge hardly stopped her insides from churning relentlessly as she and Jeremy dutifully followed the captain out the door and into the empty corridor.

"ENGAGIN THE engines...and we're off! Next stop, Riley's Station."

As his brother cackled gleefully at the control seat, Mason looked sullenly out the aft porthole. He could scarcely believe what Cyrus had in mind. Sneaking into alien skies through the back door was crazy enough, but only a madman would consider setting down on a lizard world, even if he did know where all the gold was buried. Nothing under the heavens could justify such lunacy. There was treasure enough lurking about in Terran skies, and in the time the trip would take them they probably could dig up as much as they could ever use, if they took it into their heads to work for it.

Mason stared at the silvery globe, now fading rapidly into the distance. Something had taken hold of his brother, something that hid in the shadows of his soul, and Mason doubted that anything could make Cyrus change his mind.

Soon the small ship was speeding west-to-center, toward the last outpost on Terra's northern frontier, and the alien globe disappeared into the Big Black. As it faded, unseen mysteries vanished as well—mysteries like the powerful mechanism buried deep within, which had kept the cones aligned across inconceivably vast distances through uncounted centuries; or the two dominant stars showing on its surface, which were now gas clouds expanding outward from two large gravity wells, one of which Terran spacers knew as "Newcomb's Black Hole;" or the eerie absence from the star map of two other dominant stars of the local arm of the Galaxy—stars which the g'Khruushtani called "Gl'Siesh" and "Nabana" and Terra knew as "Rigel" and Deneb," which the map showed only as tertiary star clouds, condensing spirals of interstellar gas.

And around the globe's north and south poles, at a radius of 2.742 feet, were identical sets of runes—one circling clockwise, the other counterclockwise—like random strokes of a calligrapher's pen.

JEREMY SHIFTED uncomfortably on his feet; the hallway lights were making him perspire. Janet stared at the floor. From down the corridor, they could just hear the singing from the galley, where spirits were still flowing freely.

Cook's lips stretched into a tight, humorless smile. "I hate to intrude," he began coldly. Immediately, and without knowing why, Jeremy felt defensive, and was too embarrassed to notice Janet's face turning a bright crimson. Before either of them could utter a word, the captain unloaded his bombshell.

"The ship is standing at Yellow Alert," Cook said, much as if he were discussing nothing more than another glitch in the ship's temperamental engines. Janet and Jeremy were too stunned to reply.

"You remember the pirate raid two days ago, on the supply convoy bound to Ishtar?" he continued, receiving blank looks in response. "Well, I paid no attention to it, either. But the raid so panicked the locals that their home fleet sent its starship to the rescue."

Cook's eyes darkened, as they passed from Jeremy to Janet, and back again. Janet recognized the intensity in his lowered voice. "That ship is missing— "

"Missing?!" Jeremy spluttered.

"And presumed hijacked." Cook paused for a moment to let the magnitude of what he'd said register. A starship in the hands of outlaws would put the whole frontier at risk. It was the most powerful destructive force ever unleashed by Man: a single ship could lay waste to a whole planet, or hold its population hostage to whatever ransom struck its captor's fancy.

"There's a senior staff meeting at 200 Hours tomorrow." Cook continued; he smiled lamely. "I might even make this one.

"In the meantime," Cook looked directly at Janet, his voice taut, his eyes unforgiving, "I don't want to interrupt anything, so if you two will have nothing more to drink, you may proceed to the galley, where you will remain—stone cold sober—until the last of the assembled sots leaves for quarters."

"What about— "

"Even assuming that it is Wilkes we're dealing with," Cook continued ignoring Jeremy's growing signs of dismay, "at maximum speed, the hijacked ship won't reach our vicinity for two more days at the earliest. We'll have plenty of time to get the crew sobered up."

"But the mast guns are— "

"I did track down Lt. Palmer," Cook interrupted, his eyes regaining a small twinkle. "And...well, I sent her and Chief Connors to start working on repairs. They'll have the problem isolated in no time, and will likely do it faster than any redshirt repair crew."

"And the bridge?" Mendelson interjected, her voice tinged with what Cook took to be sarcasm.

"We're heading due west at cruising speed," the captain replied blandly. "Mathison's at the radio desk. I've conscripted Chief

Andersen for the systems station, and I'll have our best navigator and—well, let's say our second-best helmsman at the controls. Since all we're doing now is cruising into position, we shouldn't need any more help there for the time being.

"Your assignment is to stay close to the crew and head off any rumors. The reports from IshCom are still little more than intelligence speculation, and I won't have any uninformed hysteria sweeping the ship." He managed a weak smile. "That isn't how we do things on Isis, you know. We prefer the well-informed variety."

He looked at Janet, then at Jeremy, then at Janet once again. "Anyway, you may as well enjoy yourselves. It may be your last chance for quite a while. If CSO is right, we have a major crisis on our hands, and it's heading in our direction."

With a sigh, Cook turned and walked down the corridor. Janet watched as he rounded the hallway arch and disappeared, heading toward the bridge. From the opposite direction, the singing from the galley soon poured through the door, sounding a three hundred-year old drinking song up and down the hall.

> *Tycoons in old New Dublin, Port Ross and Cape McCann,*
> *Are seekin' brave Demetrians, their spacin' ships to man.*
>   *And we're settin' sail in the mornin',*
>   *We're settin' sail, hey-yo!*
>   *So clear the hold, we're off for gold*
>   *Let's go, Lads, go!*
>
> *Our first stop is the Outfitter's, as honest as the day—*
> *He'll charge ye twice for half your gear,*
>   *then garnishee your pay.*
>   *And we're settin' sail in the mornin',*
>   *We're settin' sail, hey-yo!*
>   *So clear the hold, we're off for gold*
>   *Let's go, Lads, go!*

Jeremy turned to face Janet, his eyes filled with alarm. "I think we should go to the bridge," he said earnestly. "Skipper's going to need help and lots of it. I saw Talbert not twenty minutes ago. He's in no shape to navigate his way to the head, and Dickinson's ready to wash out as helmsman's apprentice any day now."

"That's not what he meant, Jeremy." Janet stared straight ahead, her eyes fixed on the bend in the corridor; from the galley the singing raged, louder than ever. "That's not what he meant at all."

> *The Captain keeps us all in trim,*
>   *good comp'ny man is he—*
> *He sets the watch at risin' and goes back to bed till tea.*
> *And we're settin' sail in the mornin',*
>   *We're settin' sail, hey-yo!*
> *So clear the hold, we're off for gold*
>   *Let's go, Lads, go!*

"But— "

She turned to him and smiled weakly; in the few months they'd served together, Jeremy had never seen her look so sad. "Trust me, Jeremy. He wasn't talking about Talbert and Dickinson. And he'll do just as well without us."

> *And when at last the journey's done*
>   *and we put in to port,*
> *We'll cast about for girls of the enthusiastic sort.*
> *And then we're settin' sail in the mornin',*
>   *We're settin' sail, hey-yo!*
> *So clear the hold, we're off for gold*
>   *Let's go, Lads, go!*

Turning toward the galley, Janet started back toward the celebration. The sounds of laughter and fun fell on her heart like tears, and she didn't feel at all like singing.

Chapter 8

CONFRONTING A CRISIS ON TOP of a hangover invariably leads to surliness, so the mood in the captain's office the next day was grim. The room was crowded; books and manuals littered the shelves. There was barely space for the ship's command staff to sit, and the perpetual mess did nothing to relieve the perception that events were spinning out of control. As was his custom, Cook gave his executive officer the task of quieting the mob.

"What was that again, Jeremy?"

Finding a place at the conference table, Jeremy sighed. "I said that the captain will be detained for a few minutes and will be along shortly."

"What?"

"Oh, for the love of— "

Jeremy sighed; he was saying nothing that he hadn't said a dozen times before in the past month. But in their present circumstances the news could do little but provoke dissension, and today he was hardly the soul of patience, himself.

"You see? I could have told you. And with the engines fritzing out on us like this—I mean, it's his own idiotic fault. That man is—"

"Oh, shut up, Talbert," snapped Jeremy. "You make me sick sometimes." The rest of the senior staff stopped their grumbling to listen; unlike the captain, Jeremy rarely singled out the ship's navigator for public rebuke. "We all know the fix we're in and crabbing about the Skipper won't help a damn bit."

Though his words were different, Jeremy winced at hearing his voice taking on the curt, abrasive tone that Cook used so often on the bridge as the captain tried to explain why so many of his maneuvers always seemed to set the ship's temperamental engines to hay-wiring. The ship's engineer interrupted before Jeremy could say anything more.

"The Skipper is going over the utility curves from the engines," said Van Horn. He was a short, stocky man, with intelligent brown eyes and a well-trimmed salt-and-pepper beard. His good-natured, Demetrian gruffness announced his disdain for cant and ceremony. Jeremy liked him, though in his own way Van Horn could be as stubborn as the captain.

Raising his eyebrows, the engineer looked the ship's navigator straight in the eye. "If you're bent on crabbing at anyone, Mr. Talbert, crab at me," said Van Horn. "I suggested that he look at the figures. And I, for one, appreciate whatever insights he has to offer."

Before Talbert's lack of response became obvious, the office door opened and in walked the captain. "As you were," he said, before anyone had the chance to jump to attention.

Cook strode to the head of the conference table and took his seat. He waited until his office door was tightly closed before he began to speak. There was no need to broadcast their situation to the rest of the crew until they could discuss it themselves, though Cook knew that rumors were sweeping the ship. Worry clouded every face in the room, except his own. He couldn't afford the luxury.

"I trust you've all read IshCom's latest dispatch," he began briskly, "so I won't belabor the obvious. The hijacking is confirmed, and IshCom is deploying all available starships to guard the planets and major colonies along the frontier."

"How did they win control of the ship?" asked Van Horn. "Surely the ship's self-destruct— "

"Once his security team was overpowered," Cook interrupted, "the captain surrendered his ship in exchange for a lifeboat and safe passage. He's in custody now, charged with treason and dereliction of duty. At least, that's what CSO says over the command channel, but the failings of civilian militias are not our immediate concern."

Cook's eyes darted around the table. He could feel disgust filling the room. Handing a security-class ship over to the enemy—any enemy—was simply unthinkable, all the more so when the enemy was a band of pirates. In all the ponderous mass of regulations on the books, it was the only peacetime offense that carried the death penalty. Even so, the Ishtar skipper's cowardice wasn't the worst of it. Every member of the bridge crew had checked the ship's heading as soon as the first rumors of a renegade starship had begun to spread.

IshCom's first obligation would be protecting the settlements along the frontier, and it was obvious that they weren't heading toward any planet.

"As you might have expected, IshCom has dispatched an expedition to intercept and engage the hijacked ship." He paused, wondering how his people would react to what he was about to say. "Owing to our proximity to the bandit's last known heading, we are that expedition. And as the Eastern Fleet can spare no other ships for the job, they've told me not to expect any help."

The news was met with silence. No CosGuard ship had ever done battle with another starship outside of maneuvers, and none of them had any doubt about which pirate captain they'd be facing.

"Glad to see we're all eager for some action," Cook said wryly. "I'm sure it will do wonders for the crew's morale."

"Do they expect us...," Talbert began, only to fall silent as all eyes focused on him.

"They expect us," said Cook, "to prevent the renegade from entering uncharted space. Reports have the bandits on the heading needed to take them anticenter-north of the outpost at Calais. We are the last ship standing between them and open skies. Assuming they maintain cruising speed, they should be in our vicinity within three cosmic days."

"Is it—I mean, do we have any real evidence that it's— "

"Wilkes, Mr. Ashton?" Cook said, through an infuriating smirk. "Well, with the simultaneous raid on the supply convoy and his recent appearance in the area, what do you think?"

Jeremy nodded uncomfortably. He resented the way the captain made him feel foolish for asking the logical question. "I guess it would be a good bet."

"Yes, Jeremy, I suspect you're right. And we lose nothing by assuming that it is Wilkes we'll be facing. Any other opponent will be an anticlimax.

"In any event, we'll all be rather busy for the next few days. I want all available scouts primed and ready for launch within the hour. Mr. Ashton, I want to see the proficiency charts of all blueshirts on board so I can decide on reconnaissance assignments. Mr. Underwood, you will arrange three clear channels for the scouts—ship to ship, ship to mother ship, and emergency. I want to know instantly, whenever any of them comes in contact with anything, and I do mean anything. In addition, I want you to check the communications equipment on each of the scouts personally. Is that understood?"

"Yes, sir."

"Mr. Ashton will also help the science officer prepare a listing of the known star systems in the area." Jeremy winced, but said nothing. It was not the time to seem faint of heart.

"I'll be studying the surrounding skies before deciding on a plan of action," continued the captain. "The rest of you will spend the next two days getting the ship ready. I'm placing the ship on battle watch, effective immediately. That will double the hands available for duty on each shift. You may commandeer any personnel needed to whip your own departments into combat trim. Any problems you have you will bring directly to me.

"Questions?" Cook looked to see nothing but shaking heads. "Good—Jeremy, until I hear from you, I will be spending most of my time in Engineering, helping Mr. Van Horn squeeze some more juice from our engines."

Van Horn smiled and shook his head. He knew full well that the only thing that would boost their power past 60 percent of capacity was an overhaul at a starbase dry dock, and knew that Cook realized it, too. But the captain was not one to let things lie, not when so much might depend on doing the impossible.

"One more thing. I've received word that IshCom has granted my request to let us participate in maneuvers."

Groans greeted the announcement.

"Yes, yes—for once I agree," smiled the captain. He knew that the rest of the ship did not share his enthusiasm for going head to head with the rest of the Eastern Fleet. "As if we don't have incentive enough to stay alive. But it's better than nothing. However clumsy the means, at least they're trying to give us some encouragement."

"I'd rather have some help."

"So would I, Mr. Van Horn," Cook said, laughing with the others. "But then, the Universe is riddled with imperfection. All right—we'll meet back here at 800 Hours to discuss progress. Until then—dismissed."

As everyone rose to leave, Cook shifted uncomfortably in his chair, then cleared his throat.

"Miss Mendelson, I'd like a word with you."

Janet's heart skipped a beat, and she quietly resumed her chair. Self-consciously, she smiled at Jeremy, who shrugged his shoulders as he passed. It had taken him long enough, she thought, but he was a born procrastinator. Finally, he was going to set things right between them. With death staring at them across the abyss, it was about time.

AS THE OTHERS scurried to their stations, Jeremy lagged behind, slowly walking down the corridor, lost in thought. Crewmen were everywhere; the loudspeaker was just announcing that they would all stand on alert, and that meant everyone's work day had just been doubled. Rumors buzzed through the hallway, as thick as the redshirts around the bulletin board. Even so, Jeremy's mind was back in Cook's office until a rough backslap ended his reverie; it was the chief engineer.

"Well, Jeremy, what do you make of all this? And what chance do you think we stand against the likes of Wilkes?"

Van Horn was smiling. Even in the face of disaster, he could be cheerfully honest. In the best of times he was an antidote to Talbert's pretentiousness, but right now Jeremy just wanted to be left alone.

"Hard to say, really," the sullen executive officer said at last. "A lot depends on those engines of yours." The grimace that crossed Van Horn's face did nothing to relieve Jeremy's anxiety. Cook might be responsible for their engine troubles, he thought, but the least the chief engineer could do was give them some reason to hope.

"But more than that," he continued, "it depends on the Skipper. And right now we have no way of knowing what will happen when the guns start blasting away."

"Right you are, Jeremy," Van Horn laughed, but the gallows humor behind his cagy grin did little to lift Jeremy's spirits. "I guess this is our chance to find out just how good the Skipper is. So long as the engines hold out, that is."

As the engineer once again clapped him good-naturedly on the back, Jeremy smiled lamely. For the next few days, it would be the only kind of smile he could manage.

"HAVE A SEAT."

Cook motioned for Janet to take her chair, only to notice that she was already sitting. This whole business made him feel like a schoolboy, and it suddenly dawned on him that this was the first time the two of them had been alone since leaving the *Constantine.*

Janet cleared her throat. "You wanted something, Captain?"

"Two things, actually," Cook replied quickly, clearing his own throat. He saw Janet blush and avert her eyes. It was a look he'd seen often in better days, and it gave him exactly the answer he wanted. There was no need to amuse his helmsman by playing the fool, he thought, and he immediately relaxed, relieved that he could still read her at a glance. They might never forget the past, but there was no point served by getting maudlin. Those good feelings would prove short-lived.

"How comfortable do you feel with the ship's helm?" he asked, after an awkward pause. Janet glared at him. Cook scratched his nose, then coughed to clear a tickle caused by the sudden dryness in his throat.

"What I mean," he continued, starting to fidget, "is that we're already carrying a heavy load into this mission—what with—well, with a green crew and engines on the brink of kickdown, and all. I have to know whether you—whether you are having any problems with the—well, with the—with the steering mechanisms."

"I am having no problems, Captain," Janet said icily. "Least of all with the steering mechanisms. I've worked my tail off getting rid of all the glitches in the helm. You should know that better than anyone. And for your information, *Captain*—I don't anticipate any problems with my performance. In battle or anywhere else you might care to imagine."

Cook swallowed hard and nodded.

"We *have* been through this before, Captain. This is hardly our first battle."

Cook glowered at his helmsman. "You are quite right, Lieutenant," he said stiffly, looking her straight in the eye. Anger flashed inside his correct, Isitian bearing. "And it probably won't be the last. But it is our first battle on this ship. And it's the first time any CosGuard vessel has faced a starship in real combat. And I cannot begin to tell you how pleased I am to hear, in such stentorian terms, that the one other officer whose performance is crucial to the fate of her ship and her crew believes that she has mastered her station well enough as to require no special assistance. That is my primary—my only concern with you, Lieutenant. And I am grateful to you for easing my mind."

Now it was Janet's turn to feel foolish. Her fingers leafed absently through the briefing binder on the table in front of her.

"What's the other thing?" she said at last.

"I beg your pardon, *Lieutenant?*"

"Two things were on your mind," she said softly. "What's the other thing?"

Cook would kick himself for responding as he did, but for the moment he was too angry to care. "Actually," he said, leaning back in his chair and smiling coldly, "the other thing really isn't any of my business now that I think of it."

Janet's face began to glow. She struggled not to show how much she was hurting.

"That will be all, Lieutenant. Return to your duties; I'll let you know if I need anything else."

Without a word, Janet rose and quickly left the room. Cook turned his chair and sighed heavily. He rose, and walked to his desk, where he picked up a paperweight and began rapping it rhythmically on the table top, the papers muffling the sound. His eyes drifted to the wall to his left, scanning each of the portraits his sister had drawn for him—eight in all, his personal heroes from Earth's past. Their eyes burned deep into his soul.

"Masterfully done, Cook," he said scornfully. His eyes flitted among the eight men, sages all, hanging from his wall. And he wondered how the wall came to know more about women than the whole lot of them.

* * *

As COOK was reflecting on the follies of men, it was just past dawn in Covington. The air was clear and crisp, and dew covered the ground. A cold front had passed in the night, leaving a hint of autumn in the air. The waking birds sang to greet the sun, now just starting to peer through the treetops.

Most mornings found the Presidential Gardens deserted , except for the groundskeeper and guards, and an occasional dappled groundmunk. Today, footsteps sounded on the macadam walkway, heading north toward the river. Two men strolled slowly toward the boat landing, one in formal business attire, the other in baggy coveralls and an old battered hat. Their conversation dulled their senses to the pristine beauty of morning.

"We getting flack from Valhalla? Zack can't be too happy about scuttling his pet project."

"Nothing we can't handle." Mikoyan smiled artfully. "Besides, Mikos, it's a little late in the day to think about that."

The president chuckled. Of course, Mikoyan was right. He'd really have no regrets, even if it did mean turning the seat over to the Tories. Winfield Zack was not his favorite senator; they'd feuded ever since Sarkisian first stepped off the space liner and into federal politics. Throwing a wrench into Zack's bid to be his planet's first four-term senator would let him kill two birds with one stone, and settle an old score while freeing money to build more starships. Their real motive, however, involved more than reclaiming an old debt.

"Of course," continued Mikoyan, "it leaves us with a big decision."

"And one we really can't avoid much longer," Sarkisian nodded.

They both stopped, and turned to face each other. Like most good friends, they could read the other's thoughts. They'd shared too many problems and triumphs to waste words. What faced them now was a watershed, one that neither relished but which both knew they could no longer avoid.

"You're wondering whether we should follow up on this Zack affair by exploring our other options?" Sarkisian nodded; Mikoyan gestured with his head and the two men resumed walking.

"I don't see much choice, Mikos. Besides, there's really little risk involved. Grant will be two hundred parsecs beyond the reach of any snooping reporters. And the worst that can happen...."

"The worst that can happen is that we start playing games we don't understand. We don't even know if the aliens, any of them, play by the same rules we do." Sarkisian stopped walking. The sound of their footsteps died in the stillness.

"So what are you saying?"

The president looked his friend in the eye. "I wonder whether we're getting in over our heads, Tony. And I wonder whether we don't owe it to the Crutchtans to bring all these new contacts to light. After all, we know about as much of these new 'friends' of ours as Old Earth knew about space travel. Maybe we're better off being honest. A showing of good faith might go a long way toward resolving our differences."

Mikoyan sighed loudly. Mikos had a strong impulse for doing the right thing. It was probably why they'd remained friends through the years, but it could be a deadly handicap in the world of politics. He doubted that it would be any more use in dealing with aliens.

"No, Mikos. That would just show weakness, and weakness is something we dare not show. Not now and especially not to the likes of them. It wouldn't do us any good, anyway. The others could always deny it and we have no way to prove that they're lying."

The president nodded, more in resignation than regret. He knew that his friend was right, but then Mikoyan's instincts were rarely wrong.

"So it's settled, then," Mikoyan said quickly, sensing that now was the time to press the point, before the president had time to reconsider. "I'll call our people on Demeter and tell them to set things in motion."

The president agreed, and Mikoyan left to go to his office. There were orders to draft and answers to send. Above all, they had to start thinking about the approach to take. If they weren't careful, Grant might offend these new aliens, whose secret overtures were proving to be irresistible. The moment would pass, the opportunity could be lost forever, and Terra would be left to go it alone, with no friends and no allies. Sarkisian watched his friend disappear amid the flowers and blossoming bushes, and at last was alone with his thoughts and fears.

Even the prettiest rose carried thorns, he thought sadly. While his life on Athena was less complicated, it was often no less ruthless. Even as a professor of history, in the days before his writings on the forces impelling Terra to union brought him to the attention of the local party, politics controlled his life. The only difference was that in a universe limited to questions of tenure or control over the university journals, there was less at stake.

Not that any of them realized it at the time, he thought. He started walking again, toward the landing by the river. Felipe, the boat master, always kept a skiff moored there in the summer, just in case the president happened by in the early morning.

No, he smiled to himself; the disputes and controversies that animated the faculty at the University of New Hellas were just as bitter, just as consuming, and just as destructive to the lives and fortunes of those who lost. Now, it all seemed so petty.

The president arrived at the boat launch. He took a fishing rod from the equipment shed. Soon the sound of creaking oars split the stillness, and for a few hours an aging fisherman found peace in a strange land.

* * *

```
cc:            143-0887.3
FILE:          Log
ACCESS:        Command.
SECURITY:      Standard
OPERATIONAL STATUS: Shakedown
LOCATION:      43-436445/xx/A-12
```

We are maintaining course heading 323/045-s; the blue giant called Jacob's Star is ahead to starboard. Minor anomalies appear on infrared sensors, but the area is otherwise clear.

Mast guns are jerryrigged to point of operability, but I have ordered work to continue. While softness will not be apparent from the outside, the entire battery is simply not up to trim. Until overhauled, it will remain the weakest point in ship's weapons system.

Morale has fallen to its lowest ebb since I assumed command. A crisis coming on the heels of a celebration makes it all the more difficult for the crew to respond with a will, and the enormity of the task ahead is starting to dawn on them. But this is understandable. One does not, after all, come toe-to-toe with a legend every day. And time remains before the engagement. I hope to see their spirits improve before long.

    Capt R Cook

* * *

TWO DAYS PASSED, and then two more. For a whole week *d'Artagnan*'s scouts ranged over a whole spatioplat of space, yet all screens remained quiet, and their sensors tracked only themselves. With each day, tension grew on the mother ship, as the crew had time to reflect on what was ahead of them. In the small scouts the days passed even more slowly, as the shipmates found the cramped quarters of a CosGuard small craft conducive to little more than petty quarreling.

On the eleventh day, two small blips appeared on the subspace radar of the westernmost scout. An hour later, the two blips had grown to six, all showing the radar signatures of swift brigantines. Soon, trailing the rest, a massive blip came onto the screen, moving east by anticenter-north at a leisurely rate of speed. At first sighting, there was no doubt about what they had found.

It was the renegade.

* * *

THE ALARM BUZZER sounded throughout the ship. On all decks, the status lights already showed the changes now trumpeted by the loudspeaker.

"Condition Red—all hands stand by battle stations. Condition Red—all hands...."

The hallways suddenly came to life. Six-hundred seventy-four men and women, in various stages of preparedness, raced to their posts. Some donned their jerseys as they trotted down the corridor. Others gobbled the last remains of lunch. Everywhere, a week's worth of anxious boredom erupted into a frenzy of purposeful chaos.

Then, as quickly as it began and with as little warning, the halls fell silent, and crewmen and officers alike awaited the call to battle stations. The seconds slowly pulsed along with six-hundred seventy-four beating hearts, and the tension on the ship began to rise again.

CHIEF CONNORS sat just outside the molecular transmitter, leaning against the bend in the sidewall. The chairs had long since been secured in preparation for battle. A frown creased his brow; he was lost in thought and felt quite alone.

"Worried, Chief?" It was Palmer; the captain was rotating his bridge crew to keep them from getting stale from the tension, and it was her turn to stand down. The bridge was a quick dash from the molly room, and she was feeling lost herself. She sat next to Connors and breathed deeply. She reflected that in the last hour, she seemed to pay attention to every breath she drew. Like everyone else, she didn't know how many she had left.

Connors looked her straight in the eye; Palmer thought she caught a brief glimpse of fear, that faded like a bad dream before the light of day. He shook his head gently. "No, Matey," he said, managing a tired smile. "I'm past worryin. It just gets in the way of the job." Connors paused; he knew he should keep his thoughts to himself. It wasn't right to start spooking the others now, especially one of the bridge officers. Too much was at stake to start them worrying more than they were already, but something troubled him, and none of his greenshirt friends was around to commiserate. Of course, he'd never have leveled with any of them; but Palmer—well, with her it was different.

"I'll tell ye, Karen, I been thinkin more an more on our situation. It's been keepin me up nights, these last few days."

Palmer smiled weakly. "I hadn't noticed."

"Yeah." He took her hand in his own, and looked into her eyes. "Well, I can't say as I regard our prospects keenly. I don't doubt for a minute who it is we'll be goin up against, but we got us a ship a-limpin like she was lame, and whatever the cause, it's too late to go castin blame."

He leaned back against the wall and drew a long breath.

"Good as the Skipper may be, we're still a rookie ship, on a maiden voyage with crippled engines and a crew full of tyros, about to go head-to-head with the outlaw elite. God help us, but it's sure to be Wilkes himself."

Palmer leaned back, letting the hexagonal bend in the sidewall support her back. It hurt to see Connors so depressed and she wanted to say something, anything, to lift his spirits. To see him talking that way on the eve of battle was enough to make her cry.

But the words wouldn't come, even as she tightly squeezed his hand. Connors was saying nothing that didn't echo in her own heart. What was worse, she realized that no one on the ship felt any differently.

And all they could do was wait.

Chapter 9

HOURS PASSED SLOWLY, as everyone on board waited for combat and tried to avoid thinking about the fiery death that would claim whoever lost the encounter. Eventually, Jeremy found himself standing at Cook's door, bringing news that the enemy was drawing near and the battle was at hand.

Getting no answer to his page, he knocked on the door.

"Captain?"

"Come in," a voice called at last.

Jeremy entered the captain's office. Through the dimmed lights he saw Cook, eyes closed and feet propped on his desk. The door closed behind him with a rush of air. In the near silence that followed, Jeremy heard a soft sound floating through the air: it was music, delicate and graceful as silken thread, woven together like a summer breeze.

"Number Ten has docked..., " Jeremy began.

Cook opened his eyes and lifted a finger to his lips. Then, silently, he closed his eyes and pointed to a portrait on his wall, the one showing a frail-looking lad, apparently in his teens. "*Sshhh*, " he whispered. "It's Mozart." He smiled mysteriously, as if enjoying his own private joke. "There's no need to raise your voice, Jeremy."

"Scout Ten has docked," Jeremy began again, his voice lowered, "and that's the last of them. Hangar deck reports the bay doors closing, and all scouts accounted for."

"Thank you, Commander," Cook said absently. In the back of his mind it registered that the last scout had returned to the mother ship and that the junior officers would be returning to duty. He mentally noted his intention to enter a commendation for the two-man crew of Scout Number Ten—Dexter for being alert enough to move toward the source of the anomalous readings that turned into the pirate convoy; Denton for putting up with Dexter for the last week.

But he wasn't really listening to his first officer, or letting the details of command distract him from the task before him. Relaxing under the soothing strains of an old friend, his mind was focusing on the enemy, now a faint but growing reading on the ship's sensors. In counterpoint to the gentle music, he had been slowly preparing himself for battle. His mind was coiled and tight, ready to pounce at the enemy, but he felt aloof from those around him, as if suspended in time and watching events unfold with amused detachment. He sensed the doubts swirling around him, the worries and fears and growing anxieties, but as the battle neared these concerns had long faded from his own consciousness. He did not allow himself the same luxuries as his crew; doubt would hobble him when his brain most needed to slip its constraints. More than this, the concept of defeat was alien to him. His mind was one with the task before him, and his crew, like his ship, was simply a tool to use, a given of existence that set the odds of the encounter and dictated the range of his tactics.

"Distance?"

"One parsec, Captain," said Jeremy. The music was sad yet uplifting, the wanderings of a soul in touch with immortality. As it drew his attention, his own mind started to drift and his eyes eased shut. "The bandit has increased speed to C-14 and seems to be changing course to meet us," he continued dreamily. "Estimated intercept is one cosmic hour."

"You may sound battle watch, Mr. Ashton." Cook's stern voice carried a resolve that Jeremy had never heard before. "I'll be along shortly."

Suddenly opening his own eyes, Jeremy started, and felt very foolish. Clear as crystal and hard as diamonds, the captain's eyes were staring straight into Jeremy's soul, as if they could read his thoughts and sense all of his growing fears.

"And give the order to secure all detachables." Cook smiled wryly. "I expect that we'll need all the fancy footwork we can muster, before long." As if on cue, the music changed movements, and from the hidden speakers a haunting piano began a wistful run along the scale, followed by a sad but sprightly orchestra.

* * *

AS *D'ARTAGNAN* SAILED through uncertain skies, another ship pierced the blackness of outer Terra. Newly christened the *Black Dragon* by her crew, her scouts had just spotted the last enemy standing between their new mother ship and the safety of open space. With a cortege of a half-dozen brigantines following in her wake, the renegades sensed a kill in the offing. Tension built within their ranks, but it was the anticipation of hunters thrilling in the chase. They had confidence in their champion and no doubts about his ability to prevail in combat against anything the Cosmic Guard could send to stop them. His valor in battle was unsurpassed; his cruelty and cunning had made him a legend far beyond the confines of his own camp. The mere mention of Chadbourne Wilkes raised a mixture of hatred and admiration across the West Terran frontier. And except for a lonely figure striding onto the bridge of the Cozzie ship now hurtling toward them, the thought of facing him even up in battle was enough to send quivers of mortality through the bravest of souls.

Slowly, the two ships closed, until they were almost within range of their close-range sensors. Then *d'Artagnan* hove to, near the gravitational limit of a planetary system circling a bright blue star, inviting the pirates to attack. Wilkes responded by doubling his speed, leading his brigantines toward the glory of what would be their crowning achievement—bringing down a starship of the Cosmic Guard, and laying the frontier at their feet.

THE KLAXONS RANG loudly, calling all hands to battle stations. Crewmen scurried about, preparing the ship for the ordeal ahead. The gun batteries signaled ready; engineering signaled ready. Soon, all stations signaled their battle status to the radio officer on the bridge, who reported each bit of news to the captain.

The mood on the bridge was tight as a metal drum. On all sides, the monitors showed the enemy starship racing toward them, ten minutes away. Jeremy's heart pounded furiously and he saw fear everywhere around him. Underwood was pale as death itself; Talbert's eyes were sunken like a tomb. Beads of sweat were forming on Palmer's brow. Even Janet's hands were starting to tremble and sweat over the helm control spheres, and Jeremy knew full well how important she was to their chances of surviving. A clear, firm voice ringing over the bridge brought them all back.

"Helm, increase sublight speed to one-half, prepare to engage subspace drive."

Jeremy looked to see Cook, hands clasped behind his head, leaning back in the command chair as serenely as at one of his bridge drills.

"Prepare to come about—and I hope you've all left your queasy stomachs in your cabins," Cook chuckled. "Nothing is more distracting than having the cleaning drones scraping vomit from the floor while I'm planning an attack."

Nervous laughter coursed through the bridge.

"Miss Palmer, half power to shields," continued the captain, his voice measured and confident. "Charge the forward and portside guns, and stand by to raise the shields.

"Helm, come about to 750 by 015 south, and increase speed to C-1—mark! Now, lift us back up to the enemy's plane of approach—slowly...that's right. And prepare for hard a-starboard at increased speed.

"Mr. Underwood, sound the clearing horn, if you would. Let's try cutting enemy ranks down to more manageable proportions."

SLOWLY, THOUGH at speeds beyond the comprehension of human senses, the giant ships lumbered toward battle. As lights on a distant shore, the stars hung silently in place. The pirates approached like a dagger, in a formation the Cosmic Guard called a "battle wedge." The *d'Artagnan* approached alone.

At a distance of ten astrokilometers, the ships made visual contact. Like minor stars in the local heavens, each reflected light from the hot, blue star that glistened in the blackness nearby. Slowly, the enemies neared each other, the pace of their progress tightening the nerves of everyone on both ships.

Suddenly, on the order of their commander, the pirates doubled their speed, charging toward the CosGuard ship like the ancient armies of Old Earth. Just as suddenly, as if reacting to a long-awaited signal, *d'Artagnan* swung hard to starboard at a sharply increased speed and dove, dipping far below her adversaries' directional plane and heading toward the area's dominant star. Baffled by the maneuver, the pirates held their course, watching dumbly as the Cozzie starship raced far out of position, almost inviting them to join a deadly game of hide and seek among the stellar debris of the nearby system. Then, suddenly and without warning, the *d'Artagnan* came about smartly and changed course, heading straight for the pirate flotilla. As the seconds passed, confusion gripped the bridge of the pirate flagship, freezing the flotilla in place for a few precious moments. As Cozzie grew closer, the pirates cut speed and began to pivot, desperately trying not to be outflanked, their leader sensing that by the time he realized what Cozzie had in mind, it could well be too late.

"POWER READINGS, Mr. Ashton."

"Holding at 60 percent of capacity."

"Miss Palmer—shields amain. Blank all guns and prepare to charge the aft batteries. Helm—slow to C-1, ease up on approach arc—that's it. Prepare for hard aport, bank even at 730—and mark! Now bring us in line with the trailing brigantine, and let's let them start sweating awhile."

"All enemy guns amain, Captain; all enemy shields at full power. They're all at sublight, trying to come about."

"Thank you, Mr. Ashton. Miss Palmer, open fire on my order.

"Aye, sir."

"Helm—increase to C-14, prepare for sublight lift due north on full stop at my command."

"Aye, aye, sir. Dead ahead at fourteen, and standing by."

AS THE PIRATES pivoted in place, *d'Artagnan* raced toward the corner ship in the formation. Within seconds, she would be within range of the powerful guns of the renegade starship, but Cook had timed the maneuver to keep the pirates' leftmost wedge between the *d'Artagnan* and the pirate leader, shielding the ship. As Wilkes fumed on his bridge, frustrated that he couldn't get a clear shot, the Cozzie ship came to full halt, training her aft guns on all brigantines within range. Soon a flash appeared in the sky, the funeral fire of the corner ship in the pirate flotilla. Cozzie had drawn first blood.

The first flash was followed almost instantly by a second; two ships were gone from their ranks and the pirates had yet to fire a shot. From his bridge, Wilkes barked orders to his wingmates, telling them to scatter to the stars and give him a clear approach. He was furious with himself for being so gullible, and it was now painfully clear that the brigantines, rather than distracting Cozzie as he'd hoped, would only be a hindrance.

Suddenly, without warning, *d'Artagnan* burst through the dying fireball of her second kill on a direct heading for the enemy starship. With no time to react, panic seized the pirate bridge. Wilkes screamed the order to dive and the *Black Dragon* jerked violently downward. Barely missing the Cozzie ship as she passed overhead, the pirates felt their mast shields shudder under the blast of enemy guns. And when they finally managed to compose themselves, the Cozzie ship was speeding into open space, daring them to follow.

By the time the pirates recovered enough to take up the chase, *d'Artagnan* had begun a leisurely starboard arc, edging ever so slightly back toward the blue star that dominated the local heavens. The *Black Dragon* alone dared to follow, and across her bridge eyes widened in amazement. Even their leader looked badly shaken, and fear was a stranger to Chadbourne Wilkes. Danger was nothing new to any of them. They were used to living on the edge of disaster, cheating death by the seat of their pants. But this was different, and the same cold chill gripped the hearts of all: they were stalking a madman.

* * *

THE SIGNAL BELL rang in short, staccato claps, then fell silent. Though still standing at battle stations, the ship was out of immediate danger. Until the alarm buzzer sounded again, the crew could relax.

On B-Deck, Crewmen Sullivan and Barrett ventured into the hallway and walked slowly to the intercom. Sully punched his entry code, then entered the alpha-numeric "DCB12A," reporting "All Clear" on behalf of Damage Control Team B-12. This accomplished, he leaned on the wall to rest. Though he could hear muted voices down the corridor in either direction, he saw nobody but his own repair crew; the arching hallway kept the others out of sight. He was too tired, and too glad to be alive, to show much interest in anything another team might have to say. He doubted that anyone else would say something worth hearing, anyway.

"Quite a ride, eh Sully?" said Barrett, coming over to sit next to him. Soon the others in their team had freed themselves from their safety restraints and were coming to join them.

Sully shook his head; beads of sweat ran down his forehead. He smiled gruffly. "Like a roller coaster it was, Denny. A bloody roller coaster. At my age, the last thing I need is to spend my time going up and down a carnival ride."

Barrett laughed. "Can't say as the Skipper makes for a boring time now, can we? Y'know, I could feel the keel guns off to blastin below. Like a champagne cork popping on New Year's. But for the life of me, I didn't feel the bandits land a shot. Not a single bloody shot."

"I hope they're not saving their hits for later," said Jensen, the young tyro from New Babylon. "Like with the Ishtar Flu—if it's up to me, I'd just as soon take the shots now and get it over with. Sure as hell makes you rest easier when you reach the climax."

The others all laughed, everyone but Sullivan and Barrett. The team leaders shook their heads as their younger comrades let jokes relieve some of the tension. They were a mite green, thought Sully. Wilkes was just a name to them, not a presence that had haunted the frontier for as long as anyone could remember. And he doubted that any of them ever saw a friend's ship sent up, its death fire lighting the heavens before fading into the blackness.

JANET LEANED BACK in the helmsman's chair, grateful for the chance to rest. The helm was on automatic, easing the ship on a lazy starboard arc toward the area's dominant star. By habit, she looked back and smiled wearily at the captain. Battles under Cook were never dull, she thought, just exhausting.

"Don't get too comfortable, Lieutenant," winked the captain, grateful that the two of them still shared their rapport on the bridge. He looked over his shoulder at the aft monitor. "Looks to me like Wilkes wants a rematch."

Too busy to join in the tension-breaking laughter, Jeremy stayed focused on the monitors at the systems station. The pirate starship was gaining rapidly; if Cook didn't increase speed soon, they'd be at it again in a matter of minutes. Sensors showed the pirate guns fully charged and their shields ready for battle; d'Artagnan's weapons were still blank, and Cook was showing no inclination to change their status. Outwardly calm as ever, the captain seemed more like a cruise director than an embattled warrior.

But like most of the bridge crew, the past few minutes had left Jeremy shaken and awestruck. For the first time, he understood Cook's stubborn insistence on drilling and timing. The ship was doing things that starships just didn't do, in battle or anywhere else. The captain knew the precise limits and capabilities of the ship and of each member of his bridge crew as well. Beyond this, Cook's mind stretched into dimensions that Jeremy could scarcely comprehend. The captain had an intuitive sense of everything and everyone around him, and a dazzling ability to reassess and change his thoughts and plans in an instant. And Cook's capacity for split-second timing, it seemed, could be every bit as frightening as his daring: if Wilkes hadn't reacted when he did to their own efforts to ram him....

Jeremy just shook his head. He didn't want to think of the consequences. Beneath the nervous smiles, Jeremy could see that none of the others did, either.

"All right," Cook's smile faded; without warning, he'd become all business, his eyes as cold as death. "Helm—resume manual control, increase speed to C-14, boost navigation arc by twelve degrees. Mr. Ashton, find the major planets in the star system and plot them on the navigational monitor. Miss Palmer, begin charging the starboard and portside guns, and stand by to charge the forward."

THE D'ARTAGNAN raced toward the blue star, her navigational arc bringing her into the planetary system at a steep angle. The pirates were right behind, just out of firing range. Suddenly, Wilkes swung his ship a few degrees north and increased speed, trying to overtake the Cozzie ship while she was still suffering the space-normal distension of high speed, drawn by sensor readings showing the Cozzie starship running at greatly reduced power. Quickly, Cook blanked the ship's side guns while the forward guns finished charging; as the pirates roared into range, he shifted power from the engines to his shields. The ship slowed violently while the pirates raced overhead. As the enemy guns missed their target, d'Artagnan's scored major hits along the pirates' keel, warping their shields to the point of buckling, and discoloring the heat shields on their outer hull. But speed carried them out of danger before their shields collapsed, and by the time the pirates slowed to come about, their power reserves had repaired the damage.

Meanwhile, d'Artagnan slowly eased toward the star system's major planet—a massive, banded world of clouds and storms a half-billion miles from its sun, circled by two dozen moons and a haunting set of rings, a thin necklace gracing the skies that could easily turn into a noose for either ship.

* * *

THE CRESCENT PLANET hung silently in the cold sky, a thin splash of color in the blackness. The sun burned a fiery blue, casting the heavens into shadow and light. Cautiously, Wilkes drew his ship toward the giant world. Despite the weakness of the Cozzie ship, he'd seen enough to respect the danger that faced him. He dared not withdraw, yet he was wary of another attack. This Cozzie was a master, and could turn on them swiftly. Wilkes knew he'd need more than the brute strength of a starship to escape with his hide.

The pirates neared the planet. Cozzie had inclined his ship's orbit about twenty degrees, and was nearing the leeward terminator, crossing the planet's equator just before passing into darkness. Soon, the Cozzie ship was nearing occultation; the planet would pass between the two ships and break contact between them, leaving each with an opportunity, and placing each in peril.

"SENSOR CONTACT severed—mark. Planet's equator in five minutes; ring density holding steady our plane of travel. Present course will bring us within five hundred miles of the outer ring."

"Thank you, Mr. Ashton. Helm, increase speed and drop us fifty thousand miles inside our present orbit. We'll be emerging from inside the planet's inner ring—and cut it as close as you can, Mendelson. I want to tear past them and double back before they know what's happening, and we'll need all the room you can give us to maneuver."

"Aye aye, Captain."

"And keep the keel facing out. I still don't trust those mast batteries."

"Yes, sir. Engaging—now!"

AS HIS ADVERSARY passed to the other side of the planet, Wilkes doubled speed and charged toward it, certain that Cozzie had something in mind, but aware that he had no idea what it might be. Across his bridge, gloom had replaced the crew's cocky confidence. They were in the fight of their lives, and each of them knew it. All the old, comfortable rules of combat had vanished, and doubt was even appearing in the eyes of their leader.

Suddenly, inspiration struck, born of the clarity of vision that only panic can inspire. Wilkes knew he could never anticipate what Cozzie might do next, and was beginning to fear that his own reactions would be too slow in a head-to-head gun battle. It was like nothing he'd seen before, and the way Cozzie danced across the skies scared him. But nothing prevented them from tailing Cozzie, keeping out of harm's way until an opportunity presented itself.

Nearing the planet, the *Black Dragon* veered leeward, passing into the shadows cast by the giant world. Soon, as her skipper had hoped, the pirates' sensors detected the fading energy waves cast by the *d'Artagnan* only moments before, tracking the Cozzie ship while the planet served as a screen.

"ANY SECOND NOW."

The planet loomed large in the portside viewers, its rings dominating the starboard screen. No one had time to admire the scenery, and not even the captain could afford to divide his attention.

From the helmsman's station, Janet felt her chest thundering. She'd been through it often enough, but nothing ever changed. The one unifying thread in all of Cook's encounters was the sense of wrenching uncertainty, and for all their past times together she had no clearer idea of what the Skipper had in mind than anyone else. But the captain had trained them well, and no one dared to utter a sound. Everyone listened for the confident voice from the command seat, telling them what to do.

"Forward screen is still clear, Captain," Jeremy called from the systems desk.

Cook sat forward in his chair, his eyes narrowed in fierce concentration. Something was wrong, he thought; something was very wrong. They should have made contact by now. Obviously, he had underestimated his opponent—and he knew that they could ill afford the miscalculation. But there was no turning back now, and there was only one way to find out what was happening.

"Helm—increase speed to one-half. Prepare to engage spacedrive. and stand by for evasive maneuvers. Mr. Ashton—put your forward monitor on screen six. I want to see what's out there."

"Yes, Captain."

"Aye aye, sir."

THE D'ARTAGNAN raced out of orbit, rising high into the northern skies over the giant planet. In all directions, her screens showed clear. For all intents and purposes, Wilkes had vanished without a trace. For a moment, confusion clouded every face on the bridge. Every face except the captain's. In a sickening instant of realization, Cook knew exactly what had happened—and was furious with himself for giving the pirates an opening.

Immediately, he ordered the ship to come about, changing course to swing toward the planet's northern pole, trying to use its gravitational pull to help them change direction, but it was too late. The pirates roared upon them with guns blazing as Wilkes raced to exploit the one chance that his enemy was likely to provide. Scoring hits across the hull, he saw Cozzie's shields bend as she twisted and darted, desperately trying to deflect the crushing blasts from the pirate guns. In the end, Wilkes was left pounding his armrest in frustration. Cozzie had absorbed everything he could throw, only to fade from view over the horizon, carried more by gravity than by the dwindling power reserves from engines taxed beyond capacity in the effort to keep their shields from crumbling.

The pirates continued ahead, slowly coming about, when their computers relayed news that fired their blood and brought the first smiles to the bridge since the engagement started: the strain of the encounter had brought Cozzie's power reserve down to 38 percent of capacity. And it was slipping.

But more than this, their second salvo had cracked Cozzie's mast shields like a brittle shell. Their sensors showed stress fractures all across the shields screening her northern hull. Cozzie lacked the reserves to restore them; one more hit and they'd crumble.

"HARD A-PORT; prepare to increase speed."

"Captain—mast shield is— "

"Yes, I know, Mr. Ashton. Palmer, blank all guns, divert maximum power to shields. Helm— "

"Aye sir."

"He's coming—six o'clock, dead astern."

"—barrel roll left. Palmer, angle shields, port and starboard."

"Five seconds."

"Helm—due north—maximum speed."

The ship shook violently under the pirate barrage. On the bridge, as across the ship, the crew strained at their safety restraints as enemy fire battered the ship. The screens went blank for an instant, before auxiliary power restored them, and the stern viewer showed the pirates coming about for another pass.

"Captain, the mast shield is almost— "

"Thank you, Mr. Ashton!" snapped Cook. He'd already checked; the shield was holding, barely, but that wasn't the immediate problem. Now that the initiative had passed to Wilkes, he had to win some time to maneuver. Otherwise, the buckling shield would only hasten the inevitable.

"Helm, hard a-starboard, heading 080—take us back around the planet, full sublight power."

"But— "

"As much as you can muster, Missy. Prepare to come about."

QUICKLY OVERTAKING HIS enemy, Wilkes swung his ship around Cozzie's left flank, before veering hard to starboard to pass directly over their mast. Responding sluggishly, *d'Artagnan* astounded the pirate by rolling directly across the line of fire just as the *Black Dragon's* guns had locked onto their target, preparing to obliterate Cozzie's shields as they passed overhead. In the process, the Cozzie captain managed to turn a flush hit into a glancing blow. But as the *Black Dragon* came about once more, Wilkes shrieked in triumph—he and every other man on his bridge. Cozzie's mast shield had finally collapsed. It gave the Cozzie skipper the kind of choice that warmed a pirate's black heart: Cozzie could try to patch it by draining his already exhausted reserves; or he could leave it open. Either way, Cozzie had cheated death for the last time. Everyone on the bridge was smelling blood. Wilkes knew that the next pass would be his last.

* * *

THE SHIP lay directly sunward of the pirates, easing her way astern. Cook saw pale, ashen faces wherever he looked, but he couldn't waste his time trying to rally their spirits. It would be enough if they simply followed orders. And he dismissed the urge to blame himself for the fact that death was staring them all in the face. If his next maneuver didn't work, it wouldn't make any difference; it wouldn't make any difference at all.

"Range, one hundred astrometers." Jeremy's voice was cracked and lifeless. "Slowing for their approach."

Frustration raged in Cook's heart. He knew exactly what he wanted to do; he could see it in his mind and feel it in his belly. But it was risky enough with engines at full power. Even then the ship had a tendency to stall out on him. With reserves this low, a stall was almost a given—though it would hardly do them any harm, he smiled darkly. Especially since they had no real choice.

"Underwood, sound the clearing horn." His voice rang with conviction, admitting no hint of the slightest doubt. "Helm, steady astern at quarter speed sublight. Prepare for spiral turn—dead astern."

"But, but— " It was Talbert; he'd have to plot the course. Mendelson was too busy adjusting her controls to worry about the fact that they had never tried this maneuver before, but the news left the navigator dumbstruck.

Cook was too busy to argue. Furiously, he searched his mind for ways to conserve power. Every ounce of energy they saved would increase his chance of pulling this off.

"Palmer—begin charging a single—repeat, a single aft battery. And prepare to blank all shields."

Stunned silence greeted his order. They didn't understand, he thought. And he didn't have time to explain.

"That was not a request, Missy."

"Aye aye."

"Mr. Talbert, plot your course. *Mr. Talbert*—!"

The forward viewer showed the pirates cruising toward them, drawing nearer, nearer. Talbert's eyes bulged wildly. His mind was a complete blank, and his hands were frozen over the instruments.

In a fluid motion, Cook released his safety restraints and bounded over the railing to the navigator's desk, quickly releasing Talbert's harness and pushing him from the navigator's station. Without glancing at the instruments, eyes riveted on the approaching enemy on the viewscreen before him, Cook's hands flew over the navigation controls and dials, setting a course on the helm console.

"Forty metes and closing."

"Talbert, strap yourself into the hot seat."

Suddenly, inspiration began to strike. "Jeremy—tell me when their guns begin the firing sequence," said the captain.

As the pirates neared, Cook drew his navigation arc ever more tightly, until it was a noose around their charging enemy. The more he thought about it, the more he was convinced. It would work; it had to work. If only they had more power, he thought. He heard Mendelson gasp; his eyes darted over to see her smile of admiration. She understood at last.

"I hope we can pull it off," she whispered. "We won't get another chance."

He smiled grimly in return, his eyes focused on the screen. "Now, ease us up toward his plane of direction," he whispered, "and keep us just below the solar plane. When I give the word, spiral turn astern, all available power."

Mendelson nodded.

"That's right," he said, his eyes fixed on the main screen at the fore of the bridge. "Now, let's— "

Suddenly, the pirates increased their speed for their final approach. And in the same instant, it dawned on him—or at least, what dawned on him seemed to make sense. It was the last bit of power they could spare—it would increase the power available to the engines by almost half a point—and more importantly, it would free the ship from the strain of trying to keep gravity constant under the stress.

"Cut gravity to all decks," he barked. Jeremy hesitated.

"Do it !!"

Jeremy deactivated the gravity generator and was surprised to find that he barely noticed the queasy sensation of sudden weightlessness. They were all feeling queasy enough already. And he couldn't tell the difference a moment later, when eternity opened beneath their feet.

"Firing se— " he screamed.

"Now!" Cook shouted; Janet fired the engines and the ship shifted underneath them, lurching violently backwards and accelerating as they rose.

"Palmer—blank all shields, prepare to fire aft battery. And Palmer—make it count."

FOLLOWING HER own tail, the *d'Artagnan* arched across the pirates' line of flight less than a second ahead of her attackers, slamming crew members against walls and into ceilings. Their sensors blinded by the sun and with no time to respond—and convinced that the Cozzies were trying to ram them again—the pirates cut sharply from the point of intersection, banking south and to starboard, their guns missing wildly as the Cozzie ship streaked past their bow. Unnoticed in the panic that seized the pirate bridge, *d'Artagnan* continued her tight spiral, coming back upon the *Black Dragon* like an echo. All her firepower concentrated in a single gun, *d'Artagnan* scored a direct hit just astern of dead center as the pirates passed helplessly below, slicing through a seam in the enemy's overhead shield and burning a hole deep into the *Black Dragon's* heart. Part of the Conning Deck and much of Engineering were vaporized instantly, and the breach sucked chairs, equipment, and bodies into the Big Black. With her power gone, the pirate ship rapidly lost speed, throwing the remains of her crew against the forward walls of the ship. Debris and atmosphere rushed toward the vacuum, and internal explosions gutted the ship. Anyone still alive heard a loud, clamorous buzzer warning of the fracture in the hull and then, in a cataclysmic blast swallowed by the silence of space, the ruptured engines exploded, consuming the ship in a blinding fireball.

VEERING STEEPLY to avoid the blast, the *d'Artagnan* slowed to a halt. The battle was over. On the bridge, the crew watched the viewer without uttering a sound.

"Nice shot, Palmer," Cook said at last. "Mr. Ashton, sound the all-clear and secure us from battle stations. You have the hot seat." Breathing deeply, he rose and started toward the door.

"I'll be in my quarters."

"Helm," Jeremy said, a hint of a quiver in his voice. "Ahead one-quarter, prepare for victory sequence—wing over wing, port over starboard."

"Belay that! " Cook snapped angrily from the ramp. "I'll have none of that foolishness on my ship. Death is nothing to celebrate, Mr. Ashton, and it could have been us, just as easily." Cook turned on his heels and stormed toward the exit.

"Yes, sir." Jeremy said weakly. He looked about the bridge. Everyone was as stunned as he was—shocked to be alive, numb to any feeling but a growing sense of wonder. All, that is, but the Skipper.

"Captain?"

Cook stopped and turned to face his first officer, anger in his eyes. "Yes, Mr. Ashton?"

Suddenly, under Cook's haughty glare, Jeremy felt quite foolish. Words were inadequate to express what he felt. What they all felt.

"Well done, sir."

A sheepish smile darted across Cook's lips. His glower softened to a proudly modest glow. There was much that a captain could never tell his crew, and much more that they would never understand. Hardest of all, he thought, would be explaining just how sloppy he'd been in his first battle as a starship commander. He'd had his moments, of course; and however belatedly, he'd finally managed to snap off a spiral turn that didn't stall the engines or send the crew scurrying to Sick Bay. As for the rest, it was his worst performance in ages.

"I'll be in my quarters, Mr. Ashton. Set us on a course for Looking Glass. We may make maneuvers yet."

Jeremy looked stunned; Underwood turned to gape at Cook in astonishment; Talbert leaned back in the captain's chair, not uttering a sound. The women on the bridge exchanged glances, wondering if they'd heard correctly.

"*Looking Glass!*" Jeremy whispered intensely, wincing at the thought. "But after—and we're just a few days away from— "

Cook grinned widely, humor returning to his eyes. "And what would you have our ladies do while we're at Riley's Station, happily contracting every communicable disease known to modern science?" he laughed. "Sit around and knit?"

"But— "

"Looking Glass."

"—but— "

"Looking Glass."

Grudgingly conceding defeat, Jeremy mumbled an acknowledgment and motioned for Talbert to resume his duty station. Soon, the ship was on its course and Cook was on his way to his cabin. The rear viewers showed the dying embers of the *Black Dragon* fading from sight, soon to be cold as the surrounding void. Through the hatch, cheers of celebration filtered onto the bridge, but except for the gentle tapping of instrument keys, the bridge kept a respectful silence. The battle had drained the crew of every emotion but two. All that was left was gratitude and awe, and a long time would pass before any of them would feel comfortable discussing the source.

* * *

LYING ON his bed, eyes closed and remaining as still as possible, Cook activated the antigrav. Soon he was floating freely in his sleep chamber, alone with his thoughts. He heard the growing commotion in the hall, as crewmen poured from their stations to cheer their good fortunes. He had no inclination to join them. He was too tired to do so, in any event.

Still, when he heard the "hurrahs" ringing through the corridors, his lips curled into a smile of serenity. Moments later, he drifted off to sleep.

The old man stroked his long, gray beard. He sat beneath a tree, along with ten young men and women seated in a semi-circle around him. The shade gave welcome relief from the summer sun. Everywhere he looked, the grass was a luscious green.

The breeze gently rustled the leaves. As was his custom, the old man had gathered his new students on the Commons. The clear sky was more conducive to clear thought than a stuffy classroom would ever be. Today, though, his face bore the barest hint of disappointment. After six weeks of instruction, he expected more from the cream of the incoming class. Before long, the regular term would start. If he did not reach them soon, other subjects would compete for their attention and they would be irredeemably distracted.

"No, Sister Okumba, it is no excuse to the paradox to say that the sage rejects violence in all things. That is worse than a syllogism: it is a sophist's trick, a mere platitude. A tool fit for lawyers and politicians, perhaps, but little use to a thinker. Such things lead only to dogma, and we have already seen that logic should not be the enemy of common sense."

Master Salisi looked at each of his pupils in turn. All held promise; the Lyceum invited none without promise to attend. But he had yet to unlock their minds. The thinking of a sage was still alien to them, though all loved disputation and argument.

Or almost all, thought Salisi, for the Northlander, the youngest member of the class and in many ways the most intriguing, was hardly the most talkative. If left to himself he seemed to withdraw into a world of his own, trapped by his shyness. Yet his eyes blazed with curiosity and conviction, and when he did speak his words rang with truth, even though the truth of an adolescent was rarely ripe.

"Brother Cook."

The young man looked startled, as if stirred from a private reverie.

"I shall repeat myself; let us hear your thoughts."

The young Northlander nodded.

"Refute the following: 'Killing is wrong.'"

Saying nothing, the lad looked at the ground. Seconds passed before he raised his eyes to meet the master's.

"It is an absolute without a context, therefore without meaning."

"That is a demurrer, not a refutation. The proper course is to correct the deficiency and supply the context."

"One attacked may kill in defense—one may kill an aggressor."

"So then survival is the ultimate good? Or is your refutation simply that two wrongs make a right?"

The boy paused, his brow crinkling in contemplation. A moment later he raised his head and looked the master squarely in the eyes. "If each willingly permits his own death," he said tentatively, a hint of wryness on his lips, "merely to vindicate some abstraction of philosophy, who will remain to smell the flowers or watch the sunrise—or to ponder the questions of existence? None but murderers."

Master Salisi smiled in return. And for the longest time, he said nothing at all.

Chapter 10

STILLNESS LURKED IN THE CATACOMBS of the Imperial Palace as Ya'Lisha hurried through the darkened hallways. Beneath each dusty cobweb his footsteps echoed amid the ghosts of history.

Yet this remained the quickest route to the Minister's quarters, and it was the one path free from the prying eyes of the Imperator's Royal Guardsmen—and thus from the ears of competing Ministries.

The Lord Deputy rounded a curve and came to a fork in the hall. He bore left, past a stone statue of an imperator long dead to history and past the tomb that his statue guarded. The dim light hid the grime-shrouded works of artists and craftsmen whom time had forgotten. Ya'Lisha remembered the younger days of his own past, before the demands of court had stolen his sense of wonder. Upon his arrival in the Capital, he had often wandered the inner reaches of the Palace, thrilled at leaving footprints in the dust of uncounted generations. Now he lacked time for such games. The demands of state weighed heavily on his shoulders, and he hurried down the corridor.

He came to a marble fountain carved into the hallway, where water once poured from the stone mouth of an animal of myth. Today, the liquid seeped through the cracked and discolored marble floor, rising from a small leak deep within the ancient walls. He passed a charged metal key before the creature's unseeing eyes and a panel opened to its side, leading to a carpeted lift chamber. On the wall, as it had for millennia, a time calibrator silently clicked away the seconds.

Nervously, Ya'Lisha stepped inside. Finding the chamber waiting was an ominous sign. Properly, it belonged just inside the wall in the Minister's chamber, awaiting his pleasure. Obviously, Cra'Jenli was getting impatient.

* * *

FAR EAST of *g'Khruuste*, where Ya'Lisha girded himself to endure his Minister's wrath, Zatar of Ibleiman was facing an ordeal of a different order on the planet Balarium, in the Grand Drawing Room of the Grand Hall of the Grand Alliance.

"So, Zatar," cooed Drubid, the Glincian Solon, "what then is your real conclusion? What shall we expect you to tell the Council at tomorrow's sitting?"

Watching from near the food table, Zatsami of Mlantza frowned in silence. Like all Veshnan women, she was used to indulging the male need for attention without taking what they said seriously. Unfortunately, in diplomatic settings like this one, the men and women of other races often listened intently, encouraging boastfulness at the expense of more productive endeavors. Or worse, they actually believed the silliest bits of male puffery. Such nonsense was one of the reasons that Veshnans rarely trusted their men with any undertaking of a delicate nature. Even when the man was as brilliant as Zatar, he was often most successful at getting himself into trouble.

Like this present slice of foolishness: Drubid was perfectly transparent, and his government's interest in the matter was well known. He wished to drain Zatar's insights in advance of tomorrow's session of the Council, to help his delegation frame its position from a stance of reasonableness and draw added support from the ranks of the uncommitted. A child could see as much, but still Zatar pressed ahead, so intent on impressing the Glincian with his mastery of the subject that the need for discretion was forgotten.

Soon, the reception would be abuzz with talk of Zatar's report on the Terrans, unmindful that Zatar could very well change his conclusions by the time the Council sat the next day. There was, after all, a wide gap between his own professionalism and the Veshnan male's instinct to assert his dominance. As with all men, the show itself was all, and beyond their preening display lurked a child's insecurity, which meant that nothing said during a man's moments of self-importance should be taken seriously. Veshnan women understood this, and were quite happy to let men keep their fond illusions so long as it came to nothing. She could hardly expect sister races to understand the quiddities of Veshnan manhood, however, and the point was near when she could defer intervention no longer.

"Surely, the Solon cannot expect the Council's own emissary to display favoritism?" Zatsami interjected, ignoring Zatar's stamping foot. "How can the council's favorite procurator reveal his thoughts to one and withhold from the rest? No, I am sorry, Lord Drubid, but I must protest. And, of course, Zatar must beg your forgiveness."

Bowing politely, the Glincian smiled and excused himself. Zatar's eyes followed him to the entrance to the Banquet Hall, where Drubid disappeared into the crowd. The council's favorite turned with a fury upon Zatsami, Veshna's senior solon.

"You seem a most popular man tonight, Zatar," Zatsami said mildly. "But then, I have never known you to want for companionship."

Pleasant memories darted between their eyes, and Zatar's anger soon faded. He even managed a smile, as he realized—after the fact, of course—that the solon's intervention had spared him even greater embarrassment on the morrow. "I have never seen such curiosity on the eve of Council, Tsami," he said, "and from all corners of the Alliance. It is as if my report holds some meaning hidden from myself. Only the Crutchtans have not sought my counsel tonight, and I doubt that the reason is a lack of interest."

Sighing, Zatsami closed her eyes and nodded. Men could be so unthinking, she thought, but Zatar had been gone a long time and re-mastering the nuances of Council politics after an absence always took time. Placing her arm in his, she led him from the Drawing Room out onto the veranda. The stars glimmered in the clear night sky, and a soft breeze blew from the south. The city lights shone like diamonds strewn over the valley below. The view from the hill was magnificent, commanding one of the grandest vistas in all the civilized universe. Yet it was the loneliest vista as well, for aside from the city the planet was uninhabited. The Grand Alliance kept its administrative center alone and isolated, on a world open to none but those with official clearance to visit. Only bureaucrats and diplomats and visiting dignitaries—and their families, once the proper forms were filed and approved—could enjoy its teeming gardens, or swim in its warm, salty seas.

Coming to rest near grRunsti Fountain near the Fidrei Gate, Zatsami turned to face her countryman, concern etched across her face. "You are aware of the divisions within the Crutchtan ranks?"

"I am not long away from the Terrans, where conflict is as natural as breathing. I found myself developing a new sense to detect it. And I have come to wonder whether conflict is any less natural to our Crutchtan friends than to their Western neighbors."

Zatsami nodded ponderously, and spoke in the lowered tones of one accustomed to the intrigues of diplomacy. "Cra'Jenli and Gal'Shenga are finally joining their battle for dominance in the Imperator's Palace, and here the Glinci and Atkvalo are casting for allies among the uncommitted. Even as we speak, plans are hatching and forming here and in every corner of the Alliance, all with the purpose of gaining sway throughout the realm. All seek to use the Terrans to their advantage. Your report is critical to everyone, Zatar, though to each for different reasons. And all wish to couch their positions in terms that comport with your own."

"And Veshna's position is— ?"

"Our position is not your concern, Zatar. You are charged with the common good, not with advancing the interests of the Motherland. And our policy will likely follow whatever you recommend. After all," she smiled, "we cannot believe that what benefits all will inure to our disadvantage—particularly since the Council will be looking at matters through the eyes of a Veshnan."

She took his arm to lead him back into the palace. As they walked, Zatar had time to reflect. He was walking into a swarm of harvestbugs, he thought, a vast host devouring all before them without thought for what might lie ahead. None of them understood the dangers they faced. Not the Crutchtans, nor the Glinci, nor the Atkvalo. Not even Zatsami and the others of his own kind. And Zatar often wondered if he himself understood any better than the rest.

"YOU HAVE failed me, Ya'Lisha."

Though his soul wished to hide, the Lord Deputy stared ahead, opening his mind to the criticism. Though he sensed the presence of others, all was dark around him; he saw only the blinding light of the judgment lamp, and the merciless face of Cra'Jenli, tetrarch of the House of Crashchilieu and the Imperator's own Minister of Foreign Relations. In the Minister's fiery eyes and twisting tongue, Ya'Lisha saw his own destruction.

"You have failed me and failed our cause," the Minister continued. Amusement coursed through his veins. Making one such as Ya'Lisha stand like a servant during correction was a humiliation he relished. Cra'Jenli disliked his Lord Deputy, disliked him with the passion of one obsessed with ambition and jealous of all around him. Now he no longer needed to conceal his disdain. Though Yagravina support was crucial,

Cra'Jenli had carefully cultivated other bonds within the clan during the past few cycles. Now that Ya'Lisha had failed to deliver the assistance promised, the ties of blood to those within Gal'Shenga's camp were too thin to incite treachery in its ranks. Having proven himself useless, Ya'Lisha was now utterly expendable; any other Yagravina would suffice to satisfy dictates of form, mused Cra'Jenli. None could find fault with purging his ranks of those serving no purpose. Even Ya'Lisha's own kin would concede that the stakes were too high to permit failure to go unpunished.

Hate flooded his thoughts and Cra'Jenli watched with delight as fear coursed over Ya'Lisha's countenance, paling the Deputy's features, contracting his eyes and draining the green from his face and gills. But all too soon it was ended, replaced by the stoic defiance of one too proud to entertain his enemies by showing emotion.

"Guards," the Minister growled. Three strong, young males emerged from the shadows, and stood behind and to either side of the Lord Deputy.

Cra'Jenli strutted, hands behind his back, twice circling around the helplessly silent Ya'Lisha.

"The Lord Deputy is deposed," the Minister hissed. "Take him to the Ministry to my private detention facility while I decide upon a suitable penance."

As the guards removed an unstruggling Ya'Lisha, another figure emerged from the darkness, smiling as blackly as the shadows. It was Balshadra, the Minister's consort. Her taunting eyes and the sensual fire of her soul made her the most haunting female in the Palace, turning the proudest lords of Crutchtan manhood into small, quivering children. A full Mistress of the Royal Concubinarium, she had her choice of any man in the Capital and once had captivated the Imperator himself, until the need for fresh amusements had led his attention to wander. Now, by fancy as well as cold ambition, she found no less than the most powerful minister in the Imperial Cabinet necessary to her contentment. Gold bracelets graced her arms; a silver pendant hung tauntingly from her neck. Teasingly, she came to Cra'Jenli, running a single finger up the boneplate of his forearm, until it came to rest upon the lower gill slit gracing his arching neck.

"And what do you suppose Gal'Shenga will do next?" she cooed, regally oblivious to the lessers in the room. "By luck or by design, he always does seem to avert disaster. Perhaps the Ancient Ones were right,

My Lord. Maybe reformers and other madmen really are the lost children of the gods. After all, those provincials in his employ are learning subtlety if nothing else, and even Ga'Glishek the Boor no longer bullies your emissaries with loose talk about his brother." She smiled greedily as her lover's slits began to darken and pulse.

Cra'Jenli placed his arm around her, rubbing his neck against the warmth of her cheek.

"We have nothing but supposition left us, My Pet," he cooed in return. "And at least this failure leaves us no worse than before." His heart urged him to wildness, though he knew he should focus his mind on the tasks confronting him. But Balshadra was so lovely; and his mind was ever lost under her spell.

The Lamp of Judgment ceased burning, and the ceiling lights came alive to reveal a large room with a winding stairwell leading down to the Minister's private chambers. Colorful murals danced across the walls, of sprites and satyrs in scenes of wild abandon. Cra'Jenli felt the fire welling in his mistress' breast.

"Leave us," he called to his remaining attendants. As they obediently filed out the arching rear doorway into the central courtyard, he looked deep into Balshadra's eyes, feeling flames of passion kindling in his soul. He led her toward the stairwell, toward the pleasure room below.

"And what of Ya'Lisha?" she asked mischievously, fully aware of her effect on her lover's temperament. "Am I to have yet another manslave that you do not trust? Or shall we do something more exhilarating this time?"

Cra'Jenli laughed heartily. "What a wicked girl you are, Love of Mine. Yes, Ya'Lisha's was a blood oath—it was all I would accept to allow him into my Inner Counsel. His life belongs to me now, until I declare myself satisfied. And I would be well within my rights to sacrifice it to your amusement. But his family is too powerful to offend and he may yet reclaim his honor. No—I shall content myself with his degradation. This is the time to impress the Imperator with my capacity for generosity, not for self-indulgence."

"Well," pouted Balshadra in mock self-pity, "if it's self-indulgence you mean to avoid."

Playfully, she slapped Cra'Jenli smartly across his cheek, then dashed down the stairwell, laughing lustily and leering wildly over her shoulder. Cra'Jenli felt the blood rushing to his face, and frenzy filled his heart. With a cry of animal lust he raced her, his mind flooded with desire.

* * *

THE MORNING sun was warm and soothing as it poured through the windows in the propylaeum. Outside, gardens teased the mind with color while the odors of summer filled the hall. The large, wooden doors at the entrance to the Chambers remained tightly closed. Waiting for the Crier to come, inviting him to address the Council, Zatar paced the halls, alone with his thoughts.

Unlike most of his colleagues, his heart held much sympathy for the Terrans, and his kindly feelings had grown even as memories of the harsh Terran landscape had faded from his mind. They were not the simple savages dismissed by Civilization's pundits and intellectuals. Across the vast gulf of alien cultures, he had seen acts of kindness and generosity, enough to convince him that Terran society was ready to flower. As a people, the quaint and guileless simians had a passion for life and zest for discovery that promised to reinvigorate the stodginess of the Grand Alliance. Though burdened with the limited vision of a primitive culture, they were reaching outward, beyond themselves, toward something dimly sensed as their destiny, just as each civilized race had done before them. Once the trauma of cosmic awareness had passed, they would need only firm, gentle guidance to assume their proper place among the older races that comprised the galactic culture.

But where others saw them as uncivilized children, Zatar saw unrestrained power rising in the west. Children did not build the Terrans' powerful spaceships, he often reminded others, though usually his words met only deafness. Fear drove Terran culture: fear of the unknown, fear of the future, fear of themselves. Now the Alliance gave them something new to fear, something more terrifying than any of the nightmares that haunted their history books. And beneath it all were the same primordial urges that lay dormant in the soul of every race that called itself human.

Zatar gazed out the window at the fragile beauty outside. We have forgotten our own past, he mused sadly—forgotten the anguish and torment that grip each adolescent culture as it unlocks the powers of the universe and gropes for answers to the riddles of existence. The Alliance was looking at the Terrans through the eyes of maturity, with perceptions just as parochial as Terra's, but without the excuse of ignorance. Like dogmatists of old, most can little imagine something of value coming from anything beyond their own experience, and refuse to acknowledge that new events might require new ways of thinking. But most dangerous of all was the refusal to see that the same Terran science that trailed the rest of the galaxy by millennia in almost every respect had a single, seminal accomplishment: spaceships.

Warships, thought Zatar, shuddering as if from the cold. What black secrets must Terran history hold, he asked himself. What ingrained terror must Terrans endure each day to bind their science to a treadmill of ever-better machines of destruction? He knew he could never fully comprehend the mystery. His own people's early history of war and conquest was mired in antiquity, almost as alien to him as the past of the odd-looking Terrans. He hoped, one day, to understand. In the meantime, the Grand Alliance had to unite; they had to agree upon a single course, to ease Terra into their fold. There was simply no other alternative.

"Ambassador?"

Zatar turned to see the High Council's First Crier, zhLunta, the Fidrei. "The Council is ready, Ambassador."

Zatar stretched his back to its full height, then straightened his robe. For this address he was wearing white, as the Council had designated him as a relator, rather than a proponent or apologist. He was, after all, advancing no cause but that of the common good.

Proudly, his head high and his eyes brimming with confidence, he strode confidently into the Council Chambers, to address the High Solonic Council of the Grand Alliance.

"AND WITH the glad fervor of devotion to our beloved Imperator...."

While Zatar strode to meet the Council, ceremonial candles lighted the tables in the Meeting Hut on the Moon *Shun'Galanga*, where all but the Foodmaster kept a respectful silence. It was, after all, a Week of Remembrance, and only the service leader spoke aloud during the Incantation.

But ceremony or not, Shl'Glisen's stomach growled like an angry animal. Not easily did the appetite of a young one still itself, much the less when the cause of the delay was a rite without relevance to what lay on the table before them.

"...and whose firm Benevolence is our inspiration and our strength...."

As the Foodmaster droned on over this and over that, Shl'Glisen permitted his eyes to roam, from the *grus'l* plate to the currymilk, from the *shul'hkh* to the yeastcakes across the table.

"Small One!"

Shl'Glisen's back stiffened, and the color drained from his face and eyes.

"Small One," his mother hissed anew. "Sit straight and pay heed. The Foodmaster does not speak to exercise his voice."

"Yes, Mother."

"...and so, as with our Fathers before us, let us hold silence."

The Meeting Hut was silent as night. Following the tradition of the ages, all held vigil for a moment, remembering those who had gone before them. Only the quiet rumbling of a small boy's hunger broke the stillness.

"Begin."

The sounds of clinking glasses and raised toasts filled the hut. The gladness of thanks had lifted many hearts today, but the service of Remembrance held special meaning for the adults this week. The Ministry had accepted their Report; soon, they would be going home. All that lay ahead were some minor tasks of completion, and restoring the land to its primitive state. Throughout the encampment, spirits were high and talk was of a task well-done. Even the children were voicing dreams of Reunion.

Shl'Glisen's hand darted across the table toward the yeastcakes, only to return in a flash, smarting from a hard slap.

"You are a young man, Small One, not a carrion wolf." It was Shl'Lanasha, his father.

Shl'Glisen bowed his head. Under the table, he flexed his hand, trying to rid it of the stinging. Beside him Lanadra, his younger sister, giggled merrily, her eyes filled with a sibling's glee that correction was visiting another this time. He felt a brief surge of annoyance that his parents persisted in correcting him while ignoring the monster seated next to him. His anger, though, was short-lived, fading in the warmth of ensuing gratitude.

"Lanash," protested his mother, "he is but a child. There is no need to treat him so. Hunger dims the judgment even of grown men."

"Yes, it does, Lanshana," replied the father. "But hunger is no excuse for bad manners."

"I am sorry, Father," Shl'Glisen said, his words but echoing his feelings of regret.

Shl'Lanasha looked at his young son. It was hard being a child, he thought; all is forbidden, yet all is expected, and all from those whom time has had little chance to teach. "Your sorriness will one day ripen into maturity, my Son."

Shl'Glisen smiled through a gladdened heart.

"In the meantime—animals grab; humans ask."

"Yes, Father."

"Here are your yeastcakes."

"Thank you, Father."

"Oh—no!— do not stuff your mouth like a Terran, Shl'Glisen!"

"*Y'ff m'ff r....*"

* * *

"BUT WHY bring the whole Alliance into such a dispute," Xiazia asked pointedly. "Is it not properly a matter for the disputants to resolve?" The Landoran's coppery puff sacks undulated as he spoke, as happened whenever a Landoran's talk became animated. Landora was officially uncommitted, but Xiazia was known to favor the claim of the Glinci and Atkvalo to a share of the Crutchtan Cloud. Through a stern visage, Zatar himself laughed at the cruel irony: each sought his own gain, and was willing to join with his enemy if need be, to prevent all efforts by the Council to seek justice.

"I must agree with my Landoran brother," said Dra'Lani, the senior Crutchtan. Zatar almost choked; Xiazia and Dra'Lani had hated each other for as long as he could remember. "What basis for action do we see? What legal grounds has the Council to intervene? For even if we grant your premise, Zatar, are not we of the *g'Khruushtani* free under the Charter to pursue our own folly?"

"A Writ of Pre-emption is discretionary with the Council," answered Zatar, "requiring only a finding that the needs of all are paramount. It supplies its own legal basis."

"But has not *g'Khruuste* the right to order affairs with her own neighbors?" snapped Ma'Lunari, another Crutchtan. Most of the Council was silent, content to watch and listen. Only those with an interest were participating, Zatar noticed, and all with a purpose of foreclosing any action by the Alliance.

"Has Crutchta the right to endanger the Peace of Ages?" countered Zatar. "I think not: 'The interests of no Member shall prevail against the Needs of the Many—' "

"— 'nor shall the interests of the many overcome the Needs of the Few,'" continued Zatsami, reciting the balance of Article I, Section 6 of the Charter. "But we have not invoked Pre-emption in more than two millennia, Ambassador Zatar."

"And in that case, as here, it involved a newcomer—our good brothers the Glinci," said Zatar, bowing in the direction of Drubid, the non-voting Glincian solon.

"But the Glinci had long since asked to join us," noted the chairman, fiKunta of the Fidrei.

"My Lord Chairman," Zatar bowed slowly, a sign that he acknowledged the point but would not concede the issue. "I submit to this Council, and its fraternity of Wisdom, that it is the height of provincialism to permit Terran ignorance of our ways to blind us to what looms in the darkness. As are we all, they are a proud race, not easily given to admitting their shortcomings. Denigrating their achievements because of a transient backwardness merely masks the danger they present. And the Ages may well take note—we underestimate Terra at our peril."

"Underestimate a race with one foot in the jungle and another in the cave?" hissed Dra'Lani.

Zatar's eyes flamed with anger, but his words carried the serenity of reason. "It is easier," he replied, "to build machines than civilizations."

Proud and unyielding—for such was the posture all procurators took when debating anything, even in the privacy of home—Zatar stood at the podium, awaiting the Council's pleasure. But silence greeted the end of his remarks. Silence and the solons' skeptical faces.

Chapter 11

A T THE OPPOSITE END of civilization from the Council chambers on Balarium, on the jagged edge of charted space, a sterile body of dreams and metal twirled slowly in the dim light of a distant mother star. As they had for twenty years, the beacon lights of Riley's Station called weary travelers to port. Thirty-four parsecs anticenter-north of Planet Calais, Riley played hostess, sooner or later, to all the spacers on the frontier. There, rough and lonely men in all stages of dishevelment moored their ships, looking for a soft smile and kind word from a pretty face, and openly seeking the other charms available from the only rounded figures within hailing distance.

But the girls at Riley's Station weren't the common, unkempt sort found on any number of frontier colonies west of the Neutral Zone. And Riley kept the riffraff in line with an iron fist, brooking none of the rough-and-tumble bawdiness that livened the streets and pubs of Ishtar. Spacers whose taste in entertainment ran to rowdiness rather than feminine charms were rudely escorted to their ships, warned never to return, and blasted from the skies if they tried. Any new arrival—even those from Cozzie ships, whose hygiene had never given Riley cause for concern—was given a thorough scrubbing and a clean set of clothes, and told to make himself look civilized. Having become as presentable as he could, the spacer invariably headed straight for what Riley dubbed the Showroom.

It was a large room, brightened by the pulsing lights of the stage. The music was subdued, its rhythm almost hypnotic. The chairs were plush and comfortable, but those nearest the stage showed signs of wear. To the left, laughter poured through the hallway leading to the gaming room, where spacers with money to lose tried their luck at games of chance. To the right, a closed door led to one of the station's six observation decks, where each of the first-class cubicles had its own stunning vista of the local heavens hanging overhead, and the low sounds of men and women pretending to be in love sliced through the thin walls. On stage, on the elevated walkway extending twenty feet out from the proscenium, two pretty girls danced to the music, smiling and waving to the cheering men beyond the footlights. In the back, the small tables were filled with men with more serious things on their minds. Lost in talk and oblivious to what was happening at the other end of the room, they talked in lowered tones. And at one table, near the door leading to the living quarters for the station's permanent residents, was a solitary man, and the only other woman in the room.

"AH, KATE, ye're still a sight for sore eyes. The years ain't changed ye. They ain't changed ye one bit."

Cyrus grinned wolfishly. Katherine Riley—"Kate" to her customers—was the first and last of her breed. Two decades on the frontier hadn't dimmed her rough good looks, or tamed her spirit. Her hair was long and flowing, vanity keeping it a deep brown, unstreaked by the gray of age. Like all of her girls, her clothing trumpeted class and style—though as matron of the establishment, she'd long since stopped wearing the brief bottoms and inviting tops of her younger days.

From her chair across the wooden table, Kate shook her head skeptically. She hadn't survived in the wilderness by being naive. One of the few women along the frontier who'd managed to scratch out a living at prospecting, mostly by being good enough with a lasergun to fend off the clutching grasps of lonely spacers, she soon realized that there were easier ways for a girl to make her fortune on the frontier. Her business sense had made her a legend in board offices from Demeter to Calais. Rumor had it that she had a standing offer to join the management of one of the largest corporations on Demeter, but couldn't afford the cut in pay. Of course, rumors spread like the CosGuard Flu in these parts, and most were little more than spacer's blarney.

"Cyrus McGee, ye always was one of me favorites, though a girl can't trust ye no further'n a Cozzie can spit. An' I knew I could count on ye for help, just as soon as the danger had passed."

A roar of approval rose from the patrons. Cyrus turned his head to see one of the dancers remove an ankle bracelet and toss it into the audience. By long-standing tradition, the dancer would give a substantial discount to anyone returned it to her before the end of the day. Turning to face Kate again, Cyrus shook his head, and a warm, rich laugh rumbled deep in his throat. They'd known each other from the old days, when she was still just starting out in business for herself and he'd just retired from a profession of even greater disrepute. He helped build the defenses around her first station, an old-style wheel hub barely bigger than a frigate. All for a fee, of course, and a prettier fee he'd never collected. Then he bolted for the Black, just before the first onslaught by his old companions, who were always hungry for feminine companionship and perfectly willing to take it by storm. Of course, he left her in good hands: spacers for parsecs around had already taken a fancy to her, and were more than willing to help. Besides, he'd had his own reasons for leaving. His late associates were not the forgiving sort, and unlikely to smile at finding one of their number on the wrong side of a fight. But she'd never forgotten, and they never failed to enjoy a laugh at his expense.

"Well, there never was much danger, Katie. Ye're too much of an institution in these parts. And ye'd beaten him back twice already, mind ye. Nah, 'twould've been a rout, just like last time. Wilkes was never man enough for the likes o'ye."

"No, Cyrus. His last raid left a burn on our sides that took a month to clean off. And this time—why, Wilkes alone was a handful. Give him a starship, and he'd send the laddies a-skitterin from here to New Babylon. None would've dared lift a finger to help us, and all the Cozzies in these parts were called away to guard the settlements. I doubt we'd a-stood much chance. I hear it took some Cozzie hotshot to spread the old bugger at last. And even then, as I hear tell, things was a mite dicey, right up to the end."

Cyrus took a sip from his glass and wiped his mouth with his sleeve. "Well, Katie, much as I hate to admit it, that ain't why I come."

"That ain't no revelation, Cyrus," grinned Kate. Mildly curious, her intelligent eyes arched fetchingly. She leaned forward, elbows on the table, resting her chin in her hand.

"I got me a little bus'ness proposition," said Cyrus. "I'm castin about for some good men. The discreet sort, ye understand, who don't mind a little adventure, with profits aplenty afore we're through."

Kate sat back, disappointed. "Sounds like little more than prospectin. An' if prospectors come ten to the credit, then ye're bein overcharged."

"It's a job out East."

"Most of them are, Cyrus."

"Way East."

"How far?"

"How far?" Cyrus sat back in his chair, grinning like a gambler with a winning hand, who's just called his opponent's bluff. When he leaned forward again, Kate felt a cold thrill grip her spine.

"Think as far East as ye can," he whispered. "Then take a day layover, to get ye rid o'cabin fever. And then, keep ye the course...an start a-watchin the instruments.

"An start ye watchin, mind ye, for blips a-carryin lizards."

The barest hint of a smile danced across Kate's lips; the two of them started laughing softly.

"How much are we talkin, Cyrus McGee?"

"We ain't a-talkin anything, Mistress Riley," laughed Cyrus. "Not yet, anyways. Not till I sees who I'll be dealin with. 'Tain't that I don't trust ye, but there's riff-raff aplenty in these parts, an I've no appetite to get me throat slit. But I'll tell ye this much—there'll be enough to give ye half a plum for helpin to set up the expedition, an your slice alone will make your pretty little mouth water."

"If ye can be gittin by the Cozzies," said Kate, interested but still wary. Cyrus did, after all, have a reputation for sharp dealing, and she fully expected him to ask her to outfit the expedition. "I hear tell they've beefed up their patrols, ye know. Been months since I heard about a laddie gittin past'em."

"Little Matey," Cyrus smiled mysteriously, "we've no need to be a-gittin by the Cozzies."

Kate looked skeptical.

"We'll be a-goin 'round them."

Her eyebrows lifted, ever so slightly.

"Way 'round them."

Kate smiled wickedly, considering the implications of what Cyrus was saying. Had he really found an anticenter course through the heart of the Cloud? Teasingly, she ran her tongue across the fullness of her upper lip.

"I'll see what I can do," she said at last. "No promises, mind ye—but I think I know some lads who'll do us both proud."

"Ah, Katie, if it weren't for your other gifts, I'd swear ye was a-wastin your talents here."

"Ye always were a charmer, Cyrus. A mite crude, but a charmer nonetheless. An' while ye be waitin, why don't ye enjoy yourself?" She motioned to her left; Cyrus looked to see his brother, seated in a stage-side seat, staring at the gyrations of one of the dancers—the tall one, with the long legs and dark brown hair. All at once, the house roared with laughter, as she flung her panties into the audience and onto Mason's face and almost into his gaping mouth.

"Your brother seems right smitten with Ilena," Kate said with a wink. "Since she's new here, she works at a discount. An' for a brother o'Cyrus McGee, I'll make it a double discount. Double any way he wants to take it."

"Well, what about— ?"

"Ye can bloody well take your girls at full price, Cyrus McGee," Kate laughed saucily. "Unless, o'course, it's maturity ye be after," she added coyly. "If so, then...well I always did have a soft spot for a old friend. And we can talk this whole business over, more private-like."

"Katherine Riley, ye be readin me mind."

* * *

"ENGINES KICKING down again, sir."

"Acchh!"

"Power reserves are— "

"Yes, thank you Mr. Ashton, I expect that they're— "

"— dropping again. Yes, sir. Stabilizing at 18 percent capacity."

"Acchh!"

"Skipper, I hate to say this again— "

"Then don't, Mr. Ashton."

"But maybe it was a— "

"No, Mr. Ashton, it wasn't a fluke. *This* is the fluke."

"For the sixth time in a row?"

"Yes, and all we have to do is find out why."

"Then what— "

"Miss Mendelson, just steer the ship, please."

"But— "

"And Mr. Ashton— "

"Sir?"

" — ! "

"Sir?"

"You have the chair, Mr. Ashton."

"Yes, sir."

"If you need me, I'll be in Engineering."

"Yes, sir."

"Or in my quarters."

"Yes, sir."

"Or in the Science Lab."

"Is he gone?"

"I think so."

"How far behind schedule will this put us, Jeremy?"

"It's academic, Janet. We're so far behind now that another week or two won't make any difference."

"What's his problem anyway?"

"I don't know, Connie. But he's been chewing bricks ever since we finished off the pirates. It's like he expected the lot of us to go stabbing him in the back."

"Jeremy—you have any idea what's eating him?"

"Uh...no."

"Janet?"

"Um, no. Not really."

* * *

"I'LL NOT BE SAYIN I don't believe ye, Cyrus. We known each other long enough not to be callin us liars, and ye ain't never steered me wrong. Leastways, not that I ever learned about. But what ye be askin is—is—"

"Is no more than to be sailin on sealed orders," snapped Cyrus, his tone angry, but his eyes filled with humor. "An that, Kenny McKeller, is somethin none of us is strangers to. Or need I remind ye o'the last time the six of us sailed together?"

As Kate brought another round of Babylonian ale to the table, Cyrus shot a menacing look at each of his companions. Each averted his eyes, and each had reason enough to do so, thought Cyrus. Their last mission together had, after all, been a total disaster: McKeller had been the lookout; Rafferty and Swenson, both old hands at cutting out an escort, had supplied the cover. McGraw had skippered the decoy sloop in case the Cozzies happened by at the wrong time. And Herzog—well, he'd blown the whole operation by panicking at the first sign of trouble, spreading the mark without warning and nearly getting them all killed. It was their last sail together as privateers, and their last stab at recapturing the spirit of adventure they'd shared in their youth, before age and a growing sense of their own mortality combined to push them toward less dangerous work.

Still, all of them had their own special talents to bring to a mission like this, and each would come through like a spacer when the chips were down. As for the rest—well, Cyrus mused, they'd just have to trust each other, even though he'd make sure that he was the only one who knew the way there and back.

"All right, ye black-hearted yammermongers," laughed Kate. "There's ale for the lot o'ye, compliments of the house."

"What's your interest in this, Katie?" asked Rafferty rougishly. He spoke as a true Ceresian, with an eye for his own advantage, as well as the ladies.

"That's not your concern," snapped Cyrus, winking playfully at Kate. "She gets a cut for pulling us together, and for old time's sake. But the way we divide this here pot is up to me, and to any o'ye who be man enough to join me."

"Even if we do succeed in slipping by them slimy brutes—which I ain't concedin, mind ye—answer me this, Cyrus McGee."

"Speak on, Rafferty."

"How ye be knowin this all-eg-ed gold is gonna be waitin for us? If it be as ye say it is—and I'm not to be callin ye a liar now, Cyrus; ye know I'd never do that—but if it's as ye say, then why won't the whole boodle be off an gone to the stars, like a virgin stranded on Ishtar?"

Cyrus laughed roughly. Rafferty was a gifted pilot, one of the best he'd ever seen. But the man had gelatin for a spine and spacer's hash where others had brains. If he ever made a decision and stuck to it, heads would shake in wonder from here to New Babylon.

"An just how bloody stupid do ye think I be," Cyrus thundered at last, laughing heartily as he saw Rafferty shrink beneath his bluster. "Or are ye simply sayin I'd make like Clintus Rafferty and make sure I handed over everything I had to the lizards a-fore biddin'em goodbye?"

With a loud thud, Cyrus brought his fist down upon the table. All voices fell silent.

"I'll tell ye this, Clintus, and the same goes for the lot o'ye," Cyrus said, in a low voice barely audible over the rush of the air ducts. "I'm sure of gettin to where I want. I need no help for that. An were that the only problem, I'd not waste me time a-yammerin with any man here. But I don't know what's to be waitin for me when I arrive. It's been a long time since the lizards chased me out, and cheated me what was rightly mine."

"So what — "

"Silence, Herzog—or I'll cut me a mug across your head. Like I says, I'm in the market for some assistance, and I'll not be miserly about payin for it. I'm willin to pay half the costs of outfittin your ships, and I'll pay the rest for ye, too, after we put back here to port with our booty. For that, and for servin double duty as commodore and navigator for our expedition, the brothers McGee will be takin half o'the prize."

"Half?"

"Ye bloody jackal—ye damn right, half. It's my treasure, my plan, and my expense. Half the treasure rightly belongs to me brother, ye dim-witted rockbuster, an I'll be takin care o'Katie out of my share, as well. As for the rest, the five o'ye can split it amongst yourselves."

"I hardly think it's fair, Cyrus."

"Then ye can bloody well stay behind, Mr. Milquetoast Swenson. In fact," Cyrus rose menacingly, his eyes glaring at his former wingmate, "ye can leave right now. On your own, or on your head."

"There's no need to be makin threats, Cyrus," Rafferty pleaded, trying to make peace before his two friends squared off before them. "Swenson here's just a mite concerned about the—well, about the arrangements."

"Them that's particular can stay here," Cyrus thundered. "Them that's queasy about the thought of goin toe to toe with the lizards—or settin sail under sealed orders—can bloody well stay here an' rot. Them that's willin to stalk a fortune is welcome to join me. That's all I got to say, except that I'll be leavin as soon as possible, with or without ye."

A long silence followed.

"How much a fortune are we bein after, Cyrus?" Rafferty asked at last.

Cyrus smiled coldly, his eyes darting from man to man. Each, in turn, averted his glance.

Finally sensing triumph, Cyrus leaned back in his seat. "How much?" he chuckled humorlessly. "By my reckoning, after expenses and all, it'll come to just under two tons o'gold."

Cyrus saw eyebrows lift on every face in the room. The size of the cache impressed even Kate—and she'd been part of some of the biggest strikes eastern Terra had ever seen. But Cyrus leaned forward to deliver what he knew would end any discussion.

"An mind ye, now...that's two tons—per man."

* * *

"COME IN."

As Jeremy entered the captain's office, Cook was busy at the computer. Soft music filled the air, and except for the dull light from the screen, the room was completely dark.

For what seemed an eternity, Jeremy stood by the desk, watching the captain at work. For the captain, the universe had ceased to exist, and reality was compressed between a single, dimly lighted screen and the expanding, all-consuming curiosity of a single mind. Cook was lost in another world, his eyes blazing intensely, his mind seeing nothing but the computer screen. But swiftly as a shifting magnetic current and with as little warning, Cook's eyes lifted and he rocked back in his chair.

"Yes?"

It took Jeremy a moment to adjust his mind to the shift in the captain's attention. "You wanted to know when we neared the Looking Glass outbases."

"Thank you, Jeremy," Cook said through a tight, humorless smile. Without another word, he returned to his computer screen.

Jeremy turned to leave, but thought better of it. Something was bothering the captain, and Jeremy had a good idea what it was. Aside from his commands on the bridge, Cook hadn't spoken to his first officer for two cosmic weeks, and he'd said nothing to his helmsman either. As much as Jeremy felt slighted, the effect on Mendelson was devastating. For the past week, she'd spent her entire off-duty time alone in her cabin, doing little more than changing hairstyles and listening to sad melodies. It was well and good to leave some things unsaid, but this was getting out of hand. Whatever problems they had lingering beneath the surface were starting to affect the ship. And if Cook couldn't see that, then a good XO would have to force the issue.

"Skipper?"

Without a word, Cook stopped what he was doing and raised his eyes to look squarely at Jeremy.

"I'm not exactly sure what's going on here, sir, and maybe it's none of my business— "

"Actually," Cook leaned back in his chair, smiling cryptically, "it probably is your business, though in more ways than you probably mean."

"Sir?"

"But that doesn't really change things, does it Jeremy?" Cook laughed quietly, amused by the look of confusion on his first officer's face.

"And I guess you're not alone. I don't really understand it all myself. But then, life itself is an endless riddle with no solution except for death. And that's really not much of a solution, is it?"

Jeremy squinted; the captain was doing it to him again.

Cook laughed out loud, rocking slowly in his chair. "You know, Jeremy," he said at last. "People are idiots. And the funny thing is that we really can't help it, either because we really are fools or because whatever turns us into fools is simply beyond our power to change."

Jeremy cleared his throat, and shifted uncomfortably on his feet.

"So where does that leave two friends, who don't know why they aren't speaking— "

" — and have no real reason to keep feuding?" Cook finished. Smiling distantly, he leaned forward in his chair and rapped his fist lightly on the desktop.

"Well, Cozzie tradition would have shipmates putting in to port heading off to get as drunk as they can without landing in the brig."

"But that's not how they do it on Isis?" smiled Jeremy.

"Actually," Cook deadpanned, "Cozzie tradition skips over the part about digging up a couple of girls and trying to get laid."

Jeremy laughed. "I'll see what I can do about that," he said at last.

* * *

/UMN/dh/EARTH/29 Sept 2451-0330 eurostd/cc:143-1036.7:
MUNICHEARTH
UPDATE—Election Return
Unofficial tabulation shows incumbent Senator E. (Ernst) Emerson Hollenbach holding a widening lead over Tory challenger David A. (Adam) Piotrowski. Vote totals as of 0300 local time: Hollenbach (F) 167,456,551; Piotrowski (T) 105,998,194; Alastair Junke (Euro. National) 14,336,998; Alan B. (Bartholomew) Carlyle (Ind. Socialist): 9,339,747; others: 4,888,901.

Bulk of votes outstanding are from Bavarian Province, where computer malfunction is delaying returns. Heavy turnout there, currently favoring native son Hollenbach in margins approaching 95%, appears to assure his reelection. In local elections, Federalists are scoring major victories across the continent; following yesterday's sweeping victories in Asian provinces, local commentators are describing results as a major vote of

confidence in the Sarkisian administration. Similar results are expected tomorrow in Africa, and the following day, in the Americas.
—UPDATE/30/

* * *

"HAVE YE gone daft?"

"Coward!"

"See here, now. Listen to reason, Cyrus."

"See here yourself, Mason McGee!" Cyrus poked an angry finger into his brother's chest, backing him toward the far wall of their room. The two of them were alone; a single light from a desk lamp was all that kept the room from darkness.

"Don't go a-pokin me, Cyrus."

"I'll poke any spacer's bitch who ain't got a manly bone in his body. Ye're a bloody coward, Mason McGee. Too damn pussy-whipped by that woman of ours to stand on your own two feet."

Mason fought the urge to rip his brother's head off. It wouldn't help win the argument, and he had yet to whip his brother in a fair fight, much less the kinds of fights at which Cyrus was a master. In his own way, Mason was just as stubborn as his older brother. He refused to give it up, not without giving it his best—though once Cyrus got something into his head, reason went out the airlock.

"Answer me this, then. What in bloody hell do we need with all that lizard gold? Can ye tell me that? We already got us enough stashed away to last a lifetime, if we can ever track down where ye insisted we hide it. Why ye be wantin to trek all over creation to take back more than we can ever hope to spend, only to be sharin it with outsiders as well? You're daft—I say, you're just plain daft."

Cyrus glared at his brother hatefully. His bloodshot eyes burned deep into Mason's heart, and his words stung like acid. "All right, Mr. Pantywaist. Stay as ye will. But I'm a-takin the ship."

"Dammit, Cyrus," Mason started toward his brother, only to be halted by a raised lasergun. Cyrus' cold eyes were narrowed with hate.

"Hold fast, ye limp-wristed bugger bait," Cyrus said coldly. "I say, I'm takin the ship. Ye can bloody well get your own worthless carcas back home, closer to your apron strings. An ye better damn well be gone by the time I get back. Both o'ye."

Cyrus stormed out of the room, slamming the door behind him. Mason sank into the nearest chair, rubbing his weary eyes with his hands. Here he was, stuck on the most expensive cat house on the frontier without a friend, without a ship, and with barely enough money to call home for more. He'd have to hitch a ride home, and the prospect hardly filled him with anticipation. Last time, after Cyrus lost the old ship in a card game, it took them two whole months to wind their way home, and another month before they finally got rid of the star-dusted skipper who'd brought them back. Tippie O'Shea, was his name, and by the time he left, there wasn't enough food left in the old place to feed a spacer's ghost, much less the spacer himself.

But all that lay in the future, Mason sighed. In the meantime, he had more immediate worries. Like finding a shipmate who wouldn't try to pick his pockets. Or slit his throat.

* * *

"REPEAT, THIS is Starbase 102, Traffic Station Number Twelve. Do you copy? Come in please."

"Hello, Number Twelve, this is CGS Two-Zero-Zero-One, requesting approach clearance and docking instructions."

"Well hello, *d'Artagnan*. Nice of you to join us at last. We've been expecting you for quite a while."

"I don't doubt that, though you can't possibly be gladder to see us than we are to see port. We've had nothing but engine trouble since we put out from IshCom, and the Skipper hasn't let us rest the whole time. There's not a soul on board who can't use a healthy dose of R&R."

"I can just imagine, *d'Artagnan*. I hope you people are up for a bit of attention. You've gotten quite an advance billing, you know."

"Great. That's the last thing we need."

"Hey, what do you expect for a ship full of heroes?"

"I'll tell you, Number Twelve—we'd prefer a good night's sleep."

"We'll see what we can do about that too, *d'Artagnan*. In the meantime, you are cleared for approach on Vector G-6. And I'm patching you through immediately to Dispatch for a docking path. You're overdue enough already. I doubt they want you to get lost."

"Thank you, Number Twelve. You're a gentleman and a scholar."

"Thank you, *d'Artagnan*, and welcome to Looking Glass."

Chapter 12

"COME."

The young secretary, trying to contain her giddy elation, entered and closed the door behind her. She was in her early twenties and usually quite mature for her years, the very picture of studied seriousness. Today, she seemed more like a giggly teenager than a Cosmic Guard yeoman. She had even changed her hair for the occasion. Usually combed back into a ponytail, today it draped fetchingly over her shoulders, lending a rich brown frame to her pretty, girlish face.

"Yes, Cathy?"

"He's here, Commodore, and falling over himself with apologies for being late. Something about new fuel pods, or engine blocks. I didn't quite follow what he was saying, but I guess they're overhauling his ship."

Miriam Wright sighed and nodded. Her intense, brown eyes crinkled in amusement, softening the angular features of her face into an image of graceful feminine charm. She had seen many different types over the years, but this newest hotshot was quite a puzzle. She'd heard stories about him, and had serious doubts about making him a wing commander. Still, the order came directly from the Fleet Office, and in the cosmic year since she'd assumed command of Looking Glass she'd never found reason to doubt Admiral Clay's judgment.

Besides, she herself was curious about what he was like, though she doubted that she'd find him quite as fascinating as her secretary did. Life on a starbase could be dull. Patrols and drills were hardly the stuff of songs. At least this rookie skipper had managed to liven things up.

"I hear he's something of an eccentric," Cathy said, her eyes glowing.

Wright put her magnopen down on her desk. "We'll just see about that," she said firmly. She sat upright in her chair and began straightening her uniform. "Send him in."

"Yes, ma'am."

"Just as soon as you can bring yourself to let him go, that is," the commodore added with a wink.

Cathy laughed as she left the office. And as the door closed behind her, Commodore Wright found herself straightening her hair, fully prepared to take advantage of the usual effects of a well-trimmed female uniform on male officers of the line.

"ALL IN ALL, your record is quite...adequate, Captain." Wright leaned back in her oversized chair, trying her best to look less impressed than she was. The diplomas and certificates on her paneled walls began to look like so much paper compared to the gifts of the young man seated on the other side of her desk. Even through the eyes of his detractors—and the Academy section of his file alone was filled with enough critical comments to fill a dozen folders—she'd never seen a dossier like the one in front of her. It was, in a word, breathtaking.

"Still, you are the youngest starship captain in the Cosmic Guard, now or ever. And you've been a captain for less time than I care to mention. What makes you think you're ready to be a wing commander?" She narrowed her eyes, looking for the slightest trace of doubt. The reply she got almost drained the color from her cheeks.

"Actually, I doubt very much that I'm ready," Cook shrugged, with the indifference of the serenely self-confident. "And to be perfectly honest, I'd rather not be stuck on a starbase at all. If I had my choice, I'd rather have IshCom send me on some deep space missions. The Yourchock Shoals off Valhalla; the Pleides. Maybe even Rigel, that's a bit closer to home. Well, at least it's in the right direction from here. And it'd give me a chance to put some of my training to use, instead of whistling away my time on routine patrol. Or worse, teaching remedial jousting to a bunch of overrated prima donnas. But no one ever asks me, so I just try to keep quiet and do the best I can."

The commodore sat up in her chair, shuffling papers and looking quite flustered. With one backhand swipe, Cook had destroyed her carefully rehearsed speech, designed to keep him from getting smug about his rapid advancement and show him just how tough a boss he'd be dealing with. Now she'd have to find another way to put him in his place. And she was starting to find that smirk on his face more than a little annoying.

"Then I take it that you're dissatisfied with your assignment to Looking Glass?"

"Dissatisfaction implies a pre-existing set of expectations," Cook replied academically. "I learned long ago that expectations are often not conducive to good mental health. At least not in the Cosmic Guard."

"In other words, the Guard just doesn't measure up to your particular...*'expectations?*'"

"Oh, no, ma'am. In many ways, the Guard often lives up to my expectations. All too often, as a matter of fact. But then, I suppose that's a problem with any large bureaucracy."

Wright's eyes narrowed angrily. Beneath his smug exterior, she was sure that this rookie starship captain was laughing at her. One way or another, she was determined to wipe that smirk off his face.

"If things are that bad," the commodore snapped, "then why did you bother applying for an Academy appointment in the first place?"

Cook squinted in dismay, wondering how he'd managed to get this interview so badly off track. It had started off so nicely, but then the commodore's perfume and flirtatious manner had made him forget that he was addressing a superior officer. Now, he had no choice but to answer her questions. Kicking himself could come later.

"Actually, Commodore," he began, half-apologetically, "I didn't apply. I was invited. After finishing my studies at the Institute for Space Studies on Earth. And CosGuard is no less efficient than any other organization of similar size. In fact, in many respects it's better, although that doesn't change its inherent structural problems. Or, for that matter, make them worth arguing about. Unless, of course, it's to consider changes, but then I rather doubt that's what you wanted to talk about."

The commodore rocked quietly in her chair, glaring at the young captain. Finally she sat upright in her chair, her voice taking on the curt tones of one unaccustomed to sass from her subordinates. "I trust that you will keep me posted of any other failings in my command," she said at last, "so that we may consider changing them to your satisfaction."

"Well," Cook offered reluctantly, "there is the matter of deployment. We're not using our forces to best advantage, you know. If we just—"

"That's quite enough, Captain," Commodore Wright said sharply. "You'll have ample opportunity to critique anything you find wanting at the next staff meeting. For now I've seen and heard all I care to."

"Yes, ma'am."

"You have a briefing book and an orientation manual?"

"Yes, ma'am."

"Have it mastered by 500 Hours tomorrow. That's when you'll assume your duties as junior wing commander. And I'm warning you, Captain—"

Cook clenched his jaw. Angry at himself for making yet another hash of things, he had the presence of mind to hold his tongue. He'd caused enough trouble for one day.

"I don't much care for having IshCom appointing my wing commanders for me. To be blunt, I dislike having a smart ass pushed onto my staff, especially some young hotshot who thinks the rest of the Guard has nothing to teach him. And I'll tell you something else, Captain Cook— "

"Ma'am?"

Wright leaned forward, lowering her voice to barely a whisper.

"I love playing mother hen to all my skippers, fussing over them when they make me proud and wiping the egg off their faces when they screw up. But for the first time since I took this job, I'm actually looking forward to watching Commodore Jones teach one of my commanders some humility, come maneuvers time."

Cook's eyes narrowed, and his voice assumed a haughty coldness that Wright found infuriating. "*That* is hardly likely, Commodore," he replied. "Will there be anything else?"

"You're dismissed, Captain. Return to your duties."

"Thank you, ma'am."

* * *

OF ALL the taverns on Looking Glass, Padzieski's Pub was the liveliest. Accents from every planet in Terra crossed the plain wooden tables, and greenshirts and crewmen alike gathered to trade gripes and insults, rumors and songs.

On the east wall opposite the bar, looking down on the revelers, hung the hulking, mottled-brown head of a mutluk, the gentle, dim-witted giant from the plains of Ceres who supplied humanity with the tenderest, most flavorful meat in all of Terra. The wild, flaming eyes and long, drooping snout gave it a comically menacing look, but it was harmless to the point of absurdity. With no natural enemies, and no innate fear of Man, it roamed freely on the plains until the Ceresian autumn, when half the adult males on the planet were slaughtered for food, their heads sent to adorn taverns as far west as Earth.

And as in any spacers' bar, in any corner of Terra, no matter the time of day, songs were raised as high as the spirits.

Serving girl, serving girl, listen to me—
Don't ever sit on a CosGuarder's knee.

As for the reason, it's plain as can be.
Why don't you try it, and see?

"Sakes alive, Connors, I'll bet it was right rugged. Eh, McFarlane? What say ye to that?"

"Rugged. Aye, Jordan. Rugged."

"Ah, rot. " Connors dismissed his friends' remarks with a wave of his hand. " 'Tweren't nothin.'"

"Hah!" snorted McFarlane, pounding the table with his beefy fist. He was a large man, nearly as wide as he was tall. In his day, he'd faced more than his share of pirates and knew exactly what any spacer would expect going up against the likes of the late Mr. Wilkes. "You and Andersen here make like you was at some lace-n-satin picnic on New Babylon. An' all the while I bet ye was shittin in your boots."

Connors shook his head, and spoke in his most patronizing manner. "Matter of timin, that's all. We was all a mite jumpy about the ship, o'course. Takin a new ship into battle always turns a few hairs gray, don't ye know. An' there were some moments—just a few, mind ye—when some o'the laddies thought she weren't quite ready. But them's the breaks. Ye live with them or die by'em, but there ain't no changin the facts o'life. An' once the fightin started...well, 'twas never really in doubt."

Sitting in the next seat, Andersen rolled his eyes, then winced as his left leg took a sharp kick aportside.

"Well, I tell ye, Connors," Jordan shook his head. "The news set the whole place to hoppin, it did. Half the fleet figured the lot o'ye for goners, an the rest never got the word till it was all over."

"Lot o'space bilge," scoffed Connors, scowling derisively.

"And the buzzin ain't stopped yet," added McFarlane, leaning forward and lowering his voice. "Scuttlebutt has it that your skipper sails by a charmed star, and that he's likely to lead an attack wing from here on maneuvers. Whenever they get around to them, that is."

"A rookie? Ain't seen the likes of that these past thirty years."

Jordan shook his head. "Well, them's the rumors, Connors. Guess we'll know soon enough."

Connors took a large swig of beer, and then filled his glass and those of his friends as well. Soon all of them were roaring with laughter as they shared spacers' stories, and joined the rest of the revelers in song.

Set sail, set sail—
    The stars are burnin' bright;
Set sail, set sail
    Through everlastin' night.
Spacers are a sorry lot,
    'Tis plain as plain can be,
So raise a glass along with us
    And set our spirits free.

Connors' mind whirled with exuberance. And when the toasts started flying across the room to the best ship in the fleet, he bellowed as loud for the *d'Artagnan* as any four tyros, almost coming to blows with a old time yeoman from the *St. George* with differing views on the relative skills of their respective skippers. Whether it was the beer or the company or the singing, it didn't make much difference. He was glad to be alive, and eager to let everyone know it.

UNLIKE THE air of rough camaraderie that filled the unrestricted taverns, the Looking Glass Officers' Club tried its best to affect an image of polish and sophistication. Its tables were the color of stained wood, with the grace and charm of molded plastic. Overhead, the pressed-glass chandeliers had the all the pretension of real crystal, with none of the sparkle.

A long, sausage-shaped bar ran through the center of the club, where off-duty officers, men and women alike, could gather for a friendly drink or wait for a dinner table. Recorded music poured from the loudspeakers, providing a soft backdrop for food or conversation. Some were there alone, waiting for friends or hoping to find one. As Jeremy Ashton looked at his watch for the twentieth time, he had the sinking feeling that he was going to be stood up, and not by the two young ladies who would be arriving any minute to join him.

He took a sip of his drink and was about to mutter something about deficiencies in the gene pool of Terra's westernmost planet when a familiar figure plopped onto the stool next to him and tossed a one-credit coin toward the bartender.

"Isitian brandy."

"Skipper!" exclaimed Jeremy, a look of long-suffering exasperation on his face. "You're late. The girls will be here any minute now. In fact, they're ten minutes late themselves."

Cook grunted in reply. Taking his drink in hand, he turned in his stool to face his first officer. He started to say something, but thought better of it and took a tall sip from his glass.

"How'd it go?"

Cook grimaced.

"What did she say?"

"Actually, I'm still trying to figure that out," Cook snapped. "I don't really know what's going on. Of course, that's not exactly rare. But this is exactly the second—no, actually, I think it's the third time—well, whatever. It's figuratively, if not literally, the first time that she and I have met."

Jeremy scratched his head, his annoyance sinking into a familiar sea of confusion.

"Um—well—what hap— "

"Anyway, I don't know what all the fuss is about."

"Well, Skipper, we did manage to— "

"And I have no idea why she'd start sniping at me like that."

Jeremy winced. Miriam Wright was one of the sharpest base commanders around, and probably the best to work for. If Cook couldn't get along with her, they were in for a long tour of duty. An awfully long tour.

"Still and all," Cook sighed, "the rumors were right. I'm the new wing commander."

"Great!" Gleefully, Jeremy clapped him on the back, his confused annoyance suddenly replaced with pride. "That's just great. The first rookie skipper ever to head an attack wing! Though for the life of me, I can't think of anyone more deserving. We're proud of you, Skipper. All of us. Congratulations."

Cook scowled. "Right. Just what we need. More headaches."

"What's wrong with you, anyhow? I thought you'd be happy to get some recognition. But damn the recognition—wing commander is quite a plum for anyone. Getting it this early means— "

"It means we'll be crapped at and carped over," Cook interrupted. "And in the meantime, we'll be locked into routines that will dull everybody's mind as well as whatever small skills they have." Absently, he tried to wipe a drop of water from the bar in front of him with his fingers, only to break it into smaller droplets, spreading a bigger mess over a much larger area.

Wearily, Jeremy rubbed his eyes. The last thing he wanted to do was make Cook any less personable than he was at the moment. Jeremy barely knew one of the girls who was coming to meet them, and her friend was a complete unknown. The reason both of them had agreed to what was essentially a blind date was that neither could resist the chance to meet the man of the hour. Introducing them to a sulking Roscoe Cook was no way to make a good impression.

"Don't let it bother you."

"It doesn't bother me, Jeremy."

"You look damn well bothered to me, Skipper."

"It doesn't bother me, Jeremy."

"There they are."

Jeremy smiled and waved to the two smiling young ladies, both attractive young lieutenants, who had just strolled into the bar area, looking quite lost.

"Try not to be sullen."

"I'm not sullen."

"And don't snap at them."

Before Cook could snap something in reply, Jeremy was waving their dates over. The girls arrived in a whirlwind of effusion, their eyes wide and eager, their voices chittering away almost too quickly to follow.

"Hello, Jeremy."

"We had such a time finding this place. Hi, my name is Jill."

"And we missed our tube stop, then had to double back, and then our directions were all mixed up."

"Yes, it's a wonder we got here at all."

Jeremy, smiling and nodding and visibly nervous, made the introductions. Sarah, the one he'd known before, had a striking face, framed by soft, auburn hair, and lighted by laughing eyes. Jill seemed a bouncy, impressionable sort, with a glittering smile and blond, curly hair, but the first words she spoke to Cook made Jeremy want to hide.

"Gee," she gushed, "I've never gone out with a hero before."

Jeremy closed his eyes and swallowed hard. The entire evening was about to be ruined, right before his eyes and before it even started. The young bluebird had just marked herself a hopeless feather-brain, he feared, at least as far as the captain was concerned. In his present mood, Jeremy thought, Cook was ready to pounce on anyone who gave him the slightest reason. Once again, the captain caught him off guard and unprepared.

"What a coincidence," Cook smiled in reply. "Neither have we."

Everyone laughed except Jeremy.

"Though you know, whenever we send our shining armor to the cleaners it always comes back rusty—right, Jeremy?"

Grinning boyishly while the two lieutenants giggled, Cook looked at the clock and suggested that they leave. They still hadn't eaten—Cook demurred to any attempt to order something from the sterile kitchen of the Officers' Club—and the Level Four film club's second show started in less than an hour.

"I love live theater," Cook said, leading them toward the door, "but there's something timeless about the old classics. It's like looking through a window at the past. And Bertucci's films have always fascinated me. Everyone thinks he's dated, and of course much of his more topical humor escapes us today. But his timing is absolutely impeccable. Two centuries later, he still hits the funny-bone like a surgeon. Besides, I think the twenty-fourth century has a lot to teach us. Especially today."

Jill nodded reflexively. She didn't know who Bertucci was; except for Cook, none of them did, but nobody was going to admit it.

As they neared the door, Jeremy took Sarah aside, letting Cook and Jill walk on ahead of them.

"I think he'll be fine."

"He seems fine to me, Jeremy. In fact, he's awfully interesting."

"He's just touchy today," Jeremy continued, undeterred. "It's been a bad day for him. Professionally I mean, though God knows he has no reason to be. Touchy, I mean. And he's still...well, he's a bit upset."

Sarah shot Jeremy a skeptical glance.

"All the same, we'd better steer clear of certain subjects." Jeremy took her arm, and they hurried to catch up to Jill and the captain, who were now far ahead of them, laughing merrily as they ambled down the arching corridor toward the main walkway.

"Just to be on the safe side, stay away from office politics. And Commodore Wright," he whispered as they walked. "And whatever you do, don't mention the new rotation rosters. That's sure to set him off. But don't worry about him. I think he'll be fine."

"You know, Jeremy...he's not the one I'm worried about."

* * *

OWING TO the ship's size, the crew's cabins on a starship were larger than those on any other ship of the line. Arranged along the circular corridors that ringed the ship, the cabins stretched twenty feet at their wider edge. All cabins came with a private bath and a separate room for sleeping. Standard furnishings were spartan but functional: a couch and guest chairs; a long counter that most used as a desk; and a communications console that included a viewing screen, intercom, and detachable pager. At the base of the console, a chronometer blinked away the seconds as they passed. A keyboard—or the intercom, depending upon the crewman's preferences—provided personal access to the centrax, the powerful electronic brain that ran the ship. The crew had unlimited access to the computer and to the library banks, and were encouraged to use the centrax for whatever purpose they could devise, to keep their minds sharp and morale high. Security programs kept anyone from damaging the programs that ran the ship, and since the needs of a modern ship of the line were incomprehensibly vast, the small fragment devoted to personal use went unnoticed.

Lying on her couch, Janet was scribbling out a letter to her parents on New Babylon. As an Academy plebe, she'd tried dictating to the computer, but the results were nothing but annoying. Without her own handwriting to add some personal warmth, her letters came out cold and sterile; worse, the writing program insisted on correcting her grammar, ignoring any instructions to let her Babylonian colloquialisms pass unmolested. So, she'd taken to writing friends and family by hand. She'd long since stopped feeling self-conscious about ignoring some miracles of modern technology. That, at least, was a gift from a lost friend who still haunted her life. As for the rest, she was making progress, though her recovery was far from over.

Hearing a knock on the door, Janet raised her head. "Come in."

Mary Mathison's head peeked through the door. "Are you busy? I don't want to intrude"

"No, don't be silly." Janet placed her writing materials on the side table and swung her feet onto the floor. "Just a note to my folks. Nothing I can't finish later."

"I can't believe that the ship's so empty. It feels deserted."

"It does, doesn't it?" Janet smiled. "But it always seems that way when we pull into port. Especially after your first voyage." She liked

Mary and relished playing big sister to the young ensign. There was something open about Mary, almost vulnerable, yet with an inner reserve of strength that surfaced during a crisis. Janet felt a special kinship toward the apprentice radio officer; it was like looking at herself just a few years ago.

"I remember drawing the short straw at Calais after my first mission on the *Constantine*, having to stay behind while the ship emptied into the port. That whole day I felt lost, and the silence was enough to drive me crazy."

Mary's laugh was too brittle to be heartfelt.

"Of course, things were different then."

Mary knew enough to change the subject. "Well, my problem hasn't changed, either," she said.

"McKenzie?"

"She is so snotty," Mary nodded. "Quoting regulations chapter and verse, but never to my face. And all the while, I can tell that she's just looking down her nose at me. Miss Fancysnips, Dexter says they used to call her. We weren't in the same class at Tech, you know, but I hear she was just as bad there."

Janet smiled sympathetically. "Well, just ask yourself whose opinion you value more—hers, or Larsen's. Besides, you couldn't change her opinion of you even if you tried. And you know, as long as Cook is in command you really have nothing to worry about. He's hardly in a position to enforce the rules. At least not that rule, anyway."

Mary cleared her throat and shook her head. "That doesn't make me feel any better. Besides, the little slut—where does she get the nerve to tell me how to run my life? Right now, the only reason she's dallying with Gerlach is because he's the ship's one Academy grad and she figures he's her ticket to advancement. But I bet she'd wag her tail in a minute if she caught Jeremy's fancy. Or the Captain's, for that matter, the tramp."

Janet's back stiffened.

"Sorry."

Janet shrugged wistfully. "Cook and Jeremy." She leaned back on the couch, a dreamy look in her eyes. "They're like two sides of the same coin. And the two of them sure patched things up in a hurry."

Mary blushed. She hadn't wanted to reopen any wounds. She could tell that were too fresh not to hurt, and hurt deeply. She wanted to crawl into a hole and hide. This time, though, it seemed that her friend actually wanted to talk.

"Now they're out tom-catting together," continued Janet, "casting about like a pair of common spacers. I can't imagine how they could do something like that—though God knows, I've never known men to behave any differently." Janet sighed loudly, and immediately perked up. Grousing with a friend always helped lift her spirits and moping about the ship would do neither of them any good. She rose from the couch and walked across the room toward the counter.

"Tea?"

"Love some."

"Maybe you can help me," Janet called over her shoulder as she drew water for the microcooker. "I don't know whether to tell my folks about our narrow escape from Wilkes. They worry about me too much already, and I don't want to add to their troubles."

"Won't they already know? It was over all the news services, I'm sure. I mean, they do know you're still with Cook, don't they?"

"They have trouble remembering which side of New Babylon is which."

Mary laughed warmly; she knew the problem.

"And—well, they've never even heard about Cook. At least, none of the details. And certainly nothing about this latest transfer."

"Isn't it about time?"

Janet shook her head; she put the creamer and sweetener on the serving tray, and reached for the tea mugs. "My father wouldn't understand. And my mother's never forgiven me for leaving home in the first place."

The bell rang on the cooker.

"Tea's ready."

Soon Janet returned to the couch, then left to fetch a plate filled with teacakes. When she came back, the steam was still rising from the mugs, so the tea was left to cool on coasters on the table. Both women preferred not to scald their tongues.

"What do you think about Palmer?"

"What have your heard? She hasn't told me anything. Not recently, anyway."

"Nothing, really. But don't they make a cute couple?"

"McKenzie won't approve."

"She never approves, the little hypocrite."

Chapter 13

A FEW DAYS LATER a call came to Looking Glass over the security scrambler. It was DemCom's commander, Admiral Weatherlee, calling to chat about nothing in particular—or so it seemed, until Commodore Wright complained about the effect that her newest wing commander was having on the rest of her staff.

"You see what I mean, Miriam?" soothed the face on the telescreen. "Can you see what I've been saying all along?"

Rocking gently in her office chair, Wright nodded her head, but skepticism began to cloud her face. For a reason she could never explain, she didn't like Weatherlee. Not that he'd ever done anything to hurt her: on the contrary, he chose his enemies as carefully as his friends. But there was something hidden, almost underhanded about the way he smiled, and in the studied charm of his manners. Today, there was also a hint of delight in his voice that seemed so at odds with the subject matter, as if he reveled in his disdain for the young Isitian. She just didn't trust him.

"Of course, I don't doubt for a minute...," Weatherlee continued, only to pause as subspace static drained the color from the screen, distorting his voice until it became unintelligible. The disturbance cleared a few moments later, and Weatherlee flashed his oily grin.

"There, that's better," he went on. "As I was saying, I don't mean to cause any trouble, and far be it from me to tell you how to run your own command. But some people are just too arrogant for their own good. They never get along with anybody and cause nothing but trouble."

"I understand what you're saying, Admiral," Wright replied. "Except for some of the girls in my office, he's hardly endeared himself to my staff. Richters in Tracking says he's been a constant pain in the backside. And McIntyre is ready to tear him apart, along with half of the contingent here."

Weatherlee nodded ponderously. "Yes—yes, that's just the sort of thing I was talking about. And I'll back you, Miriam; I'll back you if you want to take this up through channels. I've got friends who.... "

Wright shook her head. "No thank you, Winthrop. I won't give up on someone just because I don't like him. For all I know, he's just too young to know any better. He's come a long way in a short time, after all, and whatever his other faults you have to give him his due. He is brilliant. Any way you score him, he ends up at the top of any list I care to draw. If that includes the list of the most aggravating people I know—well, talent often carries a price. In the meantime, I'll just wait and see."

"Suit yourself," Weatherlee smiled mirthlessly. Within the minute, with little more than a passing word of farewell, he signed off the channel.

Miriam sank into her chair, wondering if she'd made a mistake. Perhaps she should have taken the admiral up on his offer. They'd had two staff meetings since he'd arrived, and Cook had been insufferable at both of them. Today, they'd be discussing strategy for the upcoming maneuvers with skippers from across the Eastern Fleet, and she shuddered to think what was going to happen when they began to discuss tactics.

She laughed quietly to herself. She knew, as surely as thrushes had songs, that Cook would give voice to his opinions. He always did. And wherever they came from, the supply was inexhaustible.

Shaking her head, she looked at the reports stacked on her desk. She sighed, then took the top folder from her in-basket and began reading. A commander's job, she thought, was never done. No matter what she did, the stream of paper crossing her desk was endless.

* * *

```
CGS 2001 <<D'ARTAGNAN>>
POSITION:  SB 102, 45-678933/x0/02.9w
INTRA-COMMAND REQUEST CODE IV
    CC:              143-1081.4
    TO:              Capt. R.C.Cook
    FROM:            Lt.Cmdr. R.B.Talbert, Navigator
    SECURITY:        Open
    FLAGS:           Not Applicable
    RE:              Transfer Request


Per Form TR-746/J21-2 (attached), I hereby apply for transfer from
Starship d'Artagnan to a new assignment.
   LtCmdr RBTalbert
```

* * *

THE SUN dipped below the western horizon, streaking the sky with a dazzling crimson and casting the crumbling buildings into shadows. Venus hung like a lantern over the rooftops. A few miles to the east, on a gently rolling hill, the city's space needle reached toward the heavens. Come morning, it would help a native son return to his work on a distant land. Tonight, though, was a time for celebrating.

Music poured through the open windows of the Hotel Hornung, on the Prinzregentenstrasse across from the English Gardens. The sounds were not the strident marches of a long-ago day, or the complex tapestry of long-dead masters, but the simple dances and songs that had always helped the people of the town celebrate the triumph of one of their own. The spicy fragrance of sausage wafted out of the kitchen, and from four enormous kegs, each manned by a town elder, flowed the finest beer in Bavaria, all gifts from the man of the hour, whom everyone knew simply as "Ernst."

The band played merrily in the main ballroom. Several hundred men and women kept time with their hands or feet, and a tuba marked a beat as deep as the ground beneath them. A half-dozen costumed young men danced to the center, loudly slapping their thighs in rhythm, joining an equal number of young ladies who were spinning in circles, faster and faster, in a whirling splash of color and song that tied the dancers and singers and guests and musicians to a past that grew from the hills and valleys around them.

All the while, a steady stream of people came to the dais to pay their respects to the aging but vigorous man sitting in the place of honor. He smiled in turn, returning their warmth and good wishes, and sharing their laughter and dreams. When at the end of the evening he rose to voice his thanks, he spoke to a room filled with friends, whose hearts knew nothing but affection for the local boy who'd risen to such lofty heights.

A few still remembered him as the dashing, strapping hero of their youth, who'd set the entrenched order whirling into chaos so many years ago, returning pride and dignity to the tired valleys of home. One of these was a wrinkled, elderly widow, whose back was bent with age. As the great man began to leave the hall, she slipped through the cordon of guards, and before anybody knew it had slipped a pair of withered arms around his neck.

"God bless you, Ernst Hollenbach," she whispered, her teary eyes glistening in the lights.

Hollenbach returned her embrace, then gently removed her arms from his neck. "Thank you, dear one," he said softly, a smile frozen on his face. "We couldn't have done it without you." Grandly, he waved his hand, all the while moving toward the exit. "Without all of you."

"Make us proud, Ernst. I know you'll make us proud," said the old lady. "You always have and you always will. You're all we have left, now. You're all we've ever had. I know you won't let us down."

"You can count on it," he nodded in return, easing toward the door. Bodyguards at his side, he left the hall and disappeared into the chilly Bavarian night.

* * *

//II/MISSION DISPATCH/
```
    cc:          143-1091.7/
    TO:          FtAdmPMClay, EFCmIshCom/
    FROM:        HighAdmWWPendleton, ChStfCentCom/
    SECURITY:    CodeBlue/
    PREFIX:      MissionUpdate/
    FLAGS:       red1;yellow2;yellow3/
    RE:          Foreign Ministry Transport Detail
```
This confirms our communiqué cc:143-0998.2, and recent conversation re: diplomatic mission to alien planet Girshoona.

As per Command Staff Memo 143-00231, CosGuard will transport Grant delegation to the peace conference and provide whatever further assistance he may require. As agreed, choice of ship to transport our diplomatic mission will be yours, and its replacement will come from redeployment and temporary transfer to your command of forces from detachment at CerCom B.
H Adm WPendleton//

* * *

"AND BESIDES, just where do you think all these lizards are going to come from? Shangri-la? Or maybe they'll just materialize out of thin air. Or from the Cloud itself. My God, what nonsense!"

Embarrassed, the briefing officer shifted uncomfortably on her feet. Her pretty young face blushed brightly, as if her aborted report on alien ship movements had been the cause of this latest eruption. Beside her at the lectern, just under the viewing screen. stood Commodore Wright, her face burning with disgust. Silence had fallen over the rest of the starship captains, assembled in the main auditorium for their weekly briefing. They already knew the dangers of trying to interfere. The kind of exchange they were witnessing had become all too familiar.

"I don't know, Commodore McIntyre," Cook replied sharply, standing at his seat on the left aisle. "If I did, there would be no need for this discussion, and you could spare us the witless attempts at pointed rhetoric. In the meantime, it seems to me that we would do well to start studying defenses against an enemy flanking movement, if only because the Crutchtans are unlikely to view their tactical situation as narrowly as CosGuard's finest."

McIntyre's face seethed with anger. A small man, his forceful personality and booming voice filled the hall. He was used to dominating these strategy meetings and did not take kindly to newcomers challenging him in his own domain—especially loudmouth rookies who hadn't learned their place, or how to hold their tongues.

"That's absurd, Cook—that's truly absurd."

" 'Fools see absurdity in their own reflected folly,' " Cook said, quoting a line from an old Isitian master. "What I say may well be wrong," he explained, seeing his comment evoke nothing but confusion on the faces of everyone around him, "but it's hardly absurd."

"Gentlemen..., " Wright began, as calmly as she could.

"Unlike some acquaintances of mine, I don't pretend to know all the answers," Cook continued, undaunted. "But I do know that knowledge rarely comes from ridiculing people who ask questions. If war does come, and we don't knock out the enemy with the first blow, we'll be scrambling all over creation, trying to shore up our failing flanks. In my humble opinion, that is where we should expect them to attack because that is precisely where we're weakest. No matter how strong we are elsewhere, those two starbases—117 and 121—are the keys to front. That much should be clear to anyone who can read a starmap."

"Rubbish!"

"Gentlemen— "

"If we don't reinforce them, we may well find ourselves on the short end of the war's decisive battle. Unless, of course, the war turns into something of a rout. But then that's hardly an assumption that should guide our strategic planning, so it's largely beside the point."

"Gentlemen, please...."

"They've no bases, no forces, no lines of supply, and no means of mounting an attack. And you've decided that it's all immaterial, because the lizards can suspend the laws of logistics with no more than a wave of the hand."

"*Gentlemen!*"

Cook pointed an angry finger at his antagonist. "Mark my words, McIntyre—though actually, I doubt we'll ever really know, come to think of it. It would take a war to prove me right, and from what I've seen the aliens are far too civilized to let that happen. But mark my words, anyway— "

"Cook—you're an idiot! A windbag and an idiot!"

"All right, that's quite enough!" Commodore Wright raged, her eyes on fire. "I'll see you two right here—and right now. Everyone else is dismissed. The next pre-maneuvers briefing will be posted on the Board."

Slowly, the two combatants sank into their chairs. The other starship captains started filing out of the auditorium, their feet shuffling noisily. Occasionally, one would lean over to give a word of encouragement to McIntyre while passing the senior wing commander's seat. At last the great room emptied, until just Cook, the two commodores, and the pretty young briefing officer were left. Neither Cook nor McIntyre had budged from his seat, placing them on opposite sides of the room and making it impossible for Wright to see both of them at the same time.

"I think our Isitian friend has been sniffing something besides daisies," sneered McIntrye. Before Cook could respond, the base commander erupted.

"I am sick and tired of this constant bickering!" she flamed, slapping the podium with the small stack of papers she held in her hand. "The two of you come down here—right in front of me—right in the center. Right here! Right now! I'm not about to get a stiff neck trying to yell at both of you. Come on...come...as in—*Now!*"

Reluctantly, the two men rose from their seats and ambled to the front row center. Petulantly, they kept two seats between them. Each held his tongue as Commodore Wright, index finger wagging furiously, addressed them much as a schoolteacher would scold the class troublemakers.

"There is no excuse for it. None at all! I won't have my wing commanders at each other's throats. I won't stand for it, do you hear me? And I don't care who's to blame. You're both acting like spoiled brats. Now you don't have to like each other, or talk to each other. In fact, I don't care if I hear another word spoken out loud by either one of you. Ever! And I suspect I speak for the entire contingent here at Looking Glass! But this—*gentlemen*—is the last time that you two will disrupt a staff meeting."

Wright strode to the front of the podium, and spoke in a taut voice that admitted no discussion. Her angry eyes shifted from Cook to McIntrye and back again.

"From now on, the two of you will show each other the same courtesy that you expect from the rest of the staff. In the privacy of your own quarters you may insult each other to your heart's content. But in public, you will not show the slightest hint of your differences—not on my base—not on your own ships. Not anywhere in my command. Not anywhere in the whole of Terra! And if either of you so much as thinks of starting up again, I'll have your tanned hide hanging from my wall so fast you won't even know it's gone.

"Am I clear?"

Both men nodded.

"*Am I clear?*" Wright fumed, glaring sternly at the young Isitian.

"Yes, ma'am."

"McIntyre?"

"Yes, ma'am."

Wright gathered her briefing papers and angrily stuffed them into her briefcase. "You two are confined to this auditorium for the next ten minutes. You can use it to talk over your differences, or you can sit in silence like a pair of stubborn jackasses and not say a word. I really don't care, as long as I hear nothing more about it.

"Follow me, Lieutenant. Let's leave the children alone for a while."

"Yes, ma'am."

The two women walked up the aisle toward the door. Soon the two wing commanders were alone with their thoughts, their eyes drifting everywhere around the room except toward the figure sitting two seats down. And for ten minutes—to the second—the only sound in the hall was the soft hiss of the ventilator, echoing in the stillness.

* * *

"LANE THREE is cleared, *Roustabout II*. Depart when ready."

"Thank ye, Riley, we'll be back a-fore ye know it."

Cyrus let his hands run over the controls. His main engines would soon finish priming and then the lot of them could be off. Sailing solo would take some adjustment. Rigging the command seat to let him do the jobs he usually gave to Mason had been quite a chore, but there was no other way. Besides, the added peace and quiet would do him good.

He looked at the side viewer. Riley's Station hung in the blackness, its mother star casting barely enough light at this distance to make it glimmer. Walkways connected the outstations to the central cylinder, like a snowflake frozen in time. Ships held in gravity lock circled as the station slowly spun around its focus. Soon, distance overtook the scene and the station faded into the endless night.

"All right, ye puff balls, it's time to be headin out," Cyrus called over the speaker to the other ships in his squadron. "Come about, forty-five points to starboard, twenty degrees north. Stand by to fire the overdrive."

"Where are we goin, Cyrus? I mean, really now. Ain't it about time ye told us— "

"Just follow me, Rafferty. All o'ye, just be followin me, an' stay in formation."

"But— "

"All in good time," Cyrus chuckled. "All in good time." A grim, mysterious smile crossed his lips, and he released the standby button on his throttle booster and took manual control of the helm. Seconds later, they were on their way.

* * *

"DID YOU sleep well, Zatar? I would hate to be the cause of your discomfort." Zatsami's smiling eyes reflected the soft lights and a lute's gentle melody caressed the air.

"Do I look less than refreshed?" Zatar smiled in return. Zatsami gently stroked his forearm. Her rutting scent was muted now, but would return to full force before day's end. Until her time passed, her tenderness would be unbounded. Even before they realized that her season was at hand, Zatar was grateful that she chose to attend the conference with him on *Gr'Shuna*. It was a small ship that the High Council had placed at his disposal, and its Crutchtan pilot was a study in saurian stoicism. Under the circumstances, Zatsami was a gift from the heavens. He found it gratifying to ease the passage with such pleasant company, and her present condition only heightened his sense of gratification. Even so, he was unprepared for what was about to pass between them.

"I have not spoken of this before, because I was unsure of your reaction."

Smiling blandly, Zatar rose to lean on his elbow. Her graceful curves were ravishing, he thought, but men could never know how much passion clouded their perceptions.

"You impressed the Council, Zatar. But then, you always do."

"They seemed rather unimpressed to me, Tsami. Unimpressed and disinterested. They see the Terrans as mere provincials, and primitive ones at that. I fear that I made not the slightest dent in their perceptions."

"I have overheard much, and your presentation carried more weight than you imagine, though for reasons that even I cannot discern. But that is not what I mean."

"What, then?"

Zatsami looked deeply into Zatar's eyes; a teasing, flirtatious smile darted across her lips.

"Yelina's term of office expires soon. She desires not another."

Zatar nodded. "So I have heard."

"And the Presidium has never spurned the unanimous recommendation of its own delegation to the High Solonic Council."

"You speak in gibberish, Tsami."

Smiling timidly, the solon lowered her gaze. When her eyes again met Zatar's, he saw nothing of the teasing haughtiness that rutting females used to drive their brood males to distraction. Her face still sang with affection; but respect filled her eyes.

"Would you wish for Yelina's seat on the Council?"

Slowly, the smile on Zatar's face ripened into a full grin. Then, plopping onto his back, he erupted into full-bodied laughter, much to Zatsami's consternation.

"Zatar?"

"I can barely stand them now. The pomposity and self-importance. The mindless preening of overripe egos. Even our own people are not immune, though with Yelina's departure you may well reclaim your dignity, for she is the worst offender of the lot."

"Zatar!"

"You have no idea of how much of a procurator's job is simply holding his tongue, or swallowing his pride as well as his sense of the ridiculous for long enough to make a point that the dimmest imbecile should find self-evident."

"Now really, Zatar—!"

"I find most of them boring and inane already, and all I do is bring them information. I cannot imagine having to work with them."

Zatsami sat upright, her silence bellowing profound anger.

"Present company excepted, of course."

Slowly, her angry eyes drifted to find Zatar's and he burst again into laughter, which the solon soon found irresistible. He was baiting her; he had been baiting her all along. So like a man, she thought. He had played on her sense of purpose like a child plays with sand, and still she had no notion of what he really thought about it all.

"You are incorrigible. You are all incorrigible."

Zatar smiled playfully. "We have less tolerance for idiocy than you do, at least for any that is not our own. And I must remind you, we do distract easily. That is the principal reason why what you propose is so highly impractical."

"But you will think it over?"

"I will think it over."

"Are you hungry?"

"I am famished."

"Lie there. I will send to the galley for breakfast."

As Zatsami donned a robe and left the bedchamber, Zatar reclined until his head rested once again in the soft pillows. It had been literally a millennium since the Presidium had named a male to a place on the Veshnan delegation to the High Solonic Council. If any of them had wit enough to check the history books, another millennium would pass before they considered it again. The seragliotic instinct ran strong in the females of his race, made all the worse by the male disinclination to fight it. It had wreaked havoc with what Veshnan historians now called the Council of Garak; he had little doubt that it would plague the Council of Zatar as well.

Left alone, the giddiness faded from his mind. Soon, his head was clear as the void through which they sailed. "Zatar the Solon," he said to himself. It sounded odd; but each title he had won rang strangely in his ears at first, and he knew that the strangeness would quickly pass. As for the rest, he had his doubts, but he also had a growing sense that danger loomed in the western skies. If none else would pay heed, he would have no choice but to accept whatever post the Presidium chose to give him.

* * *

"THE COMMODORE will see you now."

"Thank you...Cathy, is it?"

"Yes, Captain."

"Thank you, Cathy. It's been a pleasure."

The pretty young yeoman's spellbound smile did little to ease Cook's apprehension. After the dressing down he'd received the day before, the last place he wanted to find himself was seated in Miriam Wright's office. In another few days, perhaps; by then, the latest flap would have faded into the seamless past, but now was simply too early. Not that he had any choice in the matter, he told himself. But if he'd been scripting this whole scene—

A swallowed giggle caught his attention. He looked to see the commodore's secretary trying to hide a girlish smirk behind her hand.

Grinning, Cook simply shrugged. "Don't mind me," he said, knocking on the door to the commodore's office. "Isitians always talk to themselves. It's something of a national tradition. The only problem is that we never get any straight answers. And outworlders have a devil of a time separating us when we get into a fight."

UNLIKE HER SECRETARY, Commodore Wright did not find her junior wing commander amusing in the least. "My spies tell me that you and McIntyre still haven't buried the hatchet," said the commodore as Cook took a seat.

Ordinarily, the words would have jumped from his mouth, but Cook was prepared this time. Instead of commenting on the easy job her spies had, he waited for the appropriately innocuous response to pop into his head.

"No, ma'am."

Almost disappointed, Commodore Wright's mouth turned up into a tight, humorless smile. Slowly, she rocked in her chair, her intense glower watching for the first sign of a guilty conscience. "Do you know why I sent for you?"

"No, ma'am."

"You've heard nothing about the latest dispatch from IshCom?"

Warily, sensing a trap, Cook shook his head. "Sorry," he said at last.

Wright stroked her chin thoughtfully, wondering if the young Isitian was lying. She rocked leisurely for almost a minute before she continued.

"You have a guardian angel, Captain," she said at last, watching carefully for Cook's reaction. "IshCom informs me that—against my recommendation—they have selected you to transport Ambassador Grant and his delegation to Crutchta for the next session of the peace talks."

Cook's eyes widened with excitement, deflating Wright's suspicions about his complicity in wrangling this latest assignment. "What? The peace talks? When—how?"

Through a guileless grin and self-reflective gaze, and for the briefest of moments, Wright saw Cook's mind racing at speeds beyond her comprehension, dreaming of things which she could only guess and which to her surprise filled her with a sympathetic envy. Then, as suddenly as it began, it all came to a crashing halt.

"Why?" he asked, puzzlement furrowing his brow. "I mean, why us? And why me?"

A blank look shot across the commodore's face, as she realized that she knew as little about what was happening as her junior wing commander.

"To tell the truth...," she began sluggishly.

"And what about maneuvers?" Cook interrupted, taking no note of his own commander's perplexity. "That will be starting soon. At least, it will if IshCom ever gets around to issuing the right orders." Nonplused, Cook fell silent; where seconds earlier excitement lit his face, disappointment now hung like a shroud.

Arching her eyebrows, Wright sensed the Isitian's dilemma. And for the first time since he'd reported for duty, she found herself almost wishing there were something she could do to help. "I guess you have a decision to make, Captain," she said.

Cook grunted sullenly in reply.

"Of course, I'm sure you could decline this particular assignment... in which case they'd probably send Commodore Jones in your place."

"We'll go."

"Here are your orders," the commodore smiled despite herself. She rose and handed him a blue packet. It contained a sealed communiqué from Admiral Clay that even she was not at liberty to open. She watched Cook's eyes bulge as he read the security code.

"Ambassador Grant's party should arrive any time now. You leave in three days."

"We'll be ready," Cook grinned, his eyes flashing with pride.

* * *

TWO HOURS later Cook was in his office, rereading his orders and wondering what they meant.

Soft music filled the room. The table lamp cast shadows across Cook's face as he rocked back in his chair, lost in thought. Papers were scattered across the table, occasionally rising into discernable piles. Directly before him, on an oversized blue envelope, were three sheets of blue paper, clipped together at the upper left corner and opened to the second page.

It did not surprise him that Central Command had decided that his ship and crew would be expendable. Despite assurances of safe passage, they would be traveling deep into alien skies. However unlikely it seemed, if anything happened, keeping the peace would be more important than any single ship, and it was equally important to keep the ship from falling into unfriendly hands. Less routine, though hardly surprising, was the directive granting him full discretion to decide when to come home. Once his ship passed into Crutchtan skies, CentCom considered his a military mission, and he was on his own: "The decision to return," they had written, "will be yours and yours alone."

No, he thought, what bothered him was an obscure passage on the second page, almost buried between the instructions on permission codes needed to engage the Crutchtan relays to communicate with home and the reminder to keep his sensors open and active for the entire trip.

He leaned forward, and read it again: "You will give the Ambassador your full co-operation," Admiral Clay had written, "in his efforts to secure an agreement with the Crutchtan Government to resolve our differences over the disputed sectors. You shall also render whatever assistance he requires to pursue overtures from any other source that may surface during the course of negotiations."

Were other races courting Terran favor, Cook wondered. If so, to what end? And if they were, then why pursue separate channels when the Consortium already had its own diplomats negotiating a treaty between Terra and the Crutchtans? Something odd was happening, he thought, something that was missing from the official reports. Until the Ambassador arrived, he could only speculate, and he'd have to do it on his own, for his orders were quite specific. Aside from those details relating to the ship and its operation, he could discuss the mission, and the contents of the Code Blue packet, with no one but the Ambassador himself. Beyond that, his orders forbade him from pressing the Ambassador for details, even after they passed through the Neutral Zone.

A knock on his office door interrupted his train of thought.

"Captain?"

Cook recognized the voice; it was Talbert.

"Come in."

Talbert entered and closed the door behind him. He seemed strangely subdued, but Cook noted that he'd been that way ever since the encounter with the pirates.

"Yes, Mr. Talbert. What can I do for you?"

"My transfer orders just came through. I came to say goodbye."

Cook leaned back in his chair, his hands clasped behind his head. He'd never much cared for his navigator. Talbert's arrogance far exceeded his talent, but now that the man was leaving Cook felt genuinely sorry for him.

"Where are you going?"

"Demeter," Talbert tried to smile. "They have a trainload of new frigates waiting for crews. I'm in line for the next one to be fully manned—as navigator, not as the skipper. Guess there's little chance of that, at least for a while. Someday, perhaps."

Cook smiled and nodded.

"Well, goodbye, Captain."

Cook rose from his chair. Though he had no real desire to see Talbert stay, he disliked seeing him leave under such circumstances.

"I hate to leave you shorthanded like this," Talbert said quietly, keeping his voice under firm control. "And I'm sorry I let you down."

"I'll try not to push McKenzie as hard as I pushed you," the captain replied softly. "And remember—my style is different than most, and that's probably giving me the benefit of the doubt. Don't let the troubles we've had with each other cause you to doubt yourself." Talbert nodded lamely, embarrassed to let his captain see the gratitude he was feeling.

"And when you do get your ship," Cook continued, "remember to lighten up once in a while. Treat your crew like human beings. You'll be surprised how well they respond."

"Yes, sir."

"Good luck, Mr. Talbert."

"Thank you, sir."

They shook hands, and Talbert turned to leave. As the door closed behind him, Cook sank back into his chair. In three days he would leave on the biggest mission of his life, with an untested navigator whose biggest asset was not her navigating. To his left was a stack of supply requisitions that he'd ignored for the past week; on his right was a pile of status reports from various departments around the ship. All of them needed review and careful study. Turning to his intercom, Cook summoned his High Watch aide from the outer office, a solid though pretty yeoman of about thirty.

"Jennifer—I believe Ensign McKenzie is taking her liberty on the base. Track her down and have her report to me at 200 Hours tomorrow."

"Yes, Captain."

"And page Mr. Ashton, too. We'll be setting sail in a few days, and there's a lot of backlogged paperwork that needs his attention before we leave."

Chapter 14

MANEUVERS WERE JUST AROUND the corner, and Looking Glass was nearly bursting her seams. From across the Eastern Fleet, ships were eagerly putting into port, and in contrast to the sterile loneliness of their everyday routine, the starbase soon echoed with life. Old friends hailed each other with old memories filling their hearts, and spirits and camaraderie soon warmed the base like the summer sun. But, just as the lazy heat of summer brings mosquitoes in its wake, the arrival of starships inevitably brought their captains with them.

Misdirected by a malfunctioning interior nozzle, water spewed from the stone mouth and nose of Wadsworth Elliot, a portly past-chairman of the Senate Appropriations Committee, down his prodigious belly and into the large fountain in the atrium of Observation Deck Gamma. Stars gleamed silently overhead, through the arching, transparent canopy. On all of Looking Glass, this O-Deck gave the best view of the frontier, opening a panoramic view of the eastern skies. Astern, toward Cosmic West, the starwatcher could catch a look at the edge of Looking Glass itself, as well as the slender tendril of metal holding the concourse to the mother base.

As the cosmic clock neared Zero Hour on the 110th day of the Cosmic Year 143, the concourse was nearly deserted, though far from silent. Drowning out the calming sounds of the fountain was the percussive sound of laughter, mixed with derisive yowls and drunken hoots.

"It's a bloody shame," said Jack Chandler, lying flat on his back on the wide marble bench that edged the fountain. He and Tanana had just put into base from DemCom, the last of their attack wing to arrive. As always, the first thing they did was put in a call to their good friend, Fitz. After all, if there were anything to do on this sterile collection of girders and beams, Fitz would know about it.

"A bloody, bloody shame," he repeated. "And it just goes to show how top brass protects its own."

"What do you mean?" asked Fitz, taking a swig from their shared whiskey bottle.

"He means, it's a bloody damn outrage, is what he means," slurred Tanana. "I mean, giving an assignment like that to a—to a green-assed rookie. I mean, son of a bitch. It's—it's enough to make you puke! That green-tail, farting, double-talking son of a bitch. I mean—holy fucking son of a bitch."

"To Cookie," offered Chandler, taking the whiskey bottle and raising it toward the observation window. The stars blazed brightly in the distance; the base itself loomed, gray and dim, in the blackness. "To the snake charmer with enough friends in high places to keep his rookie ass from getting kicked across the skies—though at least the little snot has brains enough to be heading out of town when Old Jonesy goes gunning for him."

"To Cookie the rookie," chortled Tanana. In this state, he laughed at almost anything.

Fitz, slightly more sober than his two friends, just shook his head. The Isitian hotshot might be a loudmouth, he thought, but spreading Wilkes across the heavens couldn't have happened by accident. Besides, his most vivid memory of the last round of maneuvers was of a single cruiser holding a whole attack wing at bay, a wing led by McIntyre himself. The delay it bought let Jones regroup his own forces for the counterattack that won him top honors. He remembered the admiration he felt for the cruiser's unsung commander, holding the collapsing flank together by sheer willpower as Jones and the rest of the blue fleet raced, belatedly, toward the critical point of the battle. The DemCom ace had been quick to take the credit, accepting all the accolades that the gold medal brings its champion. But though the official reports never mentioned it, the cruiser's skipper was the real hero of the day, and Fitz could almost swear that the cruiser was Cook's. If that unknown commander was indeed the brash young Isitian, then the rookie had earned the right to his smart mouth.

"Well now," Fitz smiled, arching his eyebrows. "I wouldn't go selling Cookie short. He might very well surprise you."

"*Psshhh!*" scoffed Tanana, spraying disbelief all over his two companions.

"Ah, Christ!" bellowed Chandler, pulling a rag from his pocket to wipe his face. "You know, though," he added, a mischievous twinkle lighting his whiskey-soaked eyes. "If we could arrange it, there might be a way to see how good the Isitian snot really is. If we could arrange it."

"And if we find any fool daft enough to back the rookie," Tanana looked Fitz straight in the eye, "well, there might even be some money in it."

Fitz thought for the longest time. "Well now, that would all depend on the odds you're willing to give," he said at last, scratching his day-old growth of whiskers and grinning like a cat.

* * *

INTRA-SHIP MEMORANDUM No. 143-197

CC: 143-1111.7
FROM: Capt. R Cook
TO: Officers and Crew
SUBJECT: Arrival of Diplomatic Delegation

The Terran Delegation to the peace talks, headed by Ambassador Jonathan O. Grant, will arrive on board today. Ishtar Command has given us the privilege of transporting them to the conference on the Crutchtan planet Girshoona, and I expect us to leave on schedule, the day after tomorrow. To this end, liberties are cancelled, effective immediately, and the ship will maintain double shifts until further notice.

I expect all hands to show the Delegation the utmost courtesy and co-operation. They are, without exception, to be treated as distinguished guests, and I will deal harshly with any breach of hospitality or protocol. In addition, we will be making available to the diplomats and their support staff an entire corridor of crew's compartments, in order to accommodate their personal and professional needs. The Personnel Office will be contacting those affected in order to arrange new living quarters. Junior officers and enlisted personnel should make known any roommate preferences they may have.

* * *

"YOU KNOW, I find this all quite fascinating, but then, I always have. There's an aura about your world—a shroud of mystery, if you will—that's always intrigued me."

Ambassador Grant took another sip of brandy from his glass. He and Cook sat alone in the captain's office. Since the delegation had arrived earlier in the day, the two of them had been locked in conversation. He had yet to take the full measure of this young commander, but what he'd seen was every bit as mystifying as the captain's home planet.

"It has always amazed me, Captain Cook, that of all the worlds we have come to settle, Isis alone shows proof of prior habitation. And not just an idle trace, at that. You have the ruins of whole cities there, buried in the ground and rising in the forests. It's like looking through a time prism at something of incomprehensible antiquity. I'm surprised that archaeologists aren't tramping across the planet, trying to unravel the puzzle."

Grant watched the Isitian smile mysteriously, as if privy to some secret that he wasn't at liberty to reveal. When he spoke, Grant found himself offended by the tone of his host's voice. He wasn't sure why, but he was beginning to take a small dislike to the man.

"That's not really the Isitian way of doing things," Cook said at last. "We don't want people trampling over everything. In fact, that's why we settled such a small portion of the planet. In some respects, we consider ourselves guests on our world, Ambassador. And guests don't make themselves into a nuisance, uprooting everything in sight and shuffling things about like a herd of gadget-mad engineers. We like our woods and deserts and mountains just the way they are. Besides, archaeologists often make a hash of things, anyway. When the early settlers first found the underground tunnels that criss-cross the planet, archaeologists all but ruined whatever there was to be found, looking for the kinds of artifacts more properly belonging to ancient Mesopotamia than to the Ancient Isitians."

Locking his hands behind his head, Cook leaned back in his chair and smiled. "By the time we figured out what to look for, we'd destroyed or thrown away much of whatever it was that might have existed. For example, the Tubes are now useless for anything besides transportation—but we did learn our lesson. No, Ambassador, the ruins have been waiting for sixty-five million years, maybe longer. They're in no hurry to go anywhere, so we can afford to be patient. Unfortunately, that's a lesson that much of Mankind has yet to learn."

Grant chuckled, more amiably than he felt. His eyes drifted to the wall portraits: all giants of Old Earth's past, and all remarkable, in one way or another, for their accomplishments of mind. Few among his contemporaries would recognize more than one or two of the faces, and fewer still would remember their feats of imagination. Yet as intriguing as his host might be, Grant couldn't help thinking it all such a waste.

He shook his head and sighed. It shocked him to find such a wide-ranging intellect idling away his years on a CosGuard ship of the line. He would have expected the young Isitian to be engaged in some lofty social or scientific research, using Terra's magnificent universities to best advantage, in keeping with the customs of the day. That was, after all, the conventional home of the modern-day intellectual—exploring the frontiers of knowledge from the quiet sanctity of the laboratory. But there was little of the conventional about this CosGuarder, including his tastes in music. Despite the young officer's insistence that not a single piece of decent music had been written since the year 2490, it seemed that little else escaped his attention. Grant was starting to wonder just how much the captain knew about his mission, when the intercom buzzer sounded. Cook leaned over to activate the speaker.

"Yes."

"Van Horn here, sir. You wanted to know when we were ready to run the next Centrax check on the engines."

"Yes, Mr. Van Horn. How is it coming?"

"Everyone's bitching to high heaven, and most are swearing that we'll never get our certificate, but I think we've just about got it. The coils are charging like new again. Replacing those segments in B-16 has done the trick, just like we thought. And the simulator shows the mast guns coming to full power right on cue. We just need to run a few more redundancy tests before we let the base inspectors start poking around her innards. Are you coming down for the computer run?"

Exhaling slowly, Cook leaned back in his chair. "No, Vannie, you take it alone this time. If the computer gives us a green light, I'll want to come down there to run the program again. And then we'll run it once again, with me on the bridge, just to be sure."

"Aye, sir. Van Horn out."

Grinning broadly, the captain turned to face his guest.

"Would you care for something to eat, Ambassador?"

"Actually, I am a bit famished."

Cook paged the galley on his intercom and ordered some lunch. It wasn't the standard CosGuard fare, either. This meal was from the galley's special stock, which the provisions officer kept under lock and key.

"You know," the captain said, leaning back in his chair, a distant look in his eyes, "it's ironic you should mention the ruins. Most outworlders are too concerned with their own affairs to be as curious as they should be about our old, dead relics. And that has always reminded me of the scholastic schools of the Middle Ages, you see, for in those days...."

* * *

"A FINE thing. A fine thing indeed."

Sully spat on the floor, just as a robot waxer passed them by, whining and whirring and polishing to its mechanical heart's delight. Soon, the noise from its motors rounded the bend in the hallway, and the discussion resumed.

"Christ," Sully continued. "I mean, what's the Guard a-comin to?"

"It's insane, it is," agreed Denny Barrett. "Just what you'd expect from a gaggle o'desk jockeys what's never been to space. Taxi-cabbin ground-toads, indeed. It's enough to set ye to pukin in your beer."

Leaning against the wall, Barrett and Sullivan watched as Martindale and Larsen, the crewmen recruits assigned to their work detail, finished polishing the door plates on the main corridor of the Conning Deck. The Skipper had decreed that everything on board should shine, and some of the less enlightened greenshirts were taking things a bit too literally. They were about to launch into a new round of observations when their discourse was rudely interrupted.

"What in the name of mealy-mouthed malingering is goin on here?"

The two crewmen shot to their feet and looked to see Chief Connors, his arms crossed and eyes flaming, glowering at them from the bend in the corridor.

"Look here, Chief, we was— "

"Ahh—don't try to be lamin your way clear. I've seen too much first-class work-shirkin in me day, and by my word you two moldy-assed lounge lizards wouldn't pass muster for second-class stewards on a funeral freighter."

"But...."

"That's enough o'your mouthin, Mr. Barrett. You two get yourselves off your padded fannies and back to work or for your next assignment I'll slam you two so far across the ship that you'll meet each other comin round again before you know you're gone. Am I clear, Mister?"

"Aye, Chief."

"Mr. Sullivan?"

"Clear as space, Chief."

"Good. An' the next time I catch ye loafin, I'll have your fat asses in a sling and the rest o'ye in the engine coils."

Connors stormed off, rounding the bend before the two tyros dared to sneak a look.

"You heard the Chief," Sully barked at the junior members of the work team. "Back to work! And with a will this time."

The tyros shot their companions a menacing scowl before turning angrily to the next set of doors in the corridor. Moving to the center of the hallway, Barrett and Sullivan looked first in one direction, then in the other, before resuming their seats against the wall.

"What's with him?" asked Sully.

"Dunno. Prob'ly heated by the room reassignments. Hear he's not too keen on havin redshirts whoopin up and down D-Deck. Not while he's busy tryin to play stuff the cozy with his little bluebird."

"Well, I'll tell ye, I'd never stand for bein relocated neither. If that fat little personnel birdie told me to pack up an leave, why I'd tell her—I'd tell her...."

Sully never finished his sentence. One look down the corridor gave Barrett the reason why, and his jaw dropped in tandem with his crew-mate's. Two junior members of the ambassador's staff had just rounded the bend, and the curves in the hallway were no match for those on Grant's two young assistants. Each of them put Ensign McKenzie to shame, and McKenzie inspired more breaches of discipline than any other bluebird on board. One was blond, the other's hair was a rich, deep brown, but it hardly mattered to the redshirts. The girls' flowing hair and graceful, feminine gait lifted the redshirts' spirits like a gentle May breeze. Not for the first time, the two young women saw the Cosmic Guard suddenly spring to life.

As they neared the work crew, Barrett and Sullivan leaped to their feet; cleaning rag in hand, each began working the nearest brass plate with a will not seen since they'd left the ship to help Ishtar Command celebrate the Cosmic New Year.

"G'day to ye, Missies," Sully winked as they passed.

The two young ladies smiled radiantly.

"An' let me be sayin, now," he continued in his grandest Demetrian brogue, "that it's mighty nice o'ye, to be a-gracin our hunk o'metal with the presence o'yourselves. It warms the very cold o'space it does, and makes a lonely heart to shine."

One of the girls, the blond, started to giggle as they passed, and tried her best to keep from exploding. Her friend smiled brightly and nodded pleasantly, melting Sully's heart like a ray of sunshine. Then, as they neared the opposite bend in the wall, they both burst with laughter, which followed them around the turn and down the corridor.

"Well now," said Sullivan, resuming his seat, "this may not be so bad after all. From where I sit, there are advantages."

"Definite advantages," nodded Barrett, sitting beside him. "Besides which...."

"Dammit!" snapped Larsen, from across the hall. "It's hard enough getting anything done around here without listening to you two babbling like senile gorillas. You either start pulling your weight, or I'll ask the Chief to let us switch to another work team. And if he asks me, I'll tell him exactly why, so help me."

"Ah, shut your snot-nosed tyro yap!" snorted Sully. "Ye ain't got the slightest respect for your betters. And the quicker ye learn to mind your manners, the better stead ye'll be standin in the Guard."

Grudgingly, Barrett and Sullivan resumed their work, though their minds were not on the brassplates in front of their noses. A soft whistling lofted through the air, as Sully's thoughts returned to their recent guests. Curves like a pair of goddesses, he thought, with smiles like the rising sun.

"For Pete's sake," Barrett laughed heartily, finally getting his back into his work, "get them girls out o'your mind. Salutes belong on the ground, they do, an' you're old enough to know better. Except in quarters, there's no room on a ship for salutin, an' that includes the short-armed kind."

***

"CAPTAIN."

"Commodore."

Placing a small piece of paper in front of her, Miriam Wright leaned forward in her chair, staring intently at the image on the communications screen in front of her, wondering why talent seemed to carry such a price.

"I have a present for you," she began.

"Our certificate of starworthiness? I've been expecting it," Cook said. "Van Hoek finished his inspection yesterday."

"Not much for false modesty, are you Captain?"

Cook chuckled. But Wright was surprised to find that it was an amiable laugh, carrying none of the smugness that she found so annoying in her junior wing commander. This time, he seemed to be enjoying a joke at his own expense.

"I'm sorry, Commodore. I suppose I can be rather trying at times. But I am glad we passed, and I appreciate your calling to tell me personally. Most commanders would fancy themselves too busy to take the time."

"I do try to keep up morale, in my own way. Frankly, I'm surprised you noticed."

"A thick skin may lead to a thick head," Cook smiled. "Neither implies a heart of stone. I suppose I'm not the easiest man in the Guard to deal with. That doesn't mean that I don't appreciate a pat on the back, just like anybody else."

Wright visibly straightened in her chair. This was not the Roscoe Cook she had come to know.

"Anyway," he continued, "now that I'm leaving, I may as well apologize for disrupting your routine so thoroughly—though I'm not foolish enough to promise that it won't happen again when we're back from Girshoona."

"I can't say I'll miss it, even though you do keep things from getting dull."

Cook laughed and scratched his nose. "Well, we all have our roles in life."

Wright smiled.

"And I am serious about trying to get our deployment changed along the frontier."

Wright rolled her eyes, but this time, she grinned along with her junior wing commander.

"Remember—one-seventeen and one-twenty-one— "

"I'll keep it in mind," she laughed.

"That's where they'll strike, Commodore. Well, that is, they will if they ever do…."

"Goodby, Captain."

"But I suppose that the more theoretical aspects of my strategic musings can wait until our return."

"Not that I'm trying to push you off the base, you understand, but you are leaving tomorrow?"

Cook laughed and nodded. "Yes, ma'am."

"Try not to get lost, Captain."

"Thank you, Commodore. I'll stay out of trouble, too. Well, at least I'll try."

* * *

THREE HOURS later, patrons of the Looking Glass Officer's Club began casting sour glances at Table Twelve. It was not the isolated shouts, or the booming laughter that caught their attention, for such sounds were expected wherever spacers congregated. What threatened to disrupt more than one dinner were the off-key choruses and boastful toasts that were sounding across the room.

> *A jolly spacer, he*
> *Who brings us luck, say we;*
> *The stars themselves call out his fame—*
> *Captain Cook's his name.*

"Really now, people, this is getting positively emb— "

"And now, a-fore we sail tomorrow," Van Horn interrupted, his half-drunken voice booming across the table, "I think we should show our gratitude to our host, jush' one more time."

The rest of the *d'Artagnan's* senior staff responded by slapping their approval on the table.

"Now really, Mr. Van H— "

"To Captain Cook— " Van Horn continued. "The greates' skipper in all the Cosmic Guard."

"Hear, hear," the others responded.

Cook wanted to shrink into oblivion, or at least hide under the table. He couldn't even console himself by delegating the blame. This whole celebration had been his idea. He'd wanted to give his senior staff a treat on their last day in port, to show his appreciation for all their hard work and dedication. It was nice that they wanted to find some way to reciprocate, but this was not very Isitian, making themselves the center of attention like this. If he'd realized that a night on the town would lead to such a gushing, public display, he would have done things differently. Dinner at a private hall, perhaps. Or maybe just another shipside blowout.

But deep inside he was touched by his crew's display of affection, so he resigned himself to suffering through it. If he did little more than raise a mild protest, it was because he didn't have the heart to scold them for making such a fuss. That would be even less Isitian than the fuss itself.

Suddenly, Cook's musings were shattered by a rough slap on his shoulder. He looked up to see one of the starship skippers from DemCom, standing next to him and looking down through a half-drunken glaze. "Cookie...hey, Cookie, it's nice to see you, you ol' rookie-assed hotshot," he slobbered, pulling a chair up to the table.

"Hello...Chandler, is it?" Cook replied coldly. He hated his current nickname, but experience had taught him never to show it. "I suppose that DemCom is up to its old tricks again, trying to sew up top honors at maneuvers by getting half the fleet thrown in the brig with them."

Chandler laughed heartily. For as long as anyone could remember, DemCom skippers had a reputation for rowdiness. Chandler and his cronies were among the worst of the lot.

"Nah, Cookie," he slurred, stressing the name that he knew the Isitian detested. "Windup Winnie's really laid down the law. These days, we're nothing but tact and charm as far as the eye can see and the ear can hear. A base filled with regular pussycats."

Cook frowned; he knew exactly what kind of pussycats the DemCom skipper meant but didn't want to give him the chance to insult the prettier half of his bridge crew.

"No, really," Chandler laughed, the stench of drink filling the air around him. "And to show you we're on the up-and-up, I've come to make you a little proposition."

"I'm not interested."

"You haven't even heard what I have to say."

"I'm still not interested."

"Well," Chandler raised his voice, directing his remarks to the rest of the *d'Artagnan*'s senior officers, "maybe someone on your ship has a backbone filled with something besides jelly." He tapped the table with his hand, to make sure that he had everyone's attention.

"'Cause you see," he continued, his voice getting louder and louder, "some of us have been thinking that it's no coincidence that you're taking your little rookie butts off as far from here as you can. Some of us have been thinking that you all know you'll get your rookie butts kicked, once the shooting starts. And some of us think that you don't have what it takes to face the best the Guard has to offer—man-to-man—and that's why you got your friends at IshCom to save your fannies by shipping you off to Lizardland."

"What ye be sayin' Chandler?"

"That's enough, Mr. Van Horn," Cook snapped. "Whatever it is, we're not interested."

"What I'm saying," sneered Chandler in reply, "is that you just don't have the balls to take on Jefferson McKinley Jones, one-on-one—here, there, or anywhere."

Cook's eyes narrowed fiercely. He didn't care much for Jones: the blowhard had an ego ten parsecs wide and a mouth to match. This pest, however, was positively annoying. "Please give the Commodore my compliments," Cook said coldly. "But kindly tell him for me that I, for one, have nothing to prove."

"You're making a big mistake, Cookie. Ain't no way you'll look like anything but the ship-full of cowards you are, if you refuse."

"Captain, if you'll kindly excuse us, this is our last night in port. I'd hate to delay our departure because the lads from CSO need me to give a deposition at your disciplinary hearing for being drunk and disorderly. And this is a private party, after all. I'm sure you'll understand."

Indignant, Chandler reeled back to his full height, stabilizing himself by holding on to the back of Van Horn's chair.

"You ain't heard the last of this, Cookie—you—you—weak-kneed *Isitian*."

"You keep us informed, Captain Chandler. Preferably by letter."

As Chandler stormed off into the crowd, the table was silent. No one spoke a word until Cook ordered another round of drinks.

"Ye know, Skipper, he ain't no diplomat, but he is right about one thing. We ignore a challenge from Jones and it'll look like we're afraid to face him, and conceding that the *St. George* is the better ship."

"Nonsense, Mr. Van Horn," smiled the captain. "We'll have plenty of time to prove ourselves when we get back. We don't need to dignify the likes of him with anything more than the disdain he deserves.

"Besides, schoolyard dares are for bratty children and mental defectives. Not for officers of the Cosmic Guard. And certainly not for me. You know, that's not— "

"— not the way you do things on Isis," everyone said at the same time.

"Well, actually— "

"Yes, we know, Captain."

"Do ye think Isitians ever actually get around to doing anything? I mean, consid'rin all they don't do?"

"Beats me. How about it, Skipper?"

"Well...."

"You know, sometimes I think he just makes all this stuff up."

Chapter 15

T HAT'S ODD."
"What's odd?"
"There goes the *Magellan*."
"So?"

"Well, she's the sixth one to leave the dock today. Aside from *d'Artagnan*, I mean. The sixth one."

"Well here comes another."

"Where?"

"Screen Four, clearance request coming through now. There, Dudek's got it. Looks like— "

"Not the *St. George*?"

"—the *St. George*."

"Hmmm."

"They're probably getting in some space time before maneuvers. Probably just don't want to get stale waiting for IshCom to cut the orders."

"Have you ever known a starship to put out from port a second earlier than she had to?"

"Well— "

"Let alone six—no, seven of them?"

"I see your point."

"Think we should we call anyone? I mean, it's not the sort of thing that'll send a blueshirt after our butts, is it?"

"Nah. Don't be silly."

"Hmmm."

"Hey— "

"Lieutenant. . . !"

" —Lieutenant. . .!!"

* * *

"CYRUS?"

"Don't bother me, Rafferty."

"But— "

"Nor yourself, McKeller. I've had about all I can stand o'your babbling. Just keep your bloody yap shut, an let me be about my business here."

"Now, Cyrus...."

"I'll be keepin ye posted, all the lot o'ye; now just leave me be."

"Now just a minute, Cyrus Mc— "

Cyrus turned down the volume on his radio. The chattering of his wingmates was starting to drive him batty. He needed all his concentration to find where they'd gone wrong, if indeed they'd gone wrong at all. The cones had brought them well past the point that he and Mason had left off, and it was positively eerie to think that they were sailing through skies that had known neither man nor lizard. Then the cones just disappeared, and for the last six days he'd not seen a trace of them. By now, even he was beginning to worry. Unless he found another one, or something to show the buffoons traveling with him that they were on the right track, the whole expedition would likely turn and limp back to Riley's. And if left alone, he thought, he might just turn back himself.

Suddenly, a blip appeared on his screen. He set the fine tuner on his sensor and turned up the volume. At first it ebbed and surged amid a blizzard of interstellar static, but within minutes a black smile danced over his lips. He knew he had found what he'd been looking for. He checked the position, and it all matched. The path was missing a few markers, that was all. But it was still there. And the course was holding.

"All right, ye limp-wristed lizard bait—look-ee there."

"Where?"

"Medium frequency band, channel 050."

Cyrus grinned broadly to himself; forty parsecs past the Neutral Zone they'd come. Ahead, the great cloud loomed like a ghost, its faint glow growing stronger with each passing day. Once again he knew they were on the right track. There'd be a passage to meet them when the Cloud rose to cover all of heaven, he could feel it in his bones. Once through the Cloud, he chuckled darkly, the lizards could never stop him. He'd be gone before they knew he was even there.

"Like I told ye, them cones is a bloody guidepost. All we do is folly them. And on the far side of the Cloud, ye'll find riches beyond your wildest dreams."

"If there's a way through."

"There's a way through, Rafferty," Cyrus laughed. "On that ye can bank. We'll find a way through, we will, or me name ain't Cyrus McGee."

The blip on his screen was growing stronger, and Cyrus knew they'd find more along the way. He pushed his throttle ahead, jumping two full energy levels and leaving his wingmates to catch up to him.

* * *

"THERE'S ANOTHER ONE, Skipper. Six points dead under starboard."

Cook frowned. Replacing Jeremy in the command chair, the captain plopped into position and began rocking in place. He had the sinking feeling that he knew exactly what was happening. Of course, he was powerless to change things, but he was almost used to the feeling by now.

"That makes four, Skipper."

"I can count, Mr. Ashton."

"Yes, Captain."

"Make that five, Mr. Ashton," piped Dexter, from the systems desk. "Another one's showing on the screen at six o'clock, dead astern."

"Helm, maintain speed and heading. Jeremy, any idea who...."

"No, Skipper. They haven't called to let us know and they're still too far away for a scan. Unless you want Mathison to sound a hail?"

"No," snapped Cook. "If they aren't in a sociable mood, I won't be the one to break the ice. But Mathison?"

"Sir?"

"Page the rest of the bridge crew. No insult intended to the rest of you, but I think I want the first team here with me."

"Yes, Captain."

* * *

"HE'S WHERE?" thundered Hollenbach, rising from his chair to tower over the figure seated in the chair before him, his eyes almost hateful.

Nicholas Schiller's jaw twitched in anger, but he said nothing. They were too close to victory to let pride scuttle their plans. He gritted his teeth and replied in tones as measured as he could manage.

"Senator Heathcoate left Demeter two days ago. He should arrive...."

"Well, I hope he's enjoying himself," stormed Hollenbach. "I hope he's just having a grand old time getting here, because every day he delays the vote just makes it that much harder to hold onto our people. And I hope you've told him that the Cozzies decided not to wait for him. They've already sailed."

Schiller frowned. "I don't see what diff— "

"You don't see what difference it makes," sneered Hollenbach. His sarcastic tone cut like a knife.

"No, I don't really see— "

"Well hear this, my naive friend," the senator smiled coldly. "A Cozzie ship is slipping toward the Neutral Zone—and my moles tell me that Central Command isn't keeping its captain on a leash. They may even know what we have in mind."

"What do you mean, Emerson?"

Hollenbach sank back in his chair.

"What I mean, my Demetrian friend, is that once that starship crosses the Neutral Zone it's not coming back. CosGuard's treating it as a military mission, not a diplomatic one. Once that ship is in lizard skies its skipper has orders to keep sailing until he's seen all there is to see between here and the lizard's damn homeland."

Schiller's face turned ashen.

"You mean—?"

"Now you're getting the idea," sneered Hollenbach. "Looking Glass is four days from the Neutral Zone and it takes two or three days to cross it. If Old Bladderbrain doesn't get his ass back here before then...."

"I get the picture."

"I hope so, Schiller. I sincerely hope so."

Schiller sank in his chair. All this work. All this aggravation and worry, and if Heathcoate's ship was more than a day late there would be nothing they could do except revoke Grant's credentials. But doing that would make them lose face with the aliens. All of the aliens.

Even worse, he shuddered. Unless they came clean with everything they knew, it would raise a storm in the Senate, on both sides of the aisle. Disclosing what they knew would start a stampede toward the Cloud, making an orderly distribution of its riches impossible. And though the Senate's rules might prevent the Federalists from trying to topple the new government for two years, if they bungled things badly enough nothing would stop the party in power from introducing its own motion of no-confidence.

"I'll see what I can do."

"Yes, you do that," snorted Hollenbach. "You just do that."

* * *

"I'M SORRY, COMMODORE, but I can't get a response."

Miriam Wright exhaled loudly. Not only were starship skippers as stubborn as mules, they had the self-control of spoiled adolescents. "Somehow, that doesn't surprise me," she sighed, smiling at the dispatch technician seated at the control desk.

"I could order them all back to base," suggested the supervisor. "Even if they don't acknowledge the message, they're all within range. There's no way they could claim they didn't receive the order."

Wright thought a moment—but only a moment, before shaking her head. Regulations might frown on these informal jousting sessions, but they weren't exactly forbidden. Besides, she smiled, she was no different than anyone else. She was dying to know who the winner would be.

"Just keep repeating the hail," she said at last. "Let's at least cover our own fannies."

"You don't want them recalled?

"Not on your life."

Everyone laughed. Some things were more important than the rules. Even if it wouldn't be official, they all knew what was about to be settled. And somewhere east of Looking Glass, they knew that the action had already begun.

MEANWHILE, IF not action, at least something was under way on the *d'Artagnan*'s route to the Neutral Zone.

"They're moving in for another pass," announced Jeremy. "Approaching dead astern at 6 o'clock in fifteen seconds."

"Steady as she goes," Cook replied calmly. He could see the nervous faces on the bridge, but their nervousness was not born of fear. It wasn't every day that the ship was buzzed by the reigning champion, with each pass coming closer, as if determined to force the *d'Artagnan* off course one way or another.

But what was really making the crew anxious, Cook concluded, was that all of them, himself included, had no idea how they were going to respond. The dares and taunts of the *St. George* and her companions were maddening, and there seemed to be no graceful retreat open to them. Of course, that was exactly Jones' intent. The annoying thing was that it seemed to be working.

"*St. George* passing overhead...now."

The crew felt a soft shudder, as the ship crossed their rival's light wake.

"Distance?"

"One-half astromillimeter at objunction. Coming about and now passing astern. Looks like they mean to make another pass."

"Another incoming hail," added Underwood.

"Helm—hold her steady. Don't let them think we're getting rattled. Underwood, don't answer the hail."

"They've come about for another pass. This time, it looks like they're going to traverse the bow, Captain."

"Hold the course, Miss Mendelson."

"Aye, sir."

The *St. George* passed the intercept point just ahead of *d'Artagnan*, and in doing so, left a gift waiting in the skies for the *d'Artagnan*.

"Debris!" shouted Jeremy.

"Shields to hold," relayed Palmer, confirming that the ship's running shields would be sufficient to protect the ship against whatever the *St. George* had left behind.

"Analysis."

Nobody on the bridge, least of all the captain, had the slightest doubt what Jones had left for them. "Organic molecules and recycling compounds— " Jeremy began. He needed to go no further.

"All right," snapped Cook. "That's enough. That's quite enough." Though his eyes were cold as ice, fury burned in his soul. "Helm, stand by to come five points under heading 015. Mr. Underwood, sound battle stations. If they want a fight, we'll give them a fight. Helm—five under fifteen."

"Aye, aye."

"That Demetrian jackass. Jeremy, engage the mock battle computers. I don't want to blast the little bugger from here to kingdom come by mistake."

"Yes, sir; computers on."

"Palmer, raise the shields. Set the forward guns at mock strength. And remember— "

"Yes, Captain. Aim for the seams."

"Submoronic worm."

"I thought that on Isis, you didn't— "

"We are not on Isis, Jeremy."

"But— "

"And even if we were—on Isis, I mean—nobody flushes a sewage tank all over someone else's ship. That's not very Isitian no matter how you cut it."

"Look! She's coming about, range one hundred metes."

"Of course, we don't have tanks that like on Isis, either. At least not very many of them, but then that's entirely beside the point."

"Yes, sir."

"Palmer, shields to half-strength, side guns to half strength; prepare to blank all guns and charge astern. Helm—stand by for sublight cut; prepare to drop due south, on cued variant, EM-6."

"Aye, aye."

"Yes, sir; Evasive Maneuver Number Six and watch the tricks."

"Mendelson, just steer the ship."

"It's not really her fault, Skipper. We're all a bit giddy from our big night on the town, you know."

"Well, remind me to think twice about rewarding people for jobs well done, Jeremy. It's doing some odd things to discipline, here. Probably something to do with premature psychological decompression and its synergistic interaction in triggering latent forces of congenital mental abnormalities. I've been meaning to write a paper on the subject, but my case studies keep ruining my conclusions with random flashes of lucidity."

"All that drilling drives us just as batty, you know. It's probably contaminated the data, anyway."

"Yes, Miss Mendelson...well, let's hope that our performance shows more wit than our repartee."

* * *

"HE'S DONE it again."

Fitz shook his head and walked toward the main viewers, taking a place near the Systems station. Something strange was happening out there. Cook's maneuvers just didn't make sense.

The *St. George* had made its fifth pass, completely missing its target for the fifth time. Each time, at the last moment, *d'Artagnan* simply moved to one side or the other, letting the shot pass by, quite harmlessly. And each time Cook had held his fire, leaving his side batteries half-charged and oddly unprepared for the fight. If they kept this up, it would take forever for one of them to make the five kills needed to settle things, one way or the other.

"Look," said Commodore McIntyre, just one of the skippers who'd come along for the view. "Jonesy's is coming about again, all guns fully charged."

Sure enough, *St. George* made another arc, and raced toward the *d'Artagnan*. Like a charging bull, she neared Cook's ship for another pass. Like every time before, *d'Artagnan* hung as if suspended in space, floating serenely through the blackness like a dream. Only this time, as the *St. George* made its pass and *d'Artagnan* darted out of the way of the incoming fire, a single burst from *d'Artagnan*'s stern guns lit the sky and the computers on every nearby ship scored a verdict.

"It's a kill," said Hardesty, the *Magellan*'s systems officer.

Hardesty lifted his head, a quizzical look on his face. "*D'Artagnan*," he said in disbelief. "First kill to the *d'Artagnan*."

"*Hmmph*," snorted McIntyre. "Lucky shot."

Slowly, Fitz walked back and resumed his seat at the command station. The *d'Artagnan* needed a single shot for her first kill. Fitz knew how rarely first shots scored: unless your opponent's shields were drained nearly to exhaustion, your shot had to be perfect. And yet Jones had missed on six straight passes, and each time Cook had taken his ship out of harm's way with an effortless economy of motion.

"Sure looks like a freak shot to me," said Bradley; and the rest of his bridge crew nodded in agreement.

"We'll see about that," smiled Fitz, leaning back in his chair. He couldn't tell how much luck had anything to do with it. But from where he was sitting, the odds he'd gotten on Cook were starting to look awfully good.

"Chandler's on the hailing channel," announced Bradley.

"On the main speaker."

"I'm ruling that a fluke," Chandler's voice announced. "Hear that, Cook? A fluke."

There was no reply from the *d'Artagnan*.

"You can take your goddamn score or be a man and let it pass," Chandler continued. "You hear me—*Cookie*?"

D'Artagnan's silent response caught everyone off guard.

"Cook's dropped his shields," announced Hardesty.

"He what?"

"He's dropped his shields."

"Son of a bitch," Fitz whispered. By reflex, as everyone else's jaw dropped, the corners of his mouth curled upwards. He didn't know what the young Isitian had in mind; on that count, he was as mystified as anyone. No other starship skipper would dare face off without his shields, especially against the likes of Jefferson McKinley Jones. Whatever else they said about him, nobody could deny that Cook had guts. Admiringly, he shook his head.

"Son of a bitch."

SLOWLY, THE *St. George* circled *d'Artagnan*, searching for some hidden trap. Her sensors showed nothing hiding in the darkness and everything was as it seemed. *D'Artagnan* floated alone in space, taunting her adversary and daring him to make another approach, her shields down, her half-charged side guns the only sign of interest in the joust.

Finally, the *St. George* arced gracefully to port and began her run. Shields raised and guns amain she sped forward, sensors probing for *d'Artagnan*'s weak spots, her guns waiting for *d'Artagnan* to dart to one side or the other. Then, just as Jones was giving the order to ready his guns for firing, *d'Artagnan*'s side guns lost power and her engines roared to life as she arched smartly athwart her opponent's bow. Suddenly as a lightening bolt, her forward guns lit the heavens just as the *St. George* came into firing range.

"I don't believe it," said Hardesty; he swivelled his chair to face the rest of the bridge. "I just don't believe it."

"At that range?" stormed McIntyre, racing to join the systems officer. "Impossible. That's just impossible. There must be some mistake." Soon everyone on the bridge was crowding around the systems desk. No matter how dumbly they stared, or how often they reread it, the results stared back at them.

The computers had scored another kill for the *d'Artagnan*.

THE MOOD on *d'Artagnan*'s bridge was ebullient.

"*Ya-ho-eee!*"

"All right, that's enough of that."

"My God—did you see— "

"All right— !"

"I'll bet Old Jonesy's crapping in his— "

"All right, people, just calm down, now. It's not over yet. And don't get cocky. Remember, that's half of their problem."

"And the other half?"

"Well...dictates of modesty and all...."

Cook smiled as jeers and catcalls filled the air. He knew that he wasn't running his bridge by the book. This was hardly the cool, professional atmosphere that the manual recommended, but he didn't really care. He knew better than to tamper with something that was working. Besides, strictly speaking, he never did things by "The Book." And he doubted very much that its author had ever seen a battle, anyway.

"Just remember," he said loudly, making sure to be heard over the din. "A little talent can go a long way. It's all a matter of practice. Helm, ahead one-half; prepare to engage subspace drive."

"What about the shields?"

"Keep them lowered, Miss Palmer...except for the running shields, of course. Even if Jones can't touch us we don't want to be knocked off by a hunk of interstellar rock."

"Aye aye."

"But keep the port and starboard guns half-charged. I want them ready at a moment's notice, in case the *St. George* gives us another clear shot."

"Yes, sir."

"Mendelson, ahead at C-1; stand by for a starboard arc, heading 020."

"Yes, Captain."

"Let's try to rub a little salt in their wounds, shall we? That should make them good and careless. Well...at least more careless than the computer."

"Oh, no—you're not going to— "

"Well, Jeremy, that's why I want them careless. Then it won't really matter if the engines don't hold the spirals, just as long as they don't fritz out on us again."

"*Skipper!*"

"But that won't happen. At least, it shouldn't. Not since the overhaul, anyway. Just stand by for when they're ten or twenty points north. Or south, actually...and vaguely...well, sternish."

"Sternish?"

"Yes—anything from...four o'clock to eight-fifteen or so."

"But— "

"Yes...I know, I know. But I think we've got the bugs worked out, this time. And I have a few new ideas to try. They won't know what hit them. And if they do—well, it'll take them forever to figure out what to do about it."

"*St. George* coming about."

"Thank you, Mr. Ashton. Helm—increase to C-2; prepare for evasive maneuvering. McKenzie, try to remember what I showed you."

"Yes, sir."

"Remember...closed arc, keep it tight, and keep it closing. And approximate. Just keep us close. Mendelson and I will take it from there."

"I'll try, sir."

"I don't know about this, Skipper."

"Yeah, well...."

"THERE SHE goes—she's finally moving."

Fitz looked over Hardesty's shoulder, to see the *d'Artagnan*'s image on the motion monitor. Then, he lifted his eyes toward the main viewing screen. Cook's ship was moving, slowly; like a swan upon the water, she slid through the black sky, heading in the direction of Looking Glass, outwardly oblivious to the approach of danger from astern.

Fitz resumed the command seat. "Wide view on the main viewer," he said. At once, the images shrank, as his systems officer expanded their scope of vision to encompass a wider view. The two giant ships became points of light moving in the darkness against the backdrop of the local stars.

The *St. George* stormed ahead, her guns charged and ready to unleash a furious barrage against *d'Artagnan*'s unshielded hull. As the *St. George* pulled closer to her quarry, tension mounted on the *Magellan*'s bridge as everyone sensed Jones nearing his first kill. Then, at the very instant his forward guns were priming to fire, the *d'Artagnan* rolled sharply right and banked hard to starboard, darting out of the line of fire and changing course toward galactic center. The volley from the *St. George* passed harmlessly below as Cook's ship continued its serene glide across the sky—leaving the *St. George* racing headlong into the distance until she slowed to come about for another pass.

"That's eight passes without a strike," muttered McIntyre. "And I thought jousts always brought out the best in him."

"This isn't the time for Jones to have a bad day," agreed Bradley.

Seated in the captain's chair, Fitz wasn't paying attention to anything on his own bridge. His mind was riveted on what was happening in space. While everyone else wondered why nothing was going right for Jones, his own mind was seized by entirely different questions: how could the Isitian dare to leave his shields down against the deadliest shot in the Cosmic Guard? And how did Cook know exactly when to move his own ship out of danger?

"He's coming around for another pass."

"Come on, Jonesy. Show the little prick how to do it."

Fitz lifted his eyes toward the screen just in time to see Cook dart out of the way again, this time by dropping his ship due south and letting the *St. George*'s volley pass over his mast. As inertia carried Jones and his ship into the distance, Cook gracefully changed course again, heading twelve points south and west of anticenter, keeping the same leisurely pace.

Fitz mulled over the obvious. Cook was keeping his power up, but his speed down, no more than Level Two—well down from the speed many skippers used for battle, but well within the range for maximum subspace agility. After all, the faster speeds not only increased vulnerability, they flattened the parabolas for turning. But with Jones approaching at C-4, the *St. George* was at minimally increased risk; and while Cook was exploiting his maneuvering advantage to its fullest, all he was doing was stepping out of the way. Though baffled about how he was doing it, Fitz was sure that the Isitian could keep it up indefinitely. But it all looked too easy; Fitz sensed that Cook had something else in mind.

Then a thought struck and Fitz remembered Cook's long range kill: side guns half-charged, he blanked them, only to fire a second later, without warning and from a single gun. It all happened so effortlessly—*and without warning*. With everything else happening, it had passed without notice. But Fitz wondered: why did the Isitian transfer power from gun to gun? Was it just to be different? Or was there some other reason?

"*St. George* beginning her approach," Hardesty announced.

Fitz thought a moment, then activated the miniscreen on his armrest. Soon, it showed the same scene as the main viewer, only so reduced in size as to make the dimmest stars unperceivable. That was not quite what Fitz wanted.

"Fifty metes, and closing."

Fitz entered the sensor code, calling up the *Magellan*'s close range sensors and then spelled out the command he wanted: weapon scan; command analysis. While the others focused their attention on the viewer, Fitz rested his chin in his hand, watching for the smallest hint of change. Soon, his monitor showed the two ships amidscreen—*St. George* in green, *d'Artagnan* in orange— with an abbreviated listing of the systems status of each printed on either side.

"*St. George* fully armed and increasing speed."

Fitz stared at his screen, afraid to blink for fear of missing something.

"Damn!" shouted Hardesty. " He did it again. That bastard did it again." Sure enough, the main viewer showed the *d'Artagnan* waiting until the last moment, then darting out of harm's way, this time surging hard to port as the volley from the *St. George* passed impotently behind them.

In the captain's chair, Fitz fought to suppress a grin. The more he thought of it, the more he was certain: he'd discovered Cook's secret. Not that it would do him any good, he laughed to himself. To be any use, a skipper had to know exactly what he was going to do ahead of time, and give most of his commands well before the fact. Though it made Cook's showing more intelligible, it also brought chills to Fitz' spine, for it gave him a glimmer of just how far Cook stood above the rest of them.

"The firing sequence," Fitz whispered, shaking his head in admiration. Cook just waited for Jones to commit his ship's guns to fire, then used the brief notice it gave to get his ship out of the way.

"I beg your pardon, Captain?"

"Nothing, Bradley," Fitz replied quickly, a mysterious smile on his lips. "Just try to keep both ships on the monitors."

It was, thought Fitz, so simple that it reeked of genius. That was how Cook knew when to move, and probably why he took such pains to disguise any the readings from his own ship. It was why he shifted the focus of power so often, and it was how he kept his opponents so hopelessly confused. Fitz resolved to keep Cook's secret for the moment, at least, and maybe forever. After all, he doubted that the rest of them could put the Isitian's technique to use, anyway: it required split-second timing and a skipper who thought ten or twenty moves ahead. If Cook could keep track of the endless details involved in bouncing power around his ship, it was enough to make Fitz' head swim.

"The man's insane," stormed McIntyre. "Dart this way, dart that way, any which way. He may be good at darting, though God knows what good it'll do him in a real battle. But he hasn't the slightest grasp of tactics. He doesn't know how to press Jones—how to force mistakes—how to wear him down. Even how to engage the enemy one-on-one."

"Jonesy's fired ten times and missed every shot," Fitz smiled. "Cook's fired twice, for two kills. Seems to me, Mac, that you've got it backwards."

"He's a clown," snapped McIntyre. "A juggling buffoon. He's so far over his head...."

"He's baiting him, Cook is."

"What?"

"Cook's baiting him. Setting him up."

"I doubt that. And setting him up for what? An Isitian flower hunt? Or perhaps a poetry-reading contest."

"I haven't the slightest idea," laughed Fitz. "But I'll tell you this. It looks to me like he's suckering Jones into some kind of trap. And I'd be willing to bet that it'll be something sure to knock our socks off. Just be patient. You'll see. Soon enough, I'll bet we all see."

This time, there were no takers.

"SKIPPER—YOU were waiting for— "

"Yes, I noticed...dead astern, fifteen points north."

"Yes, sir, and closing at C-6—slowing now to C-4."

"Sound the clearing horn, Mr. Underwood; Mr. Ashton, prepare to cut gravity to all decks."

"Aye, sir."

"Aye, aye."

"McKenzie?"

"Eight permutations plotted, Captain."

"That should be enough. Miss Mendelson— "

"Aye, aye."

"—stand by for my command— "

"Yes, sir."

"—just as soon as he commits himself."

"Aye, aye."

* * *

"YOU'VE GOT him now," McIntyre whispered intensely. The main viewer showed the *St. George* racing toward her quarry, in a straight vector fifteen degrees above *d'Artagnan*'s stern, dead center in the prime approach window. "Go get him, Jonesy," he muttered, under his breath. "Wipe that Isitian smirk off his face."

McIntyre's eyes narrowed hatefully, true malice in his heart. For reasons even he didn't understand, he hungered to see the Isitian humbled. Cook was too damn cocky, he told himself, and didn't give a whit for tradition. Against the Isitian's haughty tone of voice and condescending smirk, the Demetrian ace was now vying with the upstart on behalf of a whole generation of starship skippers. It never crossed McIntyre's mind that until now Jones was nearly as despised as the man who now threatened to displace him.

Transfixed, Fitz watched from his position in the command seat. He couldn't see how Cook could let Jones take such an open approach. It put the *d'Artagnan* in a tactical black hole: given the angle of Jones' approach vector, her real-space distension along the approach placed her at maximum risk; with *d'Artagnan*'s shields down, and exposed for enfilading fire, the *St. George* would need a blind weapons officer to keep from scoring. The *St. George* slowed her approach to begin the pass and Fitz leaned forward and moved to the edge of his seat.

Without warning, *d'Artagnan*'s engines fired and her shields came to life. While *St. George* slowed, trying to keep Cook's ship in the line of fire, the *d'Artagnan* banked hard to starboard—and to the amazement of all, kept banking until she spiraled in on her own course, a single forward gun charging all the while. As Jones and his ship vainly struggled to follow, the *d'Artagnan* continued until she was bearing upon the *St. George* from below and astern with guns amain, and scored her third kill against the aft shields with her third shot. Then, traversing to pass over *St. George*'s mast, the *d'Artagnan* spiraled hard to port, coming north over bow to find an unprotected keel for a fourth shot, then spiraling south under starboard athwart *St. George*'s portside for a fifth. Each time, and from directions that seemed impossible moments before, she roared tightly and ever more closely in toward her opponent, whose crew was desperately trying to plot an evasive course against an opponent who was violating all rules of engagement and suspending the known laws of navigational physics. Each time, a single shot found a different seam in *St. George*'s shields. And each time, every computer within range scored another kill.

Then, silently as the blackness in which she sailed, the *d'Artagnan* banked gracefully to port, and leisurely pivoted on her directional axis to right herself to Galactic North. She faded into the distance to disappear into the darkness of the Cosmic East.

For a small eternity, an eerie stillness gripped *Magellan*'s bridge. Finally, a sister ship's hail broke the spell.

"It's the *Capricorn*, sir. It's Captain Tanana."

Fitz nodded, and Bradley put *Capricorn*'s skipper on the communications screen. Tanana had a glazed look about him. He was in Jonesy's attack wing and used to being on the receiving end of his commander's own bag of tricks. Now Tanana looked as numb as everyone, his voice little more than a whisper.

"What do you make of that, Fitz?"

"Hell if I know. Damnedest thing I ever saw."

Fitz shook his head and smiled. "But I'll tell you one thing. When he comes back, I'm going to ask him how he cuts those 'Cook Corners' of his. And dammit, you better remember our bet. It's not every day that I can fleece half the fleet at twelve-to-one."

"Somehow, Fitz, I doubt you'll let us forget about that any time soon."

Chapter 16

DAYS PASSED, AND as the *d'Artagnan* neared the Terran side of the Neutral Zone, four small ships were slowly wending their way through a yawning hole in a series of furious storms to the North, far toward Galactic Anticenter.

It was the eeriest sight Cyrus had ever seen. He wondered whether it might not also be the most beautiful. Delicate wisps laced their pathway, in shades ranging from the darkest reds to the deepest purples. Endless clouds stretched into the distance, like phantoms fleeing before the dawn. Static crackled over his radio, as his wingmates struggled to be heard, though the storms raging about them seemed equally determined to keep them silent.

"Clintus...Clintus...what do you think, Clintus?"

"McGraw here, too. Rafferty, do you read me? Rafferty?"

"I'm here and I think we're bloody lost. But I ain't a-goin back by myself."

Cyrus paid his wingmates no heed. It wouldn't do them any good, and he wasn't about to let their problems communicating distract him from what was going on around them. They'd had trouble enough sneaking past what looked to be the lone lizard outpost guarding the entrance to the pass, though once they passed it was apparent that the base itself was ancient in origin and quite deserted. All the same, caution had taken them well into the Cloud, where their sensors were all but useless. As they edged deeper and deeper into the Cloud, Cyrus needed all the concentration he could muster to keep from straying too far from the channel. Now that the storm itself made their presence undetectable, they were back in the passage to stay, and he meant to enjoy the show.

Outside their hulls, on all sides, violent storms raged. In the distance, he could see flashes of static lightning filling the heavens, turning the thin vapors of the Cloud into gentle wisps of color and lighting the sky in all directions. As far as their instruments could see, the eddies and swirls of the Cloud were parted before them, penetrating the center of the storm as if bored by an immense cosmic drill. The narrow opening through which they sailed arched toward the galactic center like a vast tunnel, leading them through the churning dust and gases. Cyrus knew that such an opening was far beyond anything Terran science had dreamed. He hoped to heaven that it was beyond the lizards' capabilities as well.

But Cyrus had no patience for pondering the imponderable. His was a practical mind, not given to whimsy or flights of fantasy, and awe passed through it like water through a sieve. Though it was on a grander scale, he knew that this pass was little different than the ones through the storms guarding Isis, and just as likely to make him lose his bearings if he didn't mind their heading. The delicate beauty of the surrounding heavens soon faded before the task at hand. His horizon stretched no further than getting safely through the pass with his raiding party intact. And he wondered about little more than the odds of finding an operational lizard base at the other end.

* * *

"Advance."

The inner doorveil parted, and gal'Fondro of *Gr'Shuna* entered the room. Ga'Glish lifted his eyes from the monitor and, seeing his father's emissary and oldest friend, bade his aides to leave.

"I hate to intrude upon the duties of office," gal'Fondro smiled, as he heard the outer door close behind the last of the departing assistants.

"We were all but done," said Ga'Glish, motioning for the emissary to seat himself, "and I would not keep an old friend waiting without need."

"Ga'Glishek sends his wishes, and your mother sends her love."

Ga'Glish sighed; *Gr'Shuna* had seen many seasons since his feet felt the soft earth of home. He had wished for a more amiable parting, and the intervening years had made him wonder if part of the fault might not be his. His own mate had often remarked that the men of the Galgravina clan were better known for their obstinacy of purpose than for their tact.

"I am glad my father sent you," he said at last. "It eliminates the need for digressions of form."

"He understands the need for frankness," returned gal'Fondro, "even if other needs sometimes escape him."

Ga'Glish rose to his feet and walked toward the anteroom, where a large spherical map of the skies protruded from the wall. Though no words passed between them, gal'Fondro rose and followed. As soon as he entered, a sliding door closed behind them, sealing the room from the prying ears of outsiders. "The walls are now deaf," said Ga'Glish, confirming that they could talk freely.

"You are aware of events in the Capitol?"

"My Ministry keeps me well-informed."

"Then you know that your uncle vies with Cra'Jenli for the post of First Minister. And so the Expanse Ministry and Foreign Ministry are locked in struggles that follow the interests of their leaders. "

Ga'Glish nodded.

"Gal'Shenga can afford no incidents, Ga'Glish. His reputation rests on avoiding the scandals of the past. And the Imperator does not like to intervene in squabbles among the contending bureaucracies."

"I propose nothing beyond— "

Gal'Fondro held up his hand, in the manner of an Elder silencing a young one, but Ga'Glish took no offense. Despite the difference in rank decreed by fate and fortune, in his mind his father's aide would always be his elder. "You seek to force a jurisdictional dispute, Ga'Glish, one that plays into the hands of the Foreign Minister."

"But Gal'Shenga— "

"Your uncle is aware of your concern, Son of my Friend, but he is stepping through a nest of vipers. A false step now will cost his post and perhaps more, if the Imperator is in a playful mood."

"So Gal'Shenga allies himself with his rival, and my own father sleeps in the face of danger, ignoring the bond of his own blood."

"Ga'Glish, you forget yourself!" hissed gal'Fondro. "And you forget how much both you and your father have for which to atone."

Ga'Glish felt the blood burn in his soul, but he also knew that gal'Fondro spoke the truth, and so he held his tongue until the rage subsided.

"You and your father are much alike," the emissary smiled. "Perhaps too much so for your own good."

"All too well do I know my own mind," Ga'Glish smiled lamely, "though I answer not for the faults of another."

"Well spoken," laughed gal'Fondro, placing a friendly hand on the younger man's shoulder. "And you underestimate your elders, Ga'Glish. They are better versed in the subtleties of politics than you can be, isolated here on a sterile haven with none but the stars and a lonely mate for companionship."

"I am listening, Old Friend."

Though none but Ga'Glish could hear, gal'Fondro spoke in the darkest of whispers. "You must trust to the wisdom of the Galgravina elders."

"I have had occasion to laugh at such wisdom, Fondro."

"Trust their good intentions, then, Ga'Glish."

"I am still listening."

"Gal'Shenga cannot release his havenmaster from obedience, and cannot afford to press this struggle— "

"This is tedious, but I listen still."

"But the Provincial Governor must pass on the Protocol for the coming Festival of Terra, and neither he nor his designee may be excluded from the ceremonies. Form will not permit it."

"I will not renounce my post, Fondro!" Ga'Glish hissed. "My father has tried before, but this— "

"*Silence!*" gal'Fondro commanded imperially. "None but fools place stones in their ears."

Ga'Glish raged inside, but struggled to listen to Fondro's words.

"Your father cannot override the Foreign Minister's command," the emissary continued sharply. "Not for reasons of blood, not even for the dictates of security. But as the Imperator's local representative, Ga'Glish-ek may defer his prerogatives to others, of like kind and higher rank."

"This talk of protocol is like the babbling of an infant."

"Meaning," gal'Fondro replied impatiently, "that Ga'Glishek may defer to another Imperial official of higher rank, a class which includes your uncle. And as an Imperial Minister, Gal'Shenga can command his own retinue."

Ga'Glish fell silent, and began to feel very young and foolish.

"You may go to Gr'Shuna, Ga'Glish, in good time and in good form. But you go not as a Havenmaster, or on ties of blood. You go as a retainer, under call of duty, to attend your Superior under his command…if you accept the charge."

"Fondro— " Ga'Glish began.

"You will await the Terrans' arrival, and watch their passage through the expanse. When they near your Haven, you may expect your uncle's call, even though he may still be in transit. This will permit you to observe the Terran craft in full operation as you travel to Gr'Shuna. As you will be serving your current Superior, you need not renounce your current post, for the duties will not conflict. And when Gal'Shenga departs for home, he will release you from your new obligations, returning you to your haven."

Though Ga'Glish said nothing, gal'Fondro felt the emotions storming within the young man's breast, emotions of elation and respect, but mostly of the profound gratitude of the undeserving. "You owe me no debt," smiled gal'Fondro, reading the thoughts of his old friend's son. "In fact, I deem it just the opposite, for your needs have led me to witness the first civil conversation between Ga'Glishek and his brother since you were a small one clinging to your mother's arms. As for the rest—it was your father's idea."

* * *

"OF COURSE, I'm sure that diplomacy is much more complicated than you pretend," smiled Cook. Hands locked behind his head, he rocked leisurely in his chair. Ambassador Grant leaned forward, intently following each thread of their conversation. They were seated at the small conference table in the anteroom to the captain's office. On the wall were drawings of some of the major features of Terran space—Solak's Nebula in the Ishtari Belt; Cahalan's Spiral in the heart of Murphy's Cloud. And of course, the Greater Nakahashi Storm. Cook often said that the drawing of the storm reminded him of home, though his executive officer often suspected that it was because the storm, like many of the captain's conversations, seemed to go on indefinitely.

"You see," the captain said, "we all have our own perspectives, and our own roles to play. Often, though, we can find new ideas and new approaches simply by sharing what we already know."

Grant nodded blandly. He knew exactly what the captain meant, but had no intention of obliging. He had problems enough with the fools on his staff; he had no desire to share his problems with amateurs.

"I know what you mean," the ambassador replied. "If you like, I can put our store of briefing papers at your disposal. There is no telling when such knowledge could be put to use, and we've a long way to go before we come to port. I'm sure you'll find it all quite fascinating."

Cook looked sternly at his guest. When it came to dealing with the aliens, the captain knew the ambassador to be the most knowledgeable man in Terra. This was the third time the captain had broached the subject, the third time he'd given Grant the chance to take him into his confidence. Each time, his guest just smiled and changed the subject.

The door alarm sounded and Jeremy entered, hoping to jaw away a few minutes until the watch changed only to let his jaw drop, the way it did whenever he stumbled across the captain and Grant engaged in one of their interminable discussions. The ambassador was one of the few men Jeremy had met who could match Cook, pontification for pontification, and just as merciless when dealing with a captive audience. Yet, oddly, Jeremy sensed no warmth or rapport between the two of them. It was as if each took the other's talents as a threat to his own.

"You know," Grant began, signaling for Jeremy to take one of the empty visitors chairs, "you'll find many aspects of Crutchtan culture fascinating, especially their use of ritual and pageantry, and their seeming obsession with manners. I've often thought that what a culture chooses to honor gives a clearer insight into its soul than a library-full of self-reflection. Old Earth saw civilizations exalting a full range of ideas and accomplishments, from conquest to martial valor, from the accretion of material wealth to the demonstration of athletic prowess."

"It's as I was saying yesterday," Cook nodded, his eyes taking a distant, lofty glaze that Jeremy had come to dread. But he needn't have worried, for just then the intercom sounded, bringing his short ordeal to an end.

"We're nearing our edge of the Neutral Zone," came Mendelson's voice over the intercom. "You said that you wanted— "

"Say no more," Cook said cheerily. "I'm on my way."

He rose to his feet. "Sorry, Ambassador, but I wanted to be on the bridge when we left Terran space."

"I understand, Captain."

"Jeremy— "

"Yes, sir."

" — duty calls."

"Yes, sir."

As they left Cook's office, Jeremy reflected that duty didn't call him so much as it simply tried his patience. As they rounded the corner, Cook sent Jeremy ahead while he tended another item of business.

Some calls, it seemed, pressed more urgently than duty.

* * *

IT WAS dawn.

Though the morning sky promised sun, the wind blew bitterly. The cold of night glazed the meadowgrass, and warmth was but a memory to Shl'Lanasha and his mate, as they waited together for word that the new probe was ready to sail to the planet.

"How long— " Lanshana began.

"The Groupleader does not keep me so well informed as you would like," smiled Shl'Lanasha. "I know not how long we shall be this time."

"The days here are endless, and never so endless as when I am alone."

"Yes, my little one."

"And each time, Glankha promises that it will be the last, and that we shall soon sail toward the warm skies of home."

"Ya'Glankha means well, but he is a scientist. Those such as he often keep time by a different clock."

"But Lanash— "

Shl'Lanasha gently placed his fingers on his mate's lips. "I hear and understand," he grinned playfully. "Patience does have its limits as a virtue. But abide as best you can. It will not be much longer."

"But— "

"I promise—we will walk the sands of home sooner than you can dream."

Before long the call came, and Shl'Lanasha stepped into the transporter. Soon he was once again in the smallcraft circling in orbit high above the moon, preparing to venture once more into the giant planet's upper atmosphere to obtain yet another sampling for analysis.

As she walked toward the hut she shared with her mate and two small ones, Lanshana felt the sorrow of loneliness grip her. The burdens of exploration fell unevenly, she thought. How much less painful it must be to depart for alien worlds, to lose oneself in work, than to stay behind and worry. Yet the mate of an engineer could not complain. It would be unseemly, a surrender to selfish despair, and she would not bring shame upon the family of one to whom she had freely given herself, in love and for life.

Soon, the warmth of the rising sun was lifting her spirits, as it lighted the day, and once her small ones arose to greet the day, any feelings of sadness would vanish. She would pass this day as she had passed the others, finding solace in the innocence of the small ones of the village, and fondly dreaming of the warm seas of home.

* * *

```
cc:              143-1329.7
FILE:            Log
ACCESS:          Command.
SECURITY:        Standard
OPERATIONAL STATUS: Normal
LOCATION:        45-872988/gg/yG-9
```

Following layover at Starbase 119, we have crossed into the Neutral Zone, en route to the peace conference at Girshoona. Course is steady at 248/005-s. An unnamed yellow star, marking the Terran border, is three parsecs astern; a red giant, marking the Crutchtan boundary, is seven parsecs ahead, five points to port. Local skies are clear of debris.

Morale on board remains high. Routine nature of our duties has let me increase liberty time, and Ambassador Grant's party has done much to boost spirits—so much so that I am considering placing limits on fraternization between his people and mine. I have my doubts, but Cmdr. Ashton has persuaded me to wait a few more days, to see if informal "admonitions" to some of the less discreet crewmen will solve the problem. For my own part, I have found the Ambassador himself to be a valuable source of information on the aliens, and more than willing to share his books and reference materials with me. Between his insights and my own more limited ones, we should both be prepared for whatever awaits us among the aliens on Girshoona—although the Ambassador still deflects my inquiries about other members of the Consortium, leading me to wonder more and more about the true nature of our mission.

Tomorrow, we will come to that portion of the Neutral Zone under alien control, and will pass into Crutchtan skies the following day. But except for the scenery, and the mystery of sailing through unfamiliar skies, the trip promises to be uneventful. The Crutchtans have promised to steer us clear of most turbulence, and we will be following their navigation beacons all the way to Girshoona. Still, I am told that the storms along the Cloud make those of Western Terra seem like a Spring drizzle on Isis. Time will show if the Crutchtans are as bad as we are at predicting interstellar weather, or whether they are even worse.

Capt R Cook

* * *

"ENTER."

Cook looked up from his work to see Ensigns Mathison and Blount leading a small group of young bluebirds into his office. Messy as ever, his office desk was covered with charts and reports, most of which he had not the slightest intention of reading. Smiling, he leaned back in his chair and watched as they marched up to his desk to stand at rigid attention.

"Permission to speak freely, sir?" asked Mary.

"Of course, Ensign," Cook replied. "At ease, all of you. What's on your mind?"

Looking uncertainly about, Mary swallowed and resolved to say her piece. "Captain, several of us wish to lodge a protest."

"A protest? Against whom?"

"Well," interjected Blount, "it's not against anyone in particular."

"Actually, Captain, it's against the way we're being treated."

"By whom?"

"By— " Mary paused, taken aback by the captain's stern gaze. "Actually, by everybody."

"Everybody?"

"We are ignored and barely tolerated," Mary continued, "by nearly everybody on board. The greenshirts routinely disobey our orders. The enlisted men leer at us whenever we walk by. Even the senior officers treat us as if we weren't there."

"Senior officers treat everyone as if they aren't there."

"All the same, Captain— "

"Well, what have you ladies done yourselves to remedy the situation?" Cook asked.

Mary looked puzzled. "I'm afraid I don't— "

"And what do you want me to do about it?" Hands locked behind his head, Cook smirked as he rocked in his chair. "Issue an order telling everyone on board to be nice to you?"

"You might tell everyone that bluebirds are entitled to the same respect as any officers," Blount interjected.

"I might," Cook replied, "but I won't." Sitting upright, Cook met the angry eyes of the junior officers with his own stern and uncompromising gaze.

"First of all, everyone already knows that," he continued. "But more importantly, respect isn't a birthright. If it isn't earned, it isn't real. You volunteered for the service, and I suspect that none of you is a babe in the woods when it comes to dealing with men. Every human being has his own cross to bear, and every officer comes with a unique set of problems as well as gifts. In your case, you can't simply wave a magic wand and repeal human nature, or turn boorish crewmen into gentlemen and saints. But if you can't deal with an oversexed crewman, or you feel intimidated by your own subordinates, how should I expect you to react when you're on convoy duty and pirates start taunting you over the radio? How are you going to command the respect and obedience of people you haven't learned to handle, if and when you finally do get a ship of your own? And how are you going to lead your crew out of danger when lives are on the line and everyone around is blaming you for screwing up? I won't be there to solve those problems for you, then—and I can't help you now.

"No," he said, rising from his chair. "If anyone assaults you or threatens you, I'll toss him in the brig and do what I can to see him drummed out of the service. As for the rest, this is a problem you have to solve on your own. Now, if you have any other complaints, I'll be glad to listen to them. If not, I have work to do. And it looks like you people have a bit of your own, as well."

Cook watched as the sulking ensigns left his office. Plopping back onto his chair, he let out a groan. Men and women, he thought. It had been untold centuries since the Garden of Eden, and after all that time they still drove each other crazy. Keep the girls away altogether, and the men bayed like wolves; toss them together, and the women whined like kittens. It was something every commander had to deal with.

And it never seemed to change.

* * *

FOUR HOURS LATER, from the depths of a sound sleep, the buzzer from the intercom exploded in the captain's brain. Half-awake, he struggled toward the noise, his primordial instincts urging him to find and destroy the source of the irritation. Stirring toward consciousness, the rest of his brain began to focus on his surroundings, and he started groping for the transmit button on the console near his bed.

"Cook here," he slurred, his voice heavy with sleep.

"This is Dexter, on the bridge."

Dexter's voice was the last sound he wanted to hear, and Cook winced. His eyes were drooping and would not focus, his muscles refused to move, and his mind longed to drift in a sea of blissful oblivion. He ached to return to unawareness and every cell in his body cried for rest.

"Go away, Dexter."

"I think you'd better get up here, Skipper."

"Go away, Dexter."

"Right away, I mean."

"I'm sure Mr. Ashton can handle it."

"Not this, he can't. It's the Government. The Government has fallen."

Like a laser piercing the fog, reality shocked Cook's mind into sharp focus. "It just came over the emergency channel, straight from IshCom," continued the young ensign. "The Government has fallen, the Tories are in power— "

"Good God."

" — and Senator Heathcoate is the new President. Not only that, but they've ordered us back to base. IshCom has, that is."

"What?!"

"I—uh—I thought you'd want to know as soon as possible, Skipper. Ishtar Command wants us to return to Starbase 119 and await further instructions. And they want our acknowledgment right away."

In an instant, Cook's thoughts of sleep disappeared. He had no doubt what the Tories had in mind for the peace conference. Heathcoate had long opposed any concessions, and Grant had told him that momentum had long been building in Covington to tie the hands of anyone sent to do the negotiating. Whatever he did, he knew that he'd be called to account, if not by his superiors, then by his own conscience. There seemed to be no way out.

"What's our position?"

"Virtually unchanged, sir. Two parsecs from the Crutchtan border. Course steady, and cruising at C-12."

"All right, page Ambassador Grant and have him meet me in my office in five minutes. In his pajamas, if need be."

"Yes, sir."

"And don't let a word of this leave the bridge. Not until I authorize it myself."

"Aye aye."

As he signed off, Cook found his mind racing, and his heart pounding. Life was so complicated, he thought, because people could be such fools. For the longest time, all he could do was stare at the ceiling, rubbing his eyes in his hands and shaking his head.

Chapter 17

O H—I'M SORRY."

Her cheeks streaked with dried tears, Suzie Yang looked up and visibly started. The President—he would remain the president until noon, she kept telling herself—smiled gently and closed the door behind him. The walls, empty now that the pictures and wall hangings were packed into boxes, seemed to swallow the two of them.

"I didn't mean to disturb you, Miss Yang," he said. "I just came by to say goodbye. And to thank you for all you've done."

"Mr. President...."

She felt the tears welling in her eyes, but was determined not to cry.

"That's all right," he said quietly. Suzie was surprised to find him taking things so well. It was almost, she thought, as if he were relieved that it was over. "I suppose that this will make your life less complicated," he continued.

"I never complained."

"So you didn't, but it can't have been easy for you." He reached into his pocket and pulled out a small paperweight, a stone from his native Athena, flat on one side, smoothed and polished until it shined, with the presidential seal etched into its rounded surface. Suzie had seen it often, lying on his desk, employed to keep his briefing papers from flying all over the room.

"They'll be other mementoes," said Sarkisian, handing her the paperweight. "My secretary is arranging for a letter of thanks, and you'll have your nameplate, of course. I imagine there will be other things, too. But I want you to have this, because I think it best represents your contribution to what we've tried to do these last few years. The paper never did seem to end, did it?"

Managing a weak smile, Suzie shook her head. "Thank you, Mr. President." She took the gift and turned it over in her hand. Sadness was welling up inside her again. She'd never lost a job before, and losing this way made her feel helpless. She looked up, only to see the president looking about the room like someone who'd quite forgotten what he was searching for.

"I must see so many people," he said, in a soft whisper. "So very many."

Suzie noticed that he seemed preoccupied, hiding his feelings of betrayal behind the shock of yesterday's no-confidence vote, and the desertion of so many he counted among his allies.

"And I would have preferred a less hurried departure," he continued, regaining his bearings.

"I understand, sir. We all do."

The President smiled sadly and nodded. "Any plans, Miss Yang?" he said, after a long pause.

"Not really, it being so sudden and all. I suppose I'll go back to my old job. If they're still holding it for me, that is."

"They've been so anxious to get you back they probably planned this whole thing."

They both laughed nervously.

"How about you, Mr. President?"

Sarkisian's eyes filled with a distant look that Suzie had come to see frequently in the recent past. Slowly, he shook his head. "Fishing," he said softly. "My plans extend no further than that, Miss Yang. Going back home—trying to make up for lost time with Mrs. Sarkisian—and fishing."

Without another word, but with a faint mist in his eyes, the President of the Terran League took Suzie's hand, kissed it, and gave it a paternal squeeze. Then he left, and as the door slowly swung itself shut, Suzie felt the tears welling in her eyes once more.

ON THE Hill, another door in the Senate Building was slamming shut.

"Schiller!"

Nicholas Schiller rose to his feet, pale as a sheet. He wasn't used to people shouting at him first thing in the morning. All around the room were boxes stuffed with books and papers. He'd have to leave it to someone else to finish packing for him. By the end of the day, he intended to claim his own office in the Executive Mansion. For now, it looked like his hands would be full.

"I want somebody's head for this. Do you hear me, Schiller? Somebody's going to pay dearly."

As the shock of Hollenbach's entrance passed, Schiller found it ironic that it was up to him to keep Earth's senior senator from losing control of his temper. Up until the final vote, Hollenbach's was the only steady hand among the lot of them, on either side of the aisle. Now, it was all he could do to keep the Earther from screaming.

"Now calm down, Emerson. It's not over yet."

"It may as well be."

"My contacts assure me—the word's gotten out. We caught them in time."

"Your contacts are as useful as tits on a statue."

"Central Command knows which side its bread is buttered on, Emerson. They'll play ball—at least, those with sense enough to look up to find the sky."

"They're not the ones who worry me, Schiller."

"But the ceremony is just a formality," Schiller sighed, exasperated. "The civil authority has already transferred and Sarkisian is just a caretaker. Even if he tried, he couldn't countermand our directives."

"And if they don't turn—if they just keep— "

"Impossible. CosGuard's already issued the order."

Mollified, but not convinced, Hollenbach walked toward the west wall. Papers and charts, arrayed haphazardly, covered the conference table. Hollenbach and Schiller removed their jackets, and sat down across from each other. Even amid the chaos of a change in government, there was work to be done.

"Well," Hollenbach grunted, "let's get down to business—Mr. Chief of Staff."

Schiller grinned through narrowed eyes. "You've brought your list—to add to the rest?"

Hollenbach reached into his vest pocket and removed two folded pieces of paper. "You've brought your veto stamp?"

Schiller laughed. "I guess things may need a few adjustments," he replied.

* * *

"WELL, LIEUTENANT?"

"Still no confirmation, sir."

Admiral Clay grunted; his executive aide scratched his head. Nearly four cosmic hours had passed since they'd issued the order, plenty of time for Cook to respond. Neither of them liked ordering him back. Like most of the Guard, they had little love for the new regime. This alien business aside, all the Tories ever wanted to do was cut the Cosmic Guard's budget. And with echoes from Heathcoate's rattling sabers still resonating along the frontier, it would be harder than ever to keep the civilians in line. But they had no choice. Until the ship finished crossing the Neutral Zone, the Government was within its rights to recall its ambassador. Whatever they thought of their new president, the recall order came straight from Central Command.

"What's his position?" asked Admiral Mohassan.

The dispatcher pressed the data button and looked at the console.

"Less than one light-year from the border," she said. "At present speed, they'll cross into Crutchtan space in twenty-five cosmic minutes."

Clay sighed deeply. Twenty-five cosmic minutes and Cook would be in defiance of a direct order. No matter what happened at the peace conference, his career would be over. The Guard—Clay's Guard, in any event—tolerated quite a bit from its starship skippers. One thing they could not tolerate was flagrant insubordination.

Suddenly, the dispatcher leaned forward in her chair.

"Message from the d'Artagnan."

"Let's have it."

"It's in code, Admiral, for you on the security scrambler,'eyes-only' prefix."

"Well, print it out."

Clay typed his security code into the computer and placed his right thumb on the visual scanner. As they waited for the printer to unscramble the communiqué, he looked at his aide, who only returned his confused shrug. When the blue light signaled that the decryption was complete, Mohassan removed it from the hopper at his boss' instance, only to laugh when he read it.

"Let me see that," Clay said gruffly, taking the single printed page into his own hands.

It read:

```
///II/PRIORITY DISPATCH/
   CC:         143-1347.7/
   TO:         FtAdmPorterMClay/
   FROM:       CaptRCook/
   SECURITY:   CodeBlue/
   PREFIX:     Eyes-only
   FLAGS:      red1;red2;red3/
```

Malfunctioning subspace communications equipment has apparently caused interference with your last communication. Only priority code came through clearly, with a garbled message about our mission and what appears to be an order that our computers cannot decipher with any reasonable degree of certainty.

Our repairs now appear complete, and I request that you repeat your last transmission. However, while our low-wave channels remain unaffected, I cannot guarantee an accurate reception on any medium-wave channel, due to insufficient testing. I do, however, recognize that time is of the essence, as we are nearing the Crutchtan border and hence the limit of civilian authority to order our return.

You are welcome to transmit a low-frequency signal, which I am certain we will receive—or risk another medium-frequency transmission, at your pleasure. As I am sailing under your personally sealed orders, I will await your personal confirmation code to confirm any command.

   Capt R Cook

"Son of a bitch," Clay chuckled, turning to wink at his chief of staff. "He's one smart, wily bastard, isn't he?"

"He is clever," grinned Mohassan. "But that does leave it up to you."

Clay looked at the dispatcher, who was starting to look rather skeptical. "The *d'Artagnan* didn't receive our last message," Clay explained, with a wink toward his chief of staff. "It was garbled in transmission— "

"A glitch in the medium-wave receiver," added Mohassan.

"So we'll need you to repeat the transmission, Lieutenant. Word for word, once it comes off the scrambler. But low-frequency this time. To be on the safe side. Their low-wave receiver is still receiving."

"The whole message? In dits and dots? It takes nearly a minute to transmit a single letter. It that rate, it'll take about an hour, Admiral. They'll be well inside— "

"Just do the best you can, Lieutenant."

"Aye aye, Admiral."

"Well," added Mohassan, "maybe you should also transmit a request to respond on the medium range channel. Just in case, you know. To be on the safe side. In case their receiver is actually working now."

"Good thinking, Tom," Clay chuckled. It was just like his chief aide to think of a finishing touch like that. Every station along the way would document the problems they were having, in case someone started asking questions. "If *d'Artagnan* responds, then we can broadcast the return order at once."

"— and if she doesn't?" asked the dispatch officer.

"Well," said Mohassan, his eyes gleaming mischievously, "then at least we've done our best."

"And Lieutenant, call me when you're almost done broadcasting. The order I mean, not the medium-wave request," added Clay. He and his aide turned and walked toward the door.

"I'll be sure to include my confirmation code with the order."

"I hope that wasn't what glitched the first transmission," laughed Mohassan.

"Well," winked Clay, "I guess we'll never really know, will we?"

* * *

"...TOWARD A different dream— a dream of hope and not of fear; of the future, and not of the cold, dim past; and of the misty vision of limitless horizons, and not the sterile limits of a withering and dying civilization. For if the mistakes of the last few years have taught us anything...."

The Senate gallery was overflowing. Bright red bunting draped across the facing of the second deck, where the public and press had gathered to listen to their new president. The press boxes overflowed with journalists, and the public seats were packed with Tory well-wishers and supporters. Even the Senate floor was filled to capacity, and each senator feared missing the chance to be interviewed after the inaugural speech. Prominently displayed over the speaker's podium and anywhere else in the cameras' line of sight, on order of the new president's chief of staff, was the Terran flag, a five-pointed golden star on a sky blue field.

"If the future holds anything, it holds a promise, one for which we are the solemn trustees. Our children—and their children—will someday follow the trails that we are blazing for them. Today, it is not only their small, innocent hands that we hold in our own. It is their fate—their destiny—that rests in our clumsy, oversized hands. And it is our courage, our foresight, and our weary but loving shoulders, that must carry them into the uncertain future that awaits us all.

"You know, the other day my own granddaughter said something to me that I'd like to share with you today. She's a bright little girl, you know, just like...."

Shifting and fidgeting in his front row seat, Earth's senior senator was finding it hard to pay attention. Out of the range of most cameras, and visibly impatient, he was waiting for a page to deliver a message of principal interest to himself and to the man sitting next to him. But Schiller, the man beside him, was not helping matters by trying to keep the senator calm. And the speaker was only aggravating things by prattling on and on when there was work to be done. And backsides to kick into gear.

"For it has always been this way, from the early light of prehistory, through the dawning of civilization, to the present day. Mankind has always struggled to overcome the odds, inch by inch, footstep by frightened, trembling footstep. We've accomplished miracles, but only by daring to dream. And it's never been enough for us to say...."

Finally, the overdue page came, bearing a single piece of paper. Gruffly, the senator snatched it from the girl's grasp, dismissing her with an angry wave of his hand. As he read it, his jaw locked like a steel trap. The Senate chamber was erupting in cheers as he crumpled the paper and dropped it on the floor. Then, he joined in the applause. A tight smile was on his lips, but his eyes stared straight ahead, cold as death.

Inconspicuously, as the applause crescendoed and the new president nodded and smiled regally, the president's new chief of staff reached onto the senate floor to recover the paper. As everyone in the chamber stood, grandly cheering Terra's new president, Schiller smoothed the wrinkles and read the message. The cheers in the Senate swelled into the first full-bodied ovation in a decade, and the two men exchanged words as the rest of Terra hailed their new leader.

"It's not the end of the world," said Schiller, in a voice barely audible over the applause. "We'll meet tomorrow and send new instructions to Grant. Something we can live with."

Hollenbach took the paper from the new chief of staff and reread it: "*D'Artagnan* crossed into alien skies at 143-1348.0," the message read. "Recall message never received; order to return garbled in transmission."

"It won't do a damn bit of good," the senator said, his teeth tightly clenched. "That sniveling weasel of an ambassador will do whatever he damn well pleases and leave us holding the bag when it blows up."

"Well, it's too late to worry about it now. We can't order them back without looking like fools. The Federalists have made sure of that. They've agreed to a list of protocols a mile long, and we can't change them without insulting the lizards and the rest of the Galaxy as well. As long as CosGuard won't back us up— "

"Yes, we'll make the best of it. You can depend on that. There's too much at stake for us to let our guard down. Even if our own Guard can't see what's in their own best interests."

His hands stinging from the prolonged applause, Hollenbach looked to see a beaming President Heathcoate wave toward the cameras, which in turn were beaming his stately image into homes on every planet in Terra. "I have a list, Schiller, a list of every demand I want our man in Lizardland to make."

"We'll incorporate it into the new instructions."

Hollenbach turned to face Schiller, glaring hatefully. "And I'm going to start another list, Schiller. And at the top of this one, I want the name of that Cozzie captain, the one on that 'Dar-tag-nan' ship. I want his name, and the name of everyone else who helped whisk Grant out from under our noses."

Nodding, Schiller turned to face the new president, who was basking in the glow of attention and approval. Standing proudly before the Terran flag, Heathcoate started waving toward those seated in the front row, as if acknowledging his debt to all of them, and inviting the rest of Terra to join his salute. Before long, Schiller found himself applauding as loudly as anyone in the chamber, and ready to burst with pride.

Chapter 18

cc: 143-1592.7
FILE: Log
ACCESS: Command.
SECURITY: Standard
OPERATIONAL STATUS: Normal
LOCATION: 46-897779/xx/BA-15
We are ninety-five parsecs inside Crutchtan skies. Our course is holding steady at 248/005n, 3.129 ps beyond last entry. Energy level remains constant at C-12; we did, however, ease power by a quarter, to scan and chart the area's dominant feature—a major binary system hidden from Terran instruments by a dense cloud of dust located at 46-883979. This is the current project of the Science Lab—analyzing spectral data from the stars we pass—and I have conscripted the junior officers, as well as myself, to help Lt. Hatfield collect the data.

The Cloud is thickening, and looms large in the distance. The aliens are keeping us well to center of the Cloud, thereby keeping the Cloud beyond range of our sensors. The skies are surprisingly clear of space traffic: since entering Crutchtan skies, we have seen only the single alien craft first mentioned in entry cc:143-1586.1, which has continued to trail us for the last six days. This leads me to wonder whether this is by design, or whether there was a good reason for the Crutchtan's impeccable observation of the agreements establishing the Neutral Zone. In any event, as it appears we can keep a stiffer pace than our friend, I am considering slowing our speed, to let him tag along.

Communications with home are clear, and all channels are remarkably free of static. Aside from the continuing water leak in the women's locker room, routine maintenance is proceeding on schedule. With clear skies ahead, I have the crew maintaining half-shifts—except for the Bridge Crew, of course: we are maintaining our drilling schedule, to keep us from getting rusty. But even the Bridge Crew is finding liberty time ample, and like the others I have much of the day free to read, write, and generally putter about. Even so, I find myself spending most of my free time trying to educate myself

about our future hosts, and wondering exactly what sorts of beings
will greet us when we arrive.
    Capt R Cook

* * *

"I THINK it's ridiculous."

"And I doubt that any of them would tolerate such a thing. You can
expect they'd be running right to the captain. And I bet he'd do
something for *them*. There'd be a repair crew dispatched so quickly—"

"Do you think we should— "

"What good would it do?"

"And who cares about the gym, anyway?

"But it's the principle of the thing, you know. I'm sorry, Mary; what
did you— "

"Look, there's Janet."

"You don't suppose— "

"Well, it might be worth a try."

"For us or for her?"

"I know, I've heard."

"Oh, Sally. "

"Really, now."

"Yes, I know. Aren't we terrible?"

"Janet?"

"—oh, Janet?"

* * *

"...AND I find that awfully hard to believe."

Cook just laughed. Like Jeremy's, his voice was slightly groggy with
drink. "I swear, Jeremy— "

"Nah, no way."

Leaning back against the soft couch cushions, Cook clasped his hands
behind his head and sighed. The observation deck was almost empty.
Aside from the two of them, only a few of the younger redshirts had
gathered to watch their progress through the sky. The plush sofas were
arranged in groups, each group forming twin semi-circles around a coffee
table. Cook and Jeremy were just to the center of the viewing screen,
looking at each other over a half-empty pitcher of beer, their second of
the day. The redshirts were off to one side, just inside the doorway
leading to the elevators, their laughter filling the lounge.

"Well, all right—have it your way, then," Cook laughed.

"I mean," Jeremy squinted, disbelieving, "you can't tell me that you don't have some magic tricks— "

"No, none."

"—to help you pull all the stunts you pull on the bridge."

"I swear. Well, actually...."

"Aha!"

"No, but really. All of that stuff is just showing off. You know, parlor tricks. Nothing magic about it."

Jeremy snorted. "Like correcting course headings because they 'don't look right?' "

Cook started laughing.

"Or telling McKenzie exactly how much she's off by 'this time'—then making the changes on her screen for her while discoursing on the literary styles of various playwrights and poets none of us have ever heard of before?"

"All right, I guess you've— "

"Or snapping your fingers just as the ready light flashes on Palmer's weapons screen?"

"How does showing off— "

"Psshh— "

"But it means nothing."

"I'll tell you what it means. It means that you've got more tricks up your sleeve than a stage magician. That, or you're one of the great geniuses of all time."

"Nonsense."

"*Skipper*...."

"Well," Cook leaned forward, smiling mysteriously and lowering his voice. "I may have some gifts for navigation— "

"That's sure an understatement."

"— but it has nothing to do with intelligence. Nothing at all. And there are no tricks to it, Jeremy. None."

"You know, if you don't want to tell me...."

The captain shook his head, then turned toward the viewer, his eyes looking beyond the stars and into the endless Black. "I don't understand it myself," he said at last. "But for as long as I can remember, I've just—well, it's a lot like having perfect pitch."

"Look, if you really don't want to explain."

"It's either there—or it's not," Cook went on. "With pitches…well, I just hear the tone. It comes out of nowhere and it's just there for me, any time, any place. There's nothing you can do about it. Well, I can't explain how I navigate, either. I just do. I just know the course to take. I can feel it in my brain. And I can see it, too. I can close my eyes, and sense it—on the screen, in the air, like it's floating in space, just waiting for me to come along and grab it. All I do is let my mind relax… and it comes. I don't have to do anything. It just comes. And I'll tell you—

He turned to face his first officer and smiled. Maybe it was the beer, Jeremy thought. But for the first time, Jeremy wondered whether, for all the captain's cocky self-confidence, Cook was as baffled by his own gifts as anyone else.

"I'll tell you something I've told to exactly one other person—whose name is none of your damn business, Jeremy Ashton. But sometimes I wonder how long it can last. How long before it just stops coming. How long before my mind goes blank, just when everyone needs me the most."

Cook emptied his beer glass with a long deep swallow, then leaned back on the couch and looked again out toward the stars. "That's why it's nothing more than parlor tricks and never will be, either. I don't know how or why I can do it. I just can.

"But whatever it is that makes me the skipper I am—whatever lets me sense things before they happen, or compute course changes in my head—has nothing to do with training, or intelligence, or anything else that promotion boards or military manuals or logical minds consider in making promotions or assignments or any other command decisions. I could have the mind of a child and I'd still see things the same way."

"And I'll bet you have some swamp land on Isis to sell me, if I believe that one," snorted Jeremy.

"Then don't, dammit," laughed Cook, turning to face his friend once again. "Have another beer instead."

"Whooshh! Whooshh!"
"Scooter—Scooter! Don't play with the wheel like that."
"Andrew, there's no need to shout."
"But he'll— "
"The ship's on automatic pilot, son. Nothing he does can throw us off course. Relax."

Andy Cook shook his head and smiled. Dad was right again. Though awfully precocious for a four-year old, the young boy couldn't really hurt the ship. Andy could see the Paddington Shoals coming into view again on the screen, the spiraling patch of interstellar rocks guarding what his father called "Paddy's Pass." They'd be coming about soon, and heading back home.

"*All right—all hands to the control deck. It's time to come about.*"

"*Thank God.*"

"*Andrew Thomas Cook, what kind of example are you setting for your firstborn?*"

"*Pop, please—* "

"*All right, all right. But I want to show you something.*"

Andy followed his father back to the control deck. "*Okay, Scooter, time to let the grownups play with the controls.*"

"*But—but Daddy!*"

"*Scooter.*"

"*Oh, he'll be all right, Andrew.*"

"*Pop—* "

"*Come on, Roscoe, want to sit on old Grandpa Tom's lap?*"

"*Yeah!*"

"*Pop!*"

"*You having fun, Roscoe?*"

"*Lots of fun.*"

"*You like it up here?*"

"*Yeah! Like a woller coaster!*"

"*Oh—a roller coaster! Did you hear that, Andrew? And it is like a bit of a roller coaster, now, isn't it, you little monkey?*"

As Scooter laughed under a ruthless barrage of tickling, Andy gave it up. His father was having too much fun. And he couldn't really blame him: Dad loved sailing. He was an accomplished pilot in his day and never lost his love of the stars, but for the last fifteen years he'd had to do it alone. Now, with the new generation, he had hope, and was taking full advantage of the chance. He'd taken Scooter sailing as often as Andy would let him. And even as a toddler, the young boy had loved it.

Andy looked at them—grandfather and first grandson, sailing together through the stars, sharing secrets and dreams. It was so touching, he always felt guilty when he had to insist that they go home.

"You remember what I told you about the controls, Roscoe?"

"Yeah." The boy nodded his head. "Well, some of it."

"Some of it—good boy. But you remember all about steering the ship, and coming about."

"Yeah."

"All right—watch this Andrew; I've been working with him. And he's awfully good. A lot better than you ever were. But then, so's his teddy bear."

"Thanks a lot, Pop."

Tom laughed. "Roscoe, you want to guess what course we should take to get back home?"

"Okay."

Andy shook his head. His father had tried the same game with him, trying to get him interested in where they were going. It was fun for a while, seeing how close the two of them could come to the proper course before checking it on the navigational computer, but it was utterly pointless. As good a navigator as Dad was, even he had trouble coming within twenty points of their true heading just by dead reckoning. Andy was lucky to come within a hundred, and he was convinced that it was the biggest single reason why sailing through space scared the wits out of him. All that kept them from getting lost was a finicky electronic brain, one that the weakest ion squall could send fritzing, leaving them to wander about from here to the end of creation.

"All right, Roscoe... how do we get back home?"

Andy chuckled as Scooter crinkled his little brow, the way he did when he was thinking as hard as he could.

"Do you remember what we did to get here?"

The boy nodded.

"Well, just take us back the other way."

"Pop— "

"Acchhh!" said Tom, waving his hand disdainfully at his son.

"That way," said Roscoe.

Andy laughed, more at his father's crestfallen look than at his son's mistake. His face all serious, Scooter was pointing just off the port bow—and halfway toward the keel. But that was exactly the opposite direction from Isis. Even a groundtoad like Andy knew that home lay west of the Shoals.

"*Good boy,*" *chuckled Andy.* "*I'll bet you hit that one right on the nose.*"

"*Well, run along, Roscoe,*" *said Tom, hiding his disappointment from his grandson.* "*You go play astern. We'll take it from here.*"

Scooter skipped playfully down the gangplank and into the hall. Andy watched his father's hands dance over the controls. The old man mumbled to himself as he set the ship's computer to take a fix on the navigational beacon orbiting Isis.

"*Son of a gun—you know, that kid's smart, Andrew,*" *Tom said at last.* "*Real smart. He wants to know about everything. And he usually does so well. I don't understand…I just don't understand.*"

"*Guess he just inherited his father's instincts for sailing. Must be something in the genes.*"

The two of them laughed, and Andy just sat back and watched his father in action. It always amazed him: at home, Dad could barely fix a leaky faucet. In space, he was a different man—calm, collected, supremely sure of himself. It gave Andy a sense of relief to know he could trust his father to get them home safely. Today, though, the feeling didn't last very long.

"*That's impossible.*"

"*What is?*"

"*We couldn't have turned ourselves around that much.*"

"*Pop—what is it?*"

His father looked up, half-worried, but with a look of burning curiosity in his eyes. "*The computer says that we're coming at the Shoals from the East.*"

"*What?*"

"*She says we've been clear around them…and we're already heading West, toward home.*"

"*Impossible.*"

They looked at the course indicator.

"*Heading to Isis,*" *it read:* "*790x122 south.*" *Looking at the pilot's display, the guide marker showed their proper relative course—just off the port bow, and almost half-way toward the keel. They looked at each other, then back at the course indicator, then at each other again.*

Then, ever so slowly, they turned to look aft. For the longest time, they did nothing but watch a small boy play with his toy dinosaurs on the cabin floor.

* * *

"HERE SHE COMES."

"Janet, over here!"

"What do you think?"

"Let's just wait until— "

"Well? What did he say?"

"I know what I'd answer him."

"Well?"

"Now hold on there. Let me— "

"Did he— "

"Yes...yes he did. It's all set."

"He did?"

"Yes, starting tomorrow, or the next day. It'll be posted."

"Well, that's a relief."

"It certainly took long enough, that's what I think."

"What if nobody shows up?"

"Wait a minute. Janet, what if— "

"Well, that's *your* problem."

"Janet? Janet...."

"— come back here. Janet— "

"I might have known."

"Really, now."

* * *

THE THREE MEN were seated in Cook's office: Jeremy, Cook, and Ambassador Grant. As usual, Cook and Grant were doing most of the talking. And, as usual, Jeremy was trying his best to follow their conversation. It was, he thought, a thoroughly hopeless undertaking.

"What I don't understand is their family structure."

"From what I gather," said Cook, patting the top of a book on the table next to his chair, "they have none."

Ambassador Grant leaned forward in his chair, but Cook interrupted before he could speak.

"Well," the captain raised his index finger and smiled, "not in our sense. Or even in the Crutchtan sense, with the tribal unit serving to extend the nuclear family."

"In fact," Grant nodded, "Crutchtan civilization does revolve around the tribe—or clan, as the unit of social organization, though in many respects, their society is quite similar to ours. More male-dominated perhaps, but by and large, surprisingly similar. And much more like ours than I would have believed only a few short years ago. The Veshnans, on the other hand, do remain something of a puzzle."

"Are we boring you again, Jeremy?" Cook smiled.

Startled to alertness, Jeremy sat upright in his chair.

"Well—, " he began, feeling quite lost in the surrounding fog of alien sociology.

"I really find it hard to understand them," Grant interjected. "The Veshnan family, I mean."

"It's just different," said Cook, "in part because their families don't look like families to us. In fact their word for it— "

Cook squinted, trying to remember the phrase.

" — 'glasenalia,' I think it was, or something like that—translates loosely into our word for 'harem.' "

Grant arched his eyebrows; Jeremy simply laughed.

"At least, that's what Zatar's translator told me. A Veshnan *glasenalia*' usually consists of sisters and cousins. Females, usually related by blood, though the degree of relationship varies from family to family. And that structure forms the basis of Veshnan society."

"And their men?"

"As I understand it, the way their chromosome structure works means that roughly one of every eight births is a male. Their men are bigger and stronger than the women, but there are far fewer of them. And apparently, they are—well—adopted by the females of a family. At least until he wears out his welcome. Or—well, whatever."

"Like the dominant male in a pride of lions," ventured Grant.

"Exactly. Well, more or less, anyway. And as with the lions, in Veshnan prehistory the females did most of the real work—the hunting, gathering, and the rest. The men, on the other hand, became so used to doing nothing that—well—it's sort of a tradition they carry to the present."

"And that's probably why," Grant said, thinking aloud, "Veshnan males tend to lag behind their females in material achievements."

"They've never really had to work," agreed Cook. "And so they developed other—well—justifications for their existence. And other—contributions, in the broadest sense of the word—to Veshnan culture."

"Then, how do we explain Zatar?"

"A prominent exception to the rule," smiled Cook. "Or a prominent extension...I'm not really in a position to say."

Grant laughed roguishly, while Cook just shrugged. By this time, Jeremy was hopelessly lost. "I think I'm needed on the bridge," the first officer said, rising to his feet. Before he could leave, the door to the office flew open, and in walked several of the angriest women Jeremy had ever seen.

"Captain Cook!" Ensign Mathison began, her voice as cold as the depths of space.

"Yes," Cook cut her off. "I know. I heard."

"Well," muttered Sally Grissom. "What— "

Cook's hands fluttered over his computer console and within seconds the printer had handed him a slip of paper. "Here," he said, handing the paper to Mathison, "give this to Cindy in the outer office. She'll make copies and you can post them on the bulletin board yourselves."

"Captain— "

"Yes, I'm sorry. And if it happens again— "

"It had better not."

"Yes, Miss Blount. I couldn't agree more."

The women left the office, and Jeremy burst out laughing. Cook leaned back in his chair, shaking his head.

"What— ?" began the ambassador.

"Repair problems," Cook explained, with a nod of his head that told the Ambassador that it was all the explanation he was likely to get.

"But why on Earth— "

"And speaking of families," Cook interjected, in the grand manner of speech that he used whenever he wanted to change the subject, "I don't think I ever told you about my Uncle Cornelius."

"Not in the last ten minutes, at least."

"Thank you, Jeremy, but I was going to tell you about his efforts in his first campaign for public office."

"I stand corrected. That's been...what would you say, Ambassador? Fifteen minutes?"

"More or less."

"It was late Spring, you see—just after the Founders' Day holidays...."

* * *

```
              INTRA-SHIP MEMORANDUM No. 143-455
CC:          143-1688.3
FROM:        The Captain
TO:          THE CREW
SUBJECT:     Clarification of ISM 143-454
```

It has been brought to my attention that some members of the crew have chosen to misconstrue the directives contained in my last Intra-Ship Memorandum.

My purpose in granting the women use of the Men's Locker Room was to permit them to use the Gym while their own facilities are undergoing repairs. I did not intend to establish a "shower-room show time" for the entertainment of the men.

Therefore, until further notice, all men on this ship are BANNED from the Men's Locker Room from 200-350 Hours each day. Violations will be dealt with severely.

* * *

THE WEEKS passed quickly; and soon, the *d'Artagnan* was within days of the Crutchtan planet. But rather than nearing Girshoona with the usual giddiness of spacers barreling in to port, the crew found itself facing the last week of their long journey with all hands at stations and the ship standing at Red Alert.

"Mr. Ashton?"

"The storm's a beauty, Captain. Scores a full seven points on Wagner's Scale, heading out from the promontory off toward port—and it's holding right on our heels. Sensors reporting electrical surges already. Green Double A-Class binary dead ahead."

The bridge was calm and orderly. Battling an ion storm was like fighting an enemy. Coolness of mind was the watchword; keeping a level head was the biggest challenge. Yet there was one big difference between a major squall and a human foe. The squall could be just as deadly, but had no real interest in destroying its opponent. For now, the captain's biggest job would be keeping everyone's mind on the job at hand, rather than on the danger swirling off the port beam. For the rest, they had to trust their experience, as well as their ship.

"Deactivate all nonessential electrical equipment," said Cook. "We don't want to serve as a lightning rod for the storm."

"Acknowledged," said Jeremy, his eyes glancing over the sensor monitors at his station desk. "I've already given the word. Just waiting for confirmation from all decks."

"Miss Palmer?"

"Weapons blanked; running shields holding steady."

"Mendelson, prepare to slow to sublight. McKenzie, as soon as we enter the star system, plot a course for the fifth planet from the leeward sun on the ancillary navigation screen. It should be on the data chart we got from the Crutchtans. The system's massive enough to shield us from the storm, and our hosts tell me that the target planet has enough plant life to sport an oxygen atmosphere. It's a bit rocky and rather dry, and sounds more like Ishtar than I care to imagine. But once we've put into orbit, at least we can molly down to stretch our legs a bit. And I think we may need it. Looks like we'll be there for a while."

"Hope our friend makes it," smiled Jeremy, nodding his head toward the rear viewer.

Cook swung his chair around to look astern, though nothing was close enough to be visible except on their long-range sensors. For weeks, they'd had no company but the single alien ship, trailing behind them. In all directions, for as far as their sensors could see, no other Crutchtan ship had come within sensor range.

From the ends of nowhere it had come, matching their course and heading exactly, as if following them to the alien homeland. Twice it neared to within sensor range, only to shy away when the Terran ship ventured a friendly hail. Then, with no advance notice, came the storm, and the trials of the small Crutchtan vessel proved a source of sympathy and fascination for the Terran captain. Starfarers shared a common bond that transcended all their differences, and for spacers of all races an ion storm was more than a passing concern. At flank speed, the alien was racing toward a neighboring star system, one with a dim red dwarf at its center, barely enough to provide cover from the squall, but within sprinting distance for the tiny craft.

"Entering gravitational limits of target stars," announced Jeremy. "Outer particulate belt passing below; we'll intersect the bi-solar plane in ten minutes. Power surges increasing; all decks report systems secure, power levels at minimum failsafe."

"Helm—slow to one-half light and arc full a-bank to starboard, heading 395 by 22 north," Cook said, still looking into the empty space astern. "We're almost out of danger, now. We've no reason to try setting speed records or go racing down to orbit. I doubt that the Crutchtans would be impressed, and they aren't close enough to notice, anyway."

"Aye, sir."

As the *d'Artagnan* came about and began descending toward the orbital plane of the host star, Cook turned to face the main viewer and the task at hand. The storm was slamming into the stiff solar wind of the binary. From here until they crossed the backwash, the magnetic cross-currents would be treacherous. He could wonder about their alien shadow later. For the moment, the storm and the ship needed his full attention.

Chapter 19

"A YIEE —*CATASTROPHE!*" WAILED Ra'Henl, the Grand Foodmaster of the Governor's Palace. As he spoke, he began to pant like an overworked beast of burden. "All our preparations—ruined. The cakes and pastries and—and all the perishables will—rot in the meantime. We must start anew—and—and— !"

Ra'Henl drank greedily from the water vessel brought by his First Apprentice. The tables of the Preparation Room were dusted with flours. Spices and sugars lined the shelves. Newly sharpened tools lay scattered over the floor, where Ra'Henl had dropped them upon hearing the news.

"Well, perhaps it is just as well," he said, calming himself for the moment. His hands fluttered about him in a fervid display of nervousness. "Perhaps this is a boon of Fate."

"What are you saying? That your servants are not up to the task?" asked his apprentice, ls'Shen. In the last few cycles, ls'Shen had become accustomed to a certain volatility on the part of his master. Such as Ra'Henl were rare among the *g'Khruushtani*. They were artists of their craft, and artists often lacked the basics of self-control. It was the price they paid for their gifts and vision. As best he could, ls'Shen purged his mind of such patronizing thoughts. He bore much affection for the kindly old foodmaster. But more than this, Shen did not wish to be called to account by one suffering from an excess of emotion.

Ra'Henl frowned. The younger generation would never understand, he sighed. And they took affront so easily—though only days before, his whole staff was in a state of alarm, wondering how they could finish the preparations in time.

"No, Son of Shenchi. Even for Chosen Ones, you have all distinguished yourselves. But this is a Royal Feast! A Royal Feast, do you understand? And for a Royal Feast, much is expected. The smallest detail must not go unnoticed. Or else—or else—*Catastrophe!*"

"Yes, Grand One."

"And you have seen the guest list, have you not? Is there any doubt but that the smallest slight will provoke an outrage, if not a Controversy of State?"

"No, Grand One."

"And now—and now—well, ours is not the work of common laborers, young Shen. Our craft is as delicate as a songbird in flight. And just as helpless before the gullethawks of passing time."

"Yes, Grand One."

"And are we not all servants of the Governor's Palace?"

"Yes, Grand One."

"And have you forgotten upon whom our smallest failing will reflect?"

"No, Grand One."

"So let us not stand here, like a crowd of idling rabble," said Ra'Henl, his hands fluttering still, having worked himself into a proper Fit of Agitation. "Let us make the most of Lady Fortune. Turn her for good instead of ill."

"Yes, Grand One," sighed ls'Shen, watching his master flit about the room like a panicked hen. For a boy with talent and ability, his station was unequaled, and he well knew that he was the envy of all his peers. Still, the passage of time had impressed his young mind with one thing, above all else: life at court was less glamorous than it seemed.

"SO THE Terrans must bide their time like the rest of us."

Drubid ran a finger over his beak-like mouth. The soothing sensations helped the Glincian focus his thoughts. As his lips stretched into a grim smile, a servant filled the two cups on the table with spirits. Drubid wanted his guest's lips to float as freely as her mind. As the two exchanged toasts, he saw that his stratagem might yet yield results. It amused him to think that the surest way to ensure that he spoke alone with the Veshnan solon Zatsami was to suggest that she bring Zatar along with her.

"It should be but a short while," smiled the Veshnan, feeling the glow of intoxicants coursing through her body. "I am told that even now the storm abates. In a few more days, they should resume their course."

"You must be curious about the reason for this meeting."

"Curiosity can be a virtue, Drubid."

"So it can," the Glincian laughed without warmth. "I hope that the differences of our governments will not keep us from talking freely."

Zatsami bowed politely. The lamp on the table threw shadows on the wall. From her pillow, she could see the Glincian's eyes reflect the soft light.

"In the current intrigues in the Crutchtan capital," Drubid continued, after a long pause, "your Government's sympathy for the reform movement is well known."

"Crutchtan intrigues know no season," the Veshnan returned blandly. "Our only interest is that of spectators."

"Of course," the Glincian added hastily. "As allies, we dare not presume to meddle in the affairs of our brother races. But we cannot help but notice the effect of the Terran controversy on our friends."

"Continue," Zatsami said noncommittally, but Drubid sensed that he had piqued her interest.

"I see no quarrel between my people and yours. And between mine and the Crutchtans—well, our real differences are too petty to warrant discussion. But the controversy will continue, as long as it suits the needs of the contenders in the Crutchtan capital."

"Controversy is not unknown in the corridors of the Grand Alliance either, Drubid."

The Glincian laughed a shallow laugh. "There is that old proverb, you know. 'There are disputes that shake the rafters, and disputes that shake the air.' We have as much to lose— "

"And twice as much to gain," smiled the Veshnan.

"Perhaps. But time is on our side, as it is not with the Crutchtan reformers. This is not the first time that one such as Gal'Shenga has risen to prominence. And like the others before him, his efforts will come to nothing, without the kiss of Fate. Or, perhaps, help from friends. Think of it, Solon: he cannot even acknowledge openly what he hopes to achieve, much less seek support for it in the palace halls. And this is the one whom your Government hopes will rise to power?"

"Our hopes have little to do with the Terrans," retorted Zatsami.

"But resolving the controversy quickly will hardly help bring change," smiled Drubid.

The Veshnan was about to respond, but the Glincian silenced her with a outraised hand. "I ask only that you consider the consequences, that is all. We each have our own interests to advance, that I willingly concede. And ours, for the moment, are in conflict with the Crutchtans —that I will grant.

"For now I see no change coming, either from within or without, not under the present circumstances. Yet alter the circumstances, and the future opens like a flower unfolding. Today's paper peace with Terra helps none but Cra'Jenli. But the longer the controversy festers, the more it helps the forces of change. If circumstances limit what we may hope to achieve, why should we decline to achieve what little is permitted?"

Zatsami rose to her feet. "I am indebted to your hospitality," she smiled. "But I have other duties to attend."

"I understand," replied Drubid, and he rose to escort her to the door.

As her footsteps faded into the distance, Drubid rested his head against the wall and breathed deeply of the perfumed air. He had learned what he wanted to know. Zatar aside, Veshna was up to its neck in Crutchtan palace politics. Otherwise, Zatsami would have left the minute he brought up the subject. That was what protocol demanded, and what Veshnan diplomats did as a matter of course in similar circumstances. But Gal'Shenga was no ordinary reformer. His words and deeds sounded deeply in the Veshnan soul; his muted cries for an easing of the Autocracy harkened to the very beginnings of Veshnan civilization. It seemed to him that the Veshnans must be deeply divided on the subject of how to accomplish their ends, torn between their duties as allies and their own parochial philosophies. If his efforts had helped sow confusion among the friends of Crutchta, or tipped the scales to those willing to admit delay in resolving the "Terran Dilemma," then he could count his mission a success.

* * *

IT WAS mid-afternoon, and the courtyard was half in shadow. A gentle breeze stirred the air, carrying the songs of birds from outside the palace gate. Within, the courtyard echoed with nervous footsteps, and worry paced along with Glishenda as she awaited word on one long lost to her home, but not her heart.

"My Lady?"

Glishenda turned with a start, but it was only fl'Shenda, the housemaster.

"Yes, Shendi, what is it?"

"It is Fondro," the servant replied with a bow. "He wishes— "

"Show him to me at once!" Glishenda interjected. "He brings word—oh, I pray it to be so."

"I know not, Lady Glishek," said fl'Shenda, smiling sadly to show he did not take offense at her shortness.

"Oh, I am sorry, fl'Shenda. It is just...."

The old housemaster raised his hand to slow the flood or words, and affection flooded his heart. "I understand, Mistress. And I do share your hopes, My Lady. As in the past, so through the morrow."

Glishenda smiled gratefully. Fl'Shenda had been part of her family since the old days, since long before she came to the House of Galgravina. If nobility were truly in the heart, as philosophers of old had written, then fl'Shenda belonged among the House of the Ages.

"Please, Shenda, bring him to me."

"Yes, My Lady."

As the old man left, Glishenda sighed deeply to regain her composure. She did not wish to show weakness, in case gal'Fondro brought news of tragedy. As she heard the approach of footsteps, her heart filled with foreboding, only to sing with relief when she sensed hope in the soul of gal'Fondro.

"He is safe?"

"The last word is that he is moving toward a safe harbor," smiled gal'Fondro. "There is still danger, but no reason to suppose the worst. We shall not know more until the storm begins to clear."

"What foolishness!" snapped Glishenda, her worry giving way to anger.

"Ga'Glish has a strong sense of duty."

"Duty can rot in the fields. It is no more than pride and foolishness that sends him chasing a ship full of longnoses. And what is the purpose, when the ship is heading straight into port, to circle the heavens in full sight of his home?"

"There is a reason."

"With men there is always a reason," Glishenda laughed tartly, "though 'reason' is hardly the term I would employ for such silliness. It is far too flattering, to my way of thinking."

Gal'Fondro laughed good-naturedly. Glishenda was a woman of many accomplishments, not the least of which was her unerring ability to captivate the men around her while deflating their egos to a manageable size.

"And what of Glishek. Does he still— "

"He professes no concern with the vicissitudes of space," Glishenda said wryly, "though he has developed a sudden interest in monitoring transmissions between *gr'Shuna* and the local skies."

"I imagine he is more worried than he admits."

"Oh, he is another one for foolishness, Fondro, though at his age, I suspect that it is as much habit as anything else. His son's excuse is not as readily apparent."

"I suspect," replied gal'Fondro, amusement flaring his eyes, "that it may be something in the blood."

Glishenda laughed merrily at the jest, and Fondro thought that it had been quite a while since she had shown such good spirits. The mate of a provincial governor could hardly see life as a succession of festivals, and Lady Glishek had known more than her share of sadness.

"Ga'Glishek should hear word of his son," gal'Fondro said at last. "I shall tell him."

"No," interrupted Glishenda. "I shall tell. Ga'Glish is my son, as well. And a mate is permitted liberties with form, even more than an old friend."

Gal'Fondro bowed. "Then I shall be— "

"Yes, I know. Attending to details.

"As in the past— "

" — so through the morrow."

"Yes, and even yet, nothing is ever done to his satisfaction. It is his failing and his strength."

"And his son's as well," laughed Glishenda, reaching to embrace her mate's old friend. "Good bye, Fondro. And may your duties fall as lightly as morning dew."

Gal'Fondro departed, leaving her alone with her thoughts. Soon, she too departed from the courtyard, to walk down the marble corridor leading to the Hallway of Rites and to the Governor's chambers. Her mate was a proud man, she thought, and she would ever thrill in his triumphs as she consoled him through adversity. But Ga'Glish was just as proud, and possessed his own lust for achievement. It was a pity that male pride was so unaccommodating as to preclude two such ones from sharing a common roof, as they shared their bond of blood.

Chapter 20

DAYS PASSED WITH the fitfulness of birds. As the storm raged furiously in the near reaches of the Shunirium, agitation spread throughout *Gr'Shuna*—in the Palace, among those charged with the orderly administration of the Festival of Welcome, but even more so among the populace, whose hearts fretted with curiosity over the approach of the Strange Ones from the west. As Fate had ordained that they play host to strangers, it now mocked their impatience, as if to say that some things were simply beyond the ken of mortals.

Soon word came that the skies were clearing. Before long the streets were filled with anticipation over the arrival of the Strange Ones. Small ones ran about, giddily shouting from one to another: "The longnoses are coming!" they cried, as their parents vainly tried to civilize their young tongues. But as with many things, their words were only echoes of their Elders' innermost thoughts, expressed aloud.

* * *

A LONE gull played in the air currents above the waves as the sea breeze brought relief from the morning sun.

"I hear that Gal'Shenga will arrive tomorrow," said Maguna, Second Translator for the Veshnan delegation to the peace talks. She and Zatar strolled together along a lonely stretch of shore, just east of the City.

Zatar frowned sourly. The last thing he needed was for the Crutchtans to start exploiting the talks for their own partisan advantage. He knew very well that the Terrans were not above such children's games themselves, and the thought that such foolishness might soon infect the *g'Khruushtani* as well did as much for his spirits as a piece of rotten fruit. If this was to be his last bit of work as procurator for the High Council, he wanted to accomplish something. Yet on all sides, events seemed to be conspiring against his efforts to forge an understanding with Terra.

"You look perturbed."

"I do not relish the prospect of dealing with yet another audience," said Zatar. "The yard is already littered with interested parties. Even we, Guna, through our own ministries and departments, have our own particular causes to advance, though I am grateful that they, at least, have the decency to try and hide it from me. But talking to crowds rarely yields worthwhile results. It usually leads to little besides courtyard gossip and mindless posturing. Under the circumstances, it will likely do nothing but confuse the Terrans."

Maguna laughed brightly. "Perhaps Tsami is right, Zatar. Maybe you have been gone too long. You are starting to see ulterior motives behind each blossoming flower. I wonder what other bad habits the simians taught you."

Zatar simply smiled in return.

On they walked, back toward the town, as the sun rose in the sky. Soon, the full force of summer beat upon their brows and they returned to the beaches, where the natives came to sun themselves on the golden sand at the foot of the Palace Dunes.

The Terrans could wait, thought Zatar, as well as the affairs of state. In the glorious sunshine, everything faded like untreated cloth. Before long, they followed the Crutchtan young ones into the warm, salty water, before joining the young ones' elders along the shore, lending a foreign sound to the laughter of their play.

* * *

SOON, DAY became night, and stars dotted the cloudless sky like ripples on the water. On the hills overlooking the sea, sand grasses danced to the breezes of night as waves kissed the timeless shore. To the west, palm trees swayed, gently bending with the soft winds of summer. Everywhere, the fragrances of blossoms filled the air.

Ls'Shen loved the hills at night. The serenity sounded deeply in his soul, and he often came to look at the sky, or the water, or simply to think. There was room enough along the coast for countless ones such as he, who came to seek peace in the night. Though the shore was host to thousands, between the darkness and the broadness of the vista, all could maintain the illusion of solitude.

But tonight was different. Tonight, he had come not for rest or solace. The weariness in his body cried for rest, but his soul had urged him toward the hills. Here, he had a matchless view of the cloudless southern sky. Half-way overhead, heading toward the east, was a light of piercing brightness. The sight spread ripples of awe from his neck down toward his toes, for this was no ordinary satellite passing silently in the night. It knew strange stars and strange skies; and it carried the Terrans.

The first stirring of dawn lighted the east. Ls'Shen narrowed his eyeslits to filter out the thin clouds of sand blown by the gusting wind. He knew that the coming day would be one of excitement. He, himself, would be among the serving party at the Banquet of Welcome, and he wondered about the strange creatures he would see. There was much speculation in the City, but little real knowledge. It was said that the Terran males were bearded beasts, much like the monsters of myth, but with long, drooping snouts that hung to their bellies. Their fierceness as predators was said to be matched only by their hunger for gold, and their appetite for both drove them to seize food or riches like a carrion shark frenzied by the smell of blood.

But ls'Shen scoffed at such thoughts. He had seen many at the Palace who deserved the appellation "Strange One," and none of them wore a simian's countenance. His mind told him that the Terrans would likely prove less fearsome than their features suggested. While his heart cowered at the prospect of meeting such creatures, something in his soul thrilled at the thought. The Terrans were so different, so alien to everything he knew. Their manner of speech, their clothing, the coarseness of their bearing, all promised dissonance with the ordered routine of a *g'Khruushtani* court.

Something about their very difference was exhilarating. Ls'Shen harbored no secret doubts about the ancient ways of the *g'Khruushtani*, but there was a whole Universe lurking beyond the pathways of his land. He watched the Terran ship as it drifted eastward, toward the early light of dawn, a speck of light amid the vastness of the night sky. The cosmos was alive with infinite diversity, thought ls'Shen; and specks of light from alien worlds gave those inclined to dreaming the deepest perspective on the meaning of existence.

He watched the Terran ship continue on its journey until it dropped below the horizon. As he walked back toward the palace, along the crest of the hills, he wondered whether such perspectives might not benefit many of his acquaintances.

* * *

INTRA-SHIP MEMORANDUM No. 143-464

CC: 143-2072.9
FROM: The Captain
TO: THE CREW
SUBJECT: Shore Leave on Planet Girshoona

Tomorrow marks our first real landfall since leaving home, our rather chilling experience on "Ishtar East" notwithstanding.

As it will also be our first experience on a planet occupied by an alien race, I expect everyone to be on his best behavior. Whatever the cause or provocation, rowdiness on the planet's surface will result in revocation of leave privileges for those affected. Any whom I deem "at fault" for creating a disturbance will have ample time to reflect upon the folly of such conduct while whiling the hours away in the brig.

Those departing on leave parties will strictly observe posted limits on visitation points. As guests on the planet, we do not wish to intrude ourselves too conspicuously on the natives. Those on leave are restricted to the visitation zones contained in the briefing packets provided by the Personnel Office.

* * *

A CLOUDLESS sky greeted the new day. The Palace halls quickly filled with the footsteps of servants, scurrying to ready the Grand Hall for the day's feast. Outside, birds filled the air with song. In the garden, newly planted flowers lined the walks with bright colors, blues and purples, yellows and pure whites. Some plants even showed vibrant, brilliant reds—or so the Veshnans said. These, of course, were mostly for show, to honor the Terrans who were said to like the color. Such tones appeared dark and dull to the eyes of the *g'Khruushtani.*

Ga'Glish paced nervously in the garden. It had been fully twelve cycles since he last walked the grounds of home; ten cycles since he had taken a mate; nine cycles since he had taken the post of havenmaster and entered into a different world, of protocol and responsibility from which there could be no retreat. The distance he had come was nothing compared to what remained before him. He had not seen his father since leaving home, and as he paced he prayed that his tongue would not desert him, leaving him mute as a stone, should Ga'Glishek consent to a meeting.

"It has been a long time, Ga'Glish," called a voice from behind him.

Ga'Glish spun around to find Gal'Shenga, grinning broadly, standing no more than an arm's length away. The centurion had been so absorbed with his own concerns that he had quite failed to notice anyone approach.

"Uncle," smiled Ga'Glish, relief washing over his face.

Gal'Shenga laughed as the two clasped each other's shoulders. "You have dragged us all through fits of worry, Ga'Glish. Your mother is in a state of exhaustion and will probably never forget my complicity in this whole affair."

"In a different sense, neither will your nephew."

The Expanse Minister bowed, accepting the compliment. "How are you, Ga'Glish? And how are Glishana and the small ones?"

"Glishana worries over me like my mother."

"And the rest?"

"The small ones grow like weeds. And eat like Terrans."

"Come," smiled Gal'Shenga. "Let us walk."

The two walked alone through the palace grounds, much as they had done when Ga'Glish was a boy, sharing insights and memories. Though neither gave voice to his innermost thoughts, Ga'Glish felt his uncle's pride in the nephew's achievements. And the elder Galgravina felt his nephew's profound gratitude at having someone for whom independence did not mean betrayal.

At last, each felt the time had come to discuss matters of importance. They stopped walking, and came to rest upon a padded bench near the Imperial fountain. There, beneath a statue of Dr'Shenda LVIII, remembered in the capital as "Shenda the Portly," their talk turned to matters of importance.

"Was your trip worth the trouble?"

"It was disturbing, but for reasons I will admit to none but you," said Ga'Glish.

"One may not expect the Imperial Weathermen to be infallible."

Gal'Shenga meant his remarks in jest. He was surprised to feel distress flooding his nephew's heart.

"The storm was a boon, greater than I could have arranged myself."

"I am listening, Nephew."

"The Terrans have three classes of major space vessels," Ga'Glish began, doubtful of his ability to relate the full import of his experience. "This Terran ship was from their top class, the one we call— "

"'Intruder.'"

"Exactly," Ga'Glish bowed, impressed by his uncle's command of detail. "This is the class of ship they send whenever they come to inspect our side of the Great Divide. Of the others, I know but little."

"Continue."

"These ships have a cruising speed a full energy level above ours. They keep and maintain a speed of two astronomical units a day, twice the pace a ship of the Imperator can sustain."

"So I have heard."

"As they neared the haven, I put to space fully two days before they passed, only to find myself chasing their wake. But then the Terrans slowed to a pace I could keep, as if inviting me to accompany them. And I followed them, as closely as I dared, until.... "

"Until the storm intruded."

"Yes," said Ga'Glish. "Until the storm."

He rose and paced, searching for a way to make his uncle understand what would follow. Gal'Shenga was well-informed on a wide range of topics, but his knowledge of the science of space had limits.

"For many days, the Terrans seemed to enjoy the company. They were almost playful, detouring from the indicated course to skirt the edges of star systems and engaging in maneuvers which were useless, except for amusing themselves, using their ship as a toy—or perhaps demonstrating its capabilities to me; I know not which. They even sought to make verbal contact on several occasions. Of course, given the edicts of the Foreign Ministry, I chose not to join them, and made no reply to any of their messages."

"A silly loss that we must accept as payment for Cra'Jenli's blindness. But, continue."

"Then," Ga'Glish said, his voice lowering to a whisper, "the storm showed on the monitors, and the haven directed us to emergency harbors. Separate, of course, and neither optimum for a disturbance of that magnitude. But each was quite sufficient and easily reached.

"Yet the Terran shipmaster would have none of it. He broadcast an inquiry asking whether my ship needed assistance. When the haven confirmed that I needed none, he requested information on another system, fully two units ahead but far better suited as a harbor, a binary system with two stars of brightest green. The Cloud's full fury would have trouble disrupting the interior of that system, Uncle. As for the storm we were facing—why, once safely to port within the harbor of that system, the storm could be safely forgotten, like a gentle night rain upon the palace windows."

Gal'Shenga felt his nephew's heart fill with wonder.

"I myself raced right to the nearest star," Ga'Glish continued. "But the Terrans.... "

He paused, groping for a way to render what he had to say understandable.

"A space storm...of any magnitude...creates vast electrical disturbances that race through the heavens," said Ga'Glish. "A major storm like the one we faced sends magnetic waves of incredible strength racing at interstellar speeds. A ship caught in the void faces catastrophe. The storm can drain power from the ship to help feed the storm until none is left for propulsion, or to support life on board. Circuits can overload until they fuse together, making maneuvering impossible. If struck by a burst of static electricity, the hull may rupture and the ship may explode. And yet proceeding to harbor in the midst of a storm is nearly as dangerous as the storm itself. Tarry, and you face the storm's rage without cover; hurry, and you traverse the solar wind as the storm crashes into the system.

"In the face of all this," Ga'Glish whispered intensely, "the Terrans showed no alarm, not even as the storm drew to within moments of ravaging their craft. They increased their speed until it matched the storm's, and then led it to harbor, moments away from destruction all the while. They increased their speed only once that I could detect—shortly before entering the system, apparently to ensure a clean entry. And then their speed so far exceeded our own capacities that it was beyond measurement. Yet then they slowed to a crawl, as if awaiting the storm's pleasure. And it was then that I realized what the Terran shipmaster was doing, and realized the extent of his ship's capabilities."

"I am afraid I do not understand," said Gal'Shenga.

Ga'Glish smiled sadly. Few would understand, he thought; and fewer still would appreciate the depth of the dangers they faced. "The safest way to enter a star system is from a clear sky," he explained. "You need fear only the star's magnetic field and any debris you encounter."

Gal'Shenga nodded.

"But the more powerful the star, the greater its field, and the more debris it will trail."

"Of what use— "

Ga'Glish raised his hand, pleading for patience. "A major storm whips a star's magnetic field into a frenzy, dislodging any debris not firmly locked into orbit. So unless one arrives well in advance of a storm, the trip to the interior of a star system may be as dangerous as the storm itself."

"But I thought— "

"Yes, Uncle," Ga'Glish smiled, reading the confusion in the mind of Gal'Shenga. "One must cross to the interior or face certain destruction. And when the storm arrives, it disrupts the star's magnetic fields, as well as casting into chaos the rocks and iceballs that follow the star's journey through the heavens. If caught crossing from outside to inside when the storm hits the star, your ship will be buffeted from all sides and torn apart just as surely as if you had simply surrendered to the storm in the interstellar void.

"So the solution," Ga'Glish's eyes widened as he spoke, "is to ride the currents. Uncertain of a clear passage to harbor, you await the storm's arrival. As it nears, magnetic currents and eddies will manifest themselves along the star's wake. You note them, and proceed to the interior along a downdraft. It is a perilous ride, and one requiring skill and a high degree of precision, but those arriving less than a half-day before the storm have little choice."

"What does this have to do with the Terrans?"

"You do not see?" smiled Ga'Glish. "But then, I am not surprised. It was not until the Terrans disappeared behind the enveloping storm that I realized it myself.

"Uncle, the storm was more of a nuisance than a danger to the Terran shipmaster. He could have dashed to any of a half-dozen stars within easy reach of his ship, though the storm would have made itself felt through any of them. Instead, he chose the one perfect harbor within the sector, his choice showing that he deemed a proper harbor of greater importance than the fury of the storm. And the easy, effortless grace of the Terran ship as it sped along shows that its master had calculated his entry maneuvers precisely, timing his arrival to precede the storm by mere moments, and enabling him to proceed to the system's interior without delay."

"This is all very interesting," Gal'Shenga said, "but I fail to see—"

"Do you not understand, Uncle? Our own ships cannot ride the early breezes of a storm. It is simply too dangerous. And riding electromagnetic currents into the heart of a star system ahead of a storm is something we avoid whenever possible. Yet this was the Terrans' maneuver of choice, undertaken merely to avoid the inconvenience of spending a few days shaking under cover as a storm passed by. Their ships are swifter than ours, and sturdier, and this places us in danger enough.

"But more importantly," Ga'Glish lowered his voice to the barest of whispers, "it seems that the Terrans, like we, are at home in the heavens, and their ships can dance among the stars. And we delude ourselves by calling them children."

SITTING ALONE in the room provided by his hosts, Cook sat on the floor near a small wooden table. Waiting for the call to dinner, he was determined not to let to let the failure of his undertaking depress him, and resumed his study of the history texts he requested from the vast library he had seen on his tour of the palace. Opening one at random, Cook began to read. He'd already lost much of his enthusiasm for his quest to understand his hosts, and grimaced to find that his latest effort seemed no more enlightening than the others.

> And thus it came that the drought of the preceding summer did not slacken the industry of the workers of the field. Chronicles of the Treasurer report that during the Seventeenth Year of the Reign of Cal'Tagla XIX, farmers in Province Galgravin produced 39,595,644 units of milling grain, 79,409,573 units of land apples, 5,975,408 units of grinding corn....

His brain rebelled against the prospect of reading what appeared to be yet another farm report, and Cook felt his eyes close and his mind begin to wander. Deactivating the translator, he leaned back and tried to restart his brain. He had not expected this to be easy, he kept reminding himself. The earliest known writings from the ancient civilizations on Old Earth had, after all, proven largely to be tax records and business ledgers. Perhaps the Crutcthans were no different. And even if they were, the hardest thing about any field of study was cracking the code—getting past the indexing systems and structural roadblocks that divided information from the reader. All he needed was a clue.

As grateful as he was to find that the Crutchtans used a searchable index to organize their research material, it had been a mistake to use "History" as a search parameter. To the Crutchtans, "history" apparently meant something closer to "bean counting" or "production reports" than it meant to him—just as "philosophy" seemed to mean "rules of etiquette," and "poetry" seemed to be a branch of Crutchtan music, at least if he was to go by the topics that appeared on his viewing screen when he called the entry up from the Library.

"Library," he whispered, wondering whether the Crutchtan's long history had somehow changed the concept of a library, as well. Rising to his feet, he began to pace about, as he often did when thinking to himself. Some things, he knew, were universal constants, like the speed of light in the natural universe, or the atomic number of carbon. Any intelligent beings would need the capacity to retrieve and store information in order to benefit from the past. It suddenly struck him as quite likely that the Crutchtan language, like any other, had undergone significant changes in the past. And if a modern researcher or student needed to understand the usage that past ages gave to a particular word or phrase, then they would need—

"A dictionary," Cook said aloud, feeling quite pleased with himself. Regardless of the culture, a dictionary would be an indispensable tool. To understand how these people organized their past and thought about themselves, all he had to do was see how they used their own language to organize their thoughts.

Impressed by his reasoning abilities, Cook returned to his seat and entered "Dictionary" onto his screen. The screen went dark for a moment, and when the green light appeared at the top of his translating machine, indicating that he had made a contact and that he was in direct communication with a file in the Crutchtan Library, he felt a surge of triumph. He had no illusions that the task would be an easy one, but for the first time he felt as if he had a glimmer of insight into his hosts' reasoning.

"[Philosophy]," he entered, "definition and synonyms." Almost at once, the machine replied. To his surprise, it showed that the Crutchtan definition was nearly the same as his own.

"Philosophy: A field of study governing various modes of thinking or conduct," read the viewing screen. Progress at last, thought Cook, as he entered a similar request for "[History]."

"History," responded the machine. "An account of what has happened in the life or development of a People, Country, or institution." Cook furrowed his brow. Something was wrong, he thought, though he didn't know what it might be. The machine was responding just as he expected and he sensed, without understanding why, that this wasn't quite right.

Trying again, he entered requests for [Literature], [Sports], [Politics], and [Music]. Each time, he received a definition that corresponded exactly to his own understanding of the word. As annoying as his lack of progress had been so far, he found himself frustrated even more by the apparent puzzle. How, he wondered, could he be asking the right questions, but getting all the wrong answers?

Slowly, the answer began to dawn on him. Crutchtan computers were just as stupid and stubborn as any in Terra. He'd found another universal constant, to add to the others he'd uncovered and forgotten over the years: computers, like the weather, were part of some vast Cosmic plan, creations of a mischievous God with an obviously warped sense of humor, intended to drive sentient beings crazy throughout the Universe.

"*Hmmm,*" he mused, entering "[God]" onto the machine, wondering how the Crutchtans viewed the question of eternity.

A supernatural, magical, often all-knowing and all-powerful being, in any of the various ancient or modern religions; see also, Allah (Islam), Jehovah (Hebrew)....

"Oh, for the love of—" Cook muttered. Quickly, he entered another name and became annoyed when the machine gave him the answer he expected.

Shakespeare: William, 1564-1616 (OE); Old Earth playwright and poet in Elizabethan England.

Trying again and again, he soon suspected that there was a good reason why all the definitions were largely what he expected them to be. He tried his best to reject the thought that he'd wasted the last half-hour chasing definitions around his own language, but a last test convinced him to give up the pretense that he had the slightest idea what he was doing.

Noun—solid bodily waste; verb—to excrete solid bodily waste. (Use note: vulgar, often used to express anger or derision).

Cook leaned back onto the pillows that his hosts had spread over the floor and rubbed his eyes wearily. He was not used to running into so many dead ends. And he hated the thought that some brainless machine could outwit him, and would probably spend the rest of the day laughing in its circuits until they shorted. He vowed that he wouldn't leave the planet until he had some understanding, however meager, into the Crutchtan mind.

* * *

"Ys'SLALT—FETCH me the kettle. Bl'Dryna—I will need the stewing spices. Gal'Kisl, the sauces will need constant monitoring. No, no—Slalt, you fool, not the simmering pot! The kettle—the large, black kettle!"

Like his friends, ls'Shen raced about trying to obey Ra'Henl's instructions, secretly cursing the old foodmaster's reluctance to see one task through to completion before commencing the next.

"Dryna—Kisl—come. Attend me. Ys'Slalt, pay heed. What we need now is the barest hint of jizril seeds in the sauce...."

As the Foodmaster's back was turned, and knowing that he would not be missed for quite a while, ls'Shen stepped lightly into the outer cooking chamber and peered through the curtain. The Banquet Hall was filled to capacity. Dignitaries of all ranks and races graced the Table of Honor. At the lesser tables he could see the courtiers in attendance, and smiled to see the jugglers and clowns and acrobats, their faces streaked with ornamental paint, frolicking on the amusement floor in the middle of the room. From the far end of the banquet hall he could hear the palace musicians, playing a sprightly dance.

But what drew his attention were not the entertainers, nor eminences that he recognized by name or by face. What captured his eyes were the four creatures seated near the center of the Table of Honor between Lady Glishenda and her brother-in-law, the Expanse Minister himself. Raptly he stared, his eyes widened like a gawkhen's, until a gentle tap on his back caused him to jump nearly to the ceiling.

"Shen—Shen," whispered Jarenda, the foodservant. Ls'Shen's gill slits paled with fright. He had been so absorbed with watching the Terrans that he had failed to sense her approach. "How come you—"

"Jarenda, please," he interrupted, vainly trying to recover his dignity. "Never approach a foodmaster or his apprentice in such a fashion. It is entirely too disruptive. And under other circumstances— "

"You mean," Jarenda smiled, her eyes laughing merrily, "had you not been gaping at the longnoses."

Ls'Shen snorted angrily, only to rediscover that this female found his temper an endless source of amusement. Jarenda was becoming entirely too familiar, he thought, but like all males he found a female's playful teasing too enticing to resist. And so long as they were alone, he took no steps to disrupt the growing warmth of their bond.

"They look different than I had imagined," he said at last, peering through the curtain once more. "Not nearly as furry. And their snouts are not at all what I expected. They are pointed, and their faces wear a comical look about them. Calling them 'longnoses' is something of a misnomer, I think. 'Pointy-snouts' would be more accurate."

"Well," Jarenda whispered, poking her own head through the curtains, "the name 'Strange Ones' is certainly appropriate."

"That I do not doubt, but why do you say so? What have you seen?"

"Look at them," she motioned with her head. "All four of them sweat like wild hogs and yet they insist on wearing clothing. All of them, without exception."

"Yes, I see," said ls'Shen. And sure enough, two of them were clad in garments of blue, and two wore clothing of varying hues. But all four of them were fully clothed, though even from this distance he could see perspiration dripping from them like water from a fountain. Even the Veshnans did not carry matters to such extremes, and of all the races of the Grand Alliance, the Veshnan approach to garments was the most impractical.

"And their eating habits leave much to be desired," Jarenda continued. "See the blueclad Terran male, the one seated next to Glishenda, the Minister's Consort-of-the Day?"

"Yes."

"After looking at his sidebowl for the longest time, he finally asked an interpreter the purpose of the washed sand."

"To aid in digestion," said ls'Shen, answering the obvious.

"Well, upon hearing the answer, the Terran sampled some—using his spoon to carry it to his mouth, of all things."

"Incredible."

"Then he spat it out—all over the table—and started coughing and protruding his tongue from his mouth like a small one with the heaves."

"Amazing," said ls'Shen, looking at the one Jarenda had mentioned, who seemed to be viewing his broadleaf salad with some degree of suspicion. The Terran jabbed the greens with his cutlery and examined each fresh pepper carefully before stuffing it into his mouth.

"How can you tell the males from the females?" asked the young apprentice. "I mean, if they are fully clothed and all. It must get rather confusing for them."

"Well," agreed Jarenda, "that does pose several problems."

Ls'Shen closed the curtain and sighed. Much about these Strange Ones simply defied explanation.

"They seem to crop their fur differently, but from what I have observed there appears to be but one sure way to tell them apart."

"And what is that, my little friend?"

"Terran females are...well, more rounded than their males," she said, searching for a way to explain the unexplainable. "And they seem to have these—these—bumps— "

"Bumps?"

"Yes—bumps—little mounds—crests really, right in the middle of their chests."

Ls'Shen peered through the curtain once more, straining to get a good look at the Terrans. By chance, one of them turned to the right, just enough to give him a view in profile, and a benevolent Fate decreed that it would be one of the Crested Ones.

"Amazing," he said. For sure enough, there they were, exactly as Jarenda had described. And now that he knew where to look, he saw that the smaller of the blueclads displayed the same prominent features. Less pronounced, perhaps, but unmistakable nonetheless.

"What are they for?"

Jarenda shrugged. "I thought it impolite to ask," she replied.

Soon, the voice of Ra'Henl came bellowing from the kitchen, summoning his apprentices from all corners of his kitchen to assist in circumventing some new disaster. Beaming with a depth of feeling, ls'Shen nodded at Jarenda, who flushed shyly as she returned to her duties.

"Ls'Shen! Shen, come at once! Where are you, Young One?"

"Yes, Grand One, I am coming." With a smiling heart, ls'Shen returned to the kitchen, where he had duties of his own that needed tending.

* * *

Perhaps the mists of age doth shroud my mem'ry.
  Yet I so clearly see my lady love
That time and distance vanish, like the shadows
  Which, like frost, the sun melts from above.

While young, we trip through fields of flowers gaily,
  For youth, like flow'rs, will blossom 'neath the sky.
But as the dearest rose too swiftly withers,
  So beauty, like all mortal things, must die.

My love and I would swoon beneath the heavens;
       O'er gods and men proud passion holds its sway.
But warmth and day fade sadly into darkness;
       The cold of death lurks never far away.

While young, we trip through fields of flowers gaily,
       For youth, like flow'rs, will blossom 'neath the sky.
But as the dearest rose too swiftly withers,
       So beauty, like all mortal things, must die.

She faded with the summer; and the breezes
       Of time eternal, ravaging my mind
As bitter truth, the freezing winds of winter,
       But bring my lifeless soul a death in kind.

While young, we trip through fields of flowers gaily,
       For youth, like flow'rs, will blossom 'neath the sky.
But as the dearest rose too swiftly withers.
       So beauty, like all mortal things, must die.

As THE troubadour sang his sad song of love, Drubid and his aides caucused in the corridor, just outside the Banquet Hall. All wore the loose-fitting, white togas of the Glincian aristocracy; their soft, feathery bodies shone with fresh, perfumed oils.

"Repulsive," spat Galek, shuddering at the memory. "They stuff themselves like animals, and their bellies are as bottomless as the vacuum in their brains."

"They are predators, Galek," replied Drubid. "And predators often dribble their manners along with their meal. But repulsive or not, we have more pressing concerns than civilizing the Terrans."

"Surely, Home cannot be serious," Salcran whispered, her eyes narrowing darkly. "Dealing with the likes of them?"

Drubid smiled blandly. "Diplomacy," he reminded, "is an art of practicality, not aesthetics. Let us first examine the possibilities before dismissing these newcomers as too savage for polite society. And who knows, perhaps savagery will be the coming rage. At least it brings relief from boredom—and that, of course, is the inevitable end to which polite society brings us."

Their laughter was interrupted by the intrusion of a Crutchtan serving girl.

"Yes," Drubid said sharply. "What is it?"

"Begging Your Excellency's pardon," said the girl, bowing respectfully. "But the next course is ready, and Master Ra'Henl wishes— "

"Yes, yes," Galek said impatiently. "We shall be along shortly."

"Thank you, Lord, and please forgive— "

"Run along now," said Drubid, motioning with his hand. "We shall follow when we are ready." The girl bowed and departed, leaving the three Glinci alone once more.

"Crutchtan hospitality carries a stiff price, don't you think?" said Galek, as the three of them started back toward their place at the Table of Honor.

"At least they do not compel us to eat," added Salcran, smiling as she refastened the chain on her toga. "That would likely lead to outright hostilities."

"Perhaps they seek to disarm us through forced contact with our putative allies," Drubid said dryly. "Of course, they underestimate the strength of our resolve, as well as our stomachs."

Laughing, the three diplomats entered the Banquet Hall and resumed their seats.

"WELL, UNCLE, what do you think?"

As the dancers danced a merry jig of entertainment, Gal'Shenga narrowed his eyes to look at the newcomers.

The Terran seated next to him, the One Called *gh'Rahn-te*, was small, almost as small as a Veshnan. He had expected the ranking simian to be somewhat larger, though Zatar had warned him that Terrans came in odd assortments. As expected from a full ambassador, this *gh'Rahn-te* appeared intelligent, even as his conversation suffered from the blandness of diplomats.

More intriguing to his nephew—and to himself, he was coming to admit—was the Terran blueclad, the One Called *Khu'ukh*. Like the Terran ambassador, *Khu'ukh* had brought his female, showing that under the Terran Order of Things the two were of equal stature. But where *gh'Rahn-te* merely smiled and nodded, the other's eyes were constantly in motion, absorbing his surroundings like a thirsty sponge. And where the ambassador seemed eager to make the small talk that diplomats shower upon each other at such affairs, *Khu'ukh* spoke mostly to his own female, as if unconcerned with the dictates of Form. When he did choose to speak, the blueclad showed a subtle and powerful intelligence that shone through the awkwardness of translation, expressing his thoughts with a grace and precision unexpected from a barbarian. Slowly, he came to agree with Ga'Glish: the Terran commander was the true head of the delegation, and the One whom they had to impress with the firmness of their purpose and the merits of their cause.

"It would seem that events are proving you correct, Ga'Glish," he whispered. "But let us put your theories to the test." The younger Galgravina nodded, then watched as his uncle rose to quiet the gathering.

"A Word of Welcome, to our honored guests," Gal'Shenga said at last, his voice silencing the hall. "Through thought and deed, let us realize harmony with the Universe, as we seek concord with each other. And in the name of His Worthiness, the Grand Imperator Ja'Rend XCVI, let us extend the gladness of our hearts to our guests from across the Divide."

"So be it," chorused the *g'Khruushtani* in the crowd, lightly tapping the tabletops in a rhythm of agreement.

Gal'Shenga turned to his right and bowed toward the Terrans, smiling politely to see the One Called *gh'Rahn-te* rise to answer his greeting. Secretly, he wondered whether he and his nephew had not been reading too much subtlety into the Terrans' behavior. After all, protocol demanded that a reply to a welcome be made by one of equivalent rank, and as the ranking *g'Khruushtani*, Gal'Shenga would expect the ranking Terran to make the response. Still and all, he did not wish to be provincial, and Terran ignorance of protocol, or differing Terran ways, could explain the facts as easily as the ambassador's status.

"The Terran ambassador states as follows," said the Veshnan interpreter, in a thickly accented voice. "'I convey thanks to our host for his humane and polite sentiments, and might otherwise fondly state that Terra's principal desire is to live in peace with all her neighbors.'"

Pausing, as the *g'Khruushtani* politely tapped agreement on their tables, the interpreter listened to the ambassador's next few words.

"He further states," she continued, a look of confusion clouding the serene blandness of the Veshnan countenance, "that if subjects of both races could learn to live in peace...," She paused, groping for a suitable translation.

"Then," she concluded warily, "we would all live in peace."

Gal'Shenga bowed for the sake of form, wondering if Terrans always talked in circles. After a short silence, and prompted by the Expanse Minister's darkest look of severity, the others politely tapped their tables. Looking pleased with himself, the Terran ambassador bowed toward the assembly, then resumed his seat.

"Uncle...," ventured Ga'Glish. But Gal'Shenga sensed that they shared the same thought, and silenced him with a raise of his hand.

"Though it be not our custom to place a guest in a position of obligation," said Gal'Shenga, "I would welcome words from our Blueclad Friend who has shared the dangers of space with my own Nephew." A hush fell over the Banquet Hall. All sensed that Gal'Shenga's breach of protocol was for a higher purpose, though none could discern its shape.

Slowly, the blueclad male rose from his place to tower over the others. His lips turning up slightly at the corners, he shook his head at his female and at *gh'Rahn-te,* who were softly yipping some Terran words, and then he spoke. When he finished, the interpreter sighed deeply before beginning her translation.

"The Terran shipmaster states that he perceives that Terran ways, and Terran manners, have occasioned no little amusement among his kind hosts, and hopes that this amusement will help lead to cordial relations between the two races."

Gal'Shenga heard sounds of laughter course through the Hall, but as he felt himself chuckle he could offer no correction.

"He also states as follows," the interpreter continued, looking quite uncomfortable. "'We humans find ourselves overwhelmed by the strangeness of alien ways, and alien customs. And I hope that the human race will neither give nor take offense by accident.'"

Silence fell over the Hall; and at a nod from his uncle, a wary Ga'Glish gave voice to the common feeling.

"Surely, Lord Shipmaster," he retorted, rising to address their guest, "Terrans are not so conceited as to consider themselves the only human beings in the Universe. And surely you are not so presumptuous as to call alien those ways which the rest of civilization has found familiar for untold eons before Terra ventured into the heavens."

As the interpreter relayed his remarks, Ga'Glish looked to see the Terran's eyes peering directly at him, and shuddered at the calm clarity of the simian's gaze. As he gave his reply to the Veshnan interpreter, the Terran stood proudly, eyes unwavering, as if daring Ga'Glish to respond.

"'I seek forgiveness for offending where no offense was intended,'" came the reply. "'My people have little experience with other races, and I am a soldier, not a polished diplomat like Ambassador *gh'Rahn-te*.'"

The translator waited for the sounds of gentle amusement to fade, before continuing.

"'Still, my words stand unaltered. A human being is often awed by the unfamiliar. But any human who is truly civilized draws no offense from another's ignorance.'"

Though his words brought loud rappings of approval through the Hall, the Terran resumed his seat without a bow of acknowledgment. Ga'Glish turned to his uncle and exchanged a smile of understanding. The crudeness of their manners could not mask the truth. As they had suspected, Terra's power lay with those who sailed her ships, not with her bureaucrats. But apparently, the Terrans also cared enough about peace to send a true leader to oversee the talks.

Now that they knew they had found the proper course, they would let the Foreign Ministry's emissaries waste their efforts without intrusion. As with one mind, they sensed the parameters of the Terran hierarchy; as with a single heart, they knew the path to follow.

THE JUGGLERS and clowns roamed freely over the open halls, opening the hall to laughter. Musicians played their lutes and harps, and singers gave voice to the ancient songs. As the next course drew near, servant girls came to clear the tables, and as time came to clear the Table of Honor, they drew lots to see who would have to clear the plates near the Terrans, for each who had gone before reported the same thing: the Terrans would bare their teeth and snarl at whoever came near them.

Jarenda felt a sense of foreboding as her turn neared; and surely as the dawn, it was she who drew the black stone from the serving bowl.

"It will be an adventure," her friend Larenga said encouragingly, but neither her words nor her thoughts carried conviction. Taking a carting tray, Jarenda strode through the curtains and toward her assigned area.

As she neared, Jarenda's abdomen shuddered and her heart pounded wildly. She could almost sense the color draining from her neck and chest, and she averted her head as she passed the wall of mirrors, fearing what she would see.

At last, she came to the Terran section of the table. Working quickly and quietly, she prayed to the stars that the Strange Ones would take no notice, even as under other circumstances she would have prayed for Lady Glishek or Lord Gal'Shenga to bestow a word of kindness. She almost escaped unnoticed, for the Terran ambassador and his female were too busy conversing with the Minister to notice her efforts.

But despite her best efforts there was no escape, for as she finished the two blueclads bared their teeth, first the Crested One, then the male. And as her heart fluttered with anxiety, the male jerked his head at her and barked, almost causing her to drop the tray on the floor.

Having gathered everything she needed, she quickly left the table, and placed the tray on the clearing counter for the junior apprentices to collect. Then, she leaned against the wall to collect her breath and her wits. It had been a harrowing experience, but it had passed quickly enough. And as the serving staff had agreed to share the burden of serving them she would not have to approach the Terrans again for several days.

As her composure slowly returned, Jarenda found herself possessed by curiosity and no small degree of resentment. Others might accept their lot meekly, and certainly they had little choice in setting their duties. Yet even as nobility carried its privileges, it struck her as unforgivable to force loyal servants to pander to guests with the manners of untutored louts.

As thoughts of rebellion briefly stirred in her heart, a Veshnan interpreter passed, one whom Jarenda recognized from past visits. Though reluctant to approach one of superior rank, she forced herself to make the effort, hoping that the Veshnan's past kindness would incline her to let the breach of protocol go unreported.

"My Lady?" Jarenda said timidly. "Lady Munshi?"

The Veshnan turned and looked at the serving girl. "Yes…what is it?"

Heartened by the lack of anger in the Veshnan's reply, Jarenda stepped closer. "My Lady does not recognize me, but she once did me a favor by taking the blame for my clumsiness before Lord Glishek at the— "

"The Feast of Departure," Munshi concluded. She smiled a bland Veshnan smile, and slowly nodded her head. "Yes, I remember. It was a rather large mess, as I recall. And you are—Jalenda?"

"Jarenda, My Lady," she replied, bowing respectfully.

"Well, Jarenda, I am flattered that you remember me."

Jarenda smiled, then forced herself to speak her mind.

"Yes, My Lady—but is there a chance that I might dare to ask yet another undeserved boon?"

"What is it?" Munshi smiled.

"At the table, you were seated next to Lady Glishenda."

"Yes…and yes, now that I recall—was it not you who cleared our table?" Munshi smiled. "Yes, I believe it was."

Nodding shyly, her heart in her throat, Jarenda looked nervously about her, hoping that none would bear witness to her lack of proper manners. "When I approached the blueclads," she whispered, "and they were baring their teeth at me, could you hear the Terrans male bark at me? I would like to know—that is, I seek to learn—why he would behave in such a manner."

Munshi laughed softly to herself, shaking her head.

"I am afraid that I was not paying attention, Jarenda," she replied. When she saw what she recognized as disappointment cross Jarenda's face, she added, "But I have heard them speak in the same manner before, and I am certain that I know what he was saying."

"Yes?"

"The Terrans' baring of teeth is the way they have of smiling," said Munshi. "And what you heard as a bark would have been the Terran word for 'thank you.' "

As the Veshnan smiled and bowed and went on her way, Jarenda felt a great sadness in her heart. Soon, tears flooded her eyes, and she turned her face toward the wall to hide her emotions. She knew that menials were supposed to derive their contentment from their work and not from the undeserved praise of their superiors, and she was ashamed to have so little self-control as to weep in public like an infant.

But the more she tried, the less she was able to stop. Her young life had seen happiness as well as sorrow, but she had known true kindness from no more than two of her betters. She could still hear the fading footsteps of one of them; despite herself, she grieved to think that she knew of the other only by chance, and that neither were of her own kind.

Chapter 21

THE NEXT DAYS SAW clear skies along the seashore. With the conference begun in earnest, most of the Terrans had little to do but pass the time.

One day, as the summer sun beat warmly overhead, two of the Terrans strolled along the sandy breach. A soft sea breeze made the brutal heat almost bearable. Sweating profusely beneath their light blue tank tops and standard shorts, and oblivious to the stares of onlookers, they stopped to face each other thirty paces from their nearest neighbors, a group of Crutchtans enjoying themselves by the water, to whom the odd-looking strangers were as much a distraction as a curiosity.

"So you're ordering me to stay."

"Order?"

Cook's voice carried a hint of exasperation that Janet mistook for sarcasm. The tropical humidity had already sapped much of his strength; the breeze from the sea, so refreshing on other worlds, now seemed hot and oppressive, and only made him feel worse.

"Tell me, Lieutenant—when is the first, last, or any time that I really ordered you to do anything? I usually don't do that. And it doesn't seem to do much good, anyway." The cold look in Janet's eyes told him that he had stumbled into a trap.

"I seem to recall," she replied archly, "a direct order on board the *Constantine*, for which there are any number of witnesses."

Cook gritted his teeth and tried to hold his tongue. He might have known, he told himself. She had the memory of a Ceresian loan shark, at least as far as he was concerned.

"All right— "

"And if your own recollection needs prodding— "

"All right, Lieutenant—but as I remember it, I prefaced my 'order' by asking you, as a personal favor, not to make me throw you in the brig."

"Well, that's not quite...."

"And as I recall, having you stand down and confining you to quarters was the coda to a rather loud and lengthy discussion— "

"That's enough, Captain."

"— done to spare us both a great deal of embarrassment—"

"That is quite—"

"—of the kind that would have done neither of our careers the slightest bit of good."

Janet snorted derisively, the contemptuous look in her eyes searing itself into Cook's soul. "Careers! Yes, I guess it's about time for you to throw that back in my face again."

"Fine." In resignation, Cook lifted his arms toward the sky. "You want to go back to the ship, go back to the ship. I give up. I just don't need the aggravation."

"If I'm such an aggravation, why did you bring me along in the first place?"

Cook laughed bitterly, dropping his arms until they slapped against his sides. "Oh, I would have been perfectly happy to come down here by myself," he said, "but Grant wanted me to bring an 'entourage.' I need Jeremy to help keep the shore parties under control. And between you and Van Horn—well, as long as I'm bringing a date along, I'd rather bring a girl.

"Besides," he added softly, "Grant told me that bringing a female along would impress our hosts...though I'd be surprised if they're impressed as easily as all that."

"Well I'm surprised," Janet shot back, "that you didn't bring along one of the Ambassador's little honeys. I hear that they're quite a lot of fun. The men on board can barely keep from drooling all over them."

"Isitian men don't drool."

Janet frowned sourly.

"We salivate, maybe."

Cook turned away, looking toward the sea. "But they're not my type, anyway," he said at last. "And I thought...well, there is old time's sake and all."

Turning back to face her, Cook saw that she'd already stomped off in a huff. He took a step toward her, only to halt in his tracks. She never would listen to reason when she was in one of her moods, he thought, and he doubted that anything he could say would do any good. Not now, and perhaps not ever.

He watched her tromp across the sand, her hair damp with sweat, her jersey darkened with perspiration. Sadly, his thoughts drifted to another day, and another beach on another world.

As she walked by herself, her eyes glistening in the bright sunlight, Janet tried in vain to keep the same image from popping into her own mind.

Closing her eyes, she listened to the sounds of the surf. The Demetrian sun warmed her body, and she wanted to lie on the sand forever. She'd deliberately chosen a deserted stretch of beach, and basked in the knowledge that for another day she could unwind without interruption. The day after tomorrow would be another land and another existence, and she tried to put it out of mind. Her leave would end soon enough, and she would get on with the rest of her life. But if it had to end, she couldn't imagine a more peaceful way to bring this chapter to a close.

All at once, she sat up with a start. Looking behind her, shading her eyes and squinting into the bright sunlight, she saw a shape. "Sorry to startle you," said a man's voice. "But, after all, there's no one else about to form a welcoming committee, and I didn't wish to seem inhospitable."

Janet tried to place the accent but found it to be impossible. "Who are you?" she asked apprehensively, drawing her beach blanket up to cover her legs.

"Just a neighbor," smiled the intruder. He plopped onto his knees on the sand a few feet away from her. She found something vaguely familiar about him—something about the eyes, she thought. But he was sporting a scraggly overgrowth of beard, and she didn't remember meeting anyone like that. Not lately, at any rate.

"I'm camped behind that sand dune," he motioned with his hand. Janet looked to see the peak of a tent, sticking out over a rise in the sand.

"And I'm really quite harmless," he continued, his eyes twinkling, "though I hate to admit that to any pretty girl. Especially one I've just met."

Despite herself, Janet laughed out loud.

"My name is Janet," she said, and extended her hand. To her surprise, the stranger took her hand and kissed it.

"My friends call me 'Skipper,'" he said, grinning mischievously. "At least, that's what they call me when I'm within earshot. I can't vouch for what they say about me when I'm not about—but then, that's largely beside the point."

"Skipper?" Janet laughed, trying to picture him in charge of a ship. "You certainly don't sound like any spacer I've ever seen before. You don't act like one, either."

"I guess I'll take that as a compliment," Skipper chuckled. "Most bluebirds aren't quite as generous, though, so I guess I've gotten my share of compliments for the year."

"Why do you think I'm with the Cosmic Guard?"

"And I'd put your rank at...ensign."

Janet's eyes widened in amazement. It was almost as if he could read her thoughts, she marveled. Despite herself, Janet found his broad smile wonderfully disarming. For the first time since leaving home, she was beginning to feel something stirring inside her. She immediately dismissed the thought. Cavorting on the beach with a common spacer might not be her idea of a proper finish to a vacation, but she was startled to realize that she was smiling and aflutter on the inside. She was pleasantly surprised to find that she could not muster the resolve to keep from beaming like a schoolgirl on the outside, as well.

"Well," Skipper said, scratching the growth of beard on his chin, his brow furrowing in thought. "Your accent says you're from New Babylon. Aside from the local girls, only a CosGuard Missy would be stuck spending a vacation alone on the Demetrian Riviera. You're too young to be a senior officer. And only an ensign would be foolish enough to wander off so far by herself, this close to the Frontier."

"Foolish?" Janet huffed, not caring to admit that the stranger was right on all counts. "Why shouldn't I be free to go anywhere I choose? I happen to like getting away from crowds, every now and then. And I notice you haven't let the Frontier prevent you from going off as far as you care to go."

"I'm not likely to find myself dragged off into space by some love-starved prospector," said Skipper, his eyes suddenly dark and serious. "And that's something you might want to keep in mind for the future."

"I can take care of myself quite nicely, thank you. And I don't need any spacer to tell me tales about the Frontier."

"I can see that," the stranger smiled cryptically, rising to his feet. "Well, Janet—I have a bottle of wine in my tent, and no one to share it with. I'll be glad to bring it back, if you want some company. If not, I'll return you to your privacy."

Janet thought a moment—but just a moment. Her better judgment told her that this arrogant young spacer had an insufferably high opinion of himself. But there was something gentle in his eyes. And his smile tugged at her heart, making her think she didn't want him to leave just yet.

"I can't stay much longer," she said. "I'm due back in two days, and have a ton of packing to do."

"I understand," said Skipper. "This is my last day on Demeter, myself. I return to my own ship tomorrow."

"Well—why not? Go get your wine. It'll be nice to have someone besides the gulls to talk to."

"What about a guitar? It may be full of sand, but it's fully paid for."

Janet laughed. "Bring it along, too. But don't expect me to embarrass myself by singing."

"Oh, I can embarrass both of us all by myself," he called back over his shoulder as he dashed off toward his tent. Janet giggled as he pretended to trip over tree roots and driftwood along the way. What was the harm, she asked herself. Despite his appearance, he was obviously bright, and might even have an intelligent thing or two to say. Egotistical or not, he was pleasant enough; and what's more, he could make her laugh. She could think of more dreadful ways to pass an afternoon.

And who could tell? she wondered. He might even help her forget about the new commanding officer she'd report to, the day after tomorrow. She'd always wanted to meet him—ever since her first days at the Academy, when she first saw his name on all the trophies and plaques, and heard the stories the upperclassmen told about his classroom jousts with the faculty. But often it was better to leave heroes on their pedestals, to avoid seeing all their warts and failings. When she actually drew the Constantine *for her first duty assignment, she found herself dreading the prospect of actually meeting him.*

Stretching out on the sand, Janet closed her eyes and felt the sun warm her golden skin. She hoped she wouldn't regret her foolishness at choosing to spend her last day on Demeter in the company of a stranger. She smiled to herself as she wondered just how foolish she would let herself be.

* * *

AMBASSADOR GRANT sat patiently on the floor at the Terran end of the table, flanked by his senior aides who, in turn, were flanked by the rest of the delegation. Though the soft, velvety pillows helped make their wait bearable, they had long since emptied the serving dishes on the table of anything that seemed remotely edible. Their hosts, it seemed, had mastered the art of procrastinating. Either that, or the Crutchtans realized that waiting drove Terrans crazy, and were eager to grasp every edge they could find to bend the will of their guests to their own advantage.

A vast mural stretched across the cavernous ceiling of the conference hall, depicting, so he was told, the ascension of the Mother of Spirits into the heavens. Rich tapestries, inlaid with threads of gold, hung on the walls, circling the room with the portraits of nobles from Crutchta's past. High overhead, skylights lined with mythical fairies admitted the light of day, while the temperature stayed within the control of some hidden thermostat. Obviously, the Crutchtans felt that science should never intrude itself upon art.

Grant marveled in silence at the Crutchtan artistry, and remembered that this was merely one room in a palace filled with thousands of similar touches. It was like the pictures he'd seen of the ancient cathedrals on Old Earth: each wall and every corner showed some forgotten craftsman's loving care. It made him wonder what his hosts must have thought of the accommodations on Ishtar, where the barren walls barely provided cover from the wind.

But he had little time for such reflections, for the entrance curtains soon parted and the Crutchtan delegation walked in. The Terrans rose to their feet to greet their hosts, only to see a single Crutchtan enter, followed by Zatar and his interpreter.

"Greetings," said the interpreter, taking her position between Zatar and the Crutchtan at the table. "Once again, we will consider a new point of contention—and may our discussions over the next few weeks prove as fruitful as our preceding talks have proved frank and enlightening."

"On behalf of my Government," Grant replied, "I renew our warmest thanks for your hospitality, and our hope that our first visit to your shores keeps bringing progress in its wake."

"The *g'Khruushtani*'s new emissary has arrived from the Capital, and is in attendance today," the interpreter said, after translating Grant's remarks for her own people. "His name is *Fra'Grandl*, Emissary of the Imperial Foreign Ministry and Voice of His Worthiness."

Grant nodded toward the Crutchtan. "I welcome Fra'Grandl to these talks, and hope that his presence is an omen of renewed good will."

The initial pleasantries exchanged, the interpreter motioned for everyone to sit, and the Crutchtan delegation took the places across the table from the Terrans. After everyone was settled, Zatar spoke first.

"Before we begin," the interpreter related, "Ambassador Zatar wishes to know the effect that the change in the Terran government will have on these talks. Specifically, he asks whether you intend to alter your last proposals with respect to settlements and exploration in the disputed areas—and if so, the nature and extent of the alterations."

Grant paused a moment before answering.

"I am instructed," he replied, "that our proposals stand as we left them on Ishtar."

"So, nothing has changed?"

Grant looked the Veshnan straight in the eye. "My Government has chosen to pursue exactly the same paths as before. As far as these discussions are concerned, everything remains unaltered." He watched as the interpreter translated his words to Zatar, and saw the Veshnan nod his head. At the same time, the Crutchtan stared straight ahead, impassive and unimpressed.

"Then are commencing, we presently thus," Zatar said in his thickly accented voice, beneath a bland, Veshnan smile.

* * *

"ALL RIGHT, Jeremy, what's the problem this time? I'm in the middle of one of those interminable Crutchtan history books, and if this takes too long I doubt I'll ever get back to it."

"Well— "

"Of course, History can be a rather dusty discipline, I suppose. But still and all, these people have the driest writers I've ever tried to wade through."

"Well, Skipper— "

"It's not the food processors again, I hope. We're almost out of our frozen stores, and I doubt that the crew would appreciate Crutchtan cuisine. It has the taste and texture of boiled cardboard, and they keep sprinkling everything with dirt."

"No, sir. This time it's Burdick. He's complaining about having nobody to man his security watches."

"So?"

"Well, you see— "

"I mean, we only have twenty or thirty people on the whole ship."

"Thirty-three, Captain."

"Well, whatever. It's not like we're carrying the crown jewels through Sherwood Forest."

"Uh...Sherwood—?"

"And if everyone's gone ashore, anyway, he won't be having a full scale riot on his hands any time soon, right?"

"Umm— "

"So what's the problem?"

"Well, there are the entry points, Captain. And regulations are rather specific about— "

"*Acchhh*— "

"Skipper!"

"Yes...well...rules are like the stars in the sky, Jeremy."

"I beg your pardon?"

"They are guideposts, not ends in themselves. They set our course, but we sail between them, not through them."

"But...."

"Well, sometimes we're stuck circling around them, I suppose, but then each simile has its own limitations."

"This is all very interesting, but what has this got to do with— "

"So when is Van Horn coming up to spell you? Or would you just as soon rest your sweat glands a while longer?"

"I give up."

"Good. Discretion is the better part of valor, you know."

"Janet still complaining about the heat?"

"Just when she's talking to me."

"So the answer is no?"

"Very funny, Jeremy."

* * *

Grant peered down from his balcony overlooking the City Square. Serpents made of the finest silk snaked through the teeming crowd, drawing dancing revelers along behind. Clowns and jugglers, their bodies streaked with brightly colored paints, dotted the square. Small children, their tiny arms filled to capacity, were strewing flowers along the streets. Wherever he looked, Crutchtans of all ages were dancing, and the sounds of their music and songs filled the air.

"It is Festival," trilled a voice from behind him. "Our hosts spend most of their lives engaging in such nonsense. It is a wonder that they accomplish anything."

Grant turned to look at the speaker, a tall, thin Glincian named *Drub'd.* They were an odd race, he thought. With fine, down-like feathers on a broad face that narrowed to a sharp beak, they looked more like wingless owls than anything else. This one—a male, he thought, from its size and the yellow coloring of its waistband—wore a gold chain around its neck, with a medallion engraved with what looked to be some sort of writing.

"Your command of our language astounds me," said Grant.

"I have studied it for some time," replied *Drub'd.* "Ever since those you call 'Crutchtans' first confirmed their contact with a new race, and the High Council forced them to distribute the language tapes that your Government was kind enough to provide.

"Of course, I do ask that you not reveal to our hosts what little mastery of your tongue I might possess. It would complicate matters for us to have such information become…'common knowledge,' as your idiom puts it."

"I understand," said Grant.

"You are aware of our contact with your Government?"

"My briefing was quite thorough, *Drub'd.*"

"And your reply?"

Grant entered the room, closing the balcony door behind him. The room was large, almost forty feet across, and was the smallest of six in his suite. Earlier that day, his security team had neutralized the last of the hidden listening devices buried in the walls. Though he was coming to wonder just how much he could trust his Crutchtan hosts, for the time being he felt he could talk freely.

"There is much we do not know about each other," said Grant.

"But we do know where our common interests lie," replied the Glincian. "We both desire to open the Cloud to commerce. On our part, it is a desire that the Crutchtans have managed to frustrate for more than two thousand of your years."

Grant nodded ponderously.

"You may rest assured, my simian friend, that if left to their own pace, eons will pass before Crutchta reconsiders the matter. But if you join with us—align yourselves with your natural friends in the inner chambers of the High Council and stand with us as we press our claims— "

Drub'd exhaled loudly, raising his hands, palms outward. "Well," he continued, "no amount of saurian stubbornness can withstand the united efforts of three neighbor races. Their claim to the area rests upon nothing but proximity, a claim that Terra can make with equal force. And their longstanding unwillingness to exploit or settle the area has long since forfeited whatever proprietary claims they might once have had."

Grant looked into the Glincian's eyes. They were as cold as his bearing, and dark as the mysteries of creation, but for reasons that he would one day regard as a mystery, the Terran did not feel the same instinctive apprehension he felt whenever he was in the presence of a Crutchtan. He would later come to wonder whether it was the softer features of the Glincian appearance, or perhaps something as deceptively simple as *Drub'd*'s facility with the Terran language, which Fate had made possible by the similarity of Glincian vocal chords with his own. Whatever the reason, Grant felt the same easy trust toward *Drub'd* that he felt toward the Veshnans, and it made him want to take the Glincian at face value. In the end, he had little choice in the matter, for his instructions were quite specific.

"I am authorized," said Grant, "to entertain whatever proposals you care to make."

The corners of *Drub'd*'s mouth twitched in what Grant had come to recognize as a smile.

"I can promise nothing," the Terran continued.

"Neither can we," the Glinci interjected. "Other than our own good intentions."

"But if your people— "

"And let us not forget the *Atkvalo,* our longstanding allies."

"…and your allies are interested in coming to an understanding about Terran intentions, and how together we can accomplish whatever mutual goals we might have, you will find my Government highly receptive."

"Well," replied *Drub'd,* choosing his words with a precision he knew would be lost on the Terran, "unlike our Crutchtan friends, we care nothing for trivial questions like sovereignty. All that interests us is knowledge, and the ability to use that knowledge to economic advantage. So long as we have access to the Cloud—and the right to use our discoveries as we see fit—we will leave the particulars entirely up to you."

"We can settle nothing in a single meeting."

"You will find, my friend," *Drub'd* nodded slowly as he talked, "that we of the Glinci have the patience of the stars themselves, and are willing to wait however long it takes for us to reach agreement. But if, as I suspect, your Government sees the future largely as we do, I wager that we will have an informal understanding by the time you leave for home.

"Now I do not doubt that you are tired from your long day, nor that you will wish to consult your Government." *Drub'd* extended his hand. "Until tomorrow, then."

Grant felt the Glincian's smooth, leathery skin as they shook hands and was surprised to find it cool to the touch. As his visitor left he began to shiver despite the heat, and found himself overcome by a feeling of vague disquiet. He quickly attributed whatever uneasiness he felt to the fact that circumstances compelled him to negotiate with two faces, and to his knowledge that he was being less than candid with his opposites, as well as his friends.

* * *

THE FOLLOWING morning, a confused Roscoe Cook found himself seated on the floor across a large, ovate table from two old friends. They had just finished breakfast—a hot mixture of cereal grains for Zatar and his interpreter, a glass of lukewarm water for the captain. On the wall were portraits of various Crutchtan dignitaries. At least, Cook supposed them to be dignitaries: in the setting of the pose and the bearing of the subject, all had the same look of pompous self-importance about them that distinguished Terrans assumed whenever they sat for likenesses. From what he'd seen of the stratified layers of Crutchtan society, he guessed that Crutchtans, like Terrans, were unlikely to hang portraits of anyone whose sole achievement was his worth as a human being.

"Zatar says that their ways are a mystery to himself as well."

The humidity had risen during the night, and the standard issue tank top Cook wore had long since become soaked with sweat. Once outside his own room he was at the mercy of the weather, even in the temperature-controlled dining room of another. He hated the extent to which the tropical climate was draining his energy, just when he was likely to need all his wits about him.

"That isn't much help, Munshi." Cook forced himself to smile.

The Veshnan smiled in return. "Well, Cook—at least you need not stand alone."

"I doubt very much that I'll be doing much standing at all," he replied. He watched and listened as Zatar and Munshi exchanged words, and wondered whether the cold of Ishtar had bothered them as much as the heat was bothering him on Girshoona.

Finally, Munshi turned to speak once more. "Zatar has no idea why the Expanse Minister wishes an audience," she said. "He has already told them that you possess no authority, but they are adamant."

"What do they want?"

"Know not I," said Zatar, shaking his head.

"No, you are not...what?" asked Cook. He could see that Zatar was as confused as he was, though he recalled that on Ishtar they were often confused about different things at the same time. Fortunately, Munshi was always there to intercede, though he often had the impression that she was laughing at one thing or another.

As the two Veshnans conversed in their own language, Cook looked outside, into the garden. It was a pretty one, filled with exotic flowers of all kinds and sizes, and trimmed around the edges by a dark hedge of deep, rich green.

"Zatar says that Gal'Shenga insists that there are things he will discuss with no one but you, Cook," said Munshi, interrupting the thread of the Terran's daydreaming. "As for the rest—well, in their own way, our Crutchtan friends can be as stubborn as those from Terra."

Cook looked to see her smiling blandly, but he had come to the point of being able to see laughter in the Veshnan's eyes. "You're lucky I'm not a diplomat," he retorted. "Otherwise, I'd be duty-bound to feel insulted."

He heard Zatar laugh out loud, in the choking, Veshnan mode of laughing. It surprised him to learn that Zatar's understanding of English, if not his ability to speak it, had improved so much in the months since Ishtar. The ambassador motioned for Munshi to listen as he went into a long monologue in his own singsong voice, complete with graceful hand and facial gestures that Cook had never seen before.

"Zatar wonders whether that is why Gal'Shenga wishes an audience," Munshi said at last. "He says that perhaps Gal'Shenga hopes to get insight into the Terran mind through one whose tongue and mind both belong to himself, rather than echoing the wishes of a distant superior."

Cook laughed. "I'm afraid my tongue is too clumsy for much besides providing cheap entertainment. More like the clowns we saw at dinner the other day, tripping over each other. And if he'll have nothing but a translating machine to interpret what I say...well, even if Ambassador Grant gives me permission to talk to this *Galshenga*, I'll count myself lucky if I don't start a war by accident."

As Munshi translated his words, and Zatar made his response, Cook's gaze returned to the garden. He didn't see Zatar's eyes focus on him, nor his head cock gently to one side. It didn't really matter, for Cook would not have sensed its meaning: an unconscious gesture of admiration and respect.

"Zatar says," Munshi replied after an extended conversation with her superior, "that you underestimate yourself, and the impression you have made among your hosts. Meanwhile, I can reassure you about the machine. Just speak slowly and clearly, and keep your remarks free of tangled idioms. It will alert you to any phrase that it cannot recognize."

"But— "

"You may have to alter your manner of speaking to express yourself more simply, but obviously, those are difficulties which you can easily overcome."

"Munshi, I don't know if— "

"As for the rest," she continued, nodding toward Zatar and blandly indifferent to Cook's efforts to make himself heard, "it is as Zatar has said. Whatever the language, the voice of reason sounds much the same."

* * *

As Terra's ambassador played different roles for different audiences, and the captain found himself sought by his hosts for reasons he could not understand, in a remote corner of Crutchta too small to appear on any but the most detailed starmaps, four small ships put in to orbit around a small planetoid circling a small, red star. Their masters were giddy with anticipation, much like schoolboys rushing to greet the first day of summer. And soon they were walking the rocks and rilles, carrying dreams as limited as the horizon of the small, barren world.

There, hidden in a rocky crag, they found what they were seeking, exactly as it had been left many months earlier. Even in the dim light of the nearby sun, the rich color of gold glistened under the airless sky. Soon, with the sweat and effort of a few lonely men, the ships circling overhead were laden almost to bursting, stuffed with more riches than the lot of them could hope to spend in a dozen lifetimes. But as they gathered in their leader's ship, to celebrate their new fortunes, one after another came to feel a great emptiness in his soul, as if they were celebrating death itself. After their long hard journey, to find their triumph over so soon and without fanfare, in the cold vacuum of space, brought them little joy and no contentment.

As drink clouded his brain, resentment welled in Cyrus McGee's soul, and he sought something to blame for the hollowness he felt after recovering riches he'd lusted after for such a long time. As drunkenness swept him along in its wake, it seemed such a waste if their trip was over so soon. Peering out the porthole, he looked at a yellow star east and to center. And as he looked, hatred churned in his breast. He thought of the lonely world circling that small star—a world of sweet air, sweet water, and everything a man could want. A world now filled with inhuman monsters, who'd chased him away from the only world that had ever given him peace.

The lizards couldn't cheat him of his gold, he thought. And he'd be damned if he'd let them take his own private world away from him.

To the last drunken man, his party agreed to follow, to take care of the last piece of business, as he put it. "A week off, or a month—it makes us no difference," slurred one of them. "We follied ye this far, Cyrus McGee. An' by God an' by golly, we'll folly ye to the end o'creation."

Chapter 22

"MAY PLEASANT TIMES always greet you, Shipmaster," Gal'Shenga spoke into the cone-shaped translating device. Ga'Glish and his uncle rose to greet their guest, who bared his teeth and nodded. Staring into the Terran's fierce gaze, the Centurion felt a cold shiver grip his body. The wariness quickly passed, however, for almost at once the Terran began peering around the room, looking at the artworks and tapestries that adorned the walls. After all this time, and the interminable delays and excuses, he seemed nearly as interested in his surroundings as in his *g'Khruushtani* hosts. Ga'Glish wondered whether the insult was intentional, to provoke his uncle into revealing more than he intended, but he remembered the words the Terran had spoken at the welcoming feast and decided to withhold judgment. Soon, they were all seated on their pillows. Once the servants had brought the refreshments and departed, the three of them were free to converse in earnest.

"I am glad," said Gal'Shenga, striving to keep his remarks simple and direct, for the sake of the cone-shaped translator, "that you consented to join us today. I hope that we find much to discuss."

Suddenly the Terran fixed his gaze on the Expanse Minister and yipped into his own translating cone. "As I before have communicated," the machine translated, "first through Zatar and then through writings, it is *gh'Rahn-te* and not myself with whom you should speak. For it is he, and not I, who speaks for my people."

Gal'Shenga nodded politely, but his reply was more pointed than diplomatic. Ga'Glish hoped that their impression was correct, and that this Terran would prefer the freshness of candor to the niceties of diplomats.

"I beg to differ, Shipmaster," said Gal'Shenga, "but you have chosen not to speak the full truth. It is you who spends his time examining us—swimming along our shores, walking among our people—while your

Ambassador sits at the table, day after day, talking to the same faces about the same stale subjects. It is you who summon books from our library and the devices to help you make sense of them, while your Ambassador goes from meeting to meeting with no time to reflect upon what he has learned. And it is your voice and your words that carry the weight of thought, while your Ambassador's merely carry weight. Please do not insult me by insisting that it is he who commands your delegation. Your protests may fool our diplomats, but not our leaders. And until I am assured of your candor, I shall have nothing further of any substance to say."

Ga'Glish saw the Terran's head move from side to side, a gesture he had come to associate with confusion. He surmised that the Terran was at a loss to refute the obvious. "Your ways are not our ways," came the reply at last. "And I do speak the truth. The Ambassador does speak for my Government. But I will accept your protests as a compliment, and in truth, I confess that I do possess a certain amount of official discretion, though its limits would do nothing but confuse you."

Gal'Shenga and his nephew shared a smile of accomplishment. And they had confirmed a point that they had long suspected: as among the g'Khruushtani, it seemed that there were divisions within the Terran ranks.

"Even so," the Terran continued, "my discretion includes areas far removed from the Ambassador's zone of responsibility. And it is he, not I, who is authorized to make demands, and offer concessions."

"Nonetheless," Gal'Shenga interjected, "I prefer speaking to you, as I would rather speak to the Master's aide, than to his servant."

Breathing deeply, the Terran smiled—this time, without bearing his teeth—and nodded for the Minister to continue.

"You have wondered, have you not, why we insist upon a separation—a division—between our people. And you have wondered why we find Terran intrusions beyond the Great Divide to be intolerable."

"Yes, I have."

"And like others of your kind, you see our way as madness?"

"Only fools ascribe madness to that which they cannot understand."

Gal'Shenga smiled and his eyes widened. He leaned forward, with the fervor of an ecclesiastic. In all his days, and in all his struggles across the width and breadth of the Imperator's domain, he could count the number of Enlightened Ones he had encountered on the fingers of a single hand. He now wondered whether the Terrans had sent one of their own—and if they did, why they chose to do so. The thought that he was about to find out made his soul soar higher than the mightiest raptor in the sky.

* * *

THE SKY was a pristine blue. The wind whipped the sand dunes overlooking the sea, pelting the eyes and face of those who chose to walk its crests. Drubid sensed a chill in the air, though he doubted that the Terran ambassador felt any such thing. The Terrans seemed inured to the cold and this Grant-Terran seemed to welcome the cooling wind. They had come to the hills because they needed privacy and the freedom to talk without fear that a prying ear lay hidden in the walls around them.

"You have news for me?"

The Terran nodded, and Drubid felt the excitement of triumph rush through his soul, but he knew better than to betray his feelings to a simian. This was a crucial phase of their discussions, and the last thing he needed was to start drums of emotions beating in the savage Terran soul. Besides, these primitives still labored under a child's sense of honor. The slightest hint of the Glinicians' true intentions could very well send them scurrying back to the Crutchtans.

"Well, Ambassador, is it a Terran custom to keep friends in suspense?"

The ambassador shook his head. "No, at least it is no custom of mine."

"You have received word from your Government?"

"I have."

"And my answer?"

"So long as we have assurances that all parties will have free access, Terra would agree to withdraw her claim of sovereignty. Permitting our scientists, explorers, and industries to use and study the Cloud would more than compensate us for any concessions. We believe that your proposal of a joint commission to administer the region is a fair one."

"And the treaty?"

The Terran breathed deeply, a gesture Drubid had seen often in the past few weeks, yet one whose significance still escaped him.

"Terra is willing to sign a treaty to that effect, at the proper time."

"Not to sound impatient, Ambassador, but what time does Terra consider to be proper?"

"When your High Council approves the arrangement, Terra will sign. Until then, we will co-operate with you in any way we can, but we will not commit ourselves without a formal commitment from all concerned, one that recognizes Terra's rights as the equal of her new allies."

Drubid smiled, a Terran-like smile that he had spent many weeks perfecting. And yet his warm smile masked a coldness that reached into the depths of his heart. The Terrans were not the innocent fools they seemed, he mused. Beneath a savage exterior, their souls were as calculating as that of any civilized creature. But it was no matter, for over time their inexperience could substitute for oafish stupidity. For the present, a Terran commitment was all they needed.

And as for the future, once Terran consent was frozen into place, use of the Cloud's unimaginable riches would fall to those with the means to exploit them. If Terra's conceit exaggerated the capabilities of her own science, there were others who suffered from no such illusions.

Soon, the crash of waves on the shore became deafening. The two diplomats strolled together along the crest of the hill, heading toward a city alien to both, yet unfamiliar only to one.

* * *

THOUGH SWEAT flowed from his brow, Cook paid little attention to the sweltering heat. He was in a world of dreams, sitting across a table from creatures so alien that he had trouble concentrating on what they were saying. This was, after all, the first time he'd ever been alone with a Crutchtan, and he was finding the experience to be unsettling.

Their skin was brown and leathery, comprised of individual scales of varying size and shape, from large and tear-shaped along the face and chest, to minute and mesh-like on the arms and six-fingered hands. Their eyes were dark green and perfectly round, with pupils slitted like a cat's, and set farther apart and lower on the face than seemed normal to a Terran, on either side of twin peaks meeting just above what passed for a nose. The nose itself was no more than a thin, ridged slit that opened and shut with every breath, hiding two large interior openings through which the Crutchtan breathed and, to Cook's amazement, spoke. And the mouth, located in the middle of what the Terrans would call a neck, was large and ovate, bearing four rows of large molars. Only the greenishness of the gill-like openings on the either side of the thick neck and the genitalia of the lower abdomen broke the uniformly light brown coloration of the skin, though Cook had observed that the precise shade of skin coloring varied between individuals. Overall, except for the limbs,

Cook thought that the Crutchtans looked as much like fish as reptiles, and not very pretty fish at that.

But if he closed his eyes and listened to their words, he could almost forget how deformed the Crutchtans seemed to his eyes. And he kept telling himself that however disturbing he found their outward appearance, his own face was probably having the same effect on them.

"You may have wondered," came the words of Gal'Shenga over the translating device, "how peace is possible between our peoples. Our disagreements loom large as the Cloud over which we contend, and we must employ intermediaries—the Veshnans—to talk for us."

"I have known such thoughts," nodded Cook, amused to find himself adopting the stilted speech patterns he heard coming from the machine. He wondered whether the translator was having the same effect on Gal'Shenga.

"Such things are inconsequential," continued the Crutchtan, "for they stem more from myth than reality. And though such things cause us present dangers, they will fade from mind as we become inured to each other's presence. But there is a greater danger that you and your kind present us, One Called *Khu'ukh*, a danger that you may never fully comprehend, yet one which poses as big a threat to you as to ourselves."

"And what is that, Gal'Shenga?"

The Crutchtan rocked in place for a moment, before answering.

"We are a conservative people, Lord Shipmaster. We are a people set firmly in our ways. We need time to adjust, and time to adapt to new things and new surroundings. And as it is with objects, so it is with our new neighbors to the West. It will take us time to accustom ourselves to the changes that Terra brings in her wake.

"But more than this, One Called *Khu'ukh*, you and your people cannot discern the changes that shake our society as the wind shakes the trees. The last dozen generations have seen things that our ancestors little dreamed, advances in science and philosophy, the dispersion of our people to far corners of the Realm in such numbers as stagger our souls, even as they rend our families. In its wake, these changes have brought new and alien ideas into our midst—ideas which threaten our old ways as surely as they cast doubt upon our ancient truths."

Cook sat quietly, his attention riveted.

"I head a movement, Shipmaster, one which our detractors call 'reformist,' for such are the hardships that change brings to those who see the future more clearly than most. Those who denounce us as heretics or changemongers have history and tradition on their side. We have nothing but our faith in the future, and in the power of our ideas, even as we seek nothing but the betterment of our people."

The Crutchtan leaned forward, his unblinking gaze searing itself into Cook's memory.

"Others of my kind have their own reasons for keeping you outside the Great Divide—our ancient myths, our distrust of newness, even our suspicion that your intrusion into our skies will grow like a storm of bloodwasps. All of this I dismiss as superstition or worse, especially since we can discern the future no better than yourselves.

"But I have reasons of my own for wanting you to keep your distance, reasons which are more selfish yet more honorable than any I have described. You see, my Terran friend, we can tolerate only so much disruption in our lives and in our society. We could adjust to internal changes that, even though they are inevitable, would inure to my own personal and political advantage. Or, perhaps, we could adjust to a Terran presence on our frontier. I fear that we cannot do both."

Cook nodded gravely.

"And as our society moves beneath forces we neither understand nor control, I am left to seek a deferment on any dealing with Terra. For the alternative is chaos—chaos, and all the dangers that it would bring, for both our peoples."

"I can see your dilemma," said Cook, "though I cannot solve it for you. Terra has internal tensions of her own, and I have neither the power nor the wisdom to reach an accord that would satisfy all concerned."

Gal'Shenga leaned back and rocked in place for several moments before continuing further. "I expect nothing of the kind," he said, "for that is beyond the power of any man. I wish only to give you the gift of insight into another's perspective of our mutual problem. In return, I expect only that you ponder it well, and act on it honorably."

"That I can promise, Gal'Shenga."

"And ponder this also, One Called *Khu'ukh,* for it may have meaning for your companions and countrymen as well as for yourself. Others would use Terra to serve their own ends, ends that include chasing the endless riches of our Great Cloud. But as we see Terra as an unsettling neighbor, they see her as a means to serve themselves. They will use you to obtain what they are after, then cast you off like a withering concubine who has outlived her usefulness."

Soon, the afternoon sun faded into dusk; but as the stars started twinkling in the clear, dark sky, the Terran and the Crutchtans kept talking into the night.

* * *

DAYS BECAME weeks; and at the end of each week, two reports would follow long, tortuous paths from the planet Gr'Shuna westward—one path ending at Ishtar Command, the other at Covington. Different eyes, with interests differing as much as shadows from sunshine, read each report with a growing sense of wonder.

Then, without fanfare, it was all over. The diplomats finally convinced the Terran ambassador that the time had come to adjourn the talks, and he convinced a reluctant ship's captain that it was time for them to go home. Two days later, after their hosts had time to organize the obligatory Feast of Departure, a wistful Terran found himself walking alone down a palace walkway, taking no merriment from the festive sounds pouring through the palace windows, and seeking a peace that he often found in solitude.

And yet wistfulness knows no boundaries, not of time, nor space, nor race. Soon, one of his hosts approached from behind, both of them seeking a clear view of the southern sky.

GA'GLISH TRIED not to look startled, but finding a Terran sitting in the favored resting spot of his youth was hardly something he expected.

The night was still; the calm breeze tickled his skin. In the distance, Ga'Glish could hear the waves pounding the shore, as they had done for countless eons before the *g'Khruushtani* ever set foot upon the world he knew as home.

Slowly he neared the Terran, who was absorbed in some private reflection of his own. It was the Terran shipmaster, and Ga'Glish chastised himself for leaving his translating device in his room. This was likely the first and only time in his life that he would encounter one of the longnoses by himself, and they would not even be able to talk. Such, however, were the imperfections of life.

Suddenly, the Terran turned to face him, and seemed almost to jump out of his skin before baring his teeth and nodding in the Terran manner of greeting. Ga'Glish could not discern the significance of this ritual, but took it to mean that the Terran was not offended by company. When the Terran moved to one side of the stone bench, freeing the other side for Ga'Glish to sit, the latter bowed and accepted without hesitation, reflecting that for all the crudeness of their bearing, the Terrans did possess at least the rudiments of proper manners.

It was an old bench on which Ga'Glish rested, as old as the palace itself. To untold generations, it had brought solace under the stars and a matchless view of the coast. Ga'Glish had almost forgotten its draw on his soul when, as a young boy, he would seek its refuge in the wake of a well-deserved scolding, or simply to think. He loved to look at the water and hear its rhythmic pounding against the ancient shore. He loved the timeless vista of the heavens, which had drawn him to chose a life among the stars. And he had spent many idle hours simply wondering about past Galgravina who had walked the same grounds, or come to sit in the same spot, wondering at the same sights that brought him such peace.

He glanced at the Terran to his left, to see the shipmaster's gaze directed not ahead or above, but toward the eastern horizon, where dawn would come within the hour. It suddenly occurred to Ga'Glish that from the vantage of space the Terran was looking toward the West—toward a home that Gr'Shuna's sun had hidden from view for almost the Terran's entire stay. With this realization, and to his amazement, a flood of empathy washed over his soul, touching the mind of his simian companion—and confirming that the Terran was, indeed, trying to catch a glimpse of home, and that this was not the first time he had done so. But this feeling was an entirely different sort than one would expect from a newfound friend, on a lower, less visceral, less telepathic plane than he would have expected, carrying a weaker bond than he had known from friendships among his own kind, one that neither offered nor drew loyalty in its wake.

All the same, Ga'Glish found it exhilarating: for the first time, Ga'Glish found himself privy to some small insight into the Terran psyche, and it was an insight as confusing at it was enlightening. He could sense a well of deep emotions, bubbling like a mystic's cauldron, raging with turmoil and conflicting passions. And he perceived as well a profound and aggressive intelligence—a mind as powerful as any he had known, commanding a wild, alien mixture of savagery and wisdom.

Yet under it all, Ga'Glish sensed the Terran's sadness at leaving, and a heart filled with good will toward his hosts. More than anything else, this discovery brought the Crutchtan new hope for the future. Silently, the two of them sat side by side, until the stars faded under the strengthening light of the rising sun.

* * *

"LANSHANA WILL be pleased."

"As will all the women, Lanash. My mate as well, though she be far removed from these shores."

Shl'Lanasha nodded as he walked with Bra'Lendt, his friend since childhood. Though he would never admit it aloud, his heart wondered whether Lendt's approach was not the better one. His family knew no privation, nor bitter cold nor empty, windswept lands. Lendtala, his mate, lived in comfort with her family at the provincial capital. Perhaps such ways were less burdensome.

But these ways were not his own. For himself, Lanasha could not bear the thought of such a separation. And where Bra'Lendt and his mate were childless, his own young ones needed a father's guidance.

"Here we are," said Lanash.

"For three days more," smiled Lendt, "then we may depart this wasteland forever."

Bidding his friend goodnight, Shl'Lanasha entered his hut. It was warm inside, and helped to speed his blood along. Soon, he was comfortable enough to shed his clothing and wash for the night. But as his mind was still too active for sleep, he sat himself near the east window, to gaze at the sky and contemplate.

"Father?"

Lanash turned to see Shl'Glisen, sitting atop his bedding. Standing, he slowly walked to the sleep quarters and sat down next to his son.

"Yes, Young One."

"Is it true?"

"Is what true, Glisen?"

"Is it true that we are departing?"

Shl'Lanasha smiled and stroked the boy's head. He could see himself in his son's young face, just as he could see the shadow of the infant his mate had cradled in her arms just a few years earlier. "Will you miss this place, Young One?"

"Oh no, Father, though it is not so bad as I thought when we arrived."

The father laughed gently. "Yes," he said, "you and your mother both.

For the longest time, I thought that you had forgotten any other subject but the horridness of our surroundings and the length of our stay."

"Mother worries about you," said the boy, though Lanash could sense that his son spoke for himself as well. "She worries about all of us—especially Lanadra, who is too young to know when the cold is beginning to affect her."

"Your sister is learning all the time, Shl'Glisen. And it is up to you to help us teach her."

"Yes, Father."

"In the meantime, shall I tell you a secret?"

The boy nodded eagerly, folding up his legs so that he could rest his chin on his knees.

"Today's mission was our next-to-last," smiled the elder Shlangri. "We will spend three more nights here, and on the day following, we will depart for home."

The boy's eyes widened with glee. "To—?"

Shl'Lanasha bowed his head. "To *Gr'Shuna*—and to a welcoming feast that will make all our hardships here fade like a bad dream."

"But— !"

"Now, speak not a word of this," Lanash cautioned, though he knew quite well that a small boy could hold secrets no better than a sieve could hold water. "We have one more trip to the planet, either tomorrow or the next day following. Then we shall depart as soon as we finish packing for the long trip home."

Shl'Glisen smiled his youthful smile, and it seemed to his father that young ones could find joy wherever they looked, whatever their surroundings. It was a shame that life often dealt so harshly with the optimism of youth, and that such boundless good spirits would someday know pain as well as gladness.

But such thoughts could wait for another day. For now, it was enough that they were going home. For his son, the chance to spend some time with friends and family would be enough to dim the reality that duty would soon call them elsewhere.

Chapter 23

//securitydispatch/cc:143-2392.2/codea26-b/destination:
covington,foreignaffairs/governmentsecuritychannel077/
diplomaticpriority:
/Have departed Girshoona/alien contact and preliminary understanding confirmed, details follow separately, alt channel, alt code/impres-
sion alien feeler seems firm, may be friendly alt to Cr/recommend next
move CovFA— direct reply, perhaps employ CG adv base past Valhalla/
JOG/end/encrypt/transmit//

"A LAST message from Girshoona, Captain, wishing us a safe trip
home."

Cook turned to look astern, at the rear viewer. The planet's star had
nearly faded from view, but there it was, just below the center of the
screen.

It had taken them ninety-seven days, nearly a full cosmic month to
get there, and they'd stayed only half that time on the planet. The
ways of diplomats seemed horribly inefficient at times, it seemed to
him, but he wouldn't have missed it for anything.

"Thank them for their hospitality and kind wishes," smiled Cook.
"Helm, increase speed to C-12. We're heading home; next stop,
Looking Glass."

"Aye aye."

* * *

INTRA-SHIP MEMORANDUM No. 143-697

CC: 143-2393.1
FROM: The Captain
TO: THE CREW
SUBJECT: Fraternization with Non-Military Personnel

Until further notice, G-Wing of Residential Deck No. 2 will be off
limits to unauthorized personnel.

In addition, pursuant to Article 37(g)(12), governing civilian
passage on military vessels, I am invoking my authority as

commanding officer to forbid any and all fraternization between
our civilian guests and any and all members of the crew.
These directives will be enforced without exception.

* * *

"MUST YOU leave so soon?"

The sun was nearing the western horizon, coloring the sky a brilliant
orange. Ga'Glish turned to face his mother and smiled. He felt the
pain in her heart. The same ache filled his heart as well, but he had
duties and a family of his own. As his uncle had discharged his own
duties, departing for other skies that very morning, so too would the
evening send Ga'Glish back to his Haven and his mate.

"You are welcome to stay," ventured gal'Fondro. "Of that, I am
quite certain."

Sadly, Ga'Glish shook his head. Fondro was a loyal friend, yet one
who also had a master to serve. It was time for all of them to return
to the life they knew best, the life that Fate had given them. Yet as
his last day at home neared its final hours, regret filled his soul, a
regret he knew he shared with his mother and gal'Fondro. None could
command the mind of another; and as time mended some wounds,
others were immune to its healing powers.

"I am needed elsewhere," he began, only to stop as if struck dumb.
Gratitude and affection flooded his heart, as a familiar, though aging
figure stepped through the arch and into the courtyard.

"Father, " Ga'Glish whispered.

His head held proudly, Lord Glishek strode down the walkway and
came to stand beside his mate. Even at his age he was an impressive
man. Tall and handsome, he was the image of his own father, much
as Ga'Glish was his own reflection. Bowing in his most regal manner,
the elder acknowledged the presence of his son for the first time in
nearly a dozen cycles of their ancestral homeland. Though the son
felt no regret in his father's soul, and each knew that neither would
ever admit being the cause of their separation, Ga'Glish found that
his own heart would not contain itself, and emotion flooded his mind
as tears flooded his eyes.

Silently, Ga'Glishek held his hand out, bidding his mate to follow.
Glishenga, her own eyes moistening, placed her hand on his, and
followed him toward the door.

"Goodbye, Son of Mine," called his mother, barely able to keep her voice from cracking.

"Goodbye Mother," Ga'Glish returned, thirsting for words, any words, that would permit him to speak to the father who had disowned him for abandoning his home to serve a distant master among the stars.

But the words never came, and soon Ga'Glishek and his mate had departed the yard, leaving their son alone with their family's most trusted retainer.

"It is a start," said gal'Fondro, sensing that the young Galgravina had regained control over himself.

Ga'Glish smiled sadly.

"One day, perhaps."

"Perhaps," nodded Ga'Glish, his voice wistful and distant. "Let us hope that we all live long enough to see it."

* * *

"BLOODY FOOLISHNESS, that's what it is."

"Aye, Chief."

Their eyes glassy with drink, Connors and Andersen sat upright on the floor of Andersen's cabin, leaning back on the sofa for support. Two other yeomen, Chambers and Powell, were snoring noisily on the floor. Whether it was a result of the Ceresian rye, or the stress of the animated discussion on the captain's latest directive to the crew, they were out for the night.

"Ye know I got the utmost respect for the Skipper."

"That's never been in doubt, Chief."

"But, I mean, there must come a limit. Ye know, Andersen? We can only take so much o'this."

"I follow you, Chief."

Connors tried to rise, fully intending to get them both another few drams of rye. But his head had other ideas and finally convinced him to stay where he was.

"Non-fraternization indeed. Why, it's a bloody insult. Next thing ye know, he'll be tryin to keep us away from our own bluebirds—and that'll be grounds for mutiny, sure as me name is Connors."

"Well, Chief, you must admit...."

"I mean, are we so bloody damn dense that we don't have the sense to act like gentlemen? At least, as far as civilian missies are concerned? Be truthful, now, Andersen—when's the last time you put your mind to tryin to wear'em down? I mean, really put your mind to it?"

"Well, now...."

"And anyway, if it's Cozzie charm they want, then who can blame the laddie who wants to give it a go?"

"Well, Chief, you must admit that whoever put the security eye in the missies' cabins hardly made us seem like the trustworthy sort. And once the Skipper caught sight of the flyers listing their daily routine—and heard about the Hangar Deck betting pool— "

Connors snorted. "Ah, rot! What's happenin to the Guard that we can't even have us some good clean fun without some do-gooder takin it all to heart? You can bank on this, Andersen—either the Skipper's lost his wits, or he's lost something further south. And I ain't about to ask him which it is."

"Well, the Skipper's hardly a fool, Chief, and he'd never sell us out just to look good for a promotions board. I bet he's just nipping a problem in the bud. And the sooner we return the problem to port, the sooner things will get back to normal."

"Bloody lot o'bilge. Ah, well...."

Andersen just shook his head. He didn't like the new rules any better than the Chief. On the other hand he could hardly blame the Skipper. At least, not with civilians under foot.

"Well, Andersen, be a good'un and get us another glass."

Andersen laughed, and with much difficulty rose to his feet. Connors could be as stubborn as the Skipper, thought Andersen. At times like this, though, at least the Chief was level-headed enough to know what was really important.

"That's a good laddie."

* * *

THE FOUR of them sat around a table in the officer's portion of the galley—two of them alert and animated, the other two trying to keep from falling asleep.

"So that was your impression as well, Captain?"

"Absolutely," Cook nodded. He edged forward on his seat, his attention focusing on the ambassador. "In fact, at times it was downright eerie."

Janet stared at the lounge viewscreen, barely following the thread of the conversation. Her eyes drifted to her left, where she spotted Jeremy, who shook his head and yawned. Janet almost choked trying not to laugh. She knew exactly how Jeremy felt: Grant and Cook could each drone endlessly on the most obscure facets of any subject imaginable. Putting them together in the same room could work a revolution in the treatment of insomnia.

"They had the most stolid, stoic look about them," Grant continued, placing the tips of his fingers together. Janet's eyes drifted back to the stars, glowing in the endless blackness.

"And yet, there was something in the eyes...."

"Exactly," Cook interjected, his interest in the subject under discussion distracting him from the yawns of his senior officers. "You got the sense of a cauldron bubbling beneath that placid exterior. Zatar explained that their emotions were private, much like our own innermost thoughts. But he said that the Crutchtans actually can sense emotions in others. Well, others of their kind, at any rate. They can feel the anger—or love, or hate, or good will—in those around them, if the feelings are strong enough. And within their family, or their circle of intimate friends, they can read the nuances of emotion like we can read a frown. So their society has evolved— "

"— to adopt a facade of stoicism," Grant began, continuing Cook's thought, "since they don't really need any outward expressiveness to communicate. And yet I suspect their private lives have an intimacy that we can scarcely comprehend. I'm told that among the Crutchtans, mates can almost experience the other's sense of love, or hope, or longing."

"It's amazing—truly amazing," marveled Cook. "And yet, Ambassador, you can't begin to comprehend the phenomena until you actually observe it in action."

"Quite right, Captain. I find that all I read on the subject didn't prepare me in the least for observing it in operation. And you know...."

As the two of them continued their dialogue, Janet found her eyes drawn from the stars toward the face of her commanding officer. She remembered another time and another place, filled with different hopes and dreams. And for the first time in quite a while, found her sense of loss fading like yesterday's twilight, and her own feelings of self-worth returning like the dawn.

She didn't know how long it would last, this time. All she knew was that she wouldn't mind going on like this forever.

* * *

"HERE HE comes."

"Do you think he suspects?"

"Him? Are you kidding?"

"Quick—out of sight, before he sees something to tip him off."

WHISTLING AS he rounded the bend in the corridor, his arms full of reading material, Dexter pressed his entry code into the security lock on his cabin door. When nothing happened, he shifted his load to one arm, trying to pry the door open with the other.

His face showing a growing frustration, as books and papers started dropping onto the floor, he entered the command to shift the lock to voice activation.

"Open," he said, juggling his armload precariously. Obediently, the door slid open, and he hurried inside to put the library materials down.

As he tripped an electric eye in his doorway, he activated a magnetic chain that ran up the foyer wall and dumped a bucketful of water on his head, drenching himself and the books and manuals he'd borrowed from the ship's library. Silently, the door closed behind him.

Leaning back against the door, Dexter slowly slid down until he had plopped onto the floor. He heard voices that he knew outside, voices of the only friends he had in the universe, fading along with their laughter as they walked down the corridor. He closed his eyes and tried to relax, telling himself over and over again that he shouldn't take it personally, and that he was too old to cry.

As he tried to calm himself, and keep the tears from flooding his cheeks, he made himself one defiant promise. Whatever it took—and however long it took him—he would make them all regret the way they'd treated him.

If he never had another friend in all of Creation, he told himself, he would see to it. He would be the best officer on the ship, in the Wing, in the whole damn fleet if he had to be. But someday, they would regret making him feel like the ship's fool.

Chapter 24

A DEATHLY SILENCE gripped the encampment. The wind alone dared to speak, gently rattling the trees and rustling the tall grass. Even the strangers' footsteps seemed to make no sound as they gathered just beyond Ra'Jordl's hut, on the far side of the stream.

Slowly, cautiously, a crowd gathered in the center of camp. Long before this, the more sensitive among them had sensed something wrong. The clear sky assured that the morning's odd thunderclaps were not thunder. Now, the presence of the chalk-skinned longnoses confirmed that what they had heard was the cracking of a sonic boom.

By instinct, they faced the newcomers in a tight arc, keeping the small ones behind them. Like everyone, the little ones burned with curiosity. But unlike the elders, the hearts of the children knew no fear, only the playful fright evoked by legends from their campfires, and they struggled to see the strange ones clad in tattered rags. Their frisky squeals struck the hearts of their parents like daggers, just as the studied caution and measured movements of the longnoses drained the parents' minds of any thoughts but danger. Soon even the children fell silent, sensing that something was terribly wrong.

Ya'Glankha, the groupleader, whispered to the foodmaster to start moving the children westward, toward the nearby woods. His eyes remained fixed on the one whom he took for the intruders' leader, a tall, hairy-faced longnose with matted black head fur and a wild gleam in his eyes. Slowly, the Terrans came to a halt on a rise in the clearing, just outside the camp. With the caution of beasts of prey, the longnoses started dispersing to either side. Breathless, the rest of his company watched as Ya'Glankha started walking toward the rise, where the black-headed one was standing.

Ya'Glankha felt his feet itch terribly, with the instinct to flee. But he urged himself forward, reminding himself that these were intelligent, sensitive beings, fully as human as any *g'Khuushtani*. He moved slowly, deliberately, careful to give the longnoses no cause for alarm. But a haunting voice echoed in his soul, repeating an obvious truth: the border was many units to the west; and no Terran could have come this far by accident.

Soon, the distance to the rise had narrowed to a dozen paces. Ya'Glankha halted and raised his hand, palm forward in the sign of friendship. Then all sensation vanished in a blinding flash of light. He never heard his mate scream in horror. Thrown violently backwards, his body collapsed onto the ground, his face burned away by a blast from a Terran laser gun.

"THEY'RE SCATTERIN!" cried Rafferty.

Cyrus gritted his teeth and didn't bother answering. He could bloody well see, and no idiot had to point out the obvious to him.

"Herzog!" he snapped angrily. "To the right. McGraw—you and McKeller circle left. The rest o'ye, follow me."

Cyrus cursed himself for a schoolboy's blunder. They should have surrounded the camp before showing themselves. That much was clear as the Void. Any fool would have known that spooked lizards would run, just like any other animal. And if they scattered in too many directions, some would get away.

"I hope to God they're slow as turtles," he muttered under his breath.

Leading the attack, Cyrus leaped down the hill and rushed past the body of the lizard he'd shot. A few bluish-green droplets trickled down the Crutchtan's leathery cheek; the lasershot had cauterized most of the blood vessels in the ugly, fish-like face. Cyrus' nostrils could taste the smell of burned flesh.

Suddenly he looked to see another lizard racing towards him, shrieking horribly as it approached the dead Crutchtan's body. With a piercing yowl, Cyrus sped forward and cracked his fist through the creature's spongy jaw. He felt something tear in the lizard's throat, and the animal collapsed onto the ground, wheezing heavily.

Angrily, Cyrus brought his boot down into the creature's face, again and again, his rage swelling with each fresh spurt of green blood. Around him, his friends were whooping and hollering with a joyful lust. He heard the lasers' high-pitched whine, and the lizards' animal squeals echoed in his ears. His head pounded with glee, and hate pulsed in his veins. Spurred by the smell of searing flesh, he howled in triumph as he rejoined the chase.

BRA'LENDT SPUN around in his chair, horror filling his eyes.

At the same time a gust of wind from the great planet buffeted their ship. Shl'Lanasha looked out the rear window to make certain that their windsock was still intact. Clouds raced past them, filling the sock to capacity and flooding the collector with the last sampling of atmosphere that they would take before returning home. Satisfying himself that their cargo was intact, he turned to face his friend.

"What is it? Lendt—?" Lanash felt the words die in his throat as he felt a great sickness sweep through Bra'Lendt's entire being.

Lendt's hand groped toward the alarm bell, summoning the subgroupleader. The aborted message from the base brought a numbing chill to his heart. Fully dilated, his eyes fixed on Lanasha, for his friend's family was on the moon. All of them—all of his friends had families on the moon. And small ones, besides. Over and over, the message pounded on the brain of Bra'Lendt like a hammer.

"Lendt...," began an impatient Fa'Jenri the subgroupleader, until the monitor's chilling fear flooded the consciousness of everyone in the room and Bra'Lendt repeated the one-word message—the last word they would hear from the base.

"Terrans," he whispered, tears flooding his eyes. "Terrans."

SHL'GLISEN WAS almost to the woods when he heard the whine of the Terran laser behind him. Spinning on his heels he turned to see his mother fall to the ground, next to the tool shed beside the food-master's hut. Flames were rising behind her, as the longnoses put torches to their homes. His sister had been separated from them in the panic, and the shrieks of young ones and elders alike were filling the air. Too numbed by terror to feel afraid, too scared to cry, he raced back to help, tugging mightily to get her to rise to her feet.

"Hurry—!" he began, his young voice quivering. He looked into his mother's eyes, only to find a calm and peacefulness that seemed alarmingly out of place.

"Mother, please...."

Lanshana shook her head, trying not to wince from the pain. She had already caught a crippling wound to her leg, and the Terran laserblast had caught her flush in the back. She feared that this last wound was mortal, and doubted that she would be able to get to safety. Yet with all that was going on about them it was the least of her worries. With a mighty effort, she raised herself onto her elbows. It took all her remaining strength not to cry out in torment.

"Listen to me, my small one," she panted, urgency filling her whispers. "You run to safety. That is my last word to you."

"But— "

"Do not argue, Glisen. You cannot carry me and I cannot walk."

"Mother— "

"I shall be along, as best I can."

"Mother— "

"And if I cannot— "

"Mother—! "

"Remember me in your thoughts."

"*Mother—!!!* "

"*Hurry,*" she whispered. Pushing her son forward, Lanshana collapsed onto the ground, tears flooding her eyes. Pain seized her back and she nearly gave herself up as lost. But as the death shrieks of friends rang in her ears, anger filled her heart—anger and despair at all she would see no more; anger and hatred at the monsters who were destroying all she had known and loved. She vowed to reach the safety of the forest. If she was to die, she thought, she meant to die in peace, not at the hands of butchers. Desperately, she began to crawl along the ground, her hands clawing the dirt as she pulled herself toward the woods, blinding pain tormenting her body with each agonizing movement she made.

"Hurry, Young One!" she called with each lurch forward, as much to herself as to her young son.

Grief filling his heart, Shl'Glisen ran as swiftly as his small legs permitted. The desperate sound of his mother's voice rang in his ears as she urged him to safety. Reaching the woods, he kept running until he tripped over the root of a tree. His face buried in the dirt, he heard a sound that would haunt the rest of his life.

It was a scream—a horrid scream that split the air like a knife, and buried itself into the deepest reaches of his soul.

He recognized the voice. It was his mother, calling to him from the grave.

* * *

EVEN AS the flames raged toward the sky, the color drained from Cyrus' face.

"Cyrus!"

"Hold your tongue."

"But— !"

"Hold, I said." Cyrus struck Rafferty squarely in the jaw, knocking him to the ground.

"It's your bloody fault anyway, for not tellin me right off."

"But...."

Cyrus kicked the prostrate pilot in the side, then stormed off, fuming at the latest turn of events. However he looked at their situation, a voice inside his head kept droning the same answer, and they really had no choice.

"Listen to me, ye pack of bilge rats," he said at last, spitting his words out bitterly. "Take what ye want and let the rest burn through to Hell. But we'd best clear out—and I mean now."

"But Cyrus—there's no— "

"Since Brother Rafferty didn't think to tell us about the lizard he cut down in the radio shed, and thought it more fun to amuse himself by seein how loud lizards can scream, there's no tellin how well known our presence has become. I ain't no expert, and I can't tell ye if the bloody thing works. But McCauley reports a vessel headin out this way from the planet, an I think it's best we clear out."

"But— "

"Or stay, as ye wish, and let the lizards make pie stuffin out o'ye. But I'm a-headin back to my ship." He turned and started walking toward the clearing where they'd left their jet packs.

"Dammit, Cyrus! Rafferty's a-hurtin."

Cyrus turned and flashed a chilling smile. "Then leave him," he said, his eyes burning coldly. "Leave him with the bloody lizards."

As Cyrus turned and continued walking, McKeller and Swenson bent over to help Rafferty to his feet.

"He's mad," said McKeller.

"No madder'n we are," retorted Swenson, taking care not to stretch Rafferty's side. "No madder'n any who'd folly the likes o'him."

"Aaah—"

"How are ye? Can ye walk?"

Rafferty nodded, wincing from the pain.

"Let's get," McKeller said, to the rest of the group. "Cyrus is right about one thing. We'd best be gone when the lizards come with reinforcements."

Soon, they were all racing toward their jet packs.

* * *

"SUBGROUPLEADER!"

Bra'Lendt looked out the viewing window again. They were just past the moon's gravitational field, but close enough to see the blue of the seas and the broad cloud patterns, as well as something that made his soul burn with hatred.

"Subgroupleader!" he repeated, his voice filled with purpose.

He looked at Lanash, feeling the pain of doubt that racked his friend's mind. Lendt's own relief at having left his family at home was almost lost in the torment he felt for his friends and comrades. He hated to think what might await them when they arrived, yet he knew such thoughts had seized most of the others on board.

Finally Fa'Jenri arrived, along with most of this, their last survey party. The sight from the window burned indelibly into their memories. Just past the curved arc of the fertile moon's horizon was a line of specks, gleaming brightly in the sunlight. In single file, they raced from the moon in tight formation, speeding outward, away from the star system's solar plane and toward the west. There were four of them, slipping through the blackness until they faded from sight.

* * *

THE ODOR of smoldering wood hung like a shroud over the encampment. A puff of wind stirred the air, raising dust and ashes, causing the leaves on the trees to shudder while the dying flames flickered in the wind. The sun was nearing the horizon, and filled the sky with strange colors—purple and orange, darkening with the coming of night.

None of this mattered to the dazed men who walked through the camp, sifting through the rubble with weak eyes and hearts numbed with grief. Without a word, they hunted through the wreckage of homes they had left hours before, searching among the dead and desperate to find some stirrings of life. They saw instead only the bodies of friends and loved ones, most of them women and small children.

They fanned out over the charred, smoking ruins. Prepared for the worst, all kept their weapons in their hands and ready to fire. But when Gra'Cranila, the boldest, most skilled pilot in the camp, nearly shot and killed a small child as she ran weeping and hysterical from her hiding place in the nearby woods, the Subgroupleader ordered all weapons sheathed. Slowly, a few small ones began to venture from their places of safety, running and clinging desperately to their fathers as if to life itself. Others ran to the nearest man to bury themselves in the nearest pair of arms. All had to be held and soothed like infants. Everywhere lurked the ghosts of demons, and the haunted faces of the children told tales beyond their comprehension.

As OTHERS around him poked through the ruins, and called out for survivors, Alternate Subgroupleader La'Shendra stepped across the rubble of the structure that had been his own hut. Scorched furniture and blackened pictures crumbled to dust beneath his feet. The smell of death was everywhere. Sickeningly sweet, like fruit rotting in the summertime, it filled his nostrils and burned itself into his memory. Following a sound he did not recognize, he stepped past the housing huts and through a small copse of flowering bushes. Moving beyond the last bush, his eyelids suddenly forced themselves shut, and warm tears filled his eyes.

Voicelessly, deep within the soul of his senses, he felt someone calling to him.

"*Please.*"

Sealing his eyelids tightly, La'Shendra shook his head violently. His brain fought against revulsion, but he felt himself weaken, and dropped to his knees, whimpering like a small child. He dared go no closer.

"*Please.*"

"I cannot," he whispered, his throat tightening with the pain he felt in the air.

"*Help me—please.*"

"I am sorry— "

"*I beg you—please.*"

Slowly opening his eyes, La'Shendra looked at the lasergun he had strapped to his side upon first hearing the news. He still dared not raise his head, but felt his heart filling with pity.

"Please."

Rising to his feet. La'Shendra took his weapon from his side. He had to do it quickly, he thought, or he would be sink to his knees again like a child. He felt the presence surrounding him suddenly take heart from his resolve. In the heartbeat it took him to aim, he recognized the eyes of Ca'Landa, the apprentice foodmaster, hanging limply from their sockets, half his skin peeled away from his body, his arms and still staked to the posts on either side of his body, insects crawling over spillage from the gaping hole in his abdomen. Around him were the dead bodies of a dozen others, mangled and mutilated in a dozen different ways.

"Quickly. Quickly, please. I can bear it no longer."

Pulling the trigger, La'Shendra fell to his knees. He felt the peace of Ca'Landa fill his heart, and began to weep like an infant. Struggling to master his emotions, he found that he was helpless to control himself. No matter how strong he tried to be, grief raged around him like an angry sea. Quickly rising to his feet, La'Shendra ran toward the ruined settlement as fast as he could, terrified by what he had seen and sickened by the memory of what he had done.

BRA'LENDT WANDERED toward the outskirts of camp, his heart sick and weak with pain. All was quiet, but it was the quiet of a graveyard. To spare his friends from any further suffering he gave no voice to his thoughts, but his heart feared that they would find no more survivors.

Suddenly, he spotted a body on the ground, near the tool shed. His soul became a bottomless well, for he recognized Lanshana, the mate of Lanash. Her chest was ripped open, her face frozen in the horrors of death. Beside her, half-eaten by scavengers, what remained of her heart lay on the ground, caked in dust. Angrily shooing away the animals from near her, he forced himself forward and kneeled beside the body. The soil was stained green; the longnose who killed her had left his footprints in her blood. Lendt felt his heart and his stomach grow weak.

Suddenly he heard a muffled sound coming from behind him. Jumping to his feet, he spun around, ready to pounce upon the source of the noise. But when he saw who it was, his soul melted into pity: it was Shl'Glisen, son of Lanash, and perhaps the last survivor they would find among the carnage. Sitting alone, he was curled into a ball by the side of the shed, dried tears staining his face.

He ran to the boy, who drew away in a panic. Bra'Lendt sensed that Shl'Glisen had not perceived his own approach. The boy was still in shock, able to see nothing but the dead body of his mother.

He sat beside the young one, letting his mind share the boy's grief and torment. He knew at once that it would be days before Shl'Glisen would be ready to talk, and that the poor boy might never recover. He could feel the young one's overwhelming sense of failure at being unable to save his mother from such a death. He placed his arm around the boy, and the two of them gently rocked back and forth, sharing their pain, until at last another came along. It was ls'Rosha, the junior meteorologist who had angrily protested his selection to the last sampling detail.

"Find Lanash," Lendt whispered tearfully. "Tell him that his son lives."

At the other side of camp, Lanash knelt in the earth, cradling a small mass of flesh in his arms. His heart was empty and his soul was numb. The smoldering ruins of the settlement filled his senses. The bodies of dead friends littered the camp. Yet his mind could grasp nothing beyond what lay, limp and lifeless in his arms.

He lowered his eyes once again toward the body of his small daughter and ran a trembling hand over her face. It was cold to the touch, cold as the planet to which he had brought her to die. He lifted her arm to grasp her small, lifeless hand, remembering how little Lanadra had laughingly clasped his fingers when she was but an infant, cooing lovingly at the fawning adults who hovered over her. A thousand memories rose to haunt his brain—her smile, her tiny cry, the deepest fears that haunted a small child's soul, the carefree laughter they had shared as he watched her grow into childhood, all flooded his heart with an impotent mix of love and rage. Letting go of her hand, it dropped to her side to dangle in the evening air.

The small body showed few signs of violence, unlike so many others whom the barbarians had mutilated beyond comprehension. Only a large, blackened wound on her left side betrayed what had killed her, but her death would haunt him forever. Like all the others, she had died in terror. And she had died alone, with no warm presence to ease her fears and share her passage into eternity. When she most needed a champion, one to protect her against the blackest of evils, he was absent, able only to wring his hands from afar, like the weakest old eunuch of antiquity.

The sun sank below the horizon, leaving the stars to shine through the gathering darkness. Shl'Lanasha raised his head and howled his pain to the sky.

Chapter 25

THE *D'ARTAGNAN* WAS six days out of Girshoona, and the last two hours had been among the worst of Cook's life. Seated on the command chair, and however he looked at it, he saw nothing but crises.

"Any luck, Mr. Underwood?"

The communications officer shook his head.

"I'm sorry, Skipper. No matter what I do, the relay won't accept our signal. It's like the Crutchtans have cut the line. And they still haven't answered our hail."

Cook rubbed his eyes and took a long breath.

"Helm, steady as she goes," he said, trying to sound as confident as he could. "Mr. Underwood, page the Ambassador and have him meet me in the my office in ten minutes. Let's see if he has any idea what this is all about."

"Aye, sir."

"In the meantime, the ship will maintain Yellow Alert. And tell Engineering to start checking all weaponry systems—especially the shields. I don't like the looks of any of this."

"Aye, aye."

HALF-ASLEEP AND looking out of sorts, Commodore Wright entered the briefing room. The bright lights hurt her eyes, and at first she didn't notice the large, portable viewscreens that lined the far wall.

"All right" she said sullenly. "What's all this about?"

A handsome young lieutenant with an air of righteous officiousness about him motioned for one of the redshirts to bring their commander a cup of coffee. Wright groaned inwardly; it meant that this was likely to be a long session.

The lieutenant turned to face her, his humorless eyes burning with purpose. "The advance bases have detected a sudden movement of alien vessels from their starbases," he began.

"Which direc—"

"All moving away from the Neutral Zone a flank speed, and toward the general direction of the Yorchuk Bend in the Cloud."

Wright shook her head. "Lieutenant, they have every right to—"

"There's more, Commodore," the junior officer smiled coldly. Making a show of taking no offense at the young blueshirt's breach of manners, Wright nodded and raised her hands as if apologizing for the interruption.

"We have also detected what can only be described as a massive mobilization of Crutchtan interstellar ships. It shows as far as our sensors can detect and from every planet we have ever been able to discern. Their ships are all converging toward a point past the Great Central Promontory."

"And shielded from our own sensors?"

"Yes, Commodore."

Wright paused; they'd never observed such maneuvers before. Their Agreement specified that both sides had to conduct any full-scale exercises out in the open, in full sight of the other side's monitors.

"What do the aliens have to say about it?"

"They won't answer our hail."

"Well, that doesn't— "

"And," the lieutenant continued, "we seem to have lost contact with the *d'Artagnan*."

Wright's eyes widened. A rush of adrenaline purged all thoughts of sleep from her mind.

"How long since the last transmission?"

"Twelve cosmic hours, ma'am. They're two hours overdue. And as their last message showed nothing seriously wrong with—"

The commodore didn't even hear the young officer finish his sentence. As long as a starship was missing, in space controlled by a force showing outward signs of hostility, Terran security was in danger. She might not know what was happening, or have any better idea of alien intentions than anyone else. Sadly, she realized that she had no clue how it all might end. But her next official act was predetermined.

Leaving the aide prattling in her wake, she walked to the intercom and called Base Dispatch onto the screen. "Open a channel to Ishtar Command," she said to the communications officer whose face appeared. "Priority One, Code Red—Command Security Alert for Admiral Clay."

* * *

"SO WHAT you're saying...."

"I am speculating, Captain." Ambassador Grant leaned back in his chair and tried to relax. He realized the danger that faced them. Though sworn to secrecy, he decided that he had to trust the captain and pool their knowledge. Keeping Cook in the dark meant that the captain would be making decisions without knowing the full story. Grant just hoped his host would know how to use the new information to get them out of their predicament.

"There is quite a bit about my mission that I have shared with no one, despite your transparent invitations to do so on our outward trip. But there are...aspects, shall we say...about what I have been doing that may shed some light on our situation."

"Specifically?"

"Specifically," Grant cleared his throat, "just after we departed from Girshoona I radioed a message home, to the Foreign Ministry in Covington. A coded message, and one which I fear may be partly the cause of the communications blackout the Crutchtans have imposed."

"Assuming that they broke the code."

Grant nodded. He tapped his fingertips together and stared off into the distance, wondering where to begin.

"You see, Captain, the peace conference was only half the reason for our trip into Crutchta."

Cook stared ahead coldly; the squeak of his chair as he rocked back and forth was beginning to unnerve the Ambassador.

"We are trying to come to terms with the Crutchtans," Grant continued. "But they are not the only aliens in the Consortium. And we have had contacts—secret contacts—with others."

Grant looked Cook squarely in the eye.

"We share borders, of a kind, with two races besides the Crutchtans. Neither wants us to surrender our claim to the Cloud, and each is willing to back us, jointly or collectively, to whatever extent is needed to force Crutchta to open the Cloud to all. I have talked at length— secretly, of course, but at length—with their representatives. And my message to Covington was that they seem prepared to meet whatever terms we have to offer."

"So you think...."

"I don't know what to think, Captain," said Grant, "except that we may be dealing with people who have decided that they have nothing to lose. If the Crutchtans have intercepted our message, they know that we are close to reaching an accord with their rivals. I know little of Consortium politics, but I do know how strongly the Crutchtans feel about the Cloud, and about keeping it off-limits to foreigners. If they are determined to prevent an alliance...well, nothing is beyond the realm of possibility."

"That doesn't make my job any easier," Cook said coldly.

Grant nodded his head. "I thought you should know."

The two men sat across the table for several moments, without saying another word, each alone with his thoughts. Before long the intercom sounded. It was Van Horn, reporting that the shields were at full strength and the main guns had passed inspection with flying colors.

"Let's hope we don't need them," Cook said impatiently, as he switched off the speaker. A cold chill made him realize that he was the only one who knew how little use the guns would be in a crisis.

Grant rose to leave, and Cook escorted him to the door.

"You know," Grant said at the doorway, a grim smile on his lips, "when we left Looking Glass—before the Sarkisian government fell—I was charged with exactly the same mission: negotiate with the Crutchtans and make the others deal in specifics. So far, the effect of the change in governments back home is too minuscule to calculate. For all the posturing the Tories have done over the past few years, in the last analysis they see Terran interests exactly the same way."

Cook watched the ambassador walk down toward the elevator until he disappeared around the bend. The status light on the wall glowed a bright yellow. The corridor was filled with purposeful crewmen, all carrying worried and determined faces. He watched them in silence, knowing that the fate of each of them rested on his shoulders. At the same time, he felt completely alone.

After several minutes, he turned and reentered his office. Debris cluttered the room, a monument to its owner. Oddly, he found his junk strangely consoling, giving him a sense of continuity with his past. As the door closed behind him, he flopped onto the sofa stretching along the inner wall. And as the rest of the crew went about its business, he lay by himself, staring at the ceiling as his heart pounded in his chest, wracking his brain as he tried to decide what to do next.

* * *

STARS BURNED in the blackness like rare gems, spreading a rainbow of color toward the Galactic Center. But the beauty of the heavens was wasted on the inhabitants of four small ships racing westward across the heavens. Massive, reddish clouds hung off to starboard, stretching into the distance as far as any could see, singing a haunting, inhuman song across most radio bands as gravity and radiation danced and swirled in violent eddies. Deep within the frozen cauldron, glowing patches of spiraling hydrogen bore testament to the slow-motion miracle of interstellar birth. Yet no one on the ships had time to wonder about the mysteries of space. While the great cloud hung like an eternal ghost to one side, a more dominating reality was closing in from the others. To a man, their minds were fixed not on the majesty of the surrounding skies, or the mass of gold lying in the hold of each ship. Their minds saw only the blips on their radar screens, closing in on them.

"Cyrus—? Cyrus—what d'ye make of it?" a colorless voice asked across the blackness of space.

"I still think it were a blunder not to go back the way we came."

"Ahhh, McKeller...you've fewer tracks in your head than McGee."

"Watch your bloody mouth, Herzog or I'll blast ye here to kingdom bloody come."

Cyrus said nothing. Cabin lights off, he sat in the darkness, his face lit only by the glowing dials of his control panel. Alone on his ship, he'd kept his own counsel for the past two days, ever since they left the lizards dead and dying on the ground and fled to the stars just ahead of the lizard posse.

Now, the moon was four parsecs behind them and the path through the cloud lay many parsecs beyond that. But it was plain to Cyrus that they'd never have made it going that way. The lizards would have closed in on them well before then. A patrol would have been waiting for them, leaving them with nowhere to go but straight into the Cloud. No, it was better this way. The Neutral Zone was forty parsecs ahead; no matter what the others thought, they stood a better chance trying to make it a straight run.

That is, Cyrus shuddered, if they stood a chance at all.

Cyrus looked out the window, into the Black. The lizards were out there, that much he knew. The slimy creatures would never rest until Cyrus and the rest were turned to ashes, spreading out over eternity.

Making a run across open space was a risky business. Even if they outfoxed the first wave of the ugly beasts, there would be more to follow. The lizards would snap at their heels all the way, leaving them no time to rest, no chance to escape. In his darker moments, he knew that one by one, sooner or later, the lot of them would probably light the sky. But it wasn't dying that scared him; spacers dodged death with every parsec they sailed. It was something to be avoided, not feared. All the same, he hated the thought of meeting his end through a slimy hand on an slimy star-blaster.

No, he thought, such notions were foolishness. Better to keep his mind focused on the chance he had, and on the vast room he had to maneuver. It would be giving up the game to be like the others, letting panic addle his mind. He turned on his radio.

"All right," he said gruffly, his voice warning against the slightest dissent. "I've heard enough o'your tongue-waggin and hand-wringin."

"Cyrus—ye buggerin bastard. Ye got us all into this fix an now...."

"Silence! Silence, McKeller, or I'll be off to home by meself and leave the rest o'ye to be lizard bait. So help me I will."

"All right, Cyrus," called another voice. It was Rafferty, his voice partly muffled by static. "Tell us what ye've go in mind."

Cyrus laughed darkly. "Ye won't be likin it; I don't much like it meself."

"Talk, ye bloody bastard!"

"Rafferty, how far away d'ye figure the lizards to be? Six, maybe seven parsecs?"

"More or less. Three days off. Four, maybe. Unless the lizards got themselves a starship, but then we're lost to be startin."

"All right, now listen. When the salymanders get within spittin distance, they'll follow us to Hell if we care to lead them."

"Don't talk gibberish, man."

Alone in the darkness of his own bridge, Cyrus sneered. "Ye be wantin plain talk, is it? Well, let this be plain enough. I'm a-headin into the Cloud and darin the lizards to follow. The rest o'ye, ye can follow or not, and the bloody devil can take ye, if ye don't."

"Are you mad ? You know how far it is to home? Must be—"

"I know, McGraw, but most o' the Cloud ain't no more dangerous than clear space. It's just the instruments what gets fouled up, leavin us blind to whatever's a-comin. If we stay close to the edge, to be rightin ourselves when we get turned around...and with a little luck, God willin...we'll make it just fine."

"For the love o'— "

"Well, Kenny McKeller, ye can love whate'er ye be wantin. But that's what I'm a-doin. For the rest o'ye, ye can bloody well fend for yourseves, for all I care."

Cyrus ended his transmission but he kept his radio tuned, listening to the others. He'd never heard such high-mouthed babbling in his life, but for all their caterwauling nobody was thinking of anything better. As the conversation returned to general moaning about their current fix, a shadowy smile crossed Cyrus' lips. Soon, convinced that his plan would work, he put his ship on automatic pilot, closed his eyes, and slept like a baby.

Chapter 26

ACROSS THE EMPIRE, emotions churned like waves on an angry sea. The blackness of space had never seemed so cold and unforgiving. And on board all the Imperator's ships, hearts beat fiercely with the heat of vengeance.

"Readings?" asked La'Stala, the groupleader. He stood behind the monitor's shoulder, his eyes fixed on the spacenormal viewer. Tall and proud, his soul flamed like the brightest star. Though few would ever see them, the Grand Haven had transmitted pictures of the atrocity at *Shun'Galanga*. The family of his brother lived on the *Shunilla* colony, barely a dozen astronomical units from 'Galanga. The Terrans could easily have chosen any nearby planet to indulge their lust for blood. Fury and hatred were all that cured his sense of revulsion. And as the detachment's commander, the responsibility for stopping the Terran butchers was his.

"Contact is still intermittent," replied the monitor. "The Cloud speaks as loudly as the intruders."

"But their course is unaltered? They still approach?"

"Yes, Groupleader, though they still track the contours of the Cloud, as they have for days." Puzzlement in his eyes, the monitor turned in his chair to face his leader. "They must know our position and know that we block their escape, just as Sh'Ilanta blocks the way east. Why they leave themselves without retreat—"

"We cannot fathom their ways," La'Stala said sharply. "Let it suffice to make them know the full lash of *g'Khruushtani* justice."

"Yes, Groupleader."

La'Stala paced, his gill slits flushing richly with his passion. He could feel the rage welling in those around him. Their hatred burned from deep within, like the embers lighting the lumescent cloud hanging in the emptiness beside them.

* * *

```
///II/COMMAND ALERT
  CC:        143-2499.8/
  TO:        CommandingOfficers-EasternFleet/
  FROM:      FtAdmPorterMClay/
  SECURITY:  Code Blue/
  PREFIX:    GeneralAlert/
  FLAGS:     red1;red2;red3/
```
Until further notice, all Eastern Fleet starbases shall maintain a Condition Green Readiness Watch.

All non-essential transmissions shall observe Article IX emergency restrictions. The following subspace channels are reserved for emergency use until further notice: High Frequency Channels 6, 8, 71-85, 91-100; Medium Wave Channels 40-100; 201-500; all Low Wave Channels. All commands shall monitor LW-2 for security bulletins and emergency information.

All CosGuard vessels between SB-102 and the Neutral Zone shall maintain Yellow Alert status until otherwise directed by their home bases. All CosGuard vessels within 5 parsecs of the Neutral Zone shall observe a Yellow Alert-Battle Watch until otherwise directed by Fleet Headquarters.

The following starbases shall maintain Red Alert status until further notice: SB-117, SB-118, SB-119, SB-120, SB-121.
ENCRYPT/TRANSMIT//

* * *

"THERE THEY are again, Mr. Ashton, same as before."

Jeremy rose from the command seat on the bridge and walked to the systems desk. Peering over Dexter's shoulder, he saw the same pattern that had teased their motion sensors for the past few days.

A triad—at the very limits of their sensing range. Three groups of ships, six ships to a group, all maintaining a distance of two parsecs and matching *d'Artagnan's* precise course and heading.

It was a tail, thought Jeremy. At least that's what it seemed to him. The Crutchtans were tracking them like hunters tracking a quarry. Only these hunters knew exactly where to find them, on the only known route home. And home was a long way away.

"Shall I page the Skipper?" asked Mathison, turning in her chair.

Jeremy shook his head. "He needs his sleep, and there's no sense bothering him until there's something new to report." Exhaling loudly, Jeremy returned to the captain's chair. Despite an undercurrent of panic among the crew, everyone was doing a yeoman's job in yeoman's fashion: ably and, in a crisis, without complaint.

But it was little more than their sense of discipline, thought Jeremy, the same discipline that the captain had instilled over countless drills and countless complaints, that kept the crew calmly at their posts. That, and the image each carried in his own mind of the captain, barking his orders on the bridge to lead them through whatever might lie ahead.

"Helm, steady as she goes."

"Aye, sir."

"And Mr. Dexter, notify the hangar deck to ready the scouts. I want reconnaissance teams to start assembling. If we've got company astern, the Skipper will want to know if they're lurking anywhere else, just out of range."

* * *

As TENSIONS mounted on both sides of the frontier, rumors were spreading across the width and breadth of Terra.

"Suzie!"

Suzie Yang looked up from her viewer to see Freddie, the office gofer, walking toward her desk.

"Brewster wants you," said Freddie. He was a gangly kid, with unkempt hair and an easy grin. Suzie liked him; in fact, now that she was back, she found that there were few people working in the Covington Bureau of UMN that she didn't like.

"Crisis meeting, sounds like. Guess you'll find out, though." Freddie's head nodded like a yo-yo, his eyes showing that his mind was miles away, dreaming idly.

"On my way," said Suzie. She rose from her desk, straightened her favorite blue dress, and started toward the back office.

"UNACCEPTABLE—THAT is totally unacceptable," thundered Hollenbach. He glowered across the table at the hapless whiteshirt who ran the public relations office of CosGuard's Central Command, a slight though intense man named Willoughby, whose chief claim to his rank was the snappiness of his memos and the fact that Mrs. Willoughby was the sister-in-law of High Admiral Pendleton.

"Senator...."

"You forget yourself, Admiral," Hollenbach continued, leaning back in his chair. "You forget who you are and who you're dealing with."

The whiteshirt snorted, his eyes flaming. He was not used to being treated like a file clerk, and in his own domain he took pride in the terror he struck in the hearts of his underlings. But underlings didn't control CosGuard's budget, and whatever he thought about the senior senator from Earth, the admiral could hardly afford to let his feelings surface. Through the window outside, he saw that the sky promised another dose of cold, winter rain. At times like these, the grayness pretty much reflected his own self-image. Unfortunately, he feared that such times would be much more common in the days ahead.

"All I am saying, Senator...."

"Let's cut the crap, shall we? You say that you lack the authority to release the information I need."

"Well, Senator Hollenbach, it's more complicated than— "

"Fine. If the Cozzies want to take care of their own and let feather-bedders run their PR departments because they're unfit to do anything useful, I don't care. That's *their* business. After all, I'm a politician. I *understand* all that."

Hollenbach smirked inwardly as he watched the whiteshirt's back stiffen. He continued without giving his host time to open his mouth. "Now if you ask me, there's something wrong when a member of the Senate—let alone, the chairman of the committee that authorizes the goddamn paychecks of all the goddamn Cozzie feather-bedders in all the goddamn Cozzie bases in all of goddamn Terra—there's something wrong when he can't get a straight answer to a simple question."

"Now look here, Senator!"

"All right, Admiral...*you* lack the authority to tell me anything." Hollenbach leaned forward, menacingly. "Well, if it's not too much trouble," he said in a low, intense whisper, "perhaps you can put me in touch with someone that Central Command trusts to make a decision."

His eyes filled with resentment, Willoughby touched the page button on his intercom. "Yes, sir?" replied a voice from the next room.

"Mrs. Gonzalez, place a call to Admiral Tuttle in the Chief of Staff's Office. Tell him that Senator Hollenbach is in my office and would like to speak to him."

"Right away, Admiral."

"Well now," Hollenbach said, oozing good nature from every pore in his body. "That really wasn't so hard now, was it?"

Willoughby's reply was a tight smile.

Hollenbach relit his cigar, amusing himself with the smoke's effect on the nose of his host.

"If you'll excuse me," said the admiral, rising from the chair behind his desk, "I'm sure I can find something to do elsewhere."

"Nonsense," Hollenbach said, his mood suddenly friendly as a favorite uncle. "Maybe we'll both learn something useful here."

"Sit—please, Admiral. Don't leave on my account."

"IT'S LIKE...."

The face on the monitor looked off-screen, shrugging as he searched for a way to describe what they had seen happening. Sam Drummond, head of UMN's Demeter Bureau was rarely at a loss for words, but events of the past week had puzzled him.

"Well, it's not really like the crisis after President Kai's heart attack, because everyone knew what was going on. And it's not like the Hawkins crisis—not exactly, anyway. Because—well, because— "

"Because we're not facing the shock of discovery. Or anything else that I can see, for that matter," ventured Ben Brewster, sitting behind the table facing the screen. Behind the plain blue transmission screen the conference room was sparsely furnished. Barren tables, and chairs badly in need of upholstering were all that filled the room. But the lowly trappings never showed on the other end of the viewer, so the company had no incentive to hire a decorator.

"I suppose it may seem that way back there," continued Drummond. "But out here, there's—well, it's not so much panic, as...as...unfocused anxiety."

"Well then," said Suzie, from her seat the table, "what exactly are we all anxious about? I mean, we don't really have any hard facts, do we? Just a lot of speculation about— "

"More than speculation," Drummond interjected, shaking his head defensively. "The facts just don't add up to anything. Nothing that we can pin down, anyway. But there's a real sense that...that...oh, you know, it's hard to describe...."

"Well, the 'fact' that the Fleet hasn't returned from maneuvers—or the broadcast restrictions—or the small upgrade in alert...none of this is unprecedented. As for all the spacer's barroom gossip," Suzie's voice trailed off, and she shook her head skeptically. "It really means nothing. At least, nothing we can broadcast."

"All I know is what I hear," shrugged Drummond. "And the spacers all say that CosGuard has clapped tight restrictions on travel. The tightest since the Hawkins Massacre. They've grounded all civilian traffic out past the Hodges system. As for the gossip, the talk isn't about the Guard. It's about the aliens. And about a missing ship—and about strange sensor readings, and odd radio messages, and—"

"Well, Sam," said Brewster, rising to his feet. "I really think we're chasing shadows here."

"But—"

"That doesn't mean I don't want you to keep your eyes and ears open. But we really have nothing solid. Nothing more than the vague musings of spacers. And that's no better than reporting the latest rumors from the local mental ward."

Drummond sighed, but nodded his agreement.

"Keep us posted."

"I will, Ben."

As they released the channel and the screen went dark, the conference room broke into a dozen conversations, with everyone wondering why someone like Sam Drummond would start jumping to all sorts of wild conclusions.

But then, none of them really wanted to confront Drummond's speculations. Or what they might mean for the future, if they proved to be true.

HOLLENBACH LOOKED sternly at the figure on the screen where Admiral Thomas Tuttle, every bit as stubborn as Earth's senior senator, folded his arms and leaned back in his chair.

"So you're telling me," Hollenbach said at last, "that the whole Eastern Fleet has had no word from the lizards for the last week?"

"No, Senator. I am telling you that the aliens have not yet responded to—"

"Well, Tuttle, what the hell is the difference?"

From his office in CosGuard's Central Command Headquarters, Tuttle fixed an angry glare at Hollenbach. The admiral had seen this type before. Willoughby might be too weak-kneed to stand up for himself, but he'd see himself damned before giving in to the likes of Emerson Hollenbach.

"Excuse me, Senator, if you would kindly let me finish, I was simply trying to tell you that the aliens have not responded to any of our concerns, or any of our questions, for the last nine days."

"And the ship? The starship you people sent over the border? You're telling me that you have no idea what's become of it?"

"We are attempting— "

"Don't give me all the bureaucratic mush, Tuttle. That claptrap may fool some of my colleagues, but it doesn't wash with me. I'm not leaving until I find out what I want to know."

Tuttle's jaw twitched angrily, but he kept his composure.

"As I was saying, Senator, we are attempting to discover exactly what is happening. As of now— "

Hollenbach snorted, looked at Willoughby, and rolled his eyes derisively.

"As of now," Tuttle persisted, "there are too many unanswered questions to say anything more. Now if you'll excuse me, I have a lot of work to do."

"Great—just great. You fools let a starship fall into lizard hands, then mealy-mouth your way around it by denying that anything's wrong."

"Senator," Tuttle said sharply, "the *d'Artagnan* will never come into enemy hands. Her captain knows that his crew is expendable. General Order Twelve commands him to self-destruct before letting his ship fall into unfriendly hands. Now I'm sorry to be rude, but I suggest that you direct the remainder of your questions to Admiral Willoughby.

"Good day, Senator."

As the screen faded to black, Hollenbach felt a surge of exhilaration that he couldn't explain. It wasn't just that he enjoyed fencing with the CosGuard brass—finding new conquests like Willoughby, or new adversaries to crush, like Tuttle. But somewhere in space, lying beyond all the secrecy and precautions and dreams and fears of a generation, he sensed that something big was building. Whatever form it took, and come what may, he was determined to be a part of it.

* * *

```
cc:              143-2532.2
FILE:            Log
ACCESS:          Command.
SECURITY:        Standard
OPERATIONAL STATUS: Yellow Alert.
LOCATION:        47-789443/xV/b0-8
```

Fourteen days out of Girshoona, the ship remains on Yellow Alert. The skies on all sides are clear, but the Cloud looms large, eight parsecs to starboard. Heading is unaltered, at 752, speed constant at C-12.

I have ordered increased surveillance of the surrounding skies. Today, scouts detected a large Crutchtan presence, approximately five parsecs to port, holding steady at bearing 480/010s and tracking a course parallel to ours. Like the contingent astern, they are tracking our movements, but have shown no inclination to interfere with our progress.

This marks the fourth day since we lost contact with home. Morale remains good under the circumstances. The crew is too well-disciplined to let anxiety interfere with their duties. But nobody is talking about what might lie ahead, as if discussing the subject will jinx us. For myself, I find the knowledge that there is little I can do to protect us to be almost more than I can bear, and yet, surrendering to despair will only doom us all.

    Capt R Cook

Chapter 27

THREE DAYS PASSED; and on the fourth, reality came between the raiding party and the stars of home.

"Don't look back," Cyrus barked over the subspace radio, his voice as calm and commanding as he could make it. Despite the directive to the rest of the men, his own eyes were drawn to the rear viewer, and each glance chilled the marrow in his bones. As they'd done for the past week, two dozen chasers were gaining on them from astern. Now, the distance was measured in seconds, rather than hours, and dead ahead another squadron blocked the lane to the Neutral Zone.

Cyrus tried not to think about what might be in store for him. In his heart, he knew that the lives of his friends were his responsibility. They had placed their trust in him, and the fact that their deaths would be his fault might someday weigh heavily on his soul. But his own survival was at stake now. He was too busy to dwell on things he could do nothing about.

"Ready your thrusters," barked Cyrus. His fingers danced on his controls, easing his ship toward what he knew would be the trickiest maneuver of his life.

"They're gaining!" Rafferty cried over the radio, his voice choked with terror. "They're starting their approach."

Cyrus looked at his rear viewer. The Crutchtan ships had doubled their speed and were racing toward them with guns at the ready. The forward screen showed the blockading squadron ready to counter any evasive measures the raiding party might take, except for the one Cyrus had in mind.

"All right, lads," Cyrus said, his voice cold as space itself. "It's time for showin 'em what kind o' spacers Terrans can be. All ships hard a-starboard. Let 'em follow us into the Cloud, if they be man enough."

Cyrus cut his forward thrust and banked hard to starboard, leading the raiding party headlong toward the Cloud. Stunned by the maneuver, the Crutchtans hesitated before pivoting smartly and matching the Terrans' heading.

His mind fixed on his rear viewer, Cyrus drummed his fingers on the control board, beside the throttle. They were heading toward the Cloud at flank speed for ships of their class—C-12, one energy level below maximum. As they neared the Cloud, he raised his eyes to watch the forward screen and saw the Cloud dead ahead, a dim reddish fog in the eternal blackness. Within seconds, they'd be inside. Soon, their sensors would be useless, as gas and debris reflected and scattered the soundings in a thousand directions.

"Enterin the Cloud," Cyrus called over the radio. "Prepare for hard a-port on my signal—and keep tight in formation."

As they penetrated deeper into the periphery of the Cloud, a grim smile crossed Cyrus' lips. Gingerly, his right hand came to rest on the throttle, just as his left hand itched to take the helm. His eyes, fierce and unforgiving, narrowed as he saw the Crutchtan ships enter the outer reaches of the Cloud, just behind them.

Suddenly as a lightening bolt and with as little warning, Cyrus cut his power to nothing and came sharply about, his ship fading like a misty phantom from the monitor screens of all around him. The last thing he heard from those he had led to their deaths was a static-shrouded shriek of hate crackling over the radio, just before the Cloud closed around the raiding party and the three doomed ships of his companions disappeared into the thickening haze..

His heart thundering in his chest, Cyrus watched breathlessly as the Crutchtans streaked past him, intent on pursuit and caring nothing for their own survival, unaware that they had just passed one of the intruders in the gassy mist. The same interstellar fog that rendered their instruments useless concealed him quite as effectively as if he had simply vanished. His instruments started registering explosions, as the ships that had passed him began meeting the ribbons of rocks and debris hidden by the Cloud's delicate wisps and vapors.

He knew that he was not out of danger. It would take all of his skill to find his way out of the Cloud. He could only pray that he didn't drift enough to lose his bearings, or meet a ship-smashing chunk of rock along the way. More than this, the Neutral Zone was still twenty parsecs away, and the lizards had come close enough to make a full sensor scan of his ship. Those readings would be burned into the collective memory of every lizard skipper along the frontier, along with the news that there was no confirmed kill to satisfy their lust for Terran blood. There was no way to know if they'd be waiting for him when he made his last sprint for home.

* * *

THE BIRD songs floated gently through the courtyard, nearly lost amid the business of court. Midday was nearing, and the music of nature was waning beneath the echoes of footsteps and sounds of purpose.

Walking over the ancient marble tiles, Cra'Jenli strode with the swift sureness of one rushing toward destiny, his pace forcing Sha'Lendrel, his aide, to trot beside him like a favored pet. They hurried toward the Palace Hall of Counselors. The Imperator had just called his eighth crisis meeting in the last three days.

"So Gal'Shenga is still in transit from *Gr'Shuna*," smiled Cra'Jenli, his eyes merciless as death. "We must act before he arrives, Sha'Lendrel. This Terran situation must be seen as a failure of his security forces, not a failure of our diplomacy. And so they are to have no access to our broadcast beacons until their failure is complete."

"Well, Excellency, the frontier remains in chaos. He is hardly in a position to press his point of view," panted the aide, trying to keep abreast of the Lord Minister. "Word of the crisis is spreading. And the consensus seems to be— "

"I do not trust him," the Minister interrupted, without breaking his stride. "They say his life is charmed by the gods, and I have seen that where Gal'Shenga is involved anything is possible. They may even catch the Terran murderers and see the entire episode pass like a forgotten summer storm. That is but a small concern here. The Imperator is not concerned about hairy simians so long as their atrocities are far removed from his sight, and the less concern he shows the better it is for us. Within his limited powers of attention, he cares more about Glincian encroachments and maintaining his supply of snuff and young provincial girls. So in Gal'Shenga's absence this Terran incident will prove doubly useful. If we can persuade His Worthiness that the incident is entirely due to our Galgravina friend's incompetence, the unpleasantness at the Divide can only divert our forces away from the Glincian and Atkvalo borders."

"And from the fact that our own problems remain unsolved, as well," Sha'Lendrel added wryly.

Cra'Jenli stopped and turned to face his deputy. Sha'Lendrel felt a numbing cold grip his mind as the Minister's face turned hard and unforgiving.

"Need I remind you," Cra'Jenli said, thoughts of revenge lifting the corners of his lips, "of the last aide of mine who disappointed me?"

Sha'Lendrel lowered his gaze to the floor.

"I shall hear no more of such things," the Minister said, "or of anything that helps Gal'Shenga rescue himself from the tangle of his own incompetence."

"Yes, Excellency," whispered Sha'Lendrel, bowing in acknowledgement. Quickly, he purged his mind of defiance, knowing that he could afford not the slightest doubt to enter his mind. A life of riches and ease lay before him, and his ambitions longed for more than spending the rest of his days as a whipping boy for one of Cra'Jenli's women.

* * *

FOR A lonely soul adrift in the void, days passed with no beginning and no end, and each minute struck the soul like a hammer. Alone in a sea of darkness, confronting the blackness of eternity, he felt nothing but fear, and had nothing but the voice of his innermost self for companionship. Between the nothingness and the shadows, that small voice began filling his mind with cries of death and echoes of his past. When at last something appeared from the depths of space to take up the chase, he was almost grateful for the distraction, and for the company.

Strapped tightly into the pilot's seat, Cyrus could feel the shocks of the lizard blasters as they glanced off his shields, all the while knowing that one good shot would be the end of it. Sweat coursed down his face. His stomach was numb with terror, and his brain raced feverishly, trying to keep one step ahead of his pursuers. The lizard ships looked to carry about the sting of a well-trimmed frigate, and that was more than enough to spread his atoms over the heavens. After all this time, it had come to this, he thought. Living minute to horrifying minute, never sure which would be his last. With safety close enough to taste, his heart felt nothing but hatred and bitterness—to have come this far by his wits only to run a gauntlet of death at the end of it all.

But he had no time for self-recrimination. What was done was done and nothing he could do would make the lizards disappear or bring back any of those he'd left along the way. He glanced at his forward screen. Two dozen ships stood between him and the Neutral Zone. Each second brought them closer, and in the meantime he had lizards taking potshots at him from astern. Motionless, the stars hung in the sky, silent witness to the dance of death taking place in the void.

A chaser suddenly doubled its speed and raced ahead for another volley. By instinct, Cyrus rolled his ship hard to port, in yet another desperate evasive measure. Then, as the alien fire glanced off his starboard shield and the shock from the blast sent shudders coursing through the keel, it struck him.

A plan.

"Saints be praised," he muttered. Though he hadn't the slightest idea whether it would work, at least it would give him something to do until the end came. He looked to his rear viewer and slowly edged his ship toward the alien's left flank. As the next Crutchtan chaser broke ranks and sped forward for yet another pass, he closed his eyes and took a deep, trembling breath.

Quickly, Cyrus diverted all power from his engines to his shields— and his speed dropped like a rock. Guns blasting away, the stunned Crutchtans raced past him, unable to react quickly enough to stay with him.

Once they had passed out of range, Cyrus fired his engines and came about, streaking madly on a course parallel to the border. Emergency speed would take him outside the web the lizards had set for him, if only for a few moments. Angling toward the Neutral Zone would stretch the lizard fleet out toward his starboard. If his engines held… and the lizards gave him an opening....

Cyrus shook his head. He knew his chances, and he knew the odds against him. Most of all, he knew that his life depended on his wits and his daring, not on his capacity for wishful thinking.

APPEARING JUST to center of the Cloud, a odd set of readings started showing on the sensor screens of Starbase 119.

"There! Screen Six."

The yeoman closed his eyes and inhaled as the shapely young ensign bent over his shoulder to look at the viewer, her perfume bringing a feast to his senses. As the years passed, he found that he appreciated these pretty young bluebirds more and more, though under the circumstances he felt a twinge of guilt at indulging his own lustful fantasies when more important things demanded his attention.

"What do you make of it, Giles?"

"Well, ma'am, it looks like one of our own civilian craft, caught on the wrong side of the Neutral Zone. I'd swear that the lizards are trying to nail him. Look here—they've formed a web to catch him and they're nipping at his heels all the way. Now that it's close enough for resolution, I'd stake my chief's stripes on it."

The ensign stepped across the aisle, to the main console, and pressed the red button, summoning the officer of the day. The base was already on red alert; the monitors were staffed, two to a console; and the mood in the monitor station was sullen. Giles wasn't the only one to notice the desperate chase on the Crutchtan side of the border, he was just the first. His instincts were the sharpest of anyone on the base. For two days he'd tracked the hunt, warning that something big was heading right for their sector.

"Neuhardt ," came the voice over the intercom.

The ensign cleared her throat.

"Lieutenant, we have activity on the other side of the border. I think we'd better get the Old Man down here right away. The lizards are chasing one of our civilians toward the Neutral Zone and they seem to be firing at him."

"Position?"

"One parsec from the border, just west of Silverman's Star and closing at top speed. And there's an alien squadron waiting for him, right at the edge of the Neutral Zone."

"Keep a close watch, Ensign. We'll be right down."

"HE HAS done it again! He passes under the nose of Kl'Shenel's group like a ghost!"

"Advance another energy level. And order Subgroup Three to take an intercept course toward the Divide."

"Yes, Groupleader."

As subordinates carried out his commands, La'Stala's heart raged in his breast like a wildfire. His anger was boundless, though directed more at himself than at those he commanded. In his soul he felt responsible for the near-escape of the Terran butcher. The barbarian was a black-hearted assassin, whom the forces of His Worthiness had pursued across half the length of the Cloud. A murderer of women and children, the monster was quite willing to sacrifice his own comrades to save himself. Others of rank had already missed their best chances to exact vengeance, though the Terran's uncommon abilities as a pilot would excuse their earlier failings in the eyes of their superiors. But La'Stala knew that he would never forgive himself if he permitted the assassin to escape again. Nor, for that matter, would those he served.

He looked at the chart on the screen before him. There would be one last chance before the Terran crossed into the Great Divide. To avoid Group Three, the longnose would have to come about once more, angling his ship toward the skies of Terra. They would have time for one more pass at him before the Terran passed beyond their jurisdiction and into skies that were the realm of diplomats. A sense of dark foreboding welled in the groupleader's heart. This assassin had more tricks than the blackest wizard, eluding them with the trickery born of desperation. Unless the Foreign Ministry gave its approval, their power to punish the butcher ended at the invisible line that was but an impotent fiction of bureaucrats and butchers.

He felt his eyes dilate with anger. And though it sickened him to the depths of his soul, he found himself obsessed, his mind raging with a single thought: the Terran must die.

Whatever the means—whatever the cost—the death cries of the innocents could not go unanswered.

The Terran must die.

HIS SHIP shuddered under the impact of blasts from a dozen directions, buffeting him until he felt adrift in time and space. With the barest of milliseconds to react, he pulled and pushed his ship this way and that, straining his hull and engines to the breaking point. A dozen alien ships lighted his screens, each firing madly as they streaked through the vacuum, confusing themselves as much as their quarry. His brain raged in an explosion of panic and terror, as events exceeded his capacity to perceive them, entering his mind like light through a prism.

And then, with no more than the dimmest recollection of what had happened, his mind came back into focus. He saw a single ship blocking his way. By reflex, he banked hard to port, then rolled back to starboard—and when his ship shuddered under the final blast of the enemy guns, seconds passed before the full impact hit him.

Slowly, Cyrus felt the numbness lift from his mind. When he looked at his forward screen for the fourth time, it finally registered.

The screen showed nothing but clear skies in front of him.

"HE'S THROUGH!" exclaimed the yeoman at the monitor's desk. "He's made it! The crazy bugger's made it!"

The screen at his station showed a lone blip breaking away from a mass of white, subspace images. The readings were still too muddy to confirm it, but nobody harbored the slightest doubt about which ship had just bolted from the pack. Cheers rang through the monitor room of Starbase 119. Somehow—by luck, or pluck, or gritty determination—the Terran ship had slipped through the Crutchtan net blocking its way to the Neutral Zone and was racing toward home. When the ship finally crossed the line, leaving alien skies behind it, the room burst into a frenzy of celebration.

"Must be a bloody pirate!" joked one young officer, and everyone laughed. It didn't matter that the jest might harbor more than a grain of truth. The tension was broken, and they were relieved to have something to laugh about at last. In another day—or two, if the Terran ship slowed to a more normal cruising speed—he'd be home, back on the Terran side of the Neutral Zone. Then the diplomats could argue at length about the incident, but that was someone else's worry. For now, all that mattered was that the crisis had resolved itself. None of them wanted to relive the last day. Not for all the gold on Ishtar.

Standing just behind Monitor Screen Six, Commodore Steven Sellers breathed a sigh of relief and struggled not to show the rest of his command just how giddy he felt. He reveled in the simple sensation of feeling his muscles starting to relax. Twenty days of lost contact with the aliens, and an entire day of having them ignore the most pointed demands for information on what they were doing, had brought everyone nearly to the point of physical collapse. Commanding a starbase wasn't supposed to be this taxing, he chuckled to himself. At least that's what Clay had said while trying to talk him into taking the assignment. Now, maybe they could start getting some answers from across the border. Especially if this Terran intruder was the cause of the alien's sudden, stubborn silence.

"Commodore...."

Maybe Clay would even consider letting them relax a little, he thought. Maybe let them secure from red alert. After all, two weeks on the edge of your chair was too much for anyone to endure.

"Commodore—?"

And they all needed the chance to unwind, he thought. Or course, the same could be said of everyone along the frontier.

"*Commodore*—!"

Sellers suddenly noticed that the yeoman's voice had taken on an edge of panic, even as the cheers continued unabated around them. As calmly as he could, he swallowed and turned to face the greenshirt.

"Yes, Giles."

Giles spun in his chair, a look of horror on his face. Sellers looked past the yeoman to see the screen and his own heart sank into his boots. The Crutchtans had just crossed into the Neutral Zone.

They had regrouped, into an arching crescent.

And they were closing on the Terran ship.

"A MESSAGE from Gal'Shenga, Centurion."

Ga'Glish nodded his head. Rising from his seat near the monitor's desk, he strode out the door and down the hallway, leaving the messenger trailing behind him. Running past engineers and technicians in the main walkway, he arrived at the radio station nearly out of breath.

"Frequency?" he asked, racing to the nearest available seat.

"It is preset," answered Sh'Lastin, the communicator. He reached across the desk and activated the speaker.

"Ga'Glish speaking. Uncle...do you hear—?"

But the voice of Gal'Shenga interrupted. With his uncle's first words, Ga'Glish felt the darkest foreboding cast shadows on his soul.

"I have received word from the Capitol," said Gal'Shenga. The distance seemed to crackle and distort his voice, but Ga'Glish could sense the anguish in his elder's heart.

"Yes, Uncle. And pray, what is the will of His Worthiness?"

"Ga'Glish—Ga'Glish—?"

"Yes, I am here."

"Are you alone?"

"No, Uncle."

Gal'Shenga paused; the static seemed a knife into the soul of Ga'Glish. When the voice of Gal'Shenga resumed, his words were crisp and discreet.

"I am informed that the Cabinet has reached a Consensus on the crisis at hand," Gal'Shenga said. "The Imperator himself has decreed that the invader must be intercepted."

"But it has already—our ships are already— and the Terrans— "

"The pursuit is not to be recalled," continued Gal'Shenga. "And Terran demands are not to be answered until after the intruder is destroyed. We are directed to see that our forces take all steps necessary to prevent the murderer from reaching a place of safety."

"But the Terrans! We are already past our boundary, Uncle! And they are transmitting demands that we— "

"The Ministry of Foreign Relations has decreed it a matter of official policy, Ga'Glish. Our forces are now at their disposal, acting under their orders. And our duty is not to question, but to obey."

"Have we lost everything, Uncle? Are we to surrender to such misguided—?"

"Hold your tongue, Nephew. You are edging toward the brink of treason!"

Ga'Glish raged inside. Beside him, Sh'Lastin hissed a warning that the havenmaster's emotions were nearing the point of no return, that soon Ga'Glish would find his anger out of control. Slowly, his rage subsided and Ga'Glish nodded in gratitude, the bitterness in his voice taking the place of defiance.

"What of the ship I trail? What plans has Cra'Jenli for dealing with the Terrans whom we invited to our skies, or has this 'Intruder' also escaped the Minister's attention?"

"There is no Consensus, Ga'Glish. And though that ship is within the jurisdiction of our own Ministry, I must confess that I fear Pre-emption at any moment. For the moment, my direction is for you to keep it within sight. In the absence of specific instructions from the Capitol, you are free to use your own discretion."

"*Uncle!*" whispered Ga'Glish, foreboding weighing deeply on his soul, "I must confess to profound misgivings about our course."

"Misgivings are no longer our prerogative, Nephew," came the reply. "The decree comes directly from His Worthiness, and you shall issue the Orders Appropriate."

"But, Uncle...."

"I wish it were otherwise, Nephew. But those are your instructions."

* * *

A LONG pause followed the admiral's bombshell. Each viewscreen greeted the news with silence. Finally, it was the screen from Looking Glass that broke the spell.

"Admiral Clay, our ships are massing along the frontier," Commodore Wright's words were measured and well-chosen. "They are ready to cross into the Neutral Zone to effect a rescue, or they can move to intercept and divert any alien effort to cross into our skies, if that is the decision. Sellers made sure of that. In this emergency, he wanted to give us maximum flexibility."

From a chair in his plush office on IshCom, Admiral Clay nodded impassively. They were taking the news about as he'd expected. He didn't like it any better himself. Nor did he like being put on the spot, forced to defend a strategy that he knew to be indefensible.

"Now you're saying that we're to sit back and do nothing? Just like that? Let the aliens flame one of our ships and we'll worry about it later?"

"That's enough, Commodore. 'Doing nothing' hardly describes our tactics. We are continuing to broadcast demands for them to come about and return to their side of the Neutral Zone, and we are gathering our forces for a retaliatory strike if it comes to that. But Covington wants there to be no mistake: if Terran blood is going to be spilled, the aliens will have to do it on our side of the border."

"When we can prevent it all by intervention? Or by a timely show of force? That's lunacy, Admiral. Nothing short of lunacy."

"That, Miss Wright, is policy. Official Terran policy. And Central Command expects it to be carried out."

* * *

THE HOURS passed tensely as Cyrus clung desperately to a shrinking lead over his pursuers. The whole time he could feel his heart flutter in his chest, and a growing sense of doom paralyzed his brain.

By the time he crossed into Terran space, he'd come to know his pursuers as well as he knew his own soul. Just as he knew that he would never outrun the voices of those he had led to death, he knew that no imaginary line in space would hold the lizards back.

He felt his ship shudder as his engines broke down under the strain. His mouth turned dry as dust. He had driven his ship as hard as he could, overridden the emergency inhibitors that would have slowed his ship as it saved the engines, knowing that to slow was to die. Now it made no difference. His ship had used the last of its power, and the lizards were still coming.

He looked for a last time at the rear viewer. As he knew they would, he saw his pursuers following him home, racing toward him at top speed—fully powered and fully armed. He wanted to scream but he was too scared. All he could do was stare at the viewer, his mind numbed by the thought of what lay ahead.

In the end, he took a deep, trembling breath and closed his eyes, desperate to know what was happening but too terrified to watch. As his ship lighted the skies for the briefest of instants, his last, bitter thought froze itself in time and space:

Where was the Cosmic Guard?

Chapter 28

THE READINGS ON THE SCREEN were ominous and unmistakable.

"Oh, my God."

"Mathison, page the Skipper at once."

"Aye, sir."

"Mr. Ashton? Mr. Ashton?"

Jeremy looked at the monitors in disbelief. There they were, on three sides, in numbers enough to block the stars and all armed to kill. "I see it, Dexter. I don't understand it, but I see it."

"My God, Jeremy, where did they all— "

"Miss Mathison, sound Red Alert. All hands to battle stations."

"Aye, aye."

"Helm, come to 875 by 015 north, stand by for evasive maneuvers. Weapons, all shields to battle strength; prepare to charge main and ancillary guns, fore and aft."

"What's happening, Jeremy?"

"I wish I knew, Palmer. I wish I knew."

As the klaxons sounded on all decks, Jeremy reflected that this wasn't his only wish. But no amount of wishing would open the channels to home that their hosts had broken, nor relieve them of responsibility for decisions that could cost lives from here to Ishtar.

And it would take more than wishing to make the armed alien ships vanish into the blackness.

* * *

/UMN/y/NEWBABYLON/02april2552/cc:143-2585.7:
COVNEWBAB-0845covstd
FLASH—
　　COSGUARD CENTRAL COMMAND REPORTS TERRAN CIVILIAN
　　CRAFT DESTROYED IN ALIEN ATTACK. SHIPS OF EASTERN

FLEET CROSSING NEUTRAL ZONE IN RETALIATION FOR ALIEN
RAID. CGS D'ARTAGNAN FEARED LOST; RADIO CONTACT WITH
STARSHIP, TRANSPORTING TERRAN PEACE DELEGATES 200
PARSECS INTO ALIEN SKIES, SEVERED TEN DAYS AGO.
DETAILS SKETCHY; MORE TO FOLLOW.
— FLASH/30/

SUZIE YANG raced from the subspace transtelex. Her face was
flushed, her hair was a mess, and the last half-hour was a blur in her
mind. The Central Command lobby was a cauldron of rumor. The
normally serene corridors had become a beehive. Bodies were rushing
about madly, in wild, frenetic motion.

Snaking her way through the mob, she crashed into Ben Brewster,
nearly knocking him to the floor. As she helped steady him on his
feet, she realized that it had been five years since she'd seen him cover
a story, maybe longer. But this was no ordinary story.

"Suzie," he said, out of breath. "Is it true?"

Suzie looked around, checking for eavesdroppers. In the chaotic
din it was impossible to overhear anything, but old habits were hard
to break. "Nobody's talking," she whispered, her voice nearly lost
amid the noise. "But one of Pendleton's senior staff aides confirmed
that Clay ordered the ships out three hours ago. I've known that aide
for ten years, Ben. He's never steered me wrong yet. And I've never
seen his face look so ashen."

"Then it's war," said Brewster.

"It's too early to tell," she answered. In her heart she knew better.

THE INTERCOM buzzed; Admiral Clay activated the screen.

It was Mrs. Dyer. Her face was haggard and she looked distracted.
These days, Clay reflected, everyone's mind was focused somewhere
east of the Neutral Zone.

"McIntyre's PSR is in, Admiral."

Clay nodded silently, and switched his screen to the incoming
message. On the tray beside his desk, his dinner sat untouched. He
read the report.

```
                 PRE-ENGAGEMENT STATUS REPORT
   cc:           143-2585.8
   TO:           ISHCOM
                 Ft Adm PORTER M CLAY
   FROM:         EF EXPED FLOT
                 Comm L JASON McINTYRE
                 Wing Commander
   SECURITY:     Code Blue
   PREFIX:       Maximum Scramble
   FLAGS:        red1;red2;red3
```

Our advance ships could not engage the bulk of the alien raiding party before they reached haven. They are now moored in the alien starbase "Dragon's Head."

Scanners show that DH is preparing for defense. They are demanding that we withdraw immediately and ignore our demand to surrender the raiders. Preliminary skirmishes with alien advance guard have produced minor casualties on both sides.

ETA DH in 0.4 chs. Our ready compliment consists of 6 starships, 10 cruisers, and 25 frigates; best estimates place alien strength at less than 35 chasers, but base defenses are unknown. Awaiting final orders.

Clay leaned back in his chair. His orders were quite specific, and yet he hesitated. He thought back to his schoolboy days, to reading of the blunders and self-serving stupidity that plunged Terra into civil war two centuries earlier, and to the endless, bloody battles of Old Earth. He'd always wondered how intelligent men could ever bring themselves to issue the commands that unleashed such madness, and how they could face the judgment of their own children once the dust of history had settled.

Now he knew. He still couldn't understand it, but he knew. He felt no malevolence, no particular hatred toward the enemy. The crush of history was a phantom in the wind, and all that was left was duty.

Sadly, he turned to the computer at his side desk to fashion his reply. It was a single sentence, one that would haunt him to his grave.

"Proceed to attack," he wrote.

* * *

"RANGE—FIVE-HUNDRED astrokilometers and closing."

Jeremy's heart was pounding. Surrounded by armed enemy vessels, a hundred and fifty parsecs from home, there wasn't a soul on the bridge who wasn't silently quaking in his boots. Sensors showed more enemy ships approaching astern at flank speed. The aliens meant to stop them, that much was certain. Under the circumstances it was unlikely that the Crutchtans wanted another chance to say goodbye. But there was no turning away; and if the aliens wanted a fight, then the *d'Artagnan* would show them what a starship could do.

"Miss Palmer, charge the forward guns. Let's give them a taste of what they're up against."

Though he knew that the captain would arrive at any moment, Jeremy's mind whirled in a dozen directions, plotting alternate battle plans, weighing evasive measures, just in case. He was totally unprepared for the next bit of news.

"The guns won't respond," cried Palmer, her voice edged with panic.

"*Jeremy*—!"

But Jeremy wasn't listening. A flashing message on the small screen on the captain's armrest had caught his attention, directing whoever had the chair to "Log Access Code," and "Summon File E."

The message on File E drained what remained of his courage.

"*Captain's override needed,*" flashed the screen.

Jeremy was dumbfounded. Regulations had no place for restricting a ship's ability to defend itself, and Cook had said nothing to him about this. Nothing at all. His eyes betrayed an angry frustration. He could not imagine the Skipper doing something like this without telling him.

Suddenly the captain arrived on the bridge. Without fanfare the crew's mood shifted, their uncertainty fading like a bad dream. Whatever might be in store for them, no one doubted that the Skipper would know exactly what to do.

Cook motioned for Jeremy to resume his systems station, and strode briskly to the captain's chair. He looked briefly at the tactical scanners, then at the main viewers. His eyes focused inward, and his brow crinkled as he scratched behind his ear. After a deep breath he had settled on his course of action.

"Range?"

"Dead ahead, four-hundred fifty klicks and closing. Alien ships astern are closing at maximum speed, range seven-hundred fifty astrokilometers."

The captain looked to see that Dexter was sitting at the systems desk. He turned his chair to face Jeremy, who was still standing beside the command seat. "Well, Mr. Ashton," Cook said, "I am relieved to learn that your voice hasn't reverted to puberty, after all. What are you doing away from your station?"

"Skipper," whispered Jeremy.

Cook looked to see the alert light flashing on his armrest. He turned it off, and smiled blandly at his first officer.

"Miss Palmer, cancel the order to charge the guns. Helm, slow to C-1; stand by for cut to sublight and prepare to come about."

"*Skipper!*"

Ignoring Jeremy for the moment, Cook turned toward the communications station where Underwood had just arrived to replace Mathison.

"Lieutenant, notify Engineering to isolate all non-essential personnel, and to stand by to seal off the Bridge and Engineering. Then notify the Hangar Deck to stand by the shuttles."

"Aye, sir."

"Aliens at four hundred klicks," reported Dexter. "Sensors show all alien ships with shields in place, and they're all armed for battle."

"Mr. Van Horn reports that it will take him five minutes to complete sealing procedures."

"Thank you, Lieutenant. Palmer, stand by to blank the shields—"

An audible gasp swept across the bridge. Though he said nothing, Cook's scowl and tone of voice registered his sharp disapproval of such theatrics.

"And Mr. Underwood, notify Engineering to begin sealing the Bridge and Engineering."

"Skipper, what the hell's going on?"

"Mr. Ashton," Cook replied coldly, his eyebrows arching imperially as his fingers entered a sequence of codes at his station computer console. "Is there a reason why you're still not at your post?"

As Jeremy stood dumbly in place, the computer began rerouting the ship's power flow. Soon, the engines started to flood several strategically placed sections of wall with an impermeable barrier of energy that would protect the heart of the ship from outside intrusion for as long as it would take to engage the ship's self-destruct mechanism. Warning bells clanged loudly, and a foreboding message echoed in every corner of the ship.

"Bridge and Engineering will be sealed in five minutes," droned the computer's mechanical voice. "All non-essential personnel are ordered to leave the Bridge and Engineering decks immediately.

"Bridge and Engineering will be sealed in four minutes and ninety seconds; all non-essential personnel...."

PUZZLEMENT FILLED the monitor's brain.

"The Terrans have lowered their screens," he said, turning to face his superior. "And they have halted their advance as if awaiting our arrival."

Raising himself to his full height, Ga'Glish took several moments to settle his mind. His brain churned with conflicting emotions. He had come to know this Terran shipmaster, the one commanding the ship that his own forces were nearing. Yet his hand held the last communiqué from the Boundary Base Number Two, and events had shown the longnoses to be without honor or mercy.

His eyes looked down again at the document, now crinkled under the weight of his own outrage.

TO THE REGIONAL DIRECTOR:
In the name of His Worthiness
GREETINGS
The Terran invaders are quickly approaching. They have damaged Four ships, leaving but Sixteen for our own defense.
Projections indicate that our protective Shielding will not last long and that without Assistance we shall surely be destroyed.
Help us, please.
Flo'Sheltari

Tears welled in the eyes of Ga'Glish, as the words of his friend tortured his soul. There was nothing anyone could have done. Sheltari's base was too distant for help to have arrived in time. Now there was another outrage to add to the list of Terran atrocities, and the deaths of an additional four hundred men, women, and children at the hands of the barbarians stirred more than anger in his heart.

Thoughts of revenge flooded his soul. Reports of the battle showed that the Terrans did not stop their attack until the base was reduced to a fragmented hulk of scrap metal, its defenseless inhabitants reduced to ashes and cast to wander the cold blackness of space. Ga'Glish had tried to listen to recordings of their last transmission but found that he could not bear it. The stars could ignore such pain, but men could not. It horrified him to feel such an empty hunger, such a mindless thirst, and he knew that from here to the soil of *g'Khruushte,* all shared his feelings. There was something ancient and sinister in their growing lust for Terran blood, and yet the stunning swiftness and brutal grandeur of the Terran attack demanded a reply in kind.

Now a Terran ship lay before them, as defenseless as the base and as helpless as the butchered women and children of the settlement at *Shun'Galanga.* It was there for capture or destruction at his whim.

Ga'Glish struggled within himself for knowledge of the proper course. His heart knew which would be the easiest, the most gratifying, but he could feel his conscience gnaw at his sense of outrage.

Worst of all, he remembered the face of the Terran shipmaster, and could still sense the contours of the Terran's mind.

"THE ALIENS are within close sensor range, Captain, and they're starting to fan out. Engineering reports sealing procedures completed," Jeremy reported from the systems desk. Fear clouded his face, and he had lots of company. Only the captain seemed unconcerned, but none of the bridge crew had ever seen him look quite so distant.

Cook pressed the intercom button on his console, opening the ship's public address system. "This is the captain," he began; his voice was calm and firm. Yet turning to face him from the helmsman's chair, Janet could tell that he was deeply troubled. His eyes were wistful, and she recognized the look: she had seen it once before, on the worst day of her life. Their eyes met briefly, and she saw a wave of sadness wash over his face before fading into the stony facade of a warrior.

"Sensors indicate that we are facing a Crutchtan force of six dozen Chaser-class ships. We have had no contact with them, nor with home for the past cosmic week, but given our present circumstances I am presuming that they bear us hostile intent.

"My sealed orders, given to me from Fleet Headquarters before we sailed, gives me wide discretion in many matters, both military and diplomatic. But in one area, they were quite specific. Should any trouble arise, on any leg of our mission and from whatever source, this ship and its crew are considered expendable."

Janet felt a cold chill grip her spine. She was surprised to find that she felt no desperation, only sorrow that it had to end like this, that so much of her life remained unfinished, and that so many things would remain unsaid.

"I have sealed off the critical portions of the ship to ensure our ability to self-destruct if the need arises. All essential personnel are now on duty in the Engineering Deck and on the bridge. I am now ordering everyone else, without exception, to begin evacuation procedures in accordance with Emergency Plan A, and I am directing the Hangar Deck crew to begin preparing the shuttles for launch. I have yet to speak to the Crutchtan commander and cannot predict what will happen when I do. Should the need arise, however, I will give the order to abandon the ship, and I expect each crewmen to help execute this order promptly and professionally. I trust that my officers and yeoman have the procedures committed to memory, and they will now take over the evacuation in accordance with General Order Twenty-nine. If the worst does come to pass and I cannot address you again, I want you all to know that you have all made me proud to serve as your commander. And my only regret is that we had to part under such circumstances.

"That is all."

Smiling tightly, Cook glanced about the bridge as he turned off the public address. He saw worry and concern, but not the slightest trace of panic. They were too well-drilled for that. He hoped to have the time to express his appreciation, but for now other worries filled his mind.

"Mr. Underwood, open a channel to the Crutchtans. Visual screen, if they'll permit it. Let's see what they have in mind for us."

"Aye aye, sir."

* * *

Ga'Glish stared intently at the image on the screen, realizing too late that it had been a mistake to permit visual contact. He could tell nothing from the shipmaster's appearance. The Terran's face seemed as emotionless as a rock, revealing nothing of its owner's innermost thoughts. Ga'Glish chastised himself for being so conceited as to think he could peer a second time into an alien soul, let alone do so across the void of space. Worse yet, the Terran seemed to have guessed that appearing on a *g'Khruushtani* scanning screen would make it all the more difficult for his pursuers to destroy him.

That is, thought Ga'Glish, if the Terran had known who was pursuing him, or even why. But he was beginning to wonder exactly how much this particular longnose had absorbed of *g'Khruushtani* culture in his short stay on *Gr'Shuna*.

"You are hardly in a position to issue demands, Shipmaster," Ga'Glish said at last. "It is not we who are surrounded."

"We did not intrude into your skies, uninvited," the Terran returned, calmly; the translating device portrayed his voice as a deep yelp, conveying the barest trace of an undefined accent. "And a reminder of a host's obligations is not a demand, my Friend. It is simply a formal politeness."

"We are not unmindful of our obligations, One Called *Khu'ukh*, but circumstances have changed, here and along our common border. And until our respective peoples resolve our current differences we deem it best for you to return to *Gr'Shuna*."

"You speak of altered circumstances, *Gaglish*, and yet you divulge nothing. Instead, you sever our contact with our own kind and offer no explanation. You yourselves change the understanding that brought us here—in peace, to talk of peace between our races—only to conceal your motives and intentions in platitudes. I am sorry, my Friend, but I cannot permit you to impede our progress. So once again, I ask that you clear our pathway home and let us proceed in the peace that brought us here."

Seated before the visual transmitter, Ga'Glish rocked thoughtfully. He sensed that purpose lurked in the Terran's mind, though he could discern neither its shape nor its meaning. Too much remained unknown to commit himself to a course of action. He needed further contemplation, and paused before he replied.

"I wish no insult by reminding you of the obvious, Shipmaster," Ga'Glish said at last, "but nothing can stop us from compelling your return. We may destroy your ship or board it, as we chose. Your own actions have ensured that we may do so at our pleasure. And I am afraid that our patience is nearing its limit."

"Ours, as well," returned the Terran, his words cold as the blackness of space. "But do not mistake our actions, *Gaglish*. We came to your skies under a pledge of peace. We mean you no harm and will do you no violence. But I cannot permit you to board my vessel."

"You have made it inevitable."

"Scan us again, my Friend. You will see that all but two areas of the ship are defenseless. Those two areas are the heart and soul of my vessel. I will not pretend that they are invulnerable, but I assure you that they are quite sufficient for our needs. You see, the time it will take you to penetrate these passive defenses is all that we will need to do what our own honor requires."

"And what is that?"

The Terran's words brought numbness to the belly of Ga'Glish.

"I do not pretend to know what misunderstanding causes you to threaten us with harm, nor why you choose to withhold such knowledge from us. I do know that our destruction here will eliminate any chance our races may have of resolving our disputes, and that permitting our return is the only hope either side has for peace. So you may destroy us, if that is your wish. Or you may permit us to go as we came—in peace, and with the hope of future friendship. But if you attempt to board us, duty will force me to destroy my own ship rather than permit its capture. And failing our safe return, our races cannot help but be locked into a long and senseless war."

Ga'Glish sat, motionless.

"I ask only a single favor, *Gaglish*, if you have indeed resolved on our destruction. And that is to permit my crew to depart my vessel in safety. I cannot surrender my ship, for that is not our way. But I will surrender my crew if it will save their lives.

"Mine, of course, will be forfeit, along with my senior subordinates. Someone must activate the detonation devices, you understand," the Terran smiled cryptically. "But whatever your decision, *Gaglish*, I ask that you make it quickly. However impolite it may be to kill your guests, it is less gracious still to prolong their wait for death."

Angrily, Ga'Glish suspended his transmission, and summoned his senior deputy. "Go to the sensor room," he hissed at Sra'Chenga. "Tell Ra'Nasha to take a complete reading of the Terran craft and all its devices."

"Yes, my Lord."

"I want to know if there is a way to transport our people into the heart of the Terran ship. And see if there is any way to penetrate whatever screens they have erected to impede us."

"At once, my Lord."

Ga'Glish glared at the cold image of the longnose called *Khu'ukh*. He wished with the deepest of hearts that Sra'Chenga would return with word that there was a flaw in the Terran defenses, and that he had the means to effect a capture. Yet his soul knew that the Terran was speaking the truth, and Ga'Glish felt the chilling realization that it was the Terran, and not he, who could peer into the other's soul.

Above all else, it appeared that the longnoses knew no fear of death. For a predator species, he suddenly realized, it would be so natural. Yet it seemed alien to all that he knew. More than all else he knew about them, this was the discovery that he found most terrifying.

"SIR?"

Admiral Clay looked up from his desk; it was Margaret Mullins, his newest junior aide. Fresh from the Academy, she'd arrived just in time for the biggest crisis to hit the frontier in two hundred years.

"McIntyre's still waiting for his orders, Admiral," she began. "You did say that you'd let him...."

Clay smiled sadly, and motioned for the aide to come closer. Ordinarily, having a fresh, pretty face around the office would have given his spirits quite a lift. Today, he scarcely noticed her rounded figure and soft brown eyes.

"The order came in from CentCom, not five minutes ago," he said, handing her a piece of paper.

"Send this out, priority one."

Her eyes widened when she read it.

"Advance another five parsecs into enemy space," it read. "Hold position around McCreedy's Star and await reinforcements."

"Send it on the scrambler, Ensign," Clay said in a soft voice. "There'll be more to follow, after the teleconference later today."

"Yes, Admiral."

"Margaret, is it—or is it Maggie?"

"My friends call me Peggy," she smiled.

"Well, Peggy, I hope you had a good night's sleep. It may be quite a while before you get another one."

"TOMORROW, YOU SAY?"

"Yes, my Lord. Such was the word that was given me."

Seated in his meditation pose, Cra'Jenli opened his eyes and peered at his attendant through the dim light of the candle. As if awakening from a long slumber he found his senses sharpened, his mind clear as crystal. And as he contemplated the alternatives, his smile carried as much mischief as pleasure.

"Perhaps it would be better to await the Expanse Minister's arrival after all," he mused. "The Imperator may one day look differently at Gal'Shenga's protests that we should take no action within his jurisdiction in his absence. Delaying the vote will change nothing, but it will fix his position and insulate us from future attack."

The attendant smiled and bowed.

"Send word to the Deputy Minister to postpone the meeting until tomorrow."

"As you desire, my Lord. Will there be anything else?"

She could sense the Minister's growing wishes.

"As you desire, my Lord," she smiled.

* * *

THE WAIT was excruciating.

As each second ticked its way into the past, Jeremy felt his life slipping away. Looking down the bridge, his stomach churning and his heart thundering in his head, he saw the same numbed expressions on the faces of his friends and comrades, the same fear of what might be waiting for them in the shadows.

It wasn't the prospect of death that so alarmed him. Death was a fact of life in space, one that every crewman was trained to accept. Besides, they were just as close to death at the hands of the pirates when the captain pulled them back across the abyss. No, Jeremy thought, this was different. The pirates gave them an enemy to fight, and something to do with their last moments. Now, the waiting was all. And it was unnerving all of them.

All except the captain, Jeremy grunted. He looked at the captain's chair, where Cook sat impassively, waiting for the alien skipper to return to the screen to pronounce their fate. Calm and untroubled, Cook dominated the bridge like a shining star, regally surveying the lesser bodies circling round him. How he could sit still, much less speak so challengingly to the alien who held their fate in its scaly hands, was simply beyond him, but one thing was certain: for the first time in his life, Jeremy questioned whether he had the makings of a real commander. Judging from the expressions he could see on the faces around him, his doubts weren't the only ones bouncing across the bridge.

Suddenly, the alien returned to the screen. Jeremy saw the rest of the bridge crew start in their seats; as for himself, he felt nothing but a gnawing fear in his belly.

In the command seat, in the center of the bridge, the captain merely bowed his head, smiling a tight, humorless smile. Around him, Jeremy could feel the tension. Everyone's emotions were held in place by a single thread— the steel in the captain's eyes, and the crisp confidence in his voice.

"I trust you've made your decision," said Cook, sitting motionless in his chair. Almost glaring at the alien, his eyes never left the screen. Equally impassive, the alien commander stared back across the void. His words nearly made most of the bridge crew faint.

"We cannot permit your ship to pose a threat to us," the alien said, its voice distorted by the translating device on the alien ship.

Slowly, Cook bowed again, repeating his gesture of greeting. "As you wish," he said, his voice steady and unwavering. "Shall I order the bulk of my crew to our lifeboats, or do you prefer that they die as well?"

Though the alien kept the same stoic facade, it paused a moment before replying. "I know you to be a man of honor, One Called *Khu'ukh*," said the Crutchtan.

"If it will ease your conscience, *Gaglish*, I will confess to my share of faults."

The Crutchtan paused again, and Jeremy grabbed his hesitation as a last straw of hope. "If I permit you to depart, will you give your solemn promise to offer no violence, so long as you remain within our skies?"

An audible sigh flooded the bridge. Jeremy felt life returning to his body, but the captain would not let down his guard. "We will offer violence to no one, *Gaglish*. Our orders forbid us from doing so—and I will gladly destroy my ship and people if necessary to avoid offering violence to you, even for the purpose of our own self-preservation. However, if it would ease your mind, I will add my personal assurance."

"And if your orders change?"

"Until we return home, I sail under our original charter. If my orders change, I am free to ignore them."

Cook sat, stoic as the alien, his crew started stirring around him, afraid to believe what they were hearing, but too emotionally charged to sit still. The captain's eyes never left the screen, until finally his opposite broke the silence.

"On your assurance of peaceful passage, you are free to return."

Cook bowed solemnly. "Your people are gracious hosts," he replied. "And I shall relate what has passed to my superiors."

As the transmission ended, and the screen went dark, the bridge erupted into cheers—and Cook sagged into the back of his chair. His face was haggard and drawn; his eyes looked as tired as the deserts of Earth.

"Janet," he said, in a voice barely above a whisper; the bridge fell silent immediately. Later, after the excitement died, Janet would realize that it had been an eternity since he'd called her by her first name. "Get us out of here, heading due west, one-half sublight. Jeremy, start scanning the computer for star systems that can hide us—'O' or 'A' class, if you can find any handy. There are several coming up. The brighter the star, the better."

He took a long, trembling breath and straightened up in his chair. "I won't let them pick us off, any time they chose, just by meeting us along the way home," he said at last. "We're not going through this again. Find us a place to hide and do your best to lose anyone who's following us. When the dust clears, we'll find our own way home.

"Underwood, sound all clear, but have the crew maintain Red Alert. Palmer, once we're past the last line of Crutchtan ships, raise the shields to full strength and have Van Horn unseal the command centers."

His spirits brightening but plainly exhausted, Cook rose from his seat and started toward his office door as Janet engaged the engines and began to ease the ship forward. Fortunately, he thought, the captain's quarters were within the confines of the sealed bridge area. Fortunate for more than one reason.

"Mr. Ashton, you have the chair." He smiled weakly. "I think I need a stiff drink—and a new pair of pants."

Everyone laughed.

"Skipper—?" Jeremy called as the exit door opened.

Cook stopped and turned to face the bridge. "Yes, Mr. Ashton," he said softly.

Jeremy squinted in confusion. Still riding the crest of their ordeal, his mind was filled with conflicting thoughts and emotions. But there was a part of this episode that simply cried for an answer. "Not that this is the time to go into it all...."

Cook smiled and shook his head. He felt the ship begin to move beneath his feet. "Nonsense, Jeremy."

"How did you know that they'd let us go?"

Cook laughed wearily. "That's easy...I didn't. But given my orders, and the state of our tactical position—well, we really had nothing to lose, now did we?" The crew laughed in response; only Janet noticed his eyes suddenly turn serious.

"Besides," he added, "the Crutchtans are too civilized to engage in murder. Not when they have a choice. And especially not when their victims are defenseless."

As Cook left the bridge, the release of emotion made everyone light-headed, and the sheer joy of being alive made them giddy as the drunkest spacer in the dirtiest dive on Ishtar. Palmer started singing the bluest spacers' ditties she knew; soon, everyone on the bridge was laughing.

Barely mindful that he still had a job to do, and that commanding the ship would remain a dicey affair until the aliens were far behind him, Jeremy darted to the captain's station and plopped into the command chair. And as he did, a startled look changed his expression from high exultation to quizzical surprise.

Quite unexpectedly, Jeremy had discovered another facet of their narrow escape, one that he would never reveal. Though nobody could tell at the time, the captain had been as scared as the rest of them. And he wasn't joking about needing a change of clothes.

* * *

TWO DAYS later, in the City of the Ages on Planet *g'Khruushte*, the morning sun streamed through the high windows of the Corridor of Songs, filling the air with light and bringing a warm radiance to the old marble walls. Outside the birds sang merrily, unconcerned with events that were shaking the black skies far to the west.

Gal'Shenga strode alone toward the Hall of Audiences. The Cabinet meeting would be starting shortly, though his presence today would be little more than a formality. Most of the important decisions had been made in his absence, he sighed bitterly, many of them precipitously, most of them irrevocable, all made by fools who had not left the confines of the Palace in years. The regret thundering in his head was nearly drowned out by the mindless chants from the streets beyond the palace. Today, any peaceful voice would be lost in the din of the clamoring masses outside.

Now they really had no choice, he told himself. The advance of the Terran fleet could mean nothing but a declaration of total war by the barbarians, a declaration following on the heels of *g'Khruushtani* folly. The mob outside was demanding that the Terran blood debt be reclaimed in kind, and His Worthiness himself had decreed, to an adoring throng in the Palace Square, that he would not rest until his legions brought to his palace the long nose cut from the face of a dead barbarian, and offered to dine with the family of the subject who first accomplished the deed.

That their souls still stirred so lustily at the sound of drums and talk of honor horrified Gal'Shenga. Unlike most of his kind, he had studied the history of his race with a keen and dispassionate eye. All this talk sounded dimly of the Lost Millennia where clan once marched upon clan to redeem insults, and the darkest recess of the *g'Khruushtani* heart flamed before the fear and horror of the dying, consuming rather than warming the sympathy and compassion that civilized men and women feel toward the weak. Civilization was grafted perilously onto the human heart, he thought, and the passions of today were never far removed from the abyss of madness.

The footsteps of Gal'Shenga were soon echoes in the ancient corridor. The vote, of course, was unanimous: the Grand One would accept nothing less, and the danger was now too great for faintness of heart. Yet alone among the advisors of His Worthiness, Gal'Shenga voiced the belief that their actions were rash and irresponsible, and expressed concern that some among them had pushed toward war with the Terrans to advance their petty, personal interests.

Such foolishness, however, came quickly to an end. The other ministers all sided with Cra'Jenli, and the Imperator arched an imperial frown toward the wayward Expanse Minister, as if to say that such treasonous pessimism would be excused but once—and even then, only because of the boiling emotions that the crisis had unleashed.

As he voted with the others to gather the forces of His Worthiness to do battle with the forces of barbarism, the mind of Gal'Shenga was tormented by the knowledge that Zatar had been right about the Terrans' willingness to war. He could only hope that modern science would prove able to beat back the forces of darkness, and that as the Flotilla of Defensive Necessity moved westward, it would not be trailing the last remnants of civilization in its wake.

Chapter 29

THE CONTENDING FLOTILLAS MET in Crutchtan skies, seven parsecs east of the Neutral Zone.

The first contingent from Looking Glass arrived a day before the Crutchtan fleet, giving the Terrans a chance to deploy their forces to maximum advantage and take full account of the swirling cloud of dust and gas north and anticenter of the Terran positions. Kelton's Cloud provided a defensive barrier to guard the Terran flank. More importantly, the pluming jetty, extending nearly a light-year from the cloud, would force the Crutchtans to swing around it to meet their adversaries, letting the Terrans lie in ambush.

For ten—twelve—fourteen cosmic hours, the Terrans waited nervously, watching enemy ships crawl toward them at a glacial pace. Both sides adopted and altered contingency plan after contingency plan, leaving the frightened souls on their ships with little to do but peer through the blackness with the painful awareness of each passing second. For all the worry on both sides, the outcome of the battle was already determined.

As the Crutchtans came within sensor range, they sent thirty-six chasers and assorted smaller craft to secure a star system south and to center of the Terran right flank. Though barren of life, the fifth planet circling the blazing blue star had a liquid ocean of nearly potable water, making it an ideal choice for a permanent base in the event of a protracted battle. Just as important to the Crutchtan strategists was the vantage it gave to both sides of the Kelton's Cloud jetty—known to Imperial scientists as *sh'Laschmang'zyth*, or "Wing of the Songbird"—to whoever controlled the system.

Unmindful of the strategic importance of the system, but reasoning that anything the enemy wanted was worth fighting over, the Terrans sent two dozen frigates, six cruisers, and three starships to intercept and engage the aliens. At the same time, a full attack wing swung past the jetty, trying to divide the Crutchtan advance force from the main body of their fleet. Just as the pincer moved into place, the two smaller groups met a half-parsec from the blue star, and the battle, or what was to pass as a battle, was joined.

As the enemies collided in what each assumed would be the first and final conflict of the war, anger filled the hearts of both races. Each saw the other as savage and inhuman, with the soul of a demon and a thirst for all things evil. And aside from the desperate fears of the actual combatants, both sides possessed a smug sense of their own superiority, making the thought of defeat seem as alien as the monsters each imagined itself fighting. But as hatred and love each allow both sides to lose, war admitted but a single victor. And so all sensors were trained toward the blue star hanging toward the galactic center, with everyone praying that their own comrades would prove the stronger.

As it was clear that the Terrans would reach them before they themselves reached the star system that was their destination, the Crutchtans formed an arching crescent and turned to face their pursuers. Nearing the Crutchtan formation, the Terran frigates formed an attack wedge, with the cruisers at the apex, seeking to break the crescent and divide the enemy forces; the starships waited in reserve to join the battle after the initial engagement of forces. At the last moment, the Crutchtans broke the crescent themselves, swung to either side, and attacked the Terrans from the flanks.

Caught in the middle, the Terran frigates fought bravely, exchanging blast for blast with the chasers, but they were caught in the web, and the Crutchtan net kept closing tighter and tighter. Ten minutes into the battle, four frigates and a cruiser were disabled, and two frigates were destroyed. Though just as fast and more maneuverable than the chasers, the outnumbered frigates were proving no match for the enemy. As the Crutchtan attackers swung smoothly and effortlessly into place, the Terran ships scrambled and struggled just to maintain their defensive formations. The precision born of countless Crutchtan millenia in space left the Terrans firing wildly into the blackness, unable to marshal an effective counterattack and giving what seemed an inevitable victory to the forces of His Worthiness. Just as Crutchtan spacemanship and numbers seemed ready to prove decisive, the starships entered the battle.

The Crutchtan commanders had long feared the large, powerful Terran ships. Six times as long as a chaser, faster and more powerful than any ship in the Consortium, the starships loomed darkly in the mind of their leader, the Tall One from *Gr'Shuna*—who had infected his subordinates with his own gnawing fears. Yet even in the heart of Ga'Glish, all doubt had vanished with the first taste of victory. The Crutchtan commander diverted two full squadrons from the ongoing battle and sent them to meet the starships, confident that the larger Terran ships would prove no more dangerous than the smaller ones.

As the starships raced toward the battle, the Crutchtans formed another crescent and moved slowly forward, planning to hold the center this time, while the arc swung around to catch the three Terran ships in a deadly envelopment, from which the only escape would be surrender. But Captain Kruskov, the Terran commander, was too worried about his frigates to appreciate the intricacies of alien strategy. Slowing just enough to permit the primitive Terran computers to aim their guns with minimal precision, the starships rammed through the alien position like stampeding cattle. Too powerful for the Crutchtan shields, the starship blasters cut through the chaser hulls like hammers through glass, shattering the alien ships and lighting the sky with their fiery remains. In twelve seconds of fire, the Crutchtans lost sixteen ships as the Terrans sped past; the others stood frozen in space, numbly wondering how the fury of death had missed them. In the same twelve seconds, the old realities of galactic civilization exploded like the hulls of the dead, Crutchtan chasers.

Seeing that the alien ships could not stand against their starships, the Terran fleet pivoted and raced toward the main body of the Crutchtan flotilla. Desperately scrambling into a mad retreat, the Crutchtans became scattered and disorganized, easy prey for the Terrans, whose blood frenzy was swirling into madness. Of the nearly three hundred warships that the Crutchtans sent to battle, only sixty-three returned safely to base; the rest were sent to fiery deaths by the Terran firestorm or surrendered to escape certain destruction.

But the three Terran attack wings did not follow their initial advantage with an assault on the alien stronghold. As panic gripped the Crutchtan base, the Terrans slowed their advance and came to rest at a planetary system circling a pale green star, six parsecs from the Crutchtan command center. Meanwhile, Crutchtan sensors detected a massive Terran force, more than a hundred dozen ships of war, moving slowly toward Crutchtan skies.

The Terrans, the Crutchtans concluded, wanted vast regions of space. Able to destroy the entire Crutchtan presence in the area merely by wishing it, they had no need to consolidate the Terran position merely to hold onto what they had captured. But if their designs included more than a few dozen light-years—if, in other words, Terra wanted the entire Cloud—then prudence dictated awaiting the bulk of their forces.

As the main body of the Terran fleet neared what had been the Neutral Zone, the Crutchtans evacuated the area. Not a scrap from a starbase, not a ship, not a navigational beacon they could find and collect was left behind for the invaders. Their minds held the hope that, having won their battle and made their kills, the Terrans would accept the withdrawal and advance no further. Yet fond illusions were never part of Crutchtan philosophy, and few had doubts that the Terrans would follow. The only question was whether the Empire could refit its ships with stronger shields and more powerful weapons in time to stop the advance of what His Worthiness was calling *sch'Galash-po'Nara*—the "Evil Empire Beyond the Cloud."

As horrifying as the speed and power of the Terran starships were to the Crutchtan ship commanders, their leaders found even more ominous the Terran ships' navigation system, which let the starships and cruisers speed in any direction, at any time, without having to bring about the bows of their ships. For all their backwardness, it seemed, the Terrans were not simple savages, after all. However rudimentary it might be, their science had discoveries that were Terra's alone, and this realization made the future all the more terrifying.

From the UMN Trans-Terran Dispatch, 9April2552:
SENATE BACKS PRESIDENT:
WAR VOTE PASSES, 98-2
by S.L. Yang
COVINGTON, New Babylon
April 8, 2552
In the streets of Covington, demonstrators marched today from Hill Street to the Executive Mansion in support of the Senate's declaration of war on the Crutchtan Empire.

In a firm vote of confidence in the President's pledge to protect Terran security in the face of what he called "the most terrifying menace Man has ever faced," the Senate today granted President Heathcoate's request for full authority to commit Terran forces to war in order to repel "the unwarranted, unprovoked, and unprecedented assault on the safety of every man, woman, and child in Terra."

Heathcoate's remarks came during an emergency session of the Senate, called within minutes of reports from the administration's Council on State Security that massive and unexplained alien ship movements were taking place in the skies just past the advance positions taken by forces of the Cosmic Guard. "Never in human history," the President told the hushed Senate chamber, "has Mankind faced a deadlier, more merciless, more implacable foe, one so dedicated to the destruction of all we hold dear.

"This Evil Empire," he said, in words that brought the chamber to its feet, "cannot be fought with good intentions or acts of kindness. By word and act and deed, they have shown themselves dedicated to our destruction. For the sake of Humanity, we cannot let them succeed."

The Senate vote was not unanimous, however. Dissenting votes were cast by the two-member Isitian delegation, headed by Irene McGinnis, the matriarch of Isitian politics. Visibly upset by the Senate vote, McGinnis and her colleague, Raymond T. Bartlett, left the Senate chamber shortly after the roll call.

"The people of Isis will not take part in a war of aggression," McGinnis said in remarks on the Senate floor. "Terra is scoffing at lessons our ancestors learned through countless, bloody millenia, and History will judge us harshly for our folly."

The two senators from Isis left New Babylon shortly after the vote, returning home to consult with planetary leaders. There is speculation in the Capital that Isis will schedule a plebiscite on the war, in response to the Senate's vote today.

Ironically, an Isitian may well have been among the first casualties of the war. CosGuard Captain Roscoe Cook, a native of Isis, is the commander of the starship *d'Artagnan*, which is missing and presumed lost deep in alien skies. It was transporting the Terran delegation home from the peace talks when the fighting started.

Chapter 30

WITHIN DAYS, the rest of the Eastern Fleet arrived from Ishtar.

Now numbering more than fifteen hundred warships, the Terrans began a slow advance into alien skies. Barely keeping the pace of an ore freighter, they flooded space in all directions with *Starhawk*-class scouts, but could find no trace of their enemy. Except for an occasional faint reading on their most powerful sensors, barely distinguishable from background static or subspace phantoms, the aliens had simply vanished into the vastness around them.

As they crept through the void, the enormity of space unfolded before them, swallowing the small ships in an endless sea. Ahead and to port lay the giant Crutchtan Cloud, hanging in the blackness like a ghost, stretching into the cosmic gulf as far as their strongest sensors could detect. On all sides, stars burned like distant beacons, beckoning them to uncharted worlds.

Inside their ships, confidence filled the heart of the lowliest crewman, and the vastness of the Black could scarcely cool their lust for victory. Though the Crutchtans were lurking somewhere, all but a handful soon forgot that their battles had not passed without loss, that the demonstrably inferior alien vessels had destroyed several of their ships and killed more than three hundred people. Emboldened by the exhortations of their leaders, their minds were as one, united for a common purpose and against a common enemy, wedded with religious certainty to the rightness of their cause. And so the fleet pressed on, slowly heading toward the alien worlds of the cosmic east.

In the meantime, along Terra's flanks, to center and to anti-center, CosGuard's outposts continued to receive messages from alien races dotting what the Consortium called the "Terran Periphery."

Some members of the alien alliance, it seemed, wanted to talk.

* * *

"So tell us, La'Drensel," said Drubid, the senior Glinci subsolon, his eyes as cold as a Terran's heart, "exactly what has changed?"

La'Drensel, Grand Ambassador from the Crutchtan Cabinet, stared at the subsolon in puzzlement. The lights from the Council chamber jarred his eyes as they focused on the rightmost podium and frustration choked his throat. He looked to Dra'Lani, but the Crutchtan solon averted his glance.

"I do not understand...," began the ambassador, but Atlanwa of the Atkvaloanz cut him short.

"Surely, you do not contend that having once blocked all efforts at pre-emption you are entitled to rescue from the consequences?"

"But who could foresee— "

"And how can you, in good conscience, ask this Council to commit the resources of the Grand Alliance to a purpose which may serve no purpose but to bring destruction upon the heads of all?"

The ambassador's eyes grew moist, but his voice carried the anger born of desperation. "The Alliance has a responsibility— " he began.

This time, it was Zatsami of Veshna who interrupted.

"The Council cannot blind itself to emerging reality," she said. "Cannot the Solons see but that the danger threatening Crutchta will one day threaten us all?"

"Has not the Charter enshrined self-determination as the basis for mutual respect and co-operation?" answered Drubid. "My people may lack a vote in these Chambers, but my sentiments do not go unechoed. Surely my Veshnan colleague does not contend that one member's folly should bind the rest?"

"Not even when the survival of a brother race is at stake?" answered the Veshnan. "I submit to the Council that we commit a greater folly by ignoring the danger on grounds of protocol, for no purpose other than insuring a temporary, transient truce with the Terrans, than we do by countenancing a member's foolishness."

The debate raged for hour upon hour, all to no purpose. And when at last the Chairman called the roll, Crutchta's plea for assistance failed, by vote of nine to six. Veshna alone stood with the *g'Khruush-tani* to commit the resources of the Grand Alliance to finding means to stop the Terran war machines while they were still in the far distant Crutchtan Perimeter. As the roll sounded, Zatsami wondered whether anyone else felt her own numbing terror at the thought that each passing moment brought the Terrans closer and closer to the population basins of the Alliance. Certainly, the vote showed the others to be blissfully unconcerned about the danger rising in the West. Perhaps if she possessed greater eloquence, she thought briefly—but then, she had long since learned the futility of such musings. It was with much relief that she awaited the Council's recess for the day. Even then, she found herself wishing to be alone.

WALKING IN the sunshine on the palace grounds after the Council session, the cold, sterile reports she had read of the battle haunted Zatsami's mind. The numbers killed, the ships lost, the details of the evacuation were all recounted so analytically, like the briefing papers the Council staff prepared for each session. But this time, she thought, the issues involved more than abstract power relationships, or the dull questions of allocating resources among contending groups and interests.

Though spring flowers swayed merrily in the breeze, thoughts of death filled her mind. The hatred between simian and saurian, too common among the lower life forms on planets across the galaxy to be mere coincidence, was ugly and terrifying when seen in civilized beings. Above all else, she found the shortsightedness of her Council colleagues as incomprehensible as the blood lust of the Terrans.

She wandered down a long winding path from the bluff toward the ribbon of beach that lined the coast. Yelina's term on the Council expired tomorrow, she reflected. Soon, Zatar would return to Balarium, this time wearing the purple robes of a solon. With the unfolding crisis, the Grand Alliance was badly in need of a leader, and not a soul among them understood the Terrans at all. Yet her doubt still lingered: with all his accomplishments, and for all his intellect, Zatar remained, after all, a man. While the ancient prejudices had long since faded before the advance of modern science, vestigial feelings were difficult to ignore. Science may have cast doubt upon the notion that the males of her species were the congenitally lazy creatures of common perception, but it was still an open question whether men could be trusted to get anything right. Even if Zatar proved to be an exception, Veshna could not control the Council. Events had long shown that each race was guided by its own self-interest—or, as Zatar would have corrected her, by its perception of its self-interest. However unexpected it might have been, the reality of Terran power would scarcely change this fact of Alliance politics. In the end, she wondered whether Zatar's insights into the Terran soul would prove any less useless than her own muddied and emotional arguments.

Lost in thought, she wandered down toward the shore. Once there, she walked down the beach, sadly watching the sky's radiant display as the sun dipped below the horizon.

* * *

"WHAT'S THE matter?"

Suzie looked up from her writing station. Lost in thought, she hadn't noticed Ben Brewster standing beside her. She shrugged, knowing exactly what the matter was, but not in a mood to share her feelings with anyone.

"After work?" suggested Brewster.

Suzie smiled and nodded. As he walked away, she rested her elbows on her desk, staring at the blank screen. She knew it was useless; she was too upset to write. Something very wrong was happening, something that transcended politics, her work, even the distant battles that dominated the headlines. The universe she knew was changing, and she feared it was not for the better. A new attitude was in the air, visible on the face of everyone she passed. It showed in the conversation of friends she'd known for years, or the voices of children she happened to overhear in the park. Perhaps it was just her concern over the war: it was, after all, Terra's first in more than two hundred years, and no one alive remembered the effect that distant battles and headline-bloated victories had on people far-removed from the fighting. Perhaps it was her guilt at feeling the same overwhelming relief that every Terran felt upon learning that their fleet was a match for anything the galaxy could muster.

Or perhaps it was something deeper, something more ominous.

But such musings would have to wait, Suzie told herself. She was a professional, and she had a job to do. She forced herself to think about the recent abandonment of federal efforts to prevent the Ceresian plains from repeating the soil erosion that widened the North American desert in the waning years of twenty-first-century Earth. Boring as the assignment might be, she had too much pride to surrender a story to the gods of dullness without a fight. Until she was ready to ask for a reassignment, to go to the East where the real story was unfolding, she knew that she'd just have to concentrate on doing her job.

THE DAY was cold, but the morning sun hung brightly in the sky as the north wind sliced through the branches of the budding trees. To the south, the sea was just visible on the horizon, glistening in the light through the clear, crisp air.

Nodding greetings as brisk as the day to passers-by, and shivering under his overcoat, Nicholas Schiller hurried toward the Senate building. He was already late for his meeting, and beginning to think that whoever had decided to repair the Tube links between the Mansion and the Hill should be shot as a traitor. It was an outrage, making the President's chief of staff ride the subway like a common tourist. And the longer he had to endure this, he thought, the likelier it was that someone's head would roll.

Today's meeting, like most of his meetings on the Hill, was with the chairman of the Governmental Affairs committee. As always, it would be about procurement. These days, it was the only subject that Hollenbach wanted to talk about: procurement, and the awarding of contracts.

Schiller cut across the grassy commons and headed up the gentle slope of Senate Hill. Of course, he thought, it wasn't so long ago that those were his only concerns as well. Back then, his company was his universe. Now the war, and the conflicting demands of running a complex government, made the bulk of his previous life seem little more than a prologue. And the pressures kept mounting, day after day.

Coming to the Senate Building, he ran up the marble stairs, almost tripping over the top step. He paused to catch his breath, and shook his head as he sighed. He had too much on his mind, he thought—monitoring what passed for progress at the front; keeping Earth's senior senator as honest as practicable.

And, of course, contacts from other races.

He started walking, more slowly this time. It was funny, he chuckled to himself. Funny how the rest of the Consortium suddenly became so eager to be friends with them after learning how easily Terra could beat all comers in a fight. He had to hand it to Hollenbach: it was exactly what Emerson had predicted. Show them what we're made of, the old politician had said, and watch them come crawling, claiming that they'd always wanted to be friends.

Hollenbach had been right, thought Schiller. But then, Hollenbach's instincts were matchless. And if Emerson was a little overbearing at times—well, that was the price they had to pay for his talent. And his support.

Besides, Schiller sighed, striding through the door and toward the east elevators, overbearing was an adjective that his own staff applied to him. Perhaps that was why he and Emerson got along so well. They understood each other.

* * *

THE LIGHT from the monitor screen lit the face of Ga'Glish, casting shadows across the room. It gave a glow of eerie disembodiment to the Tall One, whose back was weary from the weight of his responsibilities. Looking into the screen at the kindly face of his uncle, Ga'Glish longed for less troubled times. At present, necessity dictated the limits of their conversations, and their talks on the topics of life and death no longer touched upon lessons of philosophy.

"We are in your debt, Ga'Glish."

Ga'Glish bowed in acknowledgement. "I am relieved, Uncle. I was uncertain how my news would be received."

From within the palace walls of the distant Capitol, Gal'Shenga smiled a sad smile. "These days, we have little to cheer us, Nephew," he said. "Of course, we are fortunate that your disregard of selected Foreign Ministry decrees did not come to light sooner."

"I would gladly trade the Terrans' co-operation for my own dismissal," Ga'Glish hissed bitterly. "As for our show of weakness—"

"Talk such foolishness no longer," Gal'Shenga said sharply. "You were powerless to stop them."

Ga'Glish lowered his eyes. Despite his uncle's kind words, he could not help feeling responsible. "But I have failed more than our people," he said at last, raising his face to look directly at Gal'Shenga. "I have failed you, and placed your cause at the mercy of enemies."

Ga'Glish was surprised to see a somber wryness in the eyes of his uncle. "Your concern speaks highly of you, Nephew," smiled the Minster, "but you need not concern yourself with me. Fate has chosen to show me one kind turn amid this disaster. The Imperator has, at long last, seen Cra'Jenli for the self-server that he is."

A rush of astonishment came from the breath of Ga'Glish.

"Though unknown outside the palace walls, the late Foreign Minister is even now in chains, awaiting trial for treason—charged with using this crisis, and the Terrans, for his own selfish ends.

"In the meantime, you now address the new First Minister, who chooses to forgive any past sins you may have committed. As for your—how shall we say it?—your creative disregard of protocol," Gal'Shenga smiled warmly, "such indiscretions give us hope where we had none before. For this, your Government thanks you. And so does your uncle."

Ga'Glish bowed his head in gratitude.

"So," continued Gal'Shenga, his voice firm and his manner suddenly confident, "all resources at our disposal are now being directed toward repelling the Terrans. Here and, by your foresight, along the Periphery, refitting our ships is now the highest priority. You could have done no more, Nephew. As for the Terrans conspiring to make you a hero...."

For the first time in quite a while, Ga'Glish saw true humor in his uncle's eyes.

"Let us hope that they continue their co-operation. If they should happen to think of exploring the Peripheries...but then, I need not remind you of the obvious."

Ga'Glish nodded. "My instructions?"

"They remain as before. Monitor their progress, but do not engage them under any circumstances. Not until we are ready. If all goes as we hope—and we are lost if our scientists run out of time—we shall need all forces at our disposal for your plan to have any chance of success."

"I hear and understand," Ga'Glish bowed.

"May good fortune greet you."

"And smile upon all who seek her," continued Ga'Glish, completing the phrase of parting. Soon the lights returned and Ga'Glish sat alone, staring into the darkness of an empty room, his mind filled with worry.

He worried about his mate, and about the future they would leave to their children. He worried about the destruction of all they held dear, and all his people had striven toward for uncounted generations.

He also worried about his decision to leave an enemy roaming about the skies of home, free to work destruction on anything in his path. He had barely escaped the Terrans with his life; their battle had shown the longnoses to be utterly without mercy. Now he chided himself for the folly of sparing a Terran ship at the dawn of war. His foolishness was made all the more glaring by the fact that the enemy ship had simply vanished into the Void, and was now nowhere to be found. Ga'Glish swore never to forgive himself if the Terran shipmaster proved to be less than his word—if the One they called *Khu'ukh* showed himself to be as cold and ruthless as the others of his kind.

But beneath his doubts, Ga'Glish wondered whether his own honor would have permitted any other course. And he wondered whether letting his growing hatred for the Terrans destroy his own conscience would simply be another way of letting the Evil Ones win the war.

* * *

THE GENTLE smells of the Balarian spring masked the urgency of the gathering. Lamps cast dim lights across the meeting room; on the table before them, snacking cakes and the finest teas from home lay untouched. Even the playful twilling of the Glincian language seemed to mock the gravity of the topic at hand.

"You misled us, Drubid; you misled us all."

"It was not I, Excellency," replied the subsolon, his voice assuming an air of deference. "Our course of action was decided by the highest circles of the Government, and own analysts had dismissed the thought that simians could ever be anything but the uncivilized apes that the Terrans have proven to be. They are, after all, too wild and emotional for rational thought, and their capacity for anarchy has simply exceeded our capacity to discern. But then, who among us could truly know what vileness filled the souls of such semi-intelligent creatures."

The envoy, Bulitsa, was unimpressed.

"Semi-intelligent creatures do not shred space vessels like cooks shred cabbage," she replied. Her regal eyes combed Drubid like a she-falcon searching for prey. Others in the room held their tongues; at such times, it was dangerous to intrude.

"We must not let Terran power blind us to our own interests, Dame Bulitsa," Drubid smiled coldly. "The fact that such power is directed at the Crutchtans, and not against us, buys us more than time. It buys us influence."

Bulitsa, puffing her chest to emphasize her rank, whistled derisively.

"Our overtures to the simians far predated their display of force," continued Drubid. "It cannot help but bring us whatever good will these primitives are capable of extending."

"Are we not riding the back of a predator, Drubid? A predator concerned with little beyond its own appetite?"

"Perhaps," Drubid nodded, "but if the predator is going in the direction we seek, we may find the ride a useful expedient."

The envoy was about to reply, but Drubid cut her short.

"Besides, Excellency, science is universal and cannot be concealed forever. It is only a matter of time before the entire galaxy knows Terra's secrets. By then, we will be in a position to dictate our own destiny. And if not, time will still be on our side."

Grudgingly, Bulitsa nodded. There was a certain logic in Drubid's argument. But logic could hardly change the current state of affairs. "I cannot say that I like it much," she said at last, "finding us in a position of subservience to such...uncouth barbarians."

"Would you prefer the position of the Crutchtans?" Drubid asked, a note of triumph in his voice.

The envoy's reply was silence.

"Of course not. None of us would. Therefore, we must hold our tongue, and our pride. But our day will come."

Drubid puffed his chest, in a display of pride and dominance at prevailing in the disputation.

"Note my words, Dame Bulitsa—our day will come."

* * *

PAPERS SHUFFLED on the conference table as the two men turned to the last item on the agenda. The room was large and well-lighted. The sun streamed through the bay windows; outside, the budding trees promised renewal after the long winter.

"Item twelve," said Schiller. "Progress at the front."

"Or what passes for the front," snorted Hollenbach. "Dammit, Schiller—I think they're lazy. Or just plain scared. But one thing is sure. Somebody's got to light a fire under that candy-assed fleet commander. He'd just as soon saunter his way clear to their capital, rather than having it out with the lizards like a man."

As Hollenbach's monologue on the failings of the Cosmic Guard continued, Schiller wrote himself a note, reminding himself to speak to his contacts at Central Command about their slow progress into alien skies. He hated to second-guess a commander in the field; the Cozzies swore it was bad luck. But six weeks after routing the lizards, CosGuard still hadn't pressed its advantage. They hadn't even come within sight of the aliens for the last twenty days. It seemed a curious way to run a war.

Chapter 31

"OH, CHRIST!""

Heads turned on the *d'Artagnan's* bridge and looked toward the main entrance. Jeremy Ashton stormed down the ramp to take his turn on the command seat. Palmer just managed to scramble out of the chair before the angry executive officer arrived to claim it. Jeremy rarely vented his disagreements with the captain in public, but in one way or another all of them felt the same way. All but one.

Weeks had passed before Cook had let them slip out of the star system where they'd hidden from the Crutchtan patrols. Since then, they'd crawled along, moving no more than a parsec a day, often less. Now they seemed destined to hold their present position forever. But doing so almost seemed preferable to the idea that the captain was toying with.

"Janet, how long has it been since we've moved?"

"Three days," came the reply. "Three days, two hours, and sixty-nine minutes."

"Mr. Ashton, " Connie's voice was thin and reedy. "Can't you talk to him?"

Jeremy looked at the navigator. Her eyes were bleary. It had been days since she'd gotten any real sleep. But there was more pressure on her than anybody, for if Cook had his way she'd have no time to relax for the rest of the way home.

"McKenzie," he said, as patiently as he could, "I have tried talking to him. I've tried talking at him. And I've tried it at every decibel level you could possibly imagine."

Connie nodded. Like most of those on board, she couldn't comprehend why the Skipper was being so stubborn.

"Janet...."

"Leave me out of this, Jeremy."

"But— "

"I mean it. When he's like this, he listens to himself and no one else." Janet turned to her left, facing both the navigator's station and the command seat. "But to be perfectly honest, I don't think he's at all out of line. And I'm not sure I don't agree with him."

"Not again!"

"Come on, Mendelson."

"Janet," sighed Jeremy, "you can't possibly believe that. Even if we do cross through the Cloud, how do we know what's waiting on the other side?"

"And how are we supposed to find our way home from there, anyway?" Connie whimpered. "It's all uncharted space. Totally uncharted. I don't even know where we are now. How does he expect me to find our way through unknown skies?"

Janet shook her head.

They didn't understand, she thought.

After all this time, they still didn't understand.

* * *

"WELCOME TO Looking Glass, Admiral."

Clay grunted a greeting to the young commander that Wright had sent to meet them. The five-day trip from IshCom had added a touch of constipation to his other troubles, but he hated bemoaning his personal concerns. Considering all that Terra faced, complaining about the food on a CosGuard transport seemed petty, and if the food wasn't cause of it all he didn't want to know. He felt old enough without dwelling on the problems of rapidly advancing old age.

"Commodore Wright sends her apologies at not being here to meet you personally," said the commander, in a dryly officious tone of voice.

"Save the apologies, young lady," smiled Clay. "You may need them someday, for something important."

The commander seemed puzzled, trying to discern some hidden meaning behind the gallant pleasantries of a senior officer. Sadly, Clay concluded that, though bright and probably quite capable, she was probably the type who took herself and her job rather too seriously. A pity, he thought, for she wasn't unattractive, and a smile would do much to brighten her face. It was a shame that intelligence and a sense of humor didn't always share the same mind.

He gestured toward the rest of his entourage, all clad in the white shirts of flag officers. They were the last contingent of the Eastern Fleet command staff to arrive, the rest having shipped out over the past few weeks. The command relocation was all but complete, and in another week or so they could send for their families.

"We can find our way from here," he said. "Go tell the Commodore that we received her last message, and I've already gone over the briefing papers. I'll be ready to meet with her as soon as I shower and get something to eat."

"Yes, Admiral."

The commander left to deliver the message. As she hurried toward the nearby lift, the top brass of the Eastern Fleet watched her progress with a fair amount of interest.

"Youth is wasted on the young," sighed one of the whiteshirts.

"Some of us are just born middle-aged," returned Clay. The rest of his senior staff laughed, though not one of them knew what he meant.

"ADVANCE BASE FOUR reports the Terrans within sensor range, Centurion," said the monitor, removing the earphone from his ear. His voice sounded brave, though anxiety seemed to fill his heart.

Ga'Glish rose and walked to the young officer's station. Blips of light danced on the brightly colored screens surrounding his command center. Fear was a luxury of subordinates, he thought. Responsibility did not permit him to dwell on their likelihood of success. Yet buried in his soul was the sense that he had seen his family for the last time. He found it hard to imagine how refitted freighters, even with the power boosters installed by their engineers, could ever stand against the Terrans warships.

No, he told himself—as he did whenever truth seemed more important than false hope—freighters were just too slow and clumsy to match the Terran warships. It mattered not that the Terrans had shown themselves less skilled and graceful with their ships than he had foreseen, for their ships were deadlier by far than he ever imagined. Nor did it matter how vital it was to slow the advance of the longnoses, nor how many losses the forces of His Worthiness were willing to endure. The imperial fleet had neither the speed nor the power to confront the invaders. His mind told him that they had to discover— now—whether their scientists were actually on the path toward finding a way to fight them. His heart told him that they must stop the invaders at any cost. Yet reality always stared back from his map of stars whenever he tried to formulate a plan of battle, leaving him bitter and despairing. Each calculation he made seemed but further proof that their cause was hopeless. In his darker moments he knew that each order and every idea he had merely condemned more innocent souls to a fiery death.

But he also knew they had no choice. "By glacier's edge, the children's sand huts are made of snow," ran the old saying, and for now the freighters were all that they had available. Yet all the destruction and sorrow of the next few days would be meaningless if the Terrans had similar forces deployed everywhere, at future fields of battle. And if the next armada met the same fate that now awaited the current fleet, their sacrifice would be worse than worthless. There were no other forces left between the Terrans and *la'Khryshk*, and little between the tiny colony and the rest of the Empire.

"Ask for a reading," he told the monitor, "and flag the battalion commanders."

It was time to meet the longnoses, thought Ga'Glish; or rather, the time and space that allowed retreat had nearly vanished. And yet they needed more of both, desperately, and whatever the cost. This day was nearing its median phase; in a half-day more, the battle would be joined.

* * *

"GO AWAY, Jeremy."

"*Skipper!*"

Turning his chair to face directly across his desk, Cook glared at his executive officer. "I would rather not make this a direct order, Commander, but I am not entertaining any debate."

Jeremy's jaw twitched angrily. "With all due respect—*sir*—I deem it a matter of duty to raise— "

"You have voiced your objections, and they are all duly noted," Cook interrupted. "As for the rest, this ship is not a democracy, and I'll take as long as I damn well please to make whatever decisions I need to make."

"Chasing some wild goose because some wispy cloud patterns remind you of home...."

Rising to his feet the captain hammered his desk with a closed fist. Eyes narrowed angrily, Cook leaned forward, his hands resting on his desktop, amid several open files, scattered charts, spectral readings, and other scientific data from the surrounding heavens. His voice lowered until it was no more than an intense whisper. "I have heard all I need to hear from you or anyone else, Mr. Ashton. And I will do what I must in order to make an intelligent decision."

He waited until Jeremy was about to reply, before continuing.

"You—all of you—will be of enormous help, just by leaving me alone. But if I need to throw you or anyone else into the brig to get the peace and quiet I need, so help me I'll do it." Staring into Jeremy's eyes, Cook paused a moment to let his words have their desired effect.

"Now, is there anything else?"

Jeremy felt as if every eye in the room, Cook's as well as all those damn wall portraits, was watching his every move.

"No...*sir.*"

Cook leaned back in his chair, rocking and continuing his angry glower until Jeremy averted his eyes. "Good," he said at last, swiveling his chair to face the wall once again.

"Dismissed."

* * *

COMMODORE WRIGHT was smiling as she entered Admiral Clay's temporary office. It was cramped and poorly lit, with crates and boxes littering the floor. Base Maintenance promised that his new office would be ready in a day or two, but Base Maintenance was still working on things they'd promised to have ready by the last Cosmic New Year. She lifted her thumb toward the ceiling as she caught the admiral's attention.

"Visual contact is confirmed," she said. "McIntyre reports his scouts have spotted the enemy. The main body of their fleet is five parsecs away, and Mac's closing rapidly. Finally, the battle's drawing near."

Leaning back in his chair until his head brushed against the wall, Clay dismissed his junior aide with instructions to summon his tactical advisors and the rest of the command staff. He had misgivings about issuing the orders to speed the advance, but Central Command had overruled his doubts. Now, he thought, they would see whose instincts were right.

"Miriam," said the admiral, "let's get a little jump on the rest of them, shall we? It's best if the bosses can look like they know what they're talking about."

Clay ushered her down the hall and into the arching dome of the conference room. The quiet swallowed their footsteps as they strode down the walkway. Soon, they stood in front of a large, global star map near the podium at the base of the auditorium. Ventilators always kept the temperature at a constantly moderate temperature, but Clay felt uncomfortably warm just the same. He was proud of his fleet. They had demolished everything the aliens threw at them, and he knew that Terra's ships and spacers had proven themselves to the rest of the Galaxy. In fact, his fleet had set to rest all defeatist talk about the superior alien science that had lurked in the back corridors of Cos-Guard's command structure for the last four years.

Clay gazed absently at the map, unable to focus his thoughts. With the great cloud guarding his anticenter flank, McIntyre had moved the fleet past a small swirling star cloud and was approaching a clearing, twenty parsecs across, which was nearly devoid of stars. The alien planet Lagrush was at the other end of the clearing. Doubt still gnawed at his brain, and would not let him rest. Until the main alien fleet was met and defeated, and the war brought to an end, he would be too restless to permit himself the luxury of relaxing. And on top of all the other burdens that the war had dropped on his troubled head was a thought that haunted his conscience.

If the Terran starships were really invincible, the admiral thought at least once a day, did he really send his best commander and his crew uselessly to their deaths aboard the *d'Artagnan?*

For if he hadn't, then the easy Terran victories were not what they seemed.

* * *

"...THE MOST asinine— "

Palmer cut herself short, and an embarrassed silence fell over the bridge. Arching his eyebrows, Cook ignored the stares and took his seat on the bridge. The main viewer showed the same scene it had shown for the past four days. The Cloud hung to starboard and stretched westward, a dim red glow against the blackness of space; to port lay the open cosmos. Static from the Cloud shielded them from enemy sensors as long as they stayed motionless, but it was obvious that the captain had no intention of holding their position any longer.

"Helm, ahead one-quarter sublight; prepare to engage subspace drive."

"Aye, aye."

"Miss McKenzie," said the captain, smiling mirthlessly, "plot a course to starboard, into the clearing bearing 790."

"Yes, sir," replied the navigator after a short pause, and she started right to work. Across the bridge, the crew shifted uncomfortably at their stations. Though not unexpected, the decision to proceed into the Cloud had cooled morale well past freezing.

Cook leaned back in the captain's seat. He didn't want to tell the crew his real reason for wanting to proceed. If he was wrong, he didn't want to raise their hopes falsely. The opening they'd discovered seemed similar enough to Gutterman's Gap, the pass that guarded the eastern approach to Isis, but it could easily prove to be a coincidence. If it wasn't—well, he'd always wondered how Nature had cut such a clean path through the Isitian Clouds; finding another such pathway, heading off in the general direction of Isis, would finally prove to him that Nature had nothing to do with it. Though it would take them far out of harm's way if he was right, it was still a long shot. And if some of his other hunches proved correct, about the likely outbreak of war, and the directions it might take....

This was the rankest sort of speculation, he thought. But it was obvious that he had to try something—anything—to break the tension. "I sense dissension in the ranks," he said coldly. "I will permit anyone who wishes to do so the chance to voice an opinion once more—and then I will hear nothing more about it."

It was quite a while before anyone spoke.

"The book says that only foolishness or sheer desperation can justify heading into a cloud if sensors can't see all the way through it," said Palmer in an angry, challenging voice.

"I am aware of that, Lieutenant," Cook nodded, leaning forward as if waiting for her to come to a point worth making.

"Well, we don't seem in much of a panic," she added, taken aback by the response, and averting her eyes from Cook's calm, untroubled gaze. "And we're not to what I'd call the point of desperation, either."

"No. At least I hope not," said Cook. "But it's very perceptive of you to notice.

"Anyone else?"

As Palmer's eyes bulged in muffled rage, Janet smiled involuntarily. Patronizing his subordinates was one of his most effective tools for keeping them in line. She'd been the brunt of Cook's baitings too many times not to know when he was toying with those around him. After an awkward pause, Jeremy rose from his seat. Like Palmer, he found it difficult to meet the captain's gaze directly.

"If we're going to go through with this," he ventured, suddenly discovering that his mouth had gone dry, "we should send out a scouting party to see just what's ahead. It seems...well, it just seems too risky to sail off into the Cloud like that. I can't...I just can't see the need for taking a chance like this. Not when we can...well, you know...send out some scouts, instead."

Cook furrowed his brow and nodded contemplatively. "Yes—well, Jeremy, I did consider that possibility," he smiled wryly, leaning back in his chair. "But there is only one member of this crew that I could send off in a scout to reconnoiter the opening into the Cloud and be confident that he'd find his way back."

He saw Janet watching him, and winked. "And, since I'd be going that way myself anyway, I thought I may as well take the whole ship along with me.

"Helm—come to heading 790; engage subspace drive and increase speed to Level 2. On my command, increase speed to Level Eight."

"Aye, sir."

The captain looked at Jeremy and shrugged.

"This way I save myself the return trip."

A stony silence greeted Cook's little jest, convincing him to give it up. He'd never persuade them, he thought. He'd have to show them.

Soon the ship glided through the reddish outer wisps of the great cloud, her sensors probing the surrounding heavens for clues about what might lie ahead. Nobody, not even Cook himself, lacked for misgivings about the course ahead of them. Except for the captain and his helmsman, none dared to think about what they might find in the small, irregular gap they'd found in the swirling eddies of the known galaxy's greatest natural formation.

And except for the captain, no one was looking for a small, narrow channel, winding its way through the surging storms that lighted the clouds around them—just like the hidden rift that was the only safe passage through the storms filling the skies east of Isis.

* * *

AS THE *d'Artagnan* slipped into the dense fog that dominated the heavens from Terra to the outer reaches of the Crutchtan heartland, the war's second major battle was gathering in skies far to the west.

Eager for battle, with the fierce pride of their warrior ancestors burning in their blood, Terra's forces were speeding headlong toward the enemy they had found so elusive. Leaving their support ships astern with a hundred or so frigates to guard them, the Terrans hurlted toward the main body of the Crutchtan defenses. The swirls and eddies of the Crutchtan Cloud glowed in the frozen blackness to anticenter, the random noise of subspace static broken only by transmissions to a concerned but confident military command far to the west, and to the terrified leaders of a desperate people to the east.

On the 21st of June in the Earth year 2552, the two fleets met in battle less than a parsec away from a dying red star the Crutchtans were later to call *tch'rani-ghr'Schum*—the "First Blood of Terra."

"THE TERRAN warships have slowed, Centurion," said the monitor.

Ga'Glish nodded his acknowledgment. Uncertainty pulsed through his veins and his belly tightened with hate. But all doubts had melted with the realization that the Day of Atonement his ancestors faced countless times in the past was dawning anew. It was no longer a question of seeking a means to meet the threat. Thirty dozen commandeered merchant freighters now carried the last hopes of their proud race in their creaking beams and experimental engines. If this new weaponry failed them, there was no way to stop the Terrans. Worry was an empty extravagance.

The Tall One kept the regal calm expected of a leader in the space-force of His Worthiness. The brave ones he commanded deserved no less. The bridge was silent as death as he ordered the monitor to display the Terran positions for all to see.

The Terrans had formed a broad phalanx, reinforced in the center and at both flanks by the dreaded starships. The fingers of Ga'Glish gently touched the amulet hanging from his neck, a symbol of the loved ones he knew would mourn his passing. For a moment he felt emotion cleanse his soul, and wistful tears for happier times welled in his eyes. But the time for memories had passed.

"Sound the alarm," Ga'Glish said, his voice rising with defiance. "Let Death await the coward, let Death await the foe."

* * *

"COMMODORE—"

"I see it," said Commodore McIntyre. The bridge of the *Sequoia* was a cauldron of activity, as the crew recomputed the aliens' speed and direction. No longer coming toward the Terran flank, the Crutchtans had swung far to anticenter and were now heading directly toward the heart of the Terran fleet. Sensors counted twelve hundred or so chasers, and about two hundred larger, slower ships of unknown capabilities.

"Transports, I think," the commodore said, more to himself than to anyone on his bridge. "Or maybe ore freighters." A wave of concern passed just beneath his consciousness, then faded just as imperceptibly. He hated unknowns, especially in battle, but the aliens had shown nothing capable of resisting Terran power. He harbored no doubt about the outcome.

"Enemy closing; range one thousand klicks," said the systems officer. "Engagement in twelve minutes. Chasers are moving to the flanks. The new ships are leading the attack."

"All ships at battle stations," reported the radio officer.

"Defensive Formation 'A,'" commanded McIntrye. He had no idea what the enemy was doing, but he was taking no chances. If the lizards wanted to attack, it was fine with him. But he wanted his starships up front.

THE SHIP rocked violently, tossing the crew like dust in the wind. The lights on board dimmed and flickered and the beams creaked like old men. As the starship sped past, Ga'Glish counted six separate impacts like thunder crackling directly overhead. When the Terran ship was finally out of range, he heard a shout rise from his throat, as it did from everyone on board, a primitive, primordial shout that rose from the depths of the ancient past and echoed in the streets and hills on every planet in the Empire.

The shields had held.

Like everyone else who survived the first Terran assault, Ga'Glish was surprised to find himself alive.

But the shields had held.

* * *

BY ANY objective measure, *tch'rani-ghr'Schum* was no Crutchtan victory.
Less than half of the forces the Imperator sent to do battle with the
Terrans survived the two-day battle; and of the survivors, only four
hundred chasers and ninety-six battlecruisers returned safely to port.
The rest were captured or destroyed by Terran pursuit squadrons, or
abandoned by their crews as unspaceworthy.

Though unable to turn the invaders back, the battle proved to the
Crutchtans that the Terrans were not invulnerable. A hundred Terran
frigates and nearly as many cruisers fell in battle; another two dozen
frigates fell in a swift and merciless counterattack by the Crutchtan
rear guard, as the Terran fleet tried to repeat the rout of Dragon's
Head and turn the Crutchtan retreat into a panic. They now saw that
the Terran ships could be destroyed, even if the cost would be
terrible. But now time, as much as the longnoses, would be their
enemy.

As for the Terrans, their leaders hailed the battle as another grand
victory, convincing even so cautious a man as Admiral Clay to press
the advantage. After all, CosGuard had shown itself able to withstand
the fiercest onslaught by the deadliest weapons Consortium science
had to offer and still inflict devastating losses on the enemy. Driven
by pride and vengeance, and by leaders who themselves were guided
by passions and motives they understood but dimly, the Terrans
barely noticed among the cold statistics a grim fact so small that it
nearly escaped Crutchtan attention, as well: in addition to their other
losses, the Terrans lost two starships in the battle.

Terra discounted the losses as inconsequential and more a fluke of
battle than any real cause for concern. For their part, the Crutchtan
commanders were too drained by battle and grieved by the loss of
friends and comrades to feel much satisfaction at destroying only two
of the Terrans' most powerful warships. But the data, as analysts of
both sides would later report to their respective tacticians and
strategists, would show that the clumsy Crutchtan battlecruisers could
stand against the starships, if deployed in sufficient numbers to offset
their lack of maneuvearabilty. Even so, it would take many refitted
freighters to bring down a single starship, and the freighters
themselves were highly vulnerable to attack from Terra's smaller
warships.

After pausing a few days to rest from the battle and learn what few lessons the engagement seemed to offer, the Terran fleet resumed its leisurely advance toward the Crutchtan planet *la'Khrysk*, now sixteen parsecs away. This time, however, the Terran commander let his frigates lead the way: Central Command did not like risking its most expensive and sophisticated machines in the minor skirmishes that the frantic Crutchtans were offering, and issued firm instructions to its field commanders on the use of starships in unknown skies.

Meanwhile, hidden by the swirls and eddies of the Crutchtan Cloud and undetected by Terra's sensors, a massive and frantic conversion of old, new, reconstituted, and reconstructed merchant ships was nearing completion on her flanks. All the while, the Terran fleet was venturing forty—forty-five—fifty parsecs into enemy space, massing in tight formation to guard against the peripheral raids by the enemy, and ever more dependent on the thin trail of relay buoys left behind to permit communications with home, and facilitate navigation in the alien skies of Crutchta.

* * *

```
CC:            143-2602.2
FILE:          Log
ACCESS:        Command.
SECURITY:      Standard
OPERATIONAL STATUS: Yellow Alert.
LOCATION:      Uncharted, circa 47-997734
```

The crew remains restless as we continue down the channel. Although it contains numerous wisps, eddies, and cul-de-sacs, we are maintaining a constant heading of 790, which remains unaltered, despite several minor twists in the passageway. The crew, I fear, is tired of taking this on faith, since interference from the surrounding clouds has rendered many of our instruments, including our navigation equipment, non-functional.

The surrounding clouds are quite colorful, mostly reds and purples, and interstellar lightening from the storms is providing quite a display. Were the circumstances different, we would be having a lovely time sight-seeing. As matters stand, it is all I can do to keep everyone's mind on the task at hand. I am, however, convinced of one thing: the consistency of the heading, and the fact that the channel remains open despite the violent storms raging on all sides, makes it unlikely that this is an entirely natural formation. Unfortunately, it seems I will have to leave exploring the mysteries of this discovery to others. For the moment, I have my hands full trying to maintain order and morale on my ship.

I estimate that we are presently one hundred or so parsecs from the nearest starbase. Oddly enough, once through the Cloud our current heading would take us directly to Isis. After our recent misadventures on this trip, when we reach the cross-road I may have to let Jeremy and the others talk me out of simply heading straight for home.

Capt R Cook

Chapter 32

COSGUARD'S APPARENT INVINCIBILITY brought a lightheaded giddiness to the Terran capital in the summer of 2552.

Just as the first days of the Heathcoate era brought with it a conspicuous appreciation for the finer things in life—the finest wines, the finest foods, and the finest clothing, especially when worn by the finest ladies in all of Terra—so did the first news of Terran victories produce an outpouring of patriotic fervor unequaled since the darkest days of the twentieth century. Orators proclaimed the courage of the Cosmic Guard unsurpassed since the days of Thermopylae. In endless parades, faceless marchers carried flags from every planet in the Terran League—except for misguided and wayward Isis—in step to the martial sounds of countless bands. Prominently displayed on the banners and placards being waved and carried in the tumult and pageantry of people joyously marching to drums, was the face of the man whom half of Terra now saluted as a hero, and the other half, with a few malcontented exceptions, regarded as nothing less than a savior. Even on New Babylon, where most had previously regarded him as an unenlightened buffoon, Duncan Heathcoate's picture was beginning to appear in public offices and lobbies, in town halls and libraries. In the schools, the principals were starting to hang the president's picture in the lobby, right next to the Terran flag.

As the warm summer breezes began to carry the first hints of autumn, the capital filled once again with power brokers and government officials returning from vacation. As it did every year at this time, Covington became a city of song, filled with playful laughter and nights of revelry and romance. The war was light-years away, and no longer dominated the conversations of the local dilettantes, whose minds soon drifted to more important concerns—such as Senator

Herschall's impending divorce, and Mrs. DelGrado's indelicacy in seating Finance Minister McSwaggard next to Senator Ehrlich at the Covington Underwriters' Ball, just two days after the senator's daughter announced her engagement to someone other than the Minister's son.

Even as the "Delgrado Gaffe" threatened to send Covington into an uproar, military minds across the Eastern front were considering plans to bring the war to a swift and decisive end. But life in the Capital continued as usual, for there was nothing in the reports to cause any real concern. The military was, after all, paid to tend to affairs of that sort.

* * *

THE CONFERENCE room was cramped and crowded. Every available seat was taken, and the latecomers had to find space to sit on the floor. Lights filled the briefing screen, and giddiness filled the air. The easy victories over the aliens had made everyone feel cocky. It took McIntyre ten minutes to quiet the assembled squadron leaders to hear what was being said. Even then, following the briefing was next to impossible, and the Reconnaissance Officer was not exactly helping matters. But the fleet commander forced himself to listen intently as Captain Fitzgerald highlighted the findings of his latest scouting expedition.

"As you can see," said Fitz, pointing to the star map on the screen with a directed beam of light, "we are nearing a major bend in the Crutchtan Cloud. About five parsecs from here, the cloud swings far to anticenter, leaving a large clearing in the cloud about thirty-five parsecs across. The bend itself, which I've taken the liberty of calling 'Point Fitzgerald'— "

The usual catcalls and jeers that greeted Fitzgerald's announcement that he had named another cosmic landmark after himself dissolved into laughter as the flotilla's leadership realized that "Point Fitzgerald" resembled nothing so much as the distinguishing feature found on mammalian males throughout the galaxy. Undaunted, Fitz continued, his beet-red face fighting to resume its normal hue. His voice was barely audible over the crescendo of good-natured derision.

"—guards an enclave containing two dozen or so young stars, perhaps a few hundred thousand years old. Like the Plaeides, they are still lighting the dissipating gases of the mother cloud. Though the area needs more detailed scouting...."

"Mother cloud? Damn, I think Fitz needs a biology lesson," Chandler shouted from the back of the room, his piercing voice trumpeting over the growing din.

"Naw," rejoined Forestall, DemCom's junior wing commander. "His confusion is understandable. Fitz has just been in space too long, that's all. He can't tell the difference any more."

By now, even McIntyre realized that the briefing was beyond redemption. He dismissed most of the assembly and reconvened in his office with Fitzgerald and a few top aides. Fitz could brief the others later. For the time being, it seemed they were all too giddy to pay attention.

McIntyre's office did not reflect the spartan image that CosGuard liked to display to the Senate committees that controlled the budget. Plush carpeting lined the floor, a deep maroon that gave a richness and luster to the wide, paneled walls. Unlike most starships, Mc-Intyre's office had no door leading to a briefing room. The commodore had ordered the dividing wall removed. He felt cramped in the regulation-sized captain's office and liked the spacious, airy feeling that an admiral-sized office gave him. Besides, his friends in Central Command assured him that he was moving slowly but steadily up the promotion list, and he was beginning to feel impatient about waiting for roomier surroundings.

The commodore sat behind a large desk covered with a veneer of Demetrian hardwood. Leaning back in his giant, stuffed chair he struck a pose of dignified calm, listening attentively as Fitz finished the briefing. His tactical advisors, sitting on simulated leather chairs arranged in twin rows to his left and right, listened with obvious intensity, each knowing that the boss was watching all of them with the same attention to detail that he focused on Fitzgerald.

"As I was saying," the captain said, trying to ignore the sense of inadequacy that McIntyre always raised in his subordinates. "About six days past the bend in the Cloud, at the other end of the gulf, we monitored heavy enemy activity in a binary system dominated by a large, yellow star. Our scouts couldn't risk getting close enough to see exactly what they were doing."

"Why not?" asked the commodore.

Fitz was confused. "Sir?"

"Why couldn't you send your scouts in closer? You were how far away?"

"Our closest approach was about a half-parsec."

"*About* a half-parsec?" The commodore shook his head, and his brow furrowed ominously.

"Well, 0.437 parsecs, to be precise, but the point is— "

"The point is, Captain, that we're at war, in case you've forgotten. When I send you out for reconnaissance, I expect accurate information."

Fitz' dark eyes flashed angrily. His orders had been quite specific. Do not engage the enemy; find out what you can, as quickly as you can, and report back to the fleet. He was about to speak in his defense when Richardson, McIntyre's executive aide, interjected.

"Is the binary system you mentioned the alien planet Lagrush?" asked the young commander. Fitz saw that the young man tended toward the same bilious pucker worn by the commodore, and affected the polished Babylonian accent favored by CosGuard's administrators.

Fitz nodded. "The coordinates we calculated match the ones Cook broadcast when he passed by on his way to Girshoona. As for the massive ship movements we detected—well, they're consistent with an alien evacuation. But that's hardly surprising."

"I assume that you at least monitored their radio frequencies?" McIntyre asked archly.

"Their transmissions are in code," Fitz replied icily. "We did, however, record them, if you care to refer the matter to the fleet cryptographers." In the first flush of victory, he had forgotten how much he disliked the commodore. Fitz was a proud man; but pride in one's work was common among Demetrians from working-class families, a group noted more for its backbone than its tact. He had little use for snobs, especially those who wore their credentials like crown jewels. McIntyre was hardly the worst, for despite his faults he was still a fine starship commander. He was just among the most obnoxious.

Fitz finished his briefing and left to join his friends. As the office door closed behind him with a hiss of pressured air, a sour look of disapproval flashed across McIntyre's face, a look immediately reflected by the rest of his staff. At last, as if by unspoken signal, they were ready to consider their options.

All agreed that the aliens were likely to mount a last-ditch assault on the flotilla. The enemy needed the time it would buy to complete their evacuation of the planet. When and where they would attack was an open question, though McIntyre was convinced that the lizards were too weak to pose much of a threat.

The discussion continued at length and soon McIntyre found himself losing interest. There wasn't a single option anybody mentioned that he hadn't considered at least a dozen times in the last month. The commodore looked at the framed reprints on his wall, paintings of Old Earth battles when swords cut rivers of blood, and heroes rode white chargers into battle. Taking Lagrush from the aliens would give Terra a habitable planet fifty parsecs into Crutchtan skies. And Fitzgerald's description of the site, protected by the point and open expanse of the gulf on one side and by the main body of the Crutchtan Cloud on the other, promised that the planet would be almost impregnable once it fell to Terran hands.

The commodore switched the view on the table screen, and looked at the massive reddish clouds to port. The fleet was forty parsecs inside Crutchta and still the Cloud stretched into the distance as far as their sensors could reach. Barely visible from Earth, here it loomed in the heavens like a thundering god. McIntyre could scarcely begin to count the nascent star systems in the throes of birth visible even from the Cloud's perimeter. He could almost taste the riches lurking in the depths beyond view, all there for the taking.

McIntyre sighed, and smiled bitterly. He could hear his aides discussing tactics and battle plans. Although they were sitting within a few feet, they seemed parsecs away. The war would soon be over, of that he was all but certain. Now that Terra had a secure, livable planet almost within its grasp, hostilities would surely cease. The peacemongers in Covington would see to it. But McIntyre couldn't help thinking that it was a waste of military advantage to stop now, when so many riches were within their grasp.

And anyway, he thought, shaking his head, the lizards brought this all on themselves. Who knew how long the balance of power would stay tilted in Terra's favor? Better to eliminate the threat now, once and for all, than to hope for friendship from a race dedicated to their destruction. And he recalled his days at the Academy, and the philosophy professor who spoke fondly of the Old Earth philosopher who wrote of the folly of postponing an inevitable confrontation, since delay only works to your enemy's advantage.

What was his name? he asked himself; then it came to him: McEllerby. Or was it Machiabelli? He never could keep his Old Earth history straight.

* * *

"I STILL don't see what the fuss is, Lieutenant."

Commodore Medwick squinted at the monitor screen. The Cloud often played tricks on the base sensors, particularly when an ionic disturbance, a low grade ion storm, flared in the jetty that projected across what had been the Neutral Zone. The disturbance caused subspace static that interfered with the sensor sweeps and blurred images on the visual display. But several dozen pinpoints of light still appeared, off and on, along the curving edge of the Cloud as it faded into the cosmic east.

Ishao Takira, his new lieutenant's stripes still an unfaded gold on his epaulets, pointed to the irregular sparkles hugging the anticenter arc along the dull green image of Kelton's Jetty.

"Here," he said. Concern put an edge to his voice, but he was really more curious than anything else. He had never seen anything like it before. "You can see these images. Points of light, more than anything. They wink in and out of view, almost like newborn stars in a star cloud."

The commodore squinted again, then grunted. "Looks like an ion storm to me, one just starting to gather steam," he said, his gruff voice leaving no room for doubt. "Hardly cause for concern, Lieutenant."

"That doesn't look like any storm pattern I've ever seen, Commodore. And the motion patterns are random. An ion storm would be organizing itself into a spiral as it broke loose from the jetty."

Medwick gave the young lieutenant a hard look. Takira never accepted explanations, thought the commodore. He just kept digging for things that weren't there. The young troublemaker reminded the commodore of nothing so much as a Demetrian sandmole, wearing its claws away trying to burrow through a concrete embankment.

"Lieutenant," said the commodore, a hint of condescension in his voice. "When you decide exactly what it is, call me. Until then, I have more important things to do. Now, if you'll excuse me." Medwick turned on his heel and strode toward the door, leaving more than one face sour with disgust.

"If that don't beat all," said the chiseled old yeoman manning the monitor. "War's a-raging across the sky, and he's too busy to bother about unexplained blips on the radar screen."

"That's enough," Takira said sharply. "We have our own work to do. Don't bother about his."

* * *

"ADMIRAL?"

Clay looked up from his desk. He tried not to smile, but the soft perfume of Commodore Wright was starting to make him think of a distant beach on Valhalla, many years ago—and of the young girl who became the woman who now greeted him at home every day.

"Yes, Commodore."

"Our reinforcements have just passed Fishman's Star, and are nearing Point Fitzgerald. McIntyre's still awaiting final orders. Shall I schedule a briefing?"

"How far are they from the main fleet?"

"Two parsecs, at last report. But the advance guard has already joined the flotilla. They're just waiting for the support ships and the stragglers."

"And the alien planet?"

"Still no sign of the main enemy fleet. As far as we can tell, they've moved completely out of the quadrant. Except for the local planetary guard, the place looks deserted."

Clay took a long sigh and slowly released it. He had read McIntyre's reports: crisp, optimistic, not a whiff of anything to worry about. The skies were clear, the enemy was gone, and the alien planet loomed within sight. Taking Lagrush would give Terra control of more of the Crutchtan Cloud than they could see from Looking Glass. Above all, they would have a habitable planet in the heart a rich concentration of newly forming stars. It should, for all intents and purposes, end the war.

"Schedule your briefing, Commodore," smiled the admiral, leaning back in his chair. "And radio McIntrye to attack when ready."

"You know," said the commodore, just as she turned to leave, "it's ironic. And sad, in a way."

"What is?"

"Well, that it ends like this. So easily, I mean. Because the way things have gone, our most significant loss—maybe our only real loss—occurred before the fighting even started."

"You mean Cook?"

Wright nodded. "And what makes it so ironic is that if he *had* made it back, he'd probably never be able to live it down."

"Live what down?"

Smiling, the commodore shook her head. "He was so sure that the aliens would attack our flanks. In the short time he was here, he'd disrupt half our staff briefings, prattling on about this or that—and always carping about watching our flanks, watching our flanks. Always our flanks.

"But they never came close. The war was all but over when we fired our first shot. For all the effort he put into trying to change my mind, he didn't live long enough to see how wrong he was—though, Lord knows, I doubt that any of us would've let him forget it."

Clay sighed. "He was a character, all right. And truth to tell, he reminded me—just a little bit, mind you—of myself at that age: stubborn, cocksure...."

"Long-winded?"

"Well, I suppose that's better than the kind of wind I put out these days."

The two shared a laugh, though laughter was becoming a rare commodity. Soon the commodore left, leaving Clay alone with his thoughts.

For the first time since the war started, he thought, he could see the end. For once, it seemed that Central Command was right. The plan was simple and direct; it could have come from a textbook. The two thousand enemy ships massing to defend the planet seemed to pose no particular problem. The aliens had even split their forces, almost as if trying to make the Terrans' job easier. Once Lagrush fell, Terra would have an easily defensible base deep inside Crutchtan space, from which to dominate the entire sector, an expanse large enough to keep Terran science busy for a hundred years, charting stars, cataloguing resources, and guiding industry to treasures that made even the Ishtari Belt look like a galactic poverty pocket.

It was hard not to start relaxing, now that the end was near. For all the anxiety and tension that the past weeks had produced, the end promised to be routine.

At least, as far as anything in war was routine.

* * *

SOMETIMES, NIGHTMARES come in the dead of night, lurking in the shadows of forgotten terrors that spring suddenly to life. Others lurk around dark corners, lying in wait like the bandits that stalked the streets of Earth. Always, they loom just beyond reach, in the blackness of the unknown.

Feeling the comforting sense that the worst was over, and that his life would soon return to normal, Admiral Clay decided to skip his staff meeting and go straight home to his wife. He could, after all, speak directly to Commodore Wright any time he chose, but dinner at home had come to be rarer than a Tory on Isis. He stopped to buy some flowers, grown in the base conservatorium, and he walked most of the way from the Looking Glass administrative offices to the residential concourse on C-Deck. He even paused to window shop at some of the licensed private stores of the C-Deck Mall; his wife's birthday was two weeks away, and he'd neglected her for longer than he cared to remember. Yet a vague disquiet haunted his sense of well-being. It was nothing he could pinpoint, and he felt so much better than he had in months that it almost escaped his attention entirely. But as he neared his home, foreboding ripened into panic as he came to realize that he'd felt the same feeling once before in his life, twenty minutes before learning that his father had died. The thought so scared him that he forgot about the hundred other times that similar thoughts came and passed each month.

At home he found everything normal, and everyone healthy. He dismissed his fears as little more than the worries and phobias that plagued him from time to time as he passed through the rushing years of middle age. That night he slept soundly in his wife's arms. Not even the news that McIntyre was beginning the siege of Lagrush brought back the dark feelings he'd known a few hours earlier.

Those feelings did not return until shortly after Zero Hour, when his wife turned over to answer the incessant buzzing of the intercom. It was Admiral Turner, summoning Clay to an emergency meeting of the whole command staff.

Out in the blackness, far beyond what they still called the Neutral Zone, simultaneously and without warning, the communications relay buoys linking the flotilla with the rest of the Eastern Fleet had gone dead. The sentries deployed to guard the relay stations were not answering hails from any ships or starbases. At the very time Terra was preparing to celebrate her biggest victory of the war, an ominous and impenetrable curtain of silence had fallen to sever all links between CosGuard's forces and home.

Chapter 33

AS DAWN CAME to every corner of Terra, the news spread like summer wildfires across the dry plains of Ceres. The fury of Terra's leaders over their inability to affect events to the east was dwarfed by the numbing fear of people who'd gone to bed warmed by stories of conquest. Before the day ended, their fear had given way to mindless horror. As the Cosmic Guard struggled to reopen its lost communications with the flotilla, subspace sensors detected unexpected, unfamiliar, and unknown readings on the Terran flanks that admitted a single, chilling explanation.

The aliens were coming.

Silently, the Crutchtans were heading directly at Terra's weakest, most vulnerable positions, the two most undermanned, under-protected starbases along the Neutral Zone—Starbase 117, and Starbase 121, each isolated at opposite ends of Terra's prewar borders, and far beyond any hope of reinforcement before the alien counterattack reached them.

In an instant of sickening insight, all of Terra realized two terrifying facts. If both bases fell, there was no way to stop the alien advance before it reached the population centers of eastern Terra. The contingent left at Looking Glass was too small to fight two battles at once, and the ships of the Central Fleet were too far distant to arrive in time.

Even worse, in the giddy rush of martial fervor that had marked the opening days of the war, every available starship and cruiser had sailed with the invasion flotilla.

Nothing but frigates stood between the aliens and the planets of Terra.

* * *

AS CRUTCHAN attack forces sped toward the Terran flanks, a furious battle raged in the space around the Crutchtan planet *la'Khryshk*.

Seeing that the main body of the Terran forces had rounded Point Fitzgerald, the Crutchtan defenders sailed from their stronghold to meet them, forming a giant, arcing crescent. The skies between the enemy fleets was cluttered with debris from the stellar condensation of the past few million years, slowing the Terran advance to a crawl and fouling their sensors with subspace ghosts and echoes. Almost inviting the inevitable attack, the Crutchtans halted just past the reach of the Terrans' medium range subspace radar, on the other side of a small clearing in the wavelike patterns of the interstellar dust and gases.

As McIntyre, the Terran commander, radioed the message that the battle was about to begin, he had no way of knowing that, all along the slender line of communications relays strung fifty parsecs behind them, enemy ships were moving silently into position to destroy the relay buoys, and the frigate squadrons deployed to guard them. As he gave the order to the flotilla to begin the attack and his ships started streaking toward the enemy ships waiting so patiently a half-parsec away, he could not know that he had broadcast his last message home for what would prove to be an eternity.

Swiftly, confidently, the Terrans raced through the blackness, all minds intent on a single goal—destroying the enemy. Thrusting at the heart of the enemy defenses, the Terrans kept their headings straight and true, and failed to notice the moment when they lost all contact with home. That realization would come later for some, and never for many.

Soon the Terrans closed for battle, and systems officers on a hundred ships confirmed the intelligence their scouts had given them: fifteen-hundred ships lay ahead of them, preparing to defend the alien planet; five hundred more were moving toward them from the direction of Galactic Center. While F-Wing moved against the Crutchtans' peripheral force, the main body of the fleet closed to within minutes of the defenders and, entering the clear space just before the alien position, increased their speed.

Suddenly, from all sides, the sky came alive with Crutchtan warships. Concealed in the clouds of gas and debris, patiently waiting for the moment the Terrans passed into the clearing, thousands of ships appeared and pounced upon the Terran fleet. At the same time, a whole attack force emerged from the sanctuary of a stellar cloud surrounding the young stars just beyond the point, and another two thousand Crutchtan ships raced to join the battle, blocking the last path of retreat for the disoriented Terrans. Within minutes it was clear that no escape was possible for the outnumbered invaders. The trap was too complete, too cleverly sprung, and too tightly woven. Aside from surrender, their only chance was to fight their way clear, and surrender was out of the question.

Desperately, the Terran fleet moved to meet the attack. Their commander ordered one of his attack groups into a rear guard action against the enemy fleet swarming in from the west, and tried to gather the rest of his forces inside the clearing. With the two main bodies of the Crutchtan forces still a thousand astrokilometers away, the Terrans had little time to organize their defenses, and moved toward a position in the middle of the clearing, hoping to give themselves more room to maneuver.

But the Crutchtans were everywhere, and the Terran rear guard was soon isolated from the main Terran force. Enemy ships kept streaming out of the cloud and rushing toward the battle. Wave after wave of attacks came at the main body of the Terran fleet, disrupting communications between ships. Soon, the rear guard was overrun, and only sixteen of D-Wing's two hundred ships, all of them starships, managed to fight their way back to rejoin the fleet. One by one the rest were surrounded and destroyed. As the numbed and weary survivors straggled to temporary safety, every man and woman in the fleet knew the chilling truth. They were light-years away from help. Many of them were about to die. And their ashes would soon be wandering forever, through alien skies, in the cold of eternity.

* * *

COMMODORE MEDWICK'S face was haggard and pale. The overhead lights were making him sweat, and he shifted uncomfortably in his chair. Around him, faces were grim. No one dared to speak of their private fears. They all struggled to maintain a professional, businesslike facade, while they faced the biggest challenge of their lives. But inside, everyone was terrified. The aliens were heading straight for them, in greater numbers than they had ever imagined possible, and Looking Glass had made them painfully aware that they were on their own.

"Status reports."

Each department head cleared his throat, waiting for someone else to begin. Finally, Lt. Takira spoke. "The enemy is two parsecs away. At present speed, their ETA is about eight hours from now—or 143-2799, by the cosmic clock."

"How did they get so close so quickly?" Medwick asked. By this time, the rancor had left his voice. Now, there was only resignation.

"I have no idea, Commodore," Takira said, trying to keep the bitterness out of his voice. "But there's a small jetty in the cloud bank due east of their present position. I think they've had a secret base there for some time, hidden from our sensors by distance and cosmography. We've never really charted this quadrant of space. It was beyond our frontiers at the time of the Hawkins Massacre. After the peace talks started we never had the chance, and after the war began—well, for one reason or another we just never got around to it. We just don't know what's out there."

"Enemy strength?"

Lt. Commander Proust spoke this time. With Captain Detwiler gone with the flotilla, he would lead their remaining ships into battle.

"A precise count is impossible. The enemy has scouts everywhere, and ours can't get close enough for an accurate guess. All we can say for sure is that there are more than one hundred. Many more. And they keep pouring out from behind the jetty."

"Our strength?"

Commander Erhart, the base systems officer, sighed deeply and coughed. More than anyone in the room, he knew how desperate their situation was, but there could be no holding back. At least this time, he thought, the commodore could not dismiss him with a look of disdain.

"Excluding those ships in drydock, we have forty-one frigates ready for combat. We also have a good number of escorts available, but escorts have never been tested against Crutchtan chasers and are of questionable value in battle. Our scouts are no match for the Crutchtan vipers, but neither class is likely to affect the outcome.

"As to base defenses themselves, the main shields are battle ready and the base power supply is functioning at maximum capacity. But our secondary shields are in the middle of overhaul and we can expect a maximum of 50 percent secondary reserve power by the time the enemy arrives. As for the weapons systems themselves, they're tied into the secondary power system. If we start immediately, we can switch them to mainsource within three cosmic hours. Otherwise, they'll suffer from the same power deficiency as the secondary shields, and using them will drain the secondary system even further."

"But," interjected Takira, "won't mainsourcing mean that the enemy— "

"Can knock out our weapons by draining our shields?" said Ehrhardt, finishing the thought. He tried to sound professional, to keep from showing anything but the military detachment expected of an officer of the Cosmic Guard. But the truth was that he was scared to death, and all the self-control in the galaxy could not keep his voice from cracking under the strain. "Yes, that's exactly what it means. But in my opinion, we have no choice."

Soon the meeting broke up, and each officer began the job of readying the base for the attack they all knew was coming. Everyone left the room sure that the next few days would be their last, that they all faced the certainty of a death that could be delayed for a few hours, but not avoided. As they started hearing the echoes of their own mortality, each felt cheated by the cruel realization that those last hours would be spent not in savoring what little time was left, but in rallying the command for a cause that seemed futile beyond hope, in a war that had suddenly lost most of its meaning and all of its glitter.

* * *

Commander Paavola took a sip of water and tried to relax. Even two weeks after the event, it was still hard to relive the horror that had cost the lives of so many friends. Each time he thought of it, the shudders returned, and he doubted that he'd ever be able to command again. The doctors told him differently, told him that seeing others blown to bits while he escaped destruction through blind luck often created guilt and self-doubts that would pass with time. He would believe them when it happened. For now, he had a job to do, and the debriefing officers across the table were there to find a way to prevent similar disasters in the future.

"So then what happened?" asked Admiral Turner, the senior officer on the panel. Paavola breathed deeply to calm himself, and continued.

"After the remnants of D-Wing rejoined us, Commodore McIntyre formed us into three battle groups for defense. Captains Quiroz and Napp took the flanks; Captain Schmidt took charge of the center."

"Where was McIntyre at this point?" asked Commodore Wright.

"The Commodore was in the center of the formation, about fifty astrokilometers from the perimeter, coordinating ship movements."

"And how did the enemy respond?"

Paavola swallowed hard; the struggle for control was noticeable in his wavering voice, but he continued without pause.

"Once the first enemy ships emerged from the dust cloud, they never ceased attacking, and our western flank was under constant fire. The two additional enemy battle groups advanced steadily from east and anticenter, toward our forward positions."

"And where were you at this time?" asked Commodore Kassab, the third member of the board of inquiry.

"The cruisers were ordered to the front along with the frigates, as per the battle manual. My ship, the CAPE ROYALE, *was in Captain Schmidt's group."*

"Were you ever ordered to advance and engage?"

"I was not."

"Were any ships in your division ordered to advance and engage?"

"They were not."

"And did your squadron's relative position remain fixed throughout the battle?"

"Until the retreat call, yes sir."

"THE TERRANS are assuming defensive positions, Centurion."

"Almal'Loshen reports Group One pressing its attack on the left, Centurion."

"Sha'Llonshi reports that Group Two is almost into position in the center, Centurion."

Ga'Glish turned his chair to face the display map on the screen to his right, his brow raised in contemplation. However much he tried to fight it, a blood thirst was swelling his soul like a parched tongue under a merciless desert sun. The Terrans provoked such hatred, and had inflicted so much death with such ease, that lust for revenge was the most common craving in the Empire. It spread like a plague among gentry and rabble alike. Among the Imperator's fleet, which had borne the full fury of the Terran war machines, the chance to reclaim the blood debt owed was the most powerful intoxicant he had ever seen. It whipped those under his command to a frenzy of madness both compelling and repulsive. Whatever the cause, it consumed the mind and fired the heart until all souls thought and felt as one. It remade his friends and comrades, civilized souls he had known for a lifetime, into mindless instruments of destruction. As useful as it made them in war, he found the transformation profoundly disturbing.

But as their leader, he had to fight such madness in himself. The Terrans were as merciless as space itself, and would fight with the fury of desperation. It would be a spur no less potent than hatred. The battle still loomed in an uncertain future, with the fate of both peoples the prize for the victor. He could afford no such self-indulgence.

As Group Two emerged from its pre-engagement position behind Alagishi Cape, the Terran defensive strategy became clear. Though still harassed on the left flank by Alma'Loshen's battlegroup, the Terran commander was sending his right flank to face the fleet from *la'Khryshk* while his center held its position. Obviously, thought Ga'Glish, they wished him to commit to one side of the battle or the other before bringing their center into play. It would give the longnoses more room to maneuver, and increase the usefulness of their central forces.

"Message to Sha'Llonshi," Ga'Glish told the monitor, as coldly as he could. "Redouble speed and begin Attack Plan A. Move forces straight ahead, to the middle of the Terran defensive positions."

Ga'Glish allowed himself a small, self-satisfied smile. As events were unfolding, his plan was exceeding his most grandiose dreams. They did not even need his seven other contingency plans. The Terrans, as if they could not help it, were reacting better than he could have hoped for, setting themselves up for the full strength of the *g'Khruush-tani* attack.

"And signal the Capitol that the battle is nearing its crest. All thoughts are of the task at hand, and of victory."

"Where exactly was the CAPE ROYALE when the enemy began its advance?"

Admiral Turner motioned for the commander to take the map cursor.

"We were about here." Paavola moved the cursor to a point midway between the Terran right flank and the center of the arc. "In charge of a squadron consisting of four divisions, each headed by a cruiser."

"Your battle group wasn't given a starship?"

A sad, distant smile formed on Paavola's lips. Try as they might, he thought, they could never understand. The survivors of battle formed a fraternity of sorts; they could understand the terror and confusion of battle even as the war forced them to form emotional callouses. Those who knew war only from the reports or news accounts that crossed their desk would have only the dimmest shadow of comprehension. Even the right questions seemed beyond their grasp. But it was just as well, for they would find the answers incomprehensible.

"There was too much confusion for us to follow deployment guidelines, Admiral Turner. Besides, there weren't enough starships to go around. Until we got into real trouble, after the aliens routed the squadrons on either side of us and the perimeter started to buckle, we simply weren't a very high priority. The starships were needed elsewhere."

"When did the starships arrive?"

"Starship, Admiral. Only one broke through the alien breach."

"And which ship was that?" asked Commodore Wright.

"The MAGELLAN, ma'am. Captain Fitzgerald's ship."

"When did it arrive?"

The commander consulted his report.

"According to my log sheets, it was cc:143-2799.4...more or less." It had been five cosmic hours after the two main alien fleets joined the battle, about seven hours after they sprang the ambush.

THE STARBASE shuddered gently under the impact of enemy blasters. Takira noticed the images on his screens flutter. In a half-dozen half-empty cups on the table beside him the coffee swayed, as if a single unsure hand had placed them all down at the same instant. He felt his stomach rise and then fall, as the enemy fire disrupted the power system of the base ever so slightly.

And this was just the initial pass. The young lieutenant knew that it would be quite a while before the aliens could make a dent in the powerful shields protecting the base from the enemy's fire. He looked up to the command station, overlooking the monitor room. There was a frenzy of activity, as the base command staff tried to organize a counterattack. The base shuddered again; the feeling was different this time, more controlled, as the outgoing fire sought to reduce the enemy attack force to something more manageable.

He heard a muffled cheer from the overlook, and saw several officers raise their hands as if in triumph. He looked at the screen to see an enemy blip suddenly slow, stung by the blasterfire. The base shuddered a second time and the image disappeared entirely.

Takira knew better than to cheer over the downing of a single enemy attack ship. He could see the steady stream of Crutchtan ships descending on them; he could watch the outnumbered Terran defenders trying to stall the enemy advance while the Crutchtans slipped patiently into position to cut them off from the base. He also remembered what most of them had already forgotten: the last transmission from Looking Glass made it quite clear that they could expect no help.

"Reinforcements unavailable at this time," read the coded transmission. "Prudence requires that we hold forces in reserve, since they could not reach you in time to help. Situation fluid, will change if SB 121 holds. Good luck."

Medwick and the others read the message to mean that help would come if they could just hold out for a few days. But Takira was an Earther, with an Earther's resigned fatalism, and held no false hopes. If Starbase 121 was also under attack, then the alien counteroffensive was widespread and well-planned. It also meant that their leaders had blundered badly by diverting so much of the fleet to the flotilla, without providing for the defense of the eastern planets.

He looked at his watch. It was cc:143-2800.4. He could count a hundred enemy ships, with more arriving each hour from the east, against less than forty frigates left from their original contingent. They would be lucky to last the rest of the day: He doubted that 2810 would see the base still standing in the heavens, or any of them alive.

"Why wasn't a starship assigned to Squadron 87 in the first place?"

Fitz had little use for table-top commanders, especially those who asked such silly questions. Unlike most of his friends, he never entertained notions of becoming an admiral, and felt few constraints against indulging his preference for candor.

"Because, Admiral Turner, we had too many other holes to plug. If we'd had a starship there, then the buggers would have broken through someplace else."

"When did you realize," asked Commodore Wright, "that your situation was, shall we say...."

"Hopeless? About five minutes after we passed into the clearing, when the aliens kept on our heels as we tried to regroup. But that was a gut feeling, Commodore, not a reasoned analysis of our military situation."

He paused a moment, but just a moment, before adding: "Of course, I wasn't under orders to capture the alien planet, either."

"Were you the only starship in the vicinity?"

"Of course not, Commodore. That battle sector had a dozen starships milling about. But all of us were engaged in battle. Thanks to the lizard battletugs, we were fighting for our lives. It wasn't until word came that the perimeter was collapsing that anyone realized just how close the enemy was to splitting the flotilla and cutting us off from the rest of the fleet. Had they succeeded, our losses would have been...insurmountable."

"How did you organize the relief operation?"

There was a note of derision in Fitzgerald's laugh. "We didn't Commodore. We didn't have time. It was all we could do to mount whatever half-assed assault we could slap together. If we'd tried to get organized, we'd all be dead."

"Did any other ship manage to penetrate the alien line?" asked Admiral Turner.

Fitz smiled inwardly. He knew his reputation for steering his ship with all the grace of a mutluk in heat. But despite his lack of pretty maneuvers, nobody else managed to slug through to relieve the trapped squadrons on the other side of the enemy breach. Even the vaunted ST. GEORGE had to sit on the sidelines, its hotshot captain relegated to providing cover and lame *encouragement as the* MAGELLAN *bulled past the Crutchtans and raced to aid the beleaguered squadrons trapped behind the rupture in the Terran defenses.*

"No sir."

"At the time you made contact with Squadron 87, what was your plan of attack?"

"My only 'plan' was to lead them to safety, Admiral. Beyond that, I had none. There simply wasn't time."

"And when that was accomplished?"

"By the time I reached them, the retreat order had come. So we engaged the enemy to west, fighting to rejoin the main body of the flotilla as it fought its way back into the cloud."

"Not to change the subject," said Commodore Wright, "but something has been troubling me about this whole mess."

She motioned to the battle map on the hologram screen to the left.

"If we were taking such a pounding, why didn't McIntyre simply retreat dead to center, along the line of the clearing? That would have let him to deploy a rear guard against the enemy advance while he regrouped. At the least, it might have bought time to organize a more orderly retreat.

"Doesn't that sound more logical to you, Captain?"

Fitz said nothing for several moments.

The same thought had occurred to him, and to every other commander who'd survived the battle. And it had occurred to him more than once.

THE BASE rocked violently. A young yeoman was slammed against a wall, seconds before an entire monitor screen was wrenched from its floor moorings and thrown through the same wall, crushing her instantly; only her decapitated head, intact except for a face flattened beyond recognition, was left to remind her friends of the terrified young woman who'd been relaying messages between stations isolated by communications failure only moments before. Her head rolled on the floor unnoticed, as the monitor room crew struggled desperately to make sense out of the constantly changing patterns of readings that raced across their instruments.

"Lieutenant!" a crewman screamed in a hoarse, ragged voice. "Screen Six!"

Takira dashed to the crewman's station in time to be jammed against the chair by another salvo from the Crutchtan blasters. Recovering, he glanced at the monitor.

"They're still coming, Lieutenant." Tears welled in the crewman's eyes. His tired voice was barely audible over the crackling of electricity from the damaged equipment.

"Be brave," said Takira, firmly grasping the young man's shoulder. "There's always hope."

"It's no good," came the tearful reply. "We're going to die! We're all going to die." There was resignation in his voice.

Clear as Rigel on a winter's night, the monitor screen showed the cause of the crewman's terror. Two parsecs away and rapidly closing on the starbase, the blip was tracking the same course the others had taken from the jetty. From its size and brightness, it promised another squadron or two of chasers, racing to join the kill. Takira felt all feeling drain from his soul, replaced by a numbing despair. Despite massive losses, the Crutchtan attack force continued to grow while the Terrans' own strength faded with each new enemy attack. The aliens were shattering the defenses already, and the base could not hold out much longer. Reinforcements would only hasten their destruction. The crewman was right. The end of the siege was plainly in view.

And yet....

Takira dismissed the thought as soon as it came. In his final moments he would indulge no false hope, no grasping at windblown phantoms. Death was better faced honestly.

But for a moment—a brief, bracing moment—the blip looked hauntingly like a starship in the distance.

"WHY AREN'T they retreating?"

Angrily, Ga'Glish slapped his thigh with his open hand. His senior aides stood silently beside him, manners silencing their tongues. But when the Lord Commander issued his command, still under the influence of rage, it fell to Sra'Chenga, the deputy commander, to speak.

"Redouble the attack, on all fronts," hissed Ga'Glish. "I want them pushed back. Pushed back, do you hear?"

"My Lord," said Sra'Chenga, "it is time to seize the moment, not to follow our old plans blindly."

"Enough!" shouted Ga'Glish. "I am in command and it is my decision!"

"The Terrans are fighting bravely and we can push them no further," Sra'Chenga continued, calmly insistent. "We should take advantage of our penetration of their lines to divide their forces. If we do this, their cause is lost. If you insist on trying to force a retreat toward the bend in the clearing they may reorganize, and we will have lost our chance to destroy their fleet and end this madness."

Ga'Glish looked harshly into his deputy's eyes. He trusted Chenga; he knew that his aide would never try to humiliate him in public. The plan called for one final ambush, one last devastating blow to the Terrans from the rear, from ships concealed in the rocks along the clearing. Altering the course of battle would throw everything into chaos, yet there was unassailable logic in what his aide was saying.

The glare faded from the centurion's eyes as his anger passed.

"Once more," he said at last, his voice calm and controlled. "We will try to force the Terrans back one more time. If we do not succeed, we will then alter our plans."

Everyone in the room nodded in agreement. Despite his misgivings, even Chenga could not argue with such a decision, though he harbored secret, treasonous doubts about its wisdom. The moment of opportunity would not last forever. It would be a simple matter to order the final wave into battle once the Terran fleet was cut in two, to give a final, devastating blow to the invaders. Sra'Chenga closed his eyes and hoped fervently that their moment would linger.

"Captain?"

"I can only speculate on the commodore's reasons, ma'am."

"Then speculate."

Fitz shrugged, "The enemy seemed so intent on driving us back that maybe McIntyre concluded that we simply could not do it. That they'd already manipulated us into doing exactly what they wanted, and since they seemed to want us to fall back, it was the one course of action that had to be resisted at all costs."

"Doesn't that sound a bit hare-brained?" asked Turner.

Fitz did not answer.

"Now, once the retreat began...."

"When the retreat call came, we pivoted to port, and fought our way toward the main body of the fleet. The enemy forces were

pressing inward, so I detached two divisions of frigates to delay them, while I led the others to safety. Then I returned to help cover the rear guard's retreat. Before I arrived, I was called off and ordered to rejoin the fleet."

"Who called you off?"

"It was Commodore McIntyre."

* * *

FROM ALL quadrants, the base shook beneath the impact of a half-dozen Crutchtan blasters. The shields were nearly depleted, and their weaponry was reduced nearly to impotence, barely felt by the waves of battletugs that swarmed around the battered starbase. Even the chasers, reduced to a supporting role by the power of the Terran blasters, had joined the attack. But the base crew kept on fighting for their lives, their fear of death kept at bay by the endless drills and rote execution that years of training had burned into every muscle in their bodies.

Silently, amid the panic and tears that grew with each new enemy barrage, and unnoticed by the desperate command staff in the control room above, a small but growing crowd had begun to gather at Monitor Screen Six. Their fear had given way to curiosity, and a wild, unspoken hope was rising in their hearts. The readings on the screen were starting to depart from all known enemy patterns.

Though nobody dared to say it, a single thought ran through every mind, even through the pounding of the enemy guns that threatened to shatter the crumbling shields that stood between them and a quick, fiery death: could it really be?

If it could only be....

"And then?"

"Turning to fight our way back into the cloud seemed to catch the aliens completely off guard. The west flank had little trouble penetrating the alien forces on that side. When the rest of the fleet broke past the breach, the bulk of the enemy was left out of position. They couldn't bring the bulk of their ships into play without running into their own forces. The only problem was extricating as much of Squadron 87's rear guard as possible, and covering our...."

Fitz searched for the right word.

"Retreat?" suggested Turner.

"Our ass," Fitz concluded. "We had to slow the enemy down enough so that we could pass through the cloud and regroup."

"How many ships were involved in the delaying action?"

"Forty-seven."

"How many got away?"

"Twenty-six."

"And the last time you saw McIntrye?"

Fitz swallowed hard. As much as he disliked the commodore, the image of the SEQUOIA racing toward certain death continued to haunt him.

"After ordering me to rejoin the fleet, he sailed past at C-19. I overheard his command to the others to form a defensive ring, and then subspace static prevented me from monitoring the rest of the battle. I heard later that after ordering a final assault on the alien battle line, he headed toward a squadron of enemy tugs to prevent an assault from the rear as the Squadron tried one last time to rejoin the fleet. As far as I know, that's the last anyone ever saw of the SEQUOIA."

"Why...," began Commodore Wright.

"Why did he do it?" Fitz shrugged. "As our commander, he may have felt that it was his duty. Or maybe he just felt responsible for leading us into the trap."

"In any event, the aliens chose not to follow you into the cloud."

Fitz nodded. "Either they were too far out of position, or else they'd already spent themselves in the ambush and didn't have the strength to come after us. We withdrew unmolested to our present position, twelve parsecs west of Lagrush. From there, we waited for our scouts to reestablish contact with home."

Fitz watched while the panel shuffled their briefing papers. Even now, their close call made him want to vomit. There was no doubt in his mind, or anyone else's, that they had come within spitting distance of losing the war.

He watched the panel confer in whispers and look intently at their notes, and wondered whether the geniuses in charge of this fiasco had learned anything. For all the technical wizardry that made victory so easy in the early days, a simple ambush had almost ruined them. And the spectacle of watching friends and enemies blown into eternity made him question whether a wispy cloud, invisible even from the plains of Ishtar, was worth all the death and destruction.

* * *

THE NEWS was devastating.

Commodore Medwick reread the message slowly, as if lingering on each word would change the printing on the paper. Though his eyes stared at the words for what seemed an eternity, the four word message stayed the same: "Starbase 121 has fallen."

In a cracking voice, he read the message aloud, in tones barely above a whisper. Though nobody made a sound, a cold shudder passed through everyone in the command room, and their eyes widened in shock and horror. No help would be coming. They would face death alone. And their deaths would open the gates of Terra to the enemy.

Suddenly, a cry arose from the floor below them, the visceral, wrenching cry of men given over to the free, wild passions of animals. Terror choked his throat and nearly emptied his bowels until he realized that the cry was not of anguish or despair, but of triumph.

Running to the window panel, Medwick saw half the people in the monitor room crowded around a single station, laughing and hugging, shouting and dancing, with fists of defiance raised against the enemy that was about to destroy them.

"Takira!" he shouted, trying to get the supervisor's attention. But his shouts were drowned by the cheers of his crew.

Finally, the young lieutenant looked up at the command room and saw the whole senior staff leaning over the edge of the window, straining to hear the news. He climbed onto one of the monitors and screamed at the top of his voice.

"She's two parsecs away and pushing C-20," he shouted, tears streaming uncontrollably down his cheeks. "And she's the most beautiful thing I've ever seen in my life."

"What is it, dammit?" Medwick hollered back, straining to be heard over the din.

"A starship, sir! From out of nowhere—it's a bloody damn starship!"

The crash of the alien blasters and the hoarse cries of the monitor crew soon made it impossible to hear anything but noise. But each new thunderclap now raised defiance in the hearts of everyone who'd heard the news. Despair had vanished, leaving stubborn determination in its place. The starship's miraculous appearance had given them hope, and made everyone forget the mortal danger they still faced.

The starship neared, racing out of the blackness at maximum speed. Chaos preceded it, as their enemies pounded the base furiously and thoughts of rescue battered the defenders' emotions like a gathering storm. No one was even surprised when her first hail told them that the ship, like the starbase, was rising from the dead.

It was the *d'Artagnan*.

Chapter 34

EXCEPT FOR HISTORY BOOKS written on Isis, and some obscure military journals written long after the war had become a dusty memory, Terra paid little attention to the marvel of navigation that brought the *d'Artagnan* so precisely to the eastern approach to Starbase 117. Though the wizardry of such a feat was not lost on the Crutchtans—first for finding the *Khu'ukhana* Rift through the Great Cloud, and then sailing undetected for day after day through unknown and unfriendly skies—what intrigued the Terran press corps was the image of the lone, travel-weary ship sailing out of nowhere to join the battle when all seemed lost.

But as the *d'Artagnan* sliced through the black skies leading to Starbase 117, history was no concern to anyone on board. A single thought ran through the mind of every man and woman on the ship.

Terra was under attack.

Their hearts pulsed with anger. Their ship strained her seams under the pressure of maximum emergency speed. The captain and crew felt the relentless pounding of fear, but had no time to listen for echoes of mortality.

Terra was under attack.

Nothing mattered except repelling the invader—not the enemy's numerical advantage, not their ship's flagging engines, not the unending tension everyone had felt since their captain first took them into uncharted skies. No one felt the slightest hesitation when the klaxons called all hands to battle stations and word spread that the enemy force was large and strong and about to obliterate CosGuard's last remaining outpost, opening the skies of home to invasion.

Terra was under attack, and they would save her or die trying.

"THE STARBASE reports their shields starting to buckle," reported Underwood from the commuications station.

"ETA?" Cook asked, matter-of-factly.

"Approaching ten cosmic minutes...mark!" answered Jeremy. "Sensors show the enemy deploying two squadrons to intercept us. We'll have to fight our way through, sir."

Jeremy shook his head. "We may not get there in time."

Cook turned the captain's chair to face his first officer. "Nonsense," he said, his eyes narrowed in grim amusement. "Miss Palmer, prepare to divert power from weapons to the forward shields; helm, steady as she goes."

For an instant, puzzlement filled Jeremy's face, then a chill of fear widened his eyes. At this speed, their physical distention in real space would make them sitting ducks if the captain didn't slow to a more manageable speed. The Crutchtan gunners could pick them off almost without trying. It was the Achilles' heel of every starship, largely neutralizing their superior speed in battle.

Quickly, he left his station and dashed to the captain's side.

"Skipper, we can't do anyone any good if they destroy us," he whispered.

Cook smiled coldly.

"We're no use if we're delayed, Commander. Return to your station."

THE BASE shuddered under the weight of enemy fire. Takira brushed the dust from his hair. He could feel his heart racing madly. But like everyone else, he couldn't take his eyes from the screen.

"They're not going to make it," he heard a voice call from behind him.

Takira knew the dangers of racing through enemy fire at top speed. The lesson was drilled into every officer, from the first day as a lowly plebe, to the merciless simulator programs that everyone aspiring to command had to master. Distention meant disaster, and trying to race past an enemy line only made their targeting easier. Starship or no, it was beginning to look like it would make no difference. The ship's captain was about to commit a midshipman's blunder. Even if they managed to sidestep destruction, the enemy had enough ships to keep the starship at bay, and could finish off the base almost at leisure.

From the giddy elation of deliverance, he felt himself sinking back into the darkness.

* * *

"HELM, CUT to C-2, come twenty points under 730," said the captain.

As *d'Artagnan* slowed, the Crutchtan ships pivoted to form a crescent along the ship's portside, moving to block access to the Terran base. The Crutchtan commander had read the briefing reports on the starships well. He knew that the Terran ship would need a wide arc to outrace the interceptors, and would be out of position to approach the base even if it eluded the squadron. Then, on a different approach, another group could serve to deflect it. In the meantime, the attack against the base would continue. By the time the starship could fight through the periphery, it would be too late.

Seated on his bridge, Cook had even less respect for enemy battle plans that he had for tactical orthodoxy. "Sound the alarm," he exclaimed. Soon, the warning siren blared throughout the ship, warning the crew that a jolting maneuver was about to take place.

"Keep the nose steady, helm, but come to 970 over 30; prepare to jump to C-19 on my command.

"Shields?"

"Standing by," replied Lt. Palmer.

"Cut gravity—now! Helm, spiral hard to port!"

The ship strained under the changing course. Cook felt himself pressed against the side of his chair. All around, he sensed the mouting tension. His crew was too well-trained not to know how risky his next maneuver would be, but he'd trained them himself. They were too disciplined to doubt him.

"Increase speed to C-19," he said firmly. "All available power to shields.

"Mr. Ashton, sound the clearing horn again. Helm, prepare to come sharply about."

HAVING LOST her enemies by spiraling around them, the Terran ship again banked steeply, drawing the Crutchtans in for the attack. Caught off guard by the enemy's sudden change of course, the interceptors scrambled to get into position to fire at the starship's distended broadside. Pivoting right and dispersing to lengthen their line of fire, they reformed their attacking crescent to the enemy's starboard and moved closer for the kill.

"Open fire on my signal," came the squadron leader's scratchy voice over the subspace radio, and the Crutchtan gunners locked their blasters onto the target, fighting the rising wave of excitement caused by the knowledge that their destruction of the starship would ensure that the Terran base would fall.

"Slow to C-2, come about to 640, dead level."

"Enemy squadron dead ahead."

"Enemy still advancing, Captain. Range, twenty-five klicks."

"Helm, accelerate toward the center of the enemy line and continue building speed. Palmer—divert 10 percent power to weapons, target center ships in enemy formation and prepare to fire at will."

Like a raging bull, the *d'Artagnan* plunged headlong into the heart of the enemy line. Everyone on board felt the enemy fire raining upon them, thundering against the hull in wave after wave. Even through her powerful shields, jolts from the enemy blasters shook the ship, knocking crewmen down in the halls and corridors, scrambling the senses of everyone on board. Under the intense barrage, the enemy guns set *d'Artagnan's* sides to burning, the contours of her shields glowing red in the blackness of space, her heat tiles glistening under the onslaught. But the Terran captain held his fire until, as the ship neared the lines, the widening angle of attack soon made it impossible for the enemy to fire without risking damage to their own ships. Then, as the ship's own guns suddenly came to life, shattering the enemy center and clearing the way for a final dash toward the starbase, a cheer rose from the throat of each member of the bridge crew.

Each member but one.

"Eyes front and quiet on the bridge!" Cook snapped, his voice stern and unforgiving. "This is no time for nonsense. Not while lives are on the line. And this is just the beginning, people."

"I don't believe it," Takira whispered. By now, everyone was following the approach of the starship. And as the *d'Artagnan* broke through the line of interceptors and continued its race toward the base, they turned to their stations with animal zeal. They hurried to marshal what remained of their tattered defenses in a last, desperate effort to ward off the Crutchtan assaults and certain death.

Shouts of encouragement filled the command center. For the first time since the attack began hope was filling their hearts, and giving purpose to their acts.

* * *

THOUGH UNPREPARED for the speed and daring of the Terran ship's maneuvers, the Crutchtans reacted quickly. Their commander diverted half of his attack force to intercept the starship, while the rest continued to attack the Terran outpost. Meanwhile, determined to break the siege or perish with the defenders, Cook pushed his ship further and further toward the starbase, with a grace and sharpness of motion that seemed to defy the laws of physics. Banking steeply to the west, he spiraled past one enemy squadron, leaving it baffled and disoriented in his wake; as if by whim, he punished the next with a merciless barrage that left not a single enemy ship intact, raining death with a furious, deadly precision that terrified every Crutchtan who watched.

Finally, *d'Artagnan* was within seconds of her destination. Starbase 117 was visible through the blackness; blasts of enemy fire filled the ship's sensors. As it became apparent that the starship would arrive despite their best efforts, the Crutchtans broke off the attack and turned to face the newcomer, letting the smaller Terran ships start straggling back toward their base. As the starship neared, the forces of His Worthiness gathered and formed a giant crescent in the sky to confront this new and fearsome enemy. In their tightest formation, the crescent moved to meet the onrushing starship, deferring their destruction of the base until they had dealt with this new threat.

But the mind of every shipmaster was haunted by the power the Terran starship carried in its engines, and by the realization that this starship was behaving differently than any yet seen. And just as the Crutchtans converged on the Terran ship from all sides, the starship made another, unexpected, and ominous maneuver.

Suddenly, and without warning, the Terran ship halted its forward progress. It floated in the darkness just beyond their forward positions, daring its enemy to attack.

"MANEUVERING THRUSTERS operating on batteries, sir."

"Divert all power to weapons," Cook said sternly. "Helm, stand by to flag and billow.

"Weapons— "

"Ready for anything the lizards throw at us, sir."

"— target anything that moves. Mr. Underwood?"

"Sir?"

"Radio the remaining ships on base defense and tell them to attack. And Palmer—you may not use the word 'lizard' on my bridge."

THE SHIP'S maneuvering baffled the *d'Artagnan's* crew, but they were too busy executing the captain's orders to wonder what it was they were doing. The Crutchtans also had no time for contemplation, for as they surrounded the ship and began blasting at her shields from all sides, the starship's powerful guns opened a furious assault on anything that moved, and space itself seemed on fire. The merciless Terran barrage destroyed everything it could reach, lighting the skies with wreckage and death. Bobbing and weaving to help her shields deflect the Crutchtan blasters, *d'Artagnan's* fate hung by the strength of her weakening shields. Both sides knew that time favored the Crutchtans in the desperate struggle of brute strength against superior numbers. But the Terran ship fought fiercely, instinctively, propelled by what the Crutchtans called *dg'Lansh*—the Demon of Darkness.

It was only on the starbase that anyone thought to question the unexpected turn the battle had taken. And the questions didn't come from the weapons stations or the monitors. They came from the command center.

"Just what the hell does he think he's doing?" shouted an incredulous Commodore Medwick. "And how in God's name can he expect me to commit my ships to a mad battle when the enemy can resume its attack at any time?"

As the last remnants of the base defense forces crawled to safety, the *d'Artagnan* shuddered and rocked under the impact of massive and simultaneous fire from Crutchtan blasters. As the ship's weapons officer was reporting the first significant draining of power from their shields, Commodore Medwick raged at his communications officers, demanding that they open a channel to the madman who was threatening to doom them all to destruction.

THE BRIDGE crew paled at the news. The moans died in their throats as they realized that all the risks they had borne, and the ceaseless buffeting they were taking, would soon become meaningless. They would die, quickly and uselessly: the base commander had refused to release his forces to join the battle.

Cook's reaction was different.

"You pompous, ignorant little twit!" he bellowed, over the sounds of the enemy barrage. It was the first time any of them had ever seen the captain explode in anger. "How dare you condemn us all to death just because you're too damn stupid to seize your one chance to beat back the enemy!"

Medwick's eyes narrowed hatefully. "You forget yourself, Captain."

The ship rocked beneath the impact of yet another Crutchtan barrage. The overhead lights faded, then returned, perceptibly dimmer than before. Cook returned the commodore's glare, his own eyes glowering fiercely. "Commodore, you take any action you want after the battle," the captain shouted over the din. "But as of this moment I am taking command of all your tactical forces."

Cook signaled for the communications officer to cut the channel to the base. Medwick's sputtering image faded from the screen, replaced by the shaken face of Lt. Commander Jordan Proust.

"You heard my communication with the base," Cook demanded.

Proust nodded nervously.

"I am ordering you to attack."

"On whose— "

Cook was already anticipating his question. "On my responsibility as a wing commander of the Cosmic Guard," he said, his voice steady and unyielding, "I have assumed command of all ships assigned to base defense, and I am *ordering* you to attack."

"But...."

The ship rocked violently under an enemy barrage. Cook's gaze never left the screen. He stared into the soul of the junior officer he'd just handed an impossible dilemma. "Don't bother about a battle plan," Cook said firmly. "Just drive your ships straight at me. The enemy will be too busy to notice your lack of subtlety, and this is no time to get cute."

He looked directly into the eyes of the nervous, young lieutenant commander. "It's on your head now, Commander. Attack and help me try to save the starbase, or follow your chain of command to your death. Either way, you won't be court-martialed for following the order of a superior officer. But my shields will collapse in about five minutes, and you're the only relief force within twenty parsecs. And if my ship goes down, you and your base are doomed."

Cook broke contact just as a jolt from another enemy attack shook the ship. He had no time left to worry about reinforcements. With a commanding confidence he turned his attention to the battle raging around him, the force of his personality driving the fear from his crew even as the enemy guns shook every deck on the ship. The frail hulls of the Crutchtan ships were no match for the starship's powerful guns, but their advantage in numbers was too much for the Terran ship's exhausted shields. Before long, the starship's weapons officer reported growing instability in all systems and power reserves draining rapidly under the relentless enemy fire. The heat from the combined force of the Crutchtans' firepower lighted the skies, shrouding the Terran ship in an eerie green glow.

Soon, the surviving Terran frigates under Proust's command arrived to engage the enemy. The Crutchtans diverted a half-squadron of ships to delay the frigates, hoping to finish off the starship quickly and then overwhelm the remaining Terran defenses. At the first hint of an enemy redeployment, the *d'Artagnan* made another daring and unexpected maneuver: her guns fell dead, as the ship diverted power to her dormant thrusters. Then, with a swiftness and grace that caught the Crutchtans off guard, the ship dipped and turned, accelerating toward a tiny crack in the shifting enemy positions. Racing through a blinding rain of enemy guns like lightening through a cloud, the mighty ship deflected the enemy fire from her crumbling shields by rolling her flanks, then burst past the frozen Crutchtan placements and sped for the open sky, her aft shields cooling as she outraced the firestorm and left the enemy guns astern.

By the time *d'Artagnan* circled back to join Proust, with shields firming and guns aroar, the Crutchtans knew that all was lost. The Terran frigates, bewildered and disorganized moments before, suddenly came to life under the starship's command. Their thrusts into the enemy midsection now precise and deadly, they quickly forced a retreat. As the weary defenders saw the Crutchtan retreat turned into a panic, a wild celebration spread over the starbase, the narrowness of their victory fading under a flood of mindless joy.

Soon, even Commodore Medwick realized that their position would hold. The realization came with decidedly mixed feelings, for the commodore was not a man given to forgiving slights. As cheers of deliverance rang through the base, the commodore retired to his quarters to nurse his wounded ego, and await another day.

Chapter 35

"GOD ALMIGHTY, BUT IT'S GOOD TO BE ALIVE!" Chief Connors laughed as he was roughly tossed and turned about. The crowd's roar was deafening, and they were showing no signs of giving it up. As far as he could see, the docks were crammed with people—screaming, delirious people, from all ranks and all stations. Over the top of the crowd, passing from shoulder to shoulder all the way down the line, *d'Artagnan's* crew was slowly making its way in toward the main corridor and the best leave time the lot of them would have in their lives.

Looking Glass had never seen anything like it, mused Connors. What's more, he'd never seen anything like it and he'd spent the better part of the last thirty years traveling the length and breadth of Terra.

"Chief! Chief—over here!!"

Connors heard a voice rising above the crowd. He turned his head one way, then another, until he saw Kevin Ward, his buddy from their old *Constellation* days. Waving just as he was being passed, Connors fell over backwards, nearly losing himself in the crowd. When the underlookers had helped him right himself, he rolled over their outstretching arms toward his longtime friend.

"Damn it all, you Demmy-rotted old rooster!" the old yeoman laughed, giving Connors a bear hug worthy of an Old Earth grizzly. "You're not worth any of this, you know. You get yourselves lost, then have the fool luck to show up in the nick of time and everyone thinks you're goddamn heroes! It ain't fair, Connors," he roared, clapping his friend behind the neck. "It just ain't fair!"

"Come—be a laddie," Connors bellowed. "We've a ship full of spacers in need of something more than Standard Issue beer. I hope to hell you've got something for an old spacer to quench his thirst. There's lots to tell and you won't believe a word of it, but I've never been so glad to see a starbase in all my days."

"Up and away with him!" hollered Ward. "He's another Cooker for the Pot!" Those around him hoisted Connors onto their shoulders, and started passing him back.

"I'll get ye for this, ye hard-hearted bastard!" Connors laughed as he found himself headed toward the interior of the base.

"We'll meet you at McKelvey's!" Ward shouted back. "The Brass is plannin' some big bash to pin a chest-full of medals on the whole sorry lot of you. You'll be needing somewhere to get a good stiff drink a-forehand, and there are enough of the old laddies around to make a right proper time of it."

"McKelvey's it is!" Connors replied, laughing at the sight of all the *d'Artagnan's* bluebirds, squealing and squirming as they tried to avoid the prying hands that seemed to follow them along the way.

Everyone was disobeying orders, Connors chuckled to himself. It was about the farthest thing from military discipline he'd ever seen. For all the medals the Brass would be pinning on their chests, he thought, the ship would never get a finer salute, nor a more honest tribute. He leaned back and closed his eyes, listening to the approving roar. He tried not to think of what might lie ahead. It was hard enough forgetting what they'd just been through. He opened his throat at screamed at the top of his lungs.

"God Almighty, but it's good to be alive!"

THE WELCOME that greeted *d'Artagnan's* arrival at Looking Glass was like nothing the Cosmic Guard had ever witnessed.

Spontaneously and against orders, hundreds of small craft left the docks to escort the starship the last half-parsec back to port—much to the consternation of the base traffic controllers, whose computers could barely keep all the ships from colliding. Almost the whole base tried to crowd into Dock 29 to greet the crew, raising thunderous cheers each time anyone, officer or crewman, emerged through the airlock. Admiral Clay himself nearly caused a riot by announcing an amnesty over the public address for all who had disobeyed the command to remain at posts while the *d'Artagnan* docked, so long as they returned to duty at once. Aside from keeping the base brig relatively empty, his gesture did nothing to curb the celebration.

But the cheers were not universal. Two days later, upon his return from the awards banquet for Cook and his crew that Clay had hosted and personally planned, a furious admiral placed a security-scrambled call to Demeter Command, which foreshadowed more than anyone imagined at the time.

THE IMAGE on the display screen was small and snowy. An ion squall had burdened communications with IshCom with static, and the admiral's balding head almost merged with the background until his face seemed to jump out of the viewer. Even so, his voice was as clear as his anger.

"Your boy has a lot of nerve, Admiral Weatherlee," said the image.

"So does yours, Admiral Clay."

"He's serious about pressing the matter?"

Weatherlee nodded gravely. Clay had a lot of pull with Central Command, the Demetrian thought, but mutiny was mutiny. Besides, anything that deflated a second-rate prima donna like Cook was worth the cost. His eyes focused scornfully at the image on the screen. Unconsciously, his fingers began rapping on his desk, as he waited impatiently for the Clay's response. When it came, it caught Weatherlee completely by surprise.

"Fine," Clay said at last. "If Medwick is dumb enough to go gunning after Terra's first war hero in two hundred years, there's nothing I can do to stop him. But if he's really a friend of yours, I hope you explain the consequences to him. Carefully explain the consequences."

Weatherlee's puzzled look told the admiral that his message was not being received.

"You see, Winthrop," the admiral smiled menacingly, "from where I sit, Medwick has two choices. He can drop his charges and forget everything that happened. Or else I see two court-martials in the offing—the second for culpable negligence in readying Starbase 117 for attack, and dereliction of duty in not releasing his ships for battle.

"And Winthrop," he said darkly, " I can tell you right now, if you like, who will sit with me on the tribunal, and exactly what our verdict will be."

Beneath stone facades, time beat slowly for the two proud men facing one another across the void. Both convinced to the point of self-righteousness, each stared wordlessly into his screen, as if silence alone could crack the other's resolve. In the end, the victor congratulated his own strength of character for unnerving his opponent, though as happened often in Terran history, from Old Earth to the present day, it was raw power that carried the day.

"Medwick would keep his command?" There was an edge to Weatherlee's voice, but his eyes admitted defeat.

Admiral Clay smiled grimly. "I'm not a vindictive man."

Soon the transmission ended and Clay was pleased that, for once, he had beaten Weatherlee at his own game. Yet the humiliation of surrender sometimes burned in the soul like an eternal flame. And like his friend and protégé, Admiral Weatherlee was not one to forget.

THE ATMOSPHERE was festive at the Looking Glass Officers' Club, and the sweet odor of alcohol filled the air. Above the songs and laughter that filled the room, Janet Mendelson could barely hear her own thoughts, and was not surprised when the bartender brought the wrong drink. Today she was too happy to argue. A few days ago she wouldn't have taken odds on being alive long enough to enjoy anything. Picking their way through the crowd, she and Mary Mathison looked for a place to sit, having promised themselves that they wouldn't mark this celebration by moping around in quarters, feeling lonely and unappreciated.

Mary had just spotted two former classmates seated by themselves at a prime table and was dragging her friend toward their table when Janet spotted a familiar face in a far corner of the lounge. After a brief inner struggle, loyalty prevailed over her pride and she snaked her way through the crowd to the solitary figure sitting in the half-darkness. Mathison's friends would still be there when she was through, she told herself. And if not—well, Jeremy would be joining them any minute now.

"What's that?" she asked jovially upon arriving at the table furthest from the bar—and nearest to the men's head.

Cook looked up. Later, she would remember that he looked wistful, almost sad. At the time she noticed only that the captain was quieter than she'd expected from the hero of the day and wrote if off to fatigue and post-battle blues. She took a seat from a nearby table and sat across from the captain.

"It's brandy."

"Isitian brandy?" Janet chuckled.

Cook smiled distantly. "Today—what else?"

The two talked of their adventures, and of their disagreements—but avoided talking about the battle at Starbase 117, or about the private battles they'd had with each other in that last week aboard the *Constantine*. They talked of the folly of war and their hopes for a quick victory and early peace. Before she realized it, Janet found herself getting lightheaded again, listening to the cadence of his voice as he prattled on, waxing philosophical on subjects she knew little about, her spirits rising and falling with the poetry of his words. Even as they talked, she could sense that he was troubled. Gone were the mischievous eyes and irreverent wit that once filled her heart. Instead, she saw the sad smile of a philosopher, whose gentle wisdom saw all the contradictions in the human condition, but knew that he was powerless to change them.

Finally, apologizing for being such bad company, Cook rose to leave. Checking her watch, Janet was shocked to see that they'd been talking for more than an hour. When she lifted her eyes to meet Cook's, she could see that he was he was hurting. Despite herself, she found herself hurting as well.

"Skipper," she asked hesitantly, "is something wrong?"

Cook chuckled, more to himself than aloud, but the tone of his laughter gave Janet the distinct and maddening impression that in some imponderably Isitian way of viewing things, she was once again being made the butt of one of his private jokes. She was starting to feel very foolish and quite angry, until the captain spoke again.

"You really don't know, do you?" he said cryptically. "Well, no matter. You'll find out soon enough. But the fact that you haven't heard actually makes our little talk all the more meaningful.

"Thanks, Janet. For more than you'll probably ever know."

Mystified, Janet watched him walk through the lounge and out the door. Too puzzled to move, she sat with a baffled look on her face until a familiar figure plopped down onto the seat the captain had just left.

"Well?" asked an anxious Jeremy Ashton.

"Well, what?"

"So how's he taking it? And what do you think he's going to do?"

Janet was thoroughly confused. "Jeremy, what are you babbling about?"

"You mean, you haven't heard?" Jeremy sighed harshly, shaking his head in disbelief. By this time, even Jeremy was getting on her nerves. "My God, Janet," he said condescendingly. "The news is all over the headlines. How can you not know about it?"

Angry and impatient, she opened her mouth to give him a piece of her mind. Jeremy's next bit of news froze the words in her mouth.

"Isis—today—seceded from the Union."

"It appears that you are a popular young man these days, Brother Cook."

Looking at the young Northlander, Master Salisi was surprised that his own predominant emotion was pity. By all rights, this particular young scholar should be dancing on every ceiling in the Lyceum. Despite his tender years, he'd narrowly missed being class valedictorian, and the school information office had been beset with inquires from universities and colleges all over Terra, the prestigious Lunar Institute for Space Studies on Old Earth among them. The young man had practically rewritten the astronomy department's textbooks with his work in subspace communications, and his skills as a pilot and navigator were already the stuff of legend throughout the school. His hometown had chosen him as their torch-runner for the Festival Torch procession later that summer. Even the Cosmic Guard Academy on New Babylon had expressed an interest in the young man— withdrawing its offer only upon learning that he was not yet eighteen. All the attention only seemed to make the quiet Northlander more withdrawn than ever.

"Something is troubling you, is it not?"

The young man smiled. "Everyone should have such troubles, Master Salisi."

"What is the matter?"

"I doubt you'd understand."

Master Salisi sat down next to the youth and pressed him on the shoulder. "You might be surprised, Brother Cook. Everyone faces crossroads, you know. I am astonished that you find the prospect so daunting."

"Don't try to bait me," laughed the young man. "I saw through that methodology in Philosophy 444—and you're just lucky

*everybody else in the class was too unimaginative to wonder why
I spent the semester laughing my way through the idiots of the
Nihilistic Period."*

*The teacher smiled and nodded. There were few pupils of his
that he had failed to reach, in one way or another. The young
Northlander was one of the few who had truly touched the old
man's own soul.*

"What is it then?"

*"A moral dilemma," the young man smiled sadly. "More a
paradox, actually, now that I think of it."*

"What is your paradox?"

*"Conflicting duties," the youth continued. "Like the father of
four, discovering one of his children trapped inside a burning
building. Does he try to save the trapped child, knowing that if
he fails he may leave the others without a father—or does he watch
one child burn to death before his eyes, ensuring that the others
do not grow up fatherless?"*

"An easy problem, Brother Cook. I am disappointed."

*"Oh—that is not my problem, Master Salisi. I am one of the
children outside, my father is trapped inside trying to rescue my
younger brother—and now the orphanage next door has just
caught fire. The dilemma is personal on the one hand, yet the
stakes are higher on the other. And the paradox is that I may
consider any course of action to be right—and yet each, in its way,
is very wrong."*

*"Many problems have no single solution, Brother Cook. The
solution is to find the path best for you."*

"That does not ease the pain of guilt, Master Salisi."

"Is leaving Isis really so difficult for you?"

*"It is not so much leaving that bothers me," the youth sighed.
"Partings are merely a part of life, and hence unavoidable.
Choosing to leave those you love is what is difficult, especially
when you cannot be certain you will ever return."*

"I cannot solve the problem for you."

*"It is a problem without a solution," the young man shook his
head, "for there is no right answer to it. Though I can pretend this
means my own answer cannot be wrong, I can't pretend that it
doesn't hurt."*

"Most people see only self-interest and disguise it as logic," said the teacher. "But so long as love exists in the Universe, logic can never provide all the answers. You have a good heart as well as a gifted mind, my young friend. Do not forget to use both, when you confront your unanswerable problems. And remember as well that admitting a problem is unanswerable is the biggest step toward resolving the matter, in your own soul."